Praise for
All Together in One Place

"Great characters and a strong story. Jane Kirkpatrick is an excellent writer."

—T. DAVIS BUNN, BEST-SELLING AUTHOR

"Jane Kirkpatrick has performed a literary miracle. She made me—a reader who seldom ventures into Western fiction by choice—struggle across dusty plains and ford swollen rivers right along with her eleven turnaround women, then thank her for the perilous journey. She made me cheer for characters who rubbed me the wrong way until they polished clean my resistance and stole my heart. Their collective trust in God fortified my own. Read and experience this miracle of kinship and courage for yourself."

—LIZ CURTIS HIGGS, BEST-SELLING AUTHOR

"Rich in detail, *All Together in One Place* is the compelling story of a band of pioneering women as told in Jane Kirkpatrick's unique style. Here is the journey west as women saw it—burdensome and often cruel, yet not without moments of compassion, love, and humor."

—JACK CAVANAUGH, BEST-SELLING AUTHOR

All
TOGETHER
in One
PLACE

OTHER NOVELS BY JANE KIRKPATRICK

No Eye Can See

What Once We Loved

A Sweetness to the Soul

(Winner of the Wrangler Award

for Outstanding Western Novel of 1995)

Love to Water My Soul

A Gathering of Finches

Mystic Sweet Communion

NONFICTION

Homestead

A Burden Shared

Daily Guideposts, Stories for a Woman's Heart

BOOK no. ONE OF THE KINSHIP and COURAGE SERIES

All TOGETHER *in One* PLACE

JANE KIRKPATRICK

WATERBROOK
PRESS

ALL TOGETHER IN ONE PLACE
PUBLISHED BY WATERBROOK PRESS
12265 Oracle Blvd., Suite 200
Colorado Springs, Colorado 80921
A division of Random House, Inc.

All Scripture quotations, unless otherwise indicated, are taken from
the *King James Version* of the Bible. Scripture quotations marked
(NIV) are taken from the *Holy Bible, New International Version*®. NIV®.
Copyright © 1973, 1978, 1984 by International Bible Society. Used by
permission of Zondervan Publishing House. All rights reserved.

The characters and events in this book are fictional, and any resemblance
to actual persons or events is coincidental.

ISBN 978-1-57856-232-9

Library of Congress Cataloging-in-Publication Data
Kirkpatrick, Jane, 1946-
    All together in one place / by Jane Kirkpatrick.— 1st ed.
        p. cm.— (Book one in The kinship and courage historical series)
    ISBN 1-57856-232-5
    1. Frontier and pioneer life—West (U.S.)—Fiction.   2. Women pioneers—West
(U.S.)—Fiction.   I. Title.

PS3561.I712 A79   2000
813'.54—dc21
                                                        99-054725

Printed in the United States of America
2007

20   19   18   17   16

This book is dedicated to
a special
circle of women

❧

Blair, Kay, Sandy, Barb, Carol, Katy,
Jewell, Harriet, Normandie, Nancy, Jeannie, Judy,
Arlene, Sherri, Jean, Michelle, Millie, Patty, Kathleen,
Melissa, Joyce, Julie, Jacki, Patty, Marilyn, Madison,
Mariah, Pearl (my mom), Annie, Melissa,
and to Lisa and Traci, newly joined

CAST OF CHARACTERS

Madison "Mazy" and Jeremy Bacon
    Elizabeth Mueller
Hathaway and Adora Wilson
    Charles Wilson
    Tipton Wilson
Tyrell Jenkins
Antone and Lura Schmidtke
    Matt and Mariah
Joe Pepin
Suzanne and Bryce Cullver
    Clayton
    Sason

Sister Esther Maeves
Harold and Ferrel Maeves
The Celestials
    Cynthia
    Mei-Ling/Deborah
    Naomi
    Zilah
Jed and Betha Barnard
    Jason, Ned, Sarah, Jessie
Ruth Martin
Seth Forrester
Silver Bells
Ezra Meeker

"Thou maintainest my lot.
The lines are fallen unto me in pleasant places."

PSALM 16:5-6

"They were all together in one place."

ACTS 2:1 (NIV)

"You [God], the great homesickness
we could never shake off."

RAINER MARIA RILKE

"One of the incidents that made a profound impression
upon the minds of all; the meeting of eleven wagons
returning and not a man left in the entire train;
all had died, and been buried on the way,
and the women returning alone."

EZRA MEEKER OREGON TRAIL DIARY, 1852

prologue

1850
near Cassville, Wisconsin

Cold water quaked from her torso to her toes. In an instant, Madison "Mazy" Bacon understood: greedy reeds and grasses lurked beneath the river's surface. Fear surged through her. She struggled against strands yearning to tangle her ankles and knot the flounced hem of her swimming dress. Cold numbed her arms; thickening stalks sucked her under. As she fought, she scolded herself for not suspecting the danger signs. For being naive, swimming in the mighty river alone.

No, no, no, no! Determined, Mazy swallowed her panic, spit out murky water. She closed her eyes tight in concentration, then jerked her legs into a ball beneath her dress. She twisted until supine, surrendered to heaven. Then with a controlling backstroke, a thrust of her sinewy legs, and a prayer, she pushed toward warmer, safer water.

Sheltered later in their log home cradled by grassy bluffs, Mazy warmed herself before the fireplace, her thin chemise clinging hot against her back. Wet chestnut strands of hair veiled over her head as she bent and toweled it with an old quilt piece.

"There's a dangerous place of currents in the Mississippi," she told her husband of two months. "It looks safe, calm almost, then all of a sudden, and you're in it."

"It's a necessary discovery," Jeremy Bacon told her, not looking up from his book about cows and cow brutes. "Things are often not as they seem at the surface."

"True," Mazy said. She tossed the thick tousle of hair over her back. Knotting the still-damp waves into a single braid, she vowed to remember his words of warning.

She didn't.

1

mazy bacon's place

April 1852

Mazy Bacon embraced her life inside a pause that lacked premonition.

Warm sun spilled on her neck as she bent over seedlings she'd nurtured in walnut shells and pumpkin halves through a blustery winter. Humming a German song her mother'd taught her, she celebrated the plants' survival and the scent of sweet earth at her feet. Pig, her dog, lay beside her, his black head resting on paws, his brown eyes watching plump robins peck at worms in the newly tilled garden soil. She relished her life. Everything smelled of promise.

Around her legs, the wind whipped the red bloomers her mother had given her for Christmas the year before.

"Red? Mother," she had said, pulling them from the string-tied wrapping. "Hardly anyone wears them at all, let alone ones as red as radishes."

"You was needing some seasoning in your days," her mother said. "A little spice now and then, that's good. You're young. You can wear 'em."

Today, for the first time, Mazy'd donned those loose folds that billowed out at her hips, stayed tight at her sturdy ankles. She didn't wear the jacket, choosing a cream chemise instead. Her muscular arms, laid bare to the sun, already showed signs of spring freckles. And her hair, the color of earth and as unruly as wind, fluffed free of its usual braid.

Her wooden spade cut the soil. Mazy thought of the fat rattlers that moved lazily in summer sun, pleased they'd still be sleeping in the limestone rocks and caves and not surprising her. She disliked surprises. She knelt, planted, and pressed dirt around her precious love apples. Tomatoes, some called them now. They'd be fat and plump earlier than ever before.

Finished, Mazy stood, brushed dirt from her ample knees. Ample. Ever since she was twelve years old and stood head to head with her father's five-foot-nine-inch frame, she'd thought of herself as ample. By the time she turned seventeen and married Jeremy Bacon, a man twice her age and exactly her height, the image of herself as large was as set as a wagon wheel in Wisconsin's spring mud.

Jeremy, her husband of two years, said she was "like fine pine formed from sturdy stock." Mazy loved him for that and for his melting smile and for treating her as fine china. He'd been gone two weeks, but he'd be back anytime, today for certain. It was their second anniversary.

Mazy longed for the stroke of his smooth finger at her temple, the brush of his unbearded cheek against hers. She sighed. She'd prepared for him the perfect anniversary gift—a newly planted garden with the promise of abundance. His gift to her would be the Ayrshire seed cow, the "brute" Marvel, as Jeremy called him, and with it, an expansion of their herd and home.

"I am richly blessed, Pig," Mazy said.

The big dog lifted one eye and thumped his tail, then yawned. A Newfoundland, with a bearlike head, Pig had tiny ears that prompted his naming when Jeremy'd brought the ball of fur home to his wife. Mazy liked the word "Pig." Not the image of a coarse-haired shoat, but the sound itself: a light and airy word that puffed off her tongue. "Pig," she said out loud, "they should have named bubbles 'pigs.' We'd say 'Look at that baby blow pigs! Pig, pig, pig.'" Mazy laughed as the dog cocked his head from side to side at the repeated sound of his name.

Mazy stood, stretched, her fingers spread at her hips, bare toes wiggling in warm earth. A breeze dried the beads of perspiration at her temples, and she lifted the bonnet hanging loose at the back of her neck to let the air whisper it cool. Blackbirds chirped as they darted toward earth.

"The Lord knows my lot," she said aloud. "He makes my boundaries fall on pleasant places." She'd read the Psalm the day she arrived at this site not far from the Mississippi River near Cassville, Wisconsin; had found it again that morning. The verse read "lines" where Mazy had remembered "boundaries," but both meant limits to her, the safety of places secured by fences of faith.

"I won't say anything to Jeremy about fencing in the garden until after he finishes the scarecrows," Mazy told Pig. She brushed her hands toward birds trying to steal her newly planted seeds. Pig startled and took chase as the flock of intruders soared over bluffs that shadowed the house. "Good work, Pig!" she shouted as she watched the dog disappear from sight.

Later, she would be filled with ifs, the stuffing of regret, but at that moment, Mazy Bacon rested inside contentment.

An unfamiliar sound made her stand and turn toward the wooded trail. Anticipation preceded puzzlement. Was it a woman's voice? A shout or grunt? She couldn't see anyone and no one used her name; a neighbor would have called her name. Her skin prickled at her neck. She felt large and exposed in her bloomers.

"Jeremy?"

A breeze washed through the pines, gave no answer.

Suddenly, something slashed through timber, loud and unruly. She caught a flash of rust and white, braiding through the shadow of birches, poplars, and pines. Her eyes followed the sound as it shifted in the wooded thickness. She willed herself to see what she heard. She couldn't.

"Jeremy? Is that you?" She shaded the sun from her eyes with her hand, aware that her heart pounded. Sweat dribbled at her breast, her hands felt damp, her body responding to danger before her mind could make sense.

A sound behind her didn't match with the clatter coming from the timber. She twisted in the dirt. Spiders of fear inched up her spine as the truth of its source stung clear.

⁓

Jeremy Bacon cursed the branches swiping at his face. How had the animal gotten away from him? So close to home but the cow brute wasn't familiar with this corral, so he wouldn't head home on his own. He would frenzy himself in the trees, move out and be lost forever, Jeremy's investment, gone, unless he could catch up the cows and hope the brute would come to them. With all the ruckus, the milk cows had bolted too. The hemp lines trailed behind them, threatening to catch in the trees and the brambles.

If only Mazy had agreed to come along! She could have helped. Instead what he had was misery, multiplied by frantic stock. He had to get them to the corral. His eye caught something through the trees near the meadow and he stopped. What was Mazy doing in those blasted bloomers? He shouted but she turned from him. He strained to see what took her attention. When he caught sight of it, his heart thudded to his knees.

⁓

The cow brute shook his wide mahogany head weighted with horns that arched upward like parallel arrows. His nostrils and mouth sprayed foam and saliva in the air. Tilled earth spewed over his back as he pawed at the ground she'd just planted. His eyes bore into Mazy's.

Mazy's hands and feet were stumps of thickness, too heavy to move. Cold, like the dangerous place of the river, coursed through her. Her head screamed to run.

Instead, she backed away, as careful as a heron's lift and laying of limbs. She stared at the ground now, her beloved soil, the seedlings both frail and exposed. The brute snorted and then lunged. Mazy sank to the earth as though dead.

Had she read that somewhere? Had Jeremy once told her? Remembered advice from some wounded patient her father had treated? She couldn't remember. Her face fell into the seedlings, her cheek gritty with dirt, just as the brute rushed ahead.

Horns gouged the ground beside her, launched pebbles of earth to her back, pelting her like snowballs on the calves of her legs, her bonnet, her head. Spray from his nose dribbled, foamed on her arm. She could see it there, the clear bubble, wondered if it was the last thing she would see. Her eyelids folded closed on their own.

She heard and smelled and felt everything as though cut with her mother's sharp scissors. Agitated weight shook the ground beside her head. The brute's breathing labored raspy, yet he bellowed, and Mazy knew that if she opened her eyes she would see the wide, wet nose inches from her head. More dirt, then his sweated scent, and she heard the thin chemise rip at her side from the scrape of his hoof as he twisted and jerked.

Help me, help me, help me. Keep me still, don't agitate him more. Her mind journeyed then, searched for pleasant places, the things she loved: her Lord, her husband, her mother, the land. She drifted above the timber to the far corners of the boundaries of the Bacon place, to the land that bordered on bluffs cut by a year-round stream that rushed through the meadow in the hot Wisconsin summer and froze over, hard as a horseshoe, in winter. Stands of pine surrounded the meadow, spearing the sky so high nothing grew beneath them on the forest floor: shelter for deer, high perches for eagles. The cleared meadow gave up stacks of hay for wintering the Bacons' stock. At the edge of the one hundred sixty acres rose the log house Jeremy's uncle had built and when he died had left—along with the farm—to his nephew.

Mazy loved this place. She relished the routine of her days, the high vistas and views. She hoped to spend her life here, to live and till and plant and let herself be nurtured by home and the love of her husband. Wind wove through eagle's wings soaring above her.

Her mind jerked back with the grunt of the brute.

He'd gore her next, gouge her with his arched horns, throw her over his back and then stomp her, and she'd be dead at the feet of a longed-for dream. Her passing would wound her husband, grieve her mother, the two in her life she loved most. Jeremy would bear the blame; she was sorry for that when this was her doing. She shouldn't have worn the bloomers, she should have gone with him, she should have, she should.

The brute twisted then. She could tell by the spray from his nostrils and the rumble of earth beneath her head. He pawed and bawled. She smelled dirt and manure. Then fury propelled him just as the piercing pain of his horns jabbed her side, the force of it lifting her, pushing, then rolling her over. She lay on her back, the blue ribbon of her bonnet caught at her throat. Her arms were like dolls' arms, stiff and exposed. A place at her side burned like the stab of a poker.

She heard the crack the moment the brute lunged, the solid bone of her arm breaking while her elbow sank into earth. A wail formed at her throat but she held it, swallowed it, still as a new-planted seed; amazed but committed to living. The sound of wind she recognized as blood rushed through her ears, her heart pounded. Her mind willed the sounds into stillness.

Pig barked then. A clatter from the timber broke her drifting. She heard splintering in the trees and what sounded like a woman's voice and then gunshots, a lead thud close to her in the dirt. A bawl, the brute snorted, and Pig barked, standing between her and the seed cow. Earth struck her like pelts of soft rain. She heard another shot, recognized it as Jeremy's cap-and-ball revolver, heard the animal bellow but farther from her now, closer to the corral. She knew in that instant what Jeremy was doing and that she, Mazy Bacon, would live not from her husband's crack shots but from her stillness, her wit, lying dead like an uprooted plant.

She heard her husband shouting directions to the dog, then to her. "Mazy! Don't move, no sounds. We'll have him in, just hang on."

Pig barked in the distance. Mazy risked opening her eyes. White, fleecy clouds drifted above her. She pressed her left hand over her stomach and stuffed part of the bloomer against oozing blood. Her arm throbbed and burned, and when she tried to move it, she felt a thousand bee stings all at once. She panted. The bull roared in the distance.

Now all was a blur, not precise. Someone ran toward her. Relief and pain touched her stomach; a prayer of thanks pressed into her mind.

"I am so sorry, so terribly sorry," Jeremy said, scooping her shoulders to lift and pull her to him. She cried out as he rocked her, then his hand held her head while she retched. "O, Mazy! The brute…it got away from us. The cows got tangled up with the ropes and we—"

"Cows?"

"Mazy, Mazy." He wiped her forehead with his soft fingers as she buried her face into his shirt smelling of perspiration, fear, and relief. The dog bounded over and tried licking her. "No, Pig," he said. His fingers made a feathery probe in her side. "You'll be sore. Badly scraped. And the arm…" He cradled the bone of her arm, the movement forcing a gasp. "Let's get you inside," he said. "You're starting to shake."

He squatted as though to lift her, and the pain of the action and the thought of his trying to carry her and the relief she felt at being alive, at seeing him, and the dog's licking at her toes, forced a strangled sound from her throat. Parched joy she felt, mixed as it was with the rhythm of living and pain.

"I'm too big," she said. "Don't try to carry me. Just help me stand." She heard the thump of footsteps thudding across the ground. The brute bellowed. She tensed. "He's corralled," her husband said. "It's all right."

"Who's there?" Pointed shoes stopped in the dirt beside the dog. "Mother?"

"I waddle like a duck when I'm hurrying," Elizabeth Mueller said, breathless.

"Here, I got this side of her, Jeremy. Let me hold the arm steady. Is

9

it broken? We was so worried, baby," she said, kissing her daughter's forehead. To Jeremy she said, "Got the cows in too?"

"Cows?" Not just a bull? It didn't make sense what her mother was saying.

Mazy's teeth chattered. She wobbled between Jeremy and Elizabeth as cobwebs smothered her mind.

~

They set her arm, the rub of bone against bone making her sick in her stomach. They splinted it, held it firm to her chest with a sling formed from a strip of her petticoat; Mazy's swollen fingers fisted over a pair of Jeremy's gray knit socks, something soft to steady and grip. They gave her dark laudanum. It turned her mind to sleep.

"Can you wrap my arm in a poultice of fresh mullein leaves? It'll cut the swelling," Mazy said through a thick tongue when she woke.

"Tomorrow," her mother told her, the back of her palm soothing her daughter's hand. "We'll make a turmeric-and-water paste to stop bruises. Just like your papa used to."

Jeremy adjusted the sling. "We've a good supply of milk now," he said. He patted her arm. "That'll help the bones heal."

"I don't like milk," Mazy said.

"Essential for bones. Take it like medicine."

"Some chamomile tea'll help you sleep," her mother added. The older woman tugged at the tiny sticks and dirt still clinging to Mazy's hair. "Got your own little woods right here among your curls. That nose of yours'll have a bruise too, looks like. Don't look broken, though. So lucky, child."

"'Lucky' isn't the word I'd have chosen," Mazy said. Every part of her body felt riddled with rawness, and just as she wondered if she'd find sleep again without throbbing, she dozed.

"Fright," Mazy heard her mother say later when she awoke to a candlelit room. Shadowy light flickered against a framed sampler hung on the log wall. "Afterwards, that's when you worry. Folks get through their pickles and then die of surviving. That's what her papa always said." Elizabeth Mueller's bulk obscured Jeremy until she moved and Mazy saw her husband seated at the table.

At forty-eight, Elizabeth Mueller was barely ten years older than Jeremy Bacon and sometimes Mazy wondered if he didn't have more in common with his mother-in-law than with his wife. She watched them now from her refuge on the bed, the low fire flickering against their faces. Jeremy read some sort of drawing laid out before him. Elizabeth Mueller leaned over, spoke in a low voice, then returned to the hickory rocker that creaked as she lowered herself into it. Mazy felt clammy and wondered if she had raised a fever.

"Doctoring all those years, her papa saw his share of death," her mother said.

"We all go eventually," Jeremy said.

"Some folks ain't ever prepared, though. When they see how close they come, that's when they shake."

Mazy coughed.

Both Jeremy and her mother turned. "Hungry?" her mother asked.

"I'll get it," Jeremy said, standing. He filled a wooden bowl from the caldron at the fireplace and, kneeling beside her, spooned her a thin soup of beef stock and potatoes. She lay on the goosedown ticking, letting him take care of her there in the great room, close to the warmth of the heated rock hearth.

"The cows weren't...well, weren't part of the plan, you know," Jeremy began in his explaining tone.

"I did wonder if I'd missed that part," Mazy said. "It must've been them I heard in the timber first. I didn't notice the brute behind me until it was too late. If only Pig'd been around. Or if I'd realized sooner what was happening."

"Quite," Jeremy said. With a neckerchief, he dabbed at a soup dribble on her chin.

"So, the cows. How did they happen to show up in Grant County?"

He looked away from her, stood, pulled at the belt that tied his woolen pants. "Lucky for us, I'd say."

"That interesting word again," Mazy said.

"See, the original buyers failed to appear at the dock. Someone said they'd chucked everything. Headed west, I guess." He blinked his eyes, cleared his throat. "I thought it would work fine to take them all. Cows're purebred. Knew someday I'd want some, but I thought later." He paused, coughed. "I would've preferred to research their bloodlines."

"And you paid for them, how?"

He glanced over at Mazy's mother before answering. Elizabeth squinted at the cream chemise she was mending. "Did you see what good straight backs they have?" he said, turning back to Mazy. "Nice udders. Should give us quite a start on a prize herd. Good coloring, like white mushrooms inside brown ones there at their hindquarters."

"Color wasn't what I was tending to," Mazy said.

Jeremy scraped the wooden dish with the spoon and set the bowl on the table as he sat down on the floor beside her, his eyes level with hers. He reached for her, twirled a strand of her hair around his finger, lowered his voice to a whisper. "You're looking more rested."

"Some prize herd with a mad cow brute at the head of it," she said.

"He just got agitated." He pulled his finger from her hair, smoothed a wrinkle in the sling. "All the newness. Long trip. They're stout animals, Maze. Calmed down now. All of them."

"Resting peacefully, are they?"

"Quite." He took a deep breath, stood. "Not much of an anniversary for you, is it? I am sorry about your garden."

"We salvaged what we could," her mother said, looking up from the needlework spread at her lap. Mazy marveled at her mother's hearing, able to listen to conversations meant for private. "'Fraid the love apples look the worst. Still not sure it's safe to eat them. I covered what's left, case it freezes."

"Aren't you always telling me to be adventurous, Mother? I planted something new with those tomatoes, which is, by the way, what they're called."

"Advice I always thought fell on deaf ears," her mother said. She smiled then. "Excepting for them bloomers."

"Quite possibly a sign you're not to have a garden this year," Jeremy said.

"After all the work of the winter? Be forced to depend on our neighbors' success? Go hungry? No. A garden's the sign that life keeps going on, Jeremy, that people are home and happy to be there. This year more than any other, I should celebrate that. I'll replant, soon as I'm able."

"Came close to losing you," Jeremy said. He pushed the muslin sling back and bent to kiss her swollen fingers curled over his socks.

"The worst part," Mazy said, reaching for her husband's hand, "was wondering where you were and if you were all right."

He coughed. "You were quite smart to drop down. How'd you know to do that?"

"Something just said to."

"And for once," he said, "you didn't argue."

❧

It must have been near midnight when Jeremy slipped into the bed beside her.

"Would you rather I slept on the floor, so as not to bother?" he asked.

"I'd like you beside me on the anniversary of our marriage vows," Mazy said. "Lie next to the wall, though. Watch my arm."

He gentled himself over her, slid under the comforter, and lay on his side, his back to the logs, his arm arched over her head. He stroked her forehead with his fingers. He smelled of sweat and tobacco.

"Maze," he began in a whisper. "I meant to tell you."

What was that tone in his voice? Tentative?

"About the cows," she said.

"Yes. And…"

No, something different, something cool, a threatening thread that wound its way from the weave of his words to her heart.

"You were the one who had them shipped in all along, weren't you? The cows."

She felt him relax.

"You knew." He sniffed now, reached beneath the pillow for a handkerchief, and blew his nose. He rested his hand back on the rise of her hip, his fingers fisted around the damp cloth.

"I didn't want to say so in front of Mama." She whispered the words, not sorry they sounded like a hiss. "Think our business should be ours and not a part of hers." She glanced to see if her mother still slept in the rocker. Mazy turned onto her back, and Jeremy adjusted the sling. "Surprised me you brought Mama back with you. She doesn't like to travel all that much, I never thought."

He didn't respond, and she waited so long she thought he'd fallen asleep, but his breathing never slowed.

"Your mother was wanting a change," he said.

That tone again, of reeds beneath the surface.

"Cassville's a change of scenery from Milwaukee, all right."

"Now she'll have a story to tell her grandbabies when they arrive," Jeremy said.

"About their mother surviving the mad cow brute named Marvel and how their grandma chased the cows?"

"Something like that." He drew a circle in the thickness of her hair, twisting it around his finger. "She didn't want to be left behind," he said, "when we…" He mumbled something that sounded like "new place."

"She's found a new place?" She turned to face him in the dark.

He coughed and cleared his throat, blew his nose. "Our new place, Maze," he said. "She wants to see our new place."

Mazy lay still, stared at the mud chink in the ceiling, confused by his words, holding firm to familiar. "But she's visited here before."

Her husband took a deep breath, and even before he spoke, she felt struck in her stomach, empty of air. Her heart pounded loud in her ears. "Guess the time's come to tell you," he said. "I've sold the farm."

Every tendril of her hair ached. Her throat burned. Her soul felt shriveled and sliced as though the brute's horns pierced afresh. "A new place?" Her voice was tiny, distant to her ears. She tried to sit up on her elbow, couldn't, lay back down. Something heavy sat on her soul, kept her from taking a filling-up breath. "You didn't talk with me?"

"You don't like change, don't handle it well," he said. His words sounded clipped, rehearsed now. "Didn't want to alarm you unless everything went through. And it did." Jeremy's words tumbled out faster now. "I was never cut out to farm, you know that. Wouldn't have come to this place without Uncle's leaving it to us. The manure makes my hands break out in bumps, and the dirt"—he rubbed his nose—"aggravates my head. But the Ayrshires—they challenge."

"Plenty of manure and dirt where cows are."

"I can hire people to do the dirt work. I'll manage the breeding program, the matching of people and animals, building the herd. That's what I'm meant for."

"You haven't managed so far," she said. "You were aimless as a stray until your uncle left you this place. Drifting, a dockworker, not saving coins or moving toward a future. That's what you said when you met me, remember?"

"I've done this. Nearly two years."

"But no love of the earth? No loyalty to our home?"

"Dirt's dirt," he said.

Tears pressed against her nose, thickened in her throat. Had Jeremy hated this place and she'd never known? How could that be?

"We have a good life," Mazy said, her heart thudding, even in her swollen fingers. "Can't we get what you want where we already are? I love this place, Jeremy. The bluffs, the eagles..." She heard the wail in her own voice, the piercing of tears. "I'll milk the cows." Her voice broke, but she kept talking. "We can build the herd here. I'll do the work in the dirt, Jeremy, you—"

"Where did you think the money for the brute came from? Think that grew on your love apples?"

"I thought the timber, I...don't know. I don't think I can live anywhere else. I don't want to live anywhere but on this place."

"This place." He spit the words. "It would take years on this place. Denniston's 'Big Brick' hotel stands empty, acts like the plague for keeping folks away. Cassville's stagnant, Maze, done, almost folded. Titles are so messed up for most, they can't even sell no matter how hard Dewey works to clear them. We're lucky that way."

"But the ferry, the iron ore, the button factory—there're reasons to come here, to stay."

He shook his head. "It'll never lure others who'd invest in dairying, nor the people who need it."

She sank back into the down, lay there, longing, bruising from loss.

He took a deep breath. "You don't need to agree with this, Mazy. It's done. It's my responsibility to provide for us. I am, my way."

"I'll stay here, then," she said after a time.

"You're not listening. I've sold it. People are coming to live here. It's done and I'm going."

He hadn't said we, just I.

"Where then? Back to Milwaukee? Or to Chicago where there're people like...yellow jackets over trash? Why buy the cows, then? And why did my mother know, before I did?"

"I wanted you to come along, remember?" he said. He sat up in the bed, arms folded across his chest, his neck stretched, jaw pushed forward. "This, your...wounding wouldn't have happened if you had come."

"You're the wound," she said.

"It's a wound for a man to care for his wife, to invest his money in a future and not gamble or drink it away? Some wound. I know a dozen wives who'd jump at the chance to live with the pains you think I've given. And they wouldn't argue about it, not one. A dozen who'd make a good life in the west."

"My life is good. Or was." She felt sluggish, her thinking as mixed up as the dog's food. Her side throbbed. "You've sold the bluffs. The meadow. My garden. My life." She paused, her words muffled by swallowed tears. "What the brute did today was nothing."

"If you'd have been with us…three could have handled the animals better. You could have driven the wagon instead of my having to. I could have herded them. The brute wouldn't have bolted."

"You bought another wagon, too?"

He said nothing for a moment, then, "Going through Iowa, I'll need a sturdier wagon. After I cross the Missouri at Kanesville, maybe I'll join with an overland train, maybe go west alone."

Lying flat on the floor, Pig yipped in his sleep, shook, then quieted. West. Leave this place.

"You let me plant the garden," Mazy said, staring at the ceiling, "knowing I wouldn't be here to ever see the harvest? You sat there at the table, hour after hour looking at Ayrshires, finding a brute to buy and never said you planned to take him west?"

He lay back beside her, kept his arms crossed over his chest. "I didn't want to upset you."

Hotness flushed over her. "It never occurred to you that I'd be upset left out of the choice? You never thought I might want to have a say in my own life?"

"I haven't wanted to say this, Maze, but you are just a child in many ways." He paused, twirled a curl of her hair around his finger. She could almost see his lazy grin trying to slip over her emptiness. "Running around in your bloomers."

"Now what I wear bothers you?" She yanked at the comforter,

pulling it from him, brushed at his hand in her hair. "Nothing I do suits you."

"It might have been someone else coming through the trees," he lectured. "Exposing your ankles won't be wise where we're going, Maze. If you're going with me…"

"What if I go back with Mama and live in Milwaukee. What then?"

"Your mother's going too, so I need you to drive a wagon. Load up and drive and no arguments."

"My mother is…?" She stared at the woman who slept through her husband's betrayal.

"That was thoughtless, what I just said, about needing you just to drive."

"It must be the laudanum." She threaded her hand through her hair. "Why would Mother leave home? She's—"

"She wants adventure. She told me. Look." He dabbed at Mazy's eyes with his handkerchief, softening her resolve, engaging her in that way he had. "We'll find another place with boundaries that take in mountains and rivers and timber and meadows, too. You'll see."

Shadows from the hearth danced against the chinking. Her mother snored, a ruffled nightcap framing her round face that lolled back against the rocker, mouth open in the sleep of the innocent.

"And if I don't go?"

"I'm thirty-six years old, Maze. If I don't take aim now, I'll be angry with myself for however long I live for having missed this shot."

"And my choice," she said, "is to do the most foreign thing I can think of. Watch my husband walk away, maybe even my mother, or step out into a cloud of the unknown and hope I don't fall through."

"You'll have your mother with you."

She swallowed a sob and turned her face to the down. Jeremy reached to hold her, but she pulled away. "I don't understand why things need to change," she said. "I don't understand!"

The dog stirred and came to the side of the bed, his face bumping against hers as he sniffed.

"Will you come, Maze?"

She couldn't answer—her thoughts too heavy, so choking.

They lay silent beside each other.

"I know what a beaver feels like now," Mazy said as the night stepped aside for the morning. "Pushed into a trap. It's not the dying he fears. It's the change, made without choice. And knowing he'll never see home again."

His lips brushed her forehead. She stiffened and turned away.

2

choices

"You'll feel better when you're not so sore," Elizabeth told her only child the next morning. She patted Mazy's still swollen fingers, exposed from the sling. "They look like little fat sausages. Maybe the bandage is too tight. I'll ponder that."

"I'm too sore to think," Mazy said. She sat on the side of the bed, dizzy.

The dog lumbered over, made growling and slurping sounds as he nuzzled Mazy's good hand.

"Even sounds like a pig," Elizabeth said. "That how you named him?" She bent, scratched the dog's head.

"I just liked the sound of the word."

"Words, words. So much readin' and writin' you got no time for grandbabies." Elizabeth laughed.

Mazy didn't.

Elizabeth frowned, irritated with herself for making light talk with her daughter who almost always wanted serious.

"I know you're grieved," Elizabeth said, adjusting the bandage. "But change is part of living. Can't stop it no matter how you try. I remember when your papa brought me from Virginia to tend his big house in Milwaukee." Elizabeth stood, held a sun-dried sheet with her chin, and started to fold it. "The bustle of that city, all the smells of people cooking and doing, woke me up when I didn't even know I'd been sleeping." She held the flannel to her breast, inhaling the memory. "Why, I might have gone my whole life without them moments if I'd stayed put just cooking. Worse, your papa surely woulda found another to love and marry. You mighta been born to a butcher's wife instead of a tender doctor's."

She looked at her daughter, said softly, "You can either see what Jeremy's done as opportunity, or spend your days pinching your nose like he's a polecat. You'll get tired pinching, Mazy, but the choice is yours."

⤜⤛

Choice, what choice did she have? Take a job as a day lady or gather clamshells for the button factory, board herself out? Through the window, she watched her mother remove the rags from her tomatoes, placed to hold back the threat of night freeze. Elizabeth sang over the garden remains, sang over change. Mazy lay back down on the bed. What would people think if she sent her husband and mother off while she stood waving good-bye in her bloomers? Was she strong enough to stay? What then? Her eye caught the seed gourd she'd decorated with berry juice designs that now hung by hemp twine over the oak mirror. All that work of planting.

She wanted penance, that's what she wanted. Some payment for his not sharing what he'd been thinking about all those months, for excluding her from the most important decision of their marriage. All those evenings she'd watched his strong jaw profiled in the candlelight and thought he understood her while she talked about what she'd plant, how certain flowers would keep the gophers away, how she'd dry the tomatoes and imagined them deepening winter stews. But all those tender moments had been betrayals, wide breaches of faith.

The times he'd lifted his eyes, adjusted his round, wire-framed glasses, and smiled at her through moistened lips as she spoke of the eagle's flights or the area where wild daisies grew, he'd been thinking not about what she said or what she hoped for, but about some far and distant place. She might have been talking of bloomers or bunions for all the difference it made. He hadn't trusted her to understand, to want to share his dream. He'd treated her like old ironstone that could be used and broken, or simply left behind.

She'd take that mirror, she decided, and the bench and the table and the plank rocker, heavy as a horse. She'd take them all, surround herself with familiar and defiance.

⁓

Jeremy looked over the furniture items Mazy marked to bring along. The round, oak table, the saltbox, her wooden mixing bowls, the doughboy with its residue of flour permanently kneaded into the oak.

"The mirror stays. So does the chest of drawers, the bonnet dresser, the table and chairs—I'll make new ones. Don't want to kill the mules with replaceable things, especially oak. Way too heavy. Only take essentials," he said.

They stood like two dogs arguing over place. "We best get this *essential* thing straightened out," Mazy said. "If I'm going, I'm taking things that matter to me even if they don't to you." The firmness in her own voice surprised her. "Don't you agree, Mother? Grandma's chairs come?"

"Oh, you two children best work that out." Elizabeth turned back to the linen she sorted. "We'll all settle in together just fine."

"Caged birds rarely settle, especially without a perch," Mazy said. Her side throbbed, and she sat down on her grandmother's chair. "I'm taking the bonnet dresser and the bedroom set if we have to latch it to the side for the chickens to cackle at." She crossed her good arm over her chest. "The china service goes, and we take the dining room table. Take it apart if we need to and double the floor with the boards. I won't arrive without familiar things around me."

"You're so beautiful when you're giving orders," Jeremy said. He reached to pull her to him, his hands tangled in the chestnut fall at the back of her neck.

"Nobody listens," she said, felt her face flush.

He kissed her then stepped back beyond her reach. "You can't take the hickory rocker. Nor the chairs, table, or dresser. But the bed, all right." He grinned. "The essentials."

⤳

"We'll be risking our lives just to get there. West," Mazy said in disgust. She and her mother walked the rows of what was left of her garden. Cows mooed from the corral. The pain in Mazy's arm made her light-headed.

"You're exaggerating again, Madison. Something I was sure you'd outgrow."

"Horace Greeley says, with the Indian trouble and all, it's criminal for a man to take women and children across the plains."

"The Fox and Sauk Indians are quiet, I hear," Elizabeth said. "Besides, everyone knows what to do and what not to. Most don't even hire guides, the trail's so well marked. It's a good year for families to go. It's a good year for adventure. It'll be no more trouble than getting from Milwaukee to here."

"And wasn't *that* full of surprises."

Elizabeth looked into the hurt of her daughter's green eyes. "We may as well have this out now as later."

Mazy heard her heart thud in her ears. Sometimes her scoffing could take her where she didn't really want to go, jabbing with words but not getting too close. A serious conversation with her mother was a place she tried to avoid.

"The day Jeremy got to Milwaukee he said he was heading west," her mother said, leading her to a pine stump, helping her to sit. "I laughed, didn't seem like him, a man who's always rubbing oils on his hands to keep 'em soft as a baby's bottom. But he was serious. I turned selfish when I pondered. I might not see my grandbabies—if you ever have any. So I found a way to tag along." She lifted Mazy's good hand and settled it in her wide palm.

Mazy felt the calluses on her mother's fingers, the firmness of her hold, and listened, watched as her mother fluffed at the lace collar on her gray dress.

"So I said I was going if you was. Jeremy laughed, told me it'd be easier to catch a weasel asleep than selling my home that fast." Elizabeth leaned into Mazy. The scent of lavender leaned with her. "Well, I said that part about the weasel. But when I mentioned needing to sell my things, a buyer showed."

"'Wish Maze could act that fast,' Jeremy says to me when I told him I'd sold the house, which had a few surprises of its own by the time it was settled." She didn't elaborate. "But I tells him, you got your papa's ways—studied-like and loyal. He said the loyal part was something he'd be needing since he hadn't told you yet." Elizabeth's blue eyes watered. "I was sad for that, his not sharing it with you. But then I pondered, well, I can't change it. But I never woulda held something like that back."

Mazy sighed. "I couldn't have stood it if you had."

"Oh, darlin', don't you know? If a body can't stand somethin' it'll pass right out." She laughed then, her wide, fleshy face blotched red, her blue eyes brimmed. "I looked for the good in it when I found out." Elizabeth licked her lips. "Except for holidays and that short month visit here last year, we ain't spent time together as two married women, like we are now."

Mazy nodded, touched her mother's chubby cheek with her finger, surprised at the smoothness. "I'm just…afraid," Mazy said.

"I know it." She patted Mazy's hand. "My mama always said fear's just a reminder to dress good as you can while you're wearing new circumstances."

"But then," Mazy said, "Grandma hadn't heard of bloomers."

❧

The Bacons' neighbors, such as there were, planned a gathering for them at the little log church in Cassville, to celebrate the changes the Bacons were making.

"It would be a salve to my soul to have a preacher there today," Mazy said, as they rode the mules into town, "but it's too early in the year to see him."

"I'll be needing salve somewhere else before this day is done," Elizabeth said, rubbing her hip. "Always worse after I ride."

"Just hang on to that pie," Jeremy said.

"More worried about your stomach than my backside, I see," Elizabeth said. Jeremy laughed while Elizabeth checked the cloth that hung from her sidesaddle as it flopped against the neck of the black mule named Ink. Mazy hoped she would get fed at this gathering, find something to fill the emptiness of their leaving, calm the uncertainty.

❧

Jeremy Bacon stood in the center of a cluster of men shaded by the maples that arched over the log building. Lilac bushes threatened to bud. Tobacco smoke circled the face of Hathaway Wilson, who drew on his pipe, then used it to make some point, all eyes turned in his direction. His right hand he stuck in his paisley vest as though holding his heart. Jeremy stood taller than Hathaway and several others, even without the hat he'd left hooked over the saddle's horn.

Mazy couldn't hear their words, but bursts of laughter rose from the group and then quieter sounds, nods of heads, pats on suspender-crossed backs. Several men bore the sun marks of a hat wearer, forehead paler than cheeks. There seemed to be looks of admiration directed at her husband, perhaps even looks of longing. It didn't seem possible that so many men could want to uproot, take their families into danger and beyond, or that so many others would admire them for it. It stretched her understanding of how different men and women were.

"This west thing is a craze, that's what it is," Adora Wilson said. The formidable-looking woman, broad shoulders, narrow waist, now stood beside Mazy. She wore a pink bonnet with a stiff pasteboard brim that shaded a face that was just beginning to wrinkle. "You'd think they were boys discovering a new fishing hole and not sure if they want to share the news or keep the treasure to themselves. My own husband among them." She fussed at her bonnet, removed it. "I don't know how you'll manage, Mazy. I simply could not do it." The last words came out like hammer pounds.

"Hathaway's not thinking of going, surely."

"Oh, the subject was raised, but I put my foot down. And Charles balked." Adora nodded to her son, a striking man who leaned against the tree scraping at his fingernails with a knife. He wore a white, collarless shirt, button pants. One ear had a healed-over notch, visible even in the shadow of his gray hat. Mazy never liked to have him wait on her in the Wilsons' mercantile: Charles always came around the smooth counter to stand beside her, liked to brush his fingers over hers when she handed him the book of cloth. "But the west fever's affected us…" Adora continued. "Tipton's fallen in love with that Tyrell Jenkins."

Mazy's eyes wandered to the man notable for his large forearms, his short but sturdy-looking legs, and his stellar reputation. He was said to be a skilled smithy, and she'd heard that in his back room, he fed orphaned kittens from a glove.

"I imagine a farrier'd be welcomed well on a westward train," Mazy's mother said, joining the twosome, waving away flies from the table as she talked. Elizabeth had met Adora last year, had only a brief conversation, but Mazy's mother knew no strangers, could carry on as familiar as a lifelong friend. "You could do worse for your daughter."

"But Tipton's only fifteen," Adora said, lifting her chin. "And a mite headstrong."

"Ponder where she got that," Elizabeth said.

Adora frowned. "She'd make any man's head turn like an owl's, but not out of wisdom, I'm afraid. She's been whittling on her father about marriage and heading west. With Tyrell. So far, he's stood firm, which he best do. We waited seven years to marry." She straightened her broad shoulders, fidgeted with the tucks that spread across her wide bosom. "'Til he had the store going strong. No reason she can't wait until Tyrell's good and settled. He can jolly well come back to pick her up. Hathaway told him that trail runs east just the same as west." She fanned her face with her hands, lowered her voice to almost a whisper. "'Course I think she'd do much better, with Tyrell out of the picture." She leaned in. "Poor people have poor ways, you know. Did you put spices in that pie, Elizabeth? It is Elizabeth, isn't it? I never can taste a thing, but sometimes I think I can smell spices."

Elizabeth nodded her head to the questions. "No harm in wishing good things for our kin, I'd guess," Elizabeth said. "Best things we mamas do."

Then Mazy's mother left to organize the food on the table and turned back to talk with Kay Krall and Janie Switzler, women watching toddlers waddling on the grass. Mazy heard the younger women laugh, noticed her mother join in.

Her mother fit like a hand-cobbled shoe, as though she'd always been a part of Cassville. Mazy guessed it was Elizabeth's backwoods upbringing, with a dozen cousins living close by, that let her turn everyone into family. It was a trait Mazy longed for in herself.

"Is Tyrell leaving soon?" Mazy asked Adora.

"Not soon enough." She opened and closed the clasp on her wrist purse without ever looking inside. "Truth is, I've a worry she might just run off. I know I'll watch her like a cornered bear the day he leaves and for two weeks after. He could have joined up before this—I wish he had. Tipton's keeping him here, in a daze, with all her flirting. Look at her," Adora said, but Mazy heard pride rolled into the words of scold.

Tipton Wilson laughed. The girl's high cheekbones flushed rose, a color Mazy guessed she'd pinched into them just before she swirled open her parasol for shade. Petite and blond and draped in blue—including the stones in her ears—she was the Wilsons' only daughter. The girl didn't just stand between her father and Tyrell, she composed the center of the circle. She stared up at her intended, flashing even, white teeth clasped together as though she posed for a portrait and had been told not to move a muscle. Tipton blinked long eyelashes, touched a gloved finger to her cheek. She spoke and the men laughed. Tyrell Jenkins's face splotched pink in the bare places free of his rhubarb red beard.

"She'll be a handful for any husband," Adora sighed.

"Desserts are fixing to spoil," Mazy's mother interrupted. "And my stomach's agrowling."

The women signaled their men, who headed for the tables. Tipton and Tyrell walked as though weighted, their heads bent in conversation.

Mazy noticed Tipton's brother loitering behind, his gartered shirt sleeve pressed at his shoulder against the tree. That odd notch out of his ear silhouetted against the light. He tossed something shiny in his palm, coins it looked like, clinking upward without his watching. His eyes stared at Tipton instead, a glare until he noticed Mazy watching. A half smile formed at one corner of his pursed lips. He made no move to join the others.

Hathaway asked the blessing over the brown betty pudding, cobbler, cookies, and pies. Elizabeth had baked Mazy's favorite raisin pie; the plump fruit had been carried in spring water in a crock jar all the way from Milwaukee. Light conversation filtered over the eaters, in between bites and batting at horseflies, gentle chastisements of children. Toddlers scampered beneath the lilac bushes, the ribbons on the girls' dresses limp and the boys' knees covered with grass stains. A half-dozen dogs lay beneath wagons. Pig panted in the shade of a buckboard while food and well-wishing were washed down with sun tea. Mazy thought of the pleasantness of this place, these people, and swallowed back tears.

Finally filled, they said good-bye, hugs and hands patting on backs. The women expressed good wishes with a sense of relief, Mazy thought, relief that it was she leaving and not any of them. She looked around her. These were good people, but she'd become close to none these two years past. Perhaps that was a blessing.

∽

"I've made a decision," Jeremy said.

The three of them rode home through the timber, the mules clop-clopping like a grandfather clock on the packed road. The squeak of the leather and the swish of the mules' tails gave Jeremy a moment to think about what he needed to change to make this come out differently than the last announcement given to his wife. He wiped at his nose with the handkerchief Mazy had embroidered with the letter *J*, stuffed it back under the rim of his hat, and cleared his throat.

"Am I to be surprised?" Mazy asked.

"I'm speaking about it beforehand. Tyrell Jenkins wants to go west," Jeremy announced.

"Another man with a wild idea."

"Hathaway's fearful his daughter'll run off after him when he leaves," Jeremy said. "She's threatened that—"

"And probably will if Adora's words prove true."

"Quite." He plunged ahead. "With your arm so bad and you so sore and still healing, we could use someone to drive your mother's wagon. And a blacksmith's skills would be of value."

Pig yawned in the road far in front of them, stopped and sat to scratch.

"We'd just need to take the girl along, too," Mazy said.

"Quite," Jeremy said. For someone so young and untested, Mazy could surprise him with her quick conclusions. She could see what other people yearned for, when she wanted to. He couldn't believe she hadn't sensed his need to leave, to try new vistas.

"You're proposing that we mother hen that one?" Elizabeth asked. "Wouldn't be a spree."

"She could be a help to you, Maze, especially with your arm as it is," Jeremy said. "Hath's willing to pay for her passage, which would help us secure Tyrell's wage for driving. But it would mean having another around, not exactly your porridge."

"Maybe we should wait until I'm healed before we leave. We could do it ourselves then. Alone."

"No," Jeremy said. "This is the perfect time. Good grazing, before big herds come through. We'll be well over the mountains before any threat of early winter. No, April's the best time to leave so we're there by October. Tyrell's strong arms and skills are a gift, if we decide to take it."

"The true gift is that you're actually asking me," Mazy said. "Before you've committed. Or have you?"

"I haven't."

A robin chirped in an oak as they rode past a mound of grass shaped like a bird. "Old Indian burial spot, Mother," Mazy said, pointing. "There're several back in the trees."

"I told Hathaway I'd have to talk it over with you," Jeremy persisted.

"That must have taken some tongue biting on your part," Mazy said.

"Hath said he knew it was like herding cats getting a woman to go down the trail you want."

"Oh, did he?"

"Never wanted this to be torture for you, Maze." He reached, lifted her hand and cupped his over it as he held the reins, felt the pull of the leather against her palm, the coolness of her fingers. "Wanted it to be our journey together. Just didn't know how to...to bring it up, without you getting all agitated. And then you've been so off your feed, as your mother'd say."

"Would I?" Elizabeth said.

"That confirmed I made the right choice in waiting, just doing it all on my own."

Mazy started to pull away. He held her hand firm.

"All I want is some say in my own life," Mazy said.

"It's what I want too. It is, Maze. To decide things together. When we can." He was never sure how much to tell her or when.

"I still don't understand why we have to go at all, why you need such a change."

"Life is just that. All it is, and adjusting to it."

The mule twisted his head to bite at a fly. "Adora doesn't know of Hathaway's plan, does she?" Mazy said.

Jeremy settled back into the saddle. "Hathaway'll have his own price to pay tonight when he tells her what he offered me…us. Once she turns seventeen, he's willing for the marriage, but until then, we'd be asked to be her family, treat her as our own."

"She's not that much younger than you," Elizabeth said.

"Might be a friend for you, Maze," Jeremy said. "Doesn't seem you have many."

"With good reason when I have to leave them behind, unexpected." She sighed. "Well, let's talk with Tipton, then, see what she understands."

Jeremy let out a burst of held air. "Thanks, Maze. Told Hathaway to come on out tomorrow, unless I came back to tell him different. I think this could be good, really good for us. I feel it in my bones."

"I'm the one whose bones have feeling," Mazy said lifting her sling. "And good's not the word I'd choose."

❧

The new people who'd bought the Bacon place arrived early the next day, before either Tyrell or Tipton and her family. Mazy held herself

31

back from the woman, a Mrs. Malarky. Her mother proved the more invitational, showing the woman the house, the furniture they'd leave, while Jeremy and the new owner rode mules toward the bluffs and the highest boundaries of the Bacon place.

Mazy watched the Malarkys' two boys, probably three and five, who tumbled out of the wagon like puppies, exploring and chattering after the chickens. Pig had barked at them and their dog, a yellow herding type with a long tail. The dogs marked their territory then sniffed each other and decided both could stay.

"And this is Mazy's garden, what's left of it," her mother told Mrs. Malarky. The two walked over to where Mazy squatted, pulling aimlessly at weeds. Mrs. Malarky, a short, round woman, looked as though she might have put on weight with the carrying of her children and had simply forgotten to take it back off.

"A fine tilling," Mrs. Malarky said. "Little mussed up, maybe, but it's still early for setting seedlings."

"The brute," Mazy said, standing, brushing dirt from her apron. "He did some renovating. I think the beans'll be fine. They didn't get troubled much. But the tomatoes, I doubt they'll make it. I brought them back inside. One or two might recover and could be set out again and staked."

"Must be hard to leave it—all this."

"It is."

They stood silent, eyes massaged by the landscape. "Do you have a seed gourd?" Mrs. Malarky asked. "No sense my keeping my seeds when you already planted yours. I've got some maple tree seed wings, too. You're taking a lilac start, surely?"

"I'd be grateful for the seeds," Mazy said. "And now you mention it, I think I'll take a bucket of Wisconsin soil with me, too."

"Now that's essential," her mother said, and Mazy laughed.

⤙⤚

The Wilson girl left no doubt about whose heart she was after, batting eyes at her intended. Jeremy'd said she could assist with cooking. Elizabeth smiled to herself. Men. Something about that girl said she might be interested in cooking, all right, but not over an open pit.

A slender gloved hand rested on the muscled forearm of Tyrell Jenkins as the two meandered toward the house now almost empty of all Bacon things and slowly filling up with the Malarkys'. The latter had graciously decided to walk with their children to the pond dotted with ducks when the visitors arrived.

Adora and Hathaway paced behind their daughter, Adora like a boat being dragged across shallow water. Adora didn't smile as she approached, her jaw set. Even Charles had joined them for the family discourse, wearing cream-colored breeches and that halfhearted smile.

"I won't be even a smidgen of a bother," Tipton offered when they gathered in the large room on the Malarkys' chairs and the ones Mazy'd been forced to leave behind. "Papa's told me all the rules, and I'll most certainly abide." She smiled that clasped-front-teeth smile that looked as though she were delicately biting off a piece of meat without letting it touch her lips, her back bed-slat straight.

"Even if you don't like what you're asked to do," Hathaway said, "you'll do it."

"Oh, Papa, haven't I always?"

Adora wiped her nose with a white lace handkerchief. Gray, swollen eyes looked out from a puffy, grief-splotched face.

"We'll take good care of her, Adora," Mazy said, "though no one can do that so well as a mother."

"She'll be a help to you, Hath says, what with your arm and all." Adora squeezed at her nose, her fingertips white. "I'll get by. Truth is, Hath says I'll be fine without my baby."

"You still have me, Mother," Charles said from his chosen place near the door.

"Oh yes, I know."

Mazy patted Adora's clenched hand. "We'll be welcoming your help, Mr. Jenkins," she said then to Tyrell.

"Worry-free wheels when a smithy travels with you." Elizabeth grinned. "Could use that as a calling card."

Tyrell blushed. "If I had such a thing." He fingered his hat brim. Elizabeth guessed him to be in his midtwenties, but he might have been older, gauging by those experience lines flowing out from his kind eyes. He was a well-proportioned young man, with a wash of wisdom about him, something offering compassion and care. She watched him perch his hat on his knee and rest his wide hand over Tipton's while the girl twirled the reddish hairs at his wrist.

"You'll write," Adora told her daughter. She looked at Mazy. "You'll make her. They say they leave mail at the forts and riders coming east will bring them. It would be so helpful, to know what's happening… I just could not bear it if something…and I did not know."

"You heading through Iowa, then," Hathaway asked. "South overland? Not taking the river to St. Louis?"

"Just flat country straight east across the ferry," Jeremy told him.

"And you'd know that, how?" Mazy asked.

"Readings I've done. Those forty-niners heading back from the fort talk. I know what I'm doing, Maze," Jeremy said.

"Mama worries overmuch," Tipton said. "Tell her, Papa, there's nothing to worry over."

"Maybe not, but caution still needs to be heeded. In all things," her father said and raised one eyebrow to his daughter.

"So your baby'll wed in Oregon," Elizabeth said. Adora let out a little mewing sound. Hathaway put his arm around his wife and patted her shoulder. It seemed to Elizabeth that the woman stiffened when he did.

"On the day I achieve seventeen. We'll have a daguerreotype made and send you the likeness, Mama. Oh, it is such an adventure. Isn't it, Tyrellie?" She twirled at his wrist hairs again, and the square, sturdy man picked at a scrape on the leather of his boot as he blushed.

❦

Mazy and Jeremy lay on the narrow cornhusk mattress squeezed into the back of the wagon. Tonight was a trial, to see if they had what they needed before starting out in the morning. Mazy gazed at the headboard of her grandmother's old bed, but it didn't hold the bed slats. They had become part of the wagon's floor. The space beneath the canvas wagon cover confined her like a corset, stuffed as it was with shelving and barrels and trunks. And yet she felt emptied by the inevitable.

Outside, crickets clacked and Mazy wondered if there would be crickets where they were going. Or clamshells for her buttons? Ducks of a dozen names? Morel mushrooms—would they grow there? Or a hundred other things of nature that nourished her and filled her soul. *The Lord knows my lot. He makes my boundaries fall on pleasant places.* She would keep repeating the phrase along with "help me, help me, help me." It was all she could do.

She listened to Tyrell snore from his bedroll on the ground outside. Tipton and Mazy's mother shared a straw tick in Elizabeth's wagon. Mazy crept out of the wagon and dropped with a gentle thud to the dew-moistened ground. In the pink of the morning light, she made her way to the garden for one last look of longing.

Mazy watched the outline of deer etched in the distance. Morning fog lifted over the timber in the direction of the river. She wiped her face with her shawl and felt the shiver of the morning cool her swollen arm. She breathed hard, fatigued by the effort at getting out of bed. She yearned to run, to hide inside a limestone cave until this uprooting passed. But Jeremy was her husband. She'd vowed before God to stay with him 'til death. No place was worth the melting away of a marriage.

Jeremy sneezed behind her.

"Can't surprise you, with this dratted nose," he said. She felt him fumble for a handkerchief, blow his nose again. "Appreciate your change of heart, Maze." He rocked her side to side then, gentle, the way a mother rocked her baby. "Expect someday you might forgive the way I did it?" Jeremy said. "I did better, with the Wilson girl, didn't I?"

"You did. Though I think before this journey's over we may both be wondering what lapse of thinking attacked us when we agreed to take her on."

"She'll be fine. This is what she wanted. Doubt she'll challenge it."

"Men can be thick as a tree trunk," Mazy said.

"Oh, can we?" He turned her to him then, his hands on her. The wash of his words whispered at her ear, rounding the edges of her anger. "You're a good woman, Maze," he said, "doing what's right. It's a man's lot to make a way for his family. That's all I'm doing." He leaned to kiss her.

Mazy pulled away, aware of his startled eyes. "I'm keeping my vows, Jeremy," she said, "to stay with you through thick and thin. That's why I'm going. But I've plans to come back. Wisconsin is what I knew first, and I can't imagine finding anything to replace it."

"The West'll seduce you, the vistas and valleys. Just as I'd like to now," he said, pulling her to him, "before the cows need milking."

She pushed at his hands. "Mother'll hear."

She turned and stomped back to the wagon.

❧

"I don't much like good-byes," Mazy said.

"Sometimes, if we're smart, we can turn them into hellos," Elizabeth said. "They live just on the other side." Elizabeth wedged her way between Tipton and Tyrell, settling onto the seat. She smiled and lines creased out like spokes of a wagon wheel as she waved her daughter toward the lead wagon as they readied to head out.

Mazy looked back only once. She saw Mrs. Malarky, round as a pumpkin, waving from her doorway, two boys like short stakes on either side. In the distance, Mr. Malarky already strained behind a mule tilling soil. She felt a rush of blood come to her face, a feeling of envy so profound it made her ache. She memorized this last look of their place, inhaled it, vowing to remember every detail, every nuance, every smell and touch and taste of where she'd first known contentment and independence braided together as peace.

"What's that? You bringing weeds along?" Jeremy said glancing at the bucket of dirt pushed up against the dashboard that kept mud from the mules' hooves from flying at their feet.

"Wisconsin soil and a tomato plant," she said, prepared to counter a challenge. "I intend to plant them in our new home. Who knows, maybe I'll even come back here to do it."

Jeremy said nothing, slapped the reins on the mules' backs.

Ahead, Pig chased after rabbits, checking back in from time to time, and Mazy could see his black tail pointing to the sky as he flushed quail. Tiny white flowers pushed through the dark forest floor reaching up for light. The land bloomed lush and green and the air felt balmy, just a light breeze lifting the leaves of sumac and oak. Before long, the morels would expose themselves beside blue columbine in the shade of the elms. It was such an early spring. Mazy bit her lip. Her garden would have been so bountiful.

3

the gathering

What was that racket? It sounded like chickens playing marbles with the dogs. Tipton pulled the linen over her head. Hadn't she earned a good night's sleep? Hadn't she done all the Bacons had asked and then some? Milking those cows 'til her hands ached, and from behind, too. Whoever heard of such a thing? And she'd endured for days the chafing of damp clothes after the hailstorm and Mr. Bacon refusing to stop long enough for things to dry out. Had she complained? Not once, not that she didn't have cause.

She'd thrown things out of her trunk to lighten the load while Miz Bacon hung on to that bucket of Cassville dirt! It didn't seem fair. Mr. Bacon was a stern and driven man, even if he did help his wife hang the cauldron over the fire without her having to ask. Still, Miz Bacon said Tipton's was the "attitude that needed buttressing."

What attitude? She'd rarely said a word these past six weeks. She was sure she didn't roll her eyes as often as Miz Bacon did at her very own mother, especially when the older woman mentioned her aching "backside" fifteen times a day, which she did. Tipton counted.

Six weeks they'd been on the road together, jostled and bounced across Iowa's rutted roads until Tipton's neck ached more than Mrs. Mueller's behind, not that she'd be so rude as to say it. Iowa was nothing but mud sketched through the shadow of tall, towering, blocking-out-the-sun trees. Tipton felt constantly cool. Snow had sometimes spit at their faces. Snow! Only the presence of Tyrell beside her gave her warmth, that and the memory of stolen moments when he'd kissed her as Mrs. Mueller pawed for something in the wagon, or the evening she'd crept to his bedroll and he'd held her briefly before he whispered her back. Stealing the experiences made them the sweeter.

With effort, they'd reached and forded the Desmoines River in what Tyrell told her was record time. Still, they'd rarely had a day without some happening to make Mr. Bacon complain that they weren't moving fast enough or far enough or paying enough attention to "essentials."

"We're required to be in Kanesville by May fifteenth," Mr. Bacon said, tapping his finger to his temple in that way he had. The delays hadn't been anyone's fault, not that Mr. Bacon would say so. No, someone always had to be at fault with him. A broken king bolt? Mules gone lame? He blamed that on "too many worthless things being carried."

They got oxen, unruly ones, from a settler, and she'd heard Mrs. Mueller say they had to lay out cash, too. Tyrell told her they should have had oxen to begin with. But Mr. Bacon set his own pace and didn't much listen to the wisdom of others.

But Tyrell was so easygoing, such a gentleman, he always let Mr. Bacon have the last word. Tipton hoped that wasn't a sign of weakness in her future husband. She wished he'd spoken up when the women asked for time to hang clothes on a bush to dry or look for berries to supplement biscuits and flour gravy.

"We keep moving," Tyrell told her later, his mouth surrounded by that red beard. "Not much worthy of bickering over. You got to get clear about what matters and then have the courage to do it." He picked up her hand and rubbed the tips of her fingers as he talked. She loved to watch him talk.

What mattered to Tipton's way of thinking was time with Tyrell, when her feet weren't so sore from the walking, when her hands weren't so red and dry from the water and wind.

She had dreamed of making this journey together. Except for the first day out, there had been little to dream about, just long hours of riding, then walking, and sometimes just waiting while Tyrell pounded on iron to repair the wheels. They moved fallen trees from trails, crossed rushing streams. Her days were filled with the clang of Mr. Bacon's orders and Miz Bacon refusing while he brushed off dust and focused on "essentials." Tipton heard that word in her sleep.

Then last evening, they'd rattled into the valley cupping Kanesville or what some called Council Bluffs. Rounded mounds on either side marked this gateway to the Missouri, and campfires twinkled across the area. Tipton was sorry she was too tired and sore to explore. Mrs. Mueller set her sights on meeting people, invited her too. "Mazy says you can sleep past dawn tomorrow. She'll look after the cows in the morning," Mrs. Mueller told her.

Instead, Tipton did what Tyrell planned to do: crawled into bed early.

Now it was morning and the cackling and barking and what sounded like the chattering of children tore her from a dreamless sleep.

Her supple fingers with tapered nails clutched her chemise at her throat as she crawled over Mrs. Mueller. The older woman didn't budge. Tipton wrinkled her nose at the snores, the smells of old sleep. She cringed at the closeness, the assumption of intimacy.

The whispering outside grew louder. Tipton folded back the wagon flap and startled as a child's dark blue eyes peered straight into hers. They both screamed at once. Tipton jumped, and the small boy clambered off the low step, tripping over another boy, sending them both sprawling to the ground. Then they fled, kicking up dirt as they left. One was thin as a hairbrush handle, the other as round as crossed buns.

Children! Tipton prepared to scold, but what she saw outside stopped her cold.

Tents and wagons and people moved everywhere. New people, cooking next to painted wagons. Women in white aprons bent over low fires, pushing their skirts back from the flames. Dogs lounged about, some sniffing close to cackling, caged chickens. Cows and oxen bellowed in the distance. The boy who'd peeked into their wagon, his hair slick and parted in the middle, turned to pick up his cap and then slipped beneath a tethered horse that hadn't been there when Tipton had told Tyrell good night.

Her eyes sought out Tyrell's bedroll in its familiar place beside their wagon. It wasn't there.

"Got us more company," Mrs. Mueller said behind her through a yawn. "Looks like a town exploded and dribbled people everywhere. Thought you'd sleep late."

"So much to see," Tipton said. She forced her voice into lightness, Tyrell's missing bedroll an ache behind her eyes.

"Guess kids don't need no sleep to wind them up. Heard a good-size group came in from Wisconsin in the night." Mrs. Mueller stretched. "Hear 'em?"

"No, nothing."

"We've got delays crossing the river, too," Mrs. Mueller told her, cracking her knuckles. "A thousand wagons ahead of us."

"Truly? A thousand!"

"Should have been here last week, Jeremy's saying."

"His precious Ayrshires'll be 'diluted of grass,' I suppose," Tipton said, pouring tepid water into a bowl. "Worries more about them than us."

Mrs. Mueller didn't answer.

Tipton splashed water onto her face. In silence, she plaited her tawny hair into a long braid, then twisted it on top of her head. She stared at the dark blue eyes gazing back at her from the section of broken mirror. Her mother said they were the color of Lake Michigan in a cold October. She pinched her cheeks and smoothed her blond brows with a wet finger. Her mind returned to Tyrell's missing bedroll. Where could he have gone? Her fingers shook as she tied on her skirt hoop.

"What's your hurry, girl?" Mrs. Mueller said, her head cocked to one side.

Tipton said nothing, trying not to look fretted.

"With additional womenfolk around now, we'll finally have a few more skirts to circle with in our necessary times," Elizabeth continued.

Tipton's cheeks burned hot with embarrassment. Why must she speak of such a private thing as if it were nothing more than washing dishes?

"Don't tell me that talk of ladies' latrines puts a blush on that pretty face," Mrs. Mueller told her. "You best learn to loosen up—hey, I made a joke," she said, "or your old bowels'll be packed like a cannon."

Tipton buried her head in a bachelor-button blue lingerie dress. When she reached Mrs. Mueller's age, she'd never talk about her bowels with others, not ever. She pulled the line-dried folds over her head, settled the waist, then sat to pull on her stockings and slippers, keeping her head low. When she sat up, she tied on a satin ribbon hat, wiped glycerin on her hands to soften them from the dry air, and pretended the pink on her cheeks came from the dot of rouge she rubbed there, not from the subject at hand.

"I'm a bit grieved by Jeremy's talk of going it alone," Mrs. Mueller said. "You ask my noggin," she continued, undoing her own long braid laced with gray and snubbing her fingers through it to untangle the plaits, "shouldn't be on one of these overland trips without at least five women. Six'd be better. We've had trees for our necessary circle so far, but come the prairies, you'll be pleased as pigs in heaven to have the backs of women's skirts to hide you while you squat."

"A lady doesn't…squat," Tipton said. "She *relieves* herself, which I intend to do right now." She felt her neck blotch hot. "I mean, relieve myself. Of this conversation."

Tipton stepped backwards down the steps, one hand managing her hoop skirt and the other grasping the side of the canvas for balance. She heard Mrs. Mueller's hearty laugh as she left.

It was one thing to lack privacy with personal hygiene and quite another to have it openly discussed. Tipton inhaled a deep breath just as Tyrell had said to whenever she felt rattled or flushed.

She looked up. Wispy clouds streaked across a blue canvas. Tipton stood a moment, savoring the light over the misted river, distant dust rising with sun streaks like gold thread woven through it. Deciding to risk continued conversation with her bedmate, she stepped back up, leaned inside to get her parasol, and plucked the pink silk from beneath the straw tick. Mrs. Mueller never even saw her. She stood with her back to the opening, one hand rubbing her hip.

Outside, Tipton scanned the wagons and the men standing in clusters, listening to the hum of conversations broken by an occasional burst of guffaws, the clank of iron against cauldron, the chatter of children at play. She smelled crackling cookies frying, felt the wetness of mud seep into her slippers. She decided to stand right where she was and scan until she found him. Now her breath came in short gasps.

She wondered why Tyrell hadn't thought to find her this morning. Maybe he wanted time away from her. Perhaps with others around now, he'd find more amiable companions, older and wiser.

She felt the familiar sensation press against her chest, the sense that air would not come through, and then the tingling numbness beginning in her fingers. Where was he? Why couldn't she see him? Maybe he and Mr. Bacon had had words. A buzz formed at the top of her head. If Tyrell left the train, she would run away with him. He wouldn't take her willingly, she knew that; he'd given his word to her parents. But she'd never be left with the Bacons. She'd escape to follow him on her own. She swallowed, her throat dry. She couldn't even make her saliva go down when she wanted.

"Did you sleep all right?"

Miz Bacon's words startled her from behind. She was light as a bird on her feet despite being as tall as most men. Tipton's eyes flickered, tightness stretched across her temples. No, it couldn't happen, not now, not here with all these people, not with Tyrell nowhere around to ease it away.

"Have some cornbread and sweet cream. Fixed it fresh this morning."

Miz Bacon put her good arm around the girl and eased her toward the Bacons' fire. There was no resisting the firmness. Miz Bacon's apron smelled of cabbage and something sour Tipton couldn't place. Still, the woman's arm felt comforting as a quilt. "Set a spell and keep me company," Miz Bacon said, and it sounded like a sigh.

Lonely, that's what she is. Loneliness could happen married to a man like Mr. Bacon; that and her being already so old with no children. Why, Miz Bacon must be almost nineteen.

Tipton let herself be helped to the milking stool set beside the embers.

"Haven't had enough of me yet?" Tipton said. Her voice sounded wispy even to herself. Her fingers felt so numb. She lowered her head below her knees. Sometimes that helped. She pretended to be gazing at the fire, blotting dampness at her slipper.

"We've a long way ahead of us to be tired of each other," Miz Bacon said. Her voice was always so gentle when she wasn't talking at her husband. "I've written a good report to your mama." The woman rubbed at the wrapped arm she now moved without a sling.

Tipton took a breath and held it. Sometimes if she did that, the tingling in her arm went away.

"Have you seen Tyrellie, Miz Bacon?" She exhaled it as a blast of air.

"I'll bet his mother named him that specifically so no one could add an *ie* at the end. Mothers'll do that, you know," Miz Bacon said. "Not want someone calling their six-foot-tall boy 'Mikie' someday, so they name him 'Jeremy' to begin with or something solid like Isaac or Tyrell. Then some sweet thing comes along and rearranges it. Tyrellie." She rolled her eyes.

"It's no one's business excepting ours, his and mine." Tipton's voice took on strength, and the tingling in her hand lessened. She sat up straighter.

Miz Bacon bit off a hunk of the cornbread and chewed. She winced as she tried to catch the crumbs in the palm of her bad hand.

"Have you seen him then, Miz Bacon?" Tipton let her eyes scan the area.

"After all this time, don't you think 'Mazy' is in order?"

"Not like him to wander from the wagons before we've had our good mornings."

"There'll be more folks around now, Tipton." Miz Bacon's voice got all soft. "People needing work done on their wagons, their horses trimmed. That's Tyrell's job. It's what a blacksmith does, why his work is so valued. Not looking after you." She said it with kindness, but still the words stung. "Your mama and papa delegated that task to us, at least for a while."

"Do tell, ma'am," Tipton said, lifting her chin. A songbird warbled into the silence. The scent of fried bacon drifted from a fire across the circle.

Pig, lying on his side in the wagon shade, let out a sharp, quick bark, woke himself, and trotted over to the women. Miz Bacon fed him bread from her palm. The dog slobbered. "You fat little pig," she said as she brushed at the dog's head in tenderness. Tipton looked away.

"What's with you? Are you worried? You strike me as so sure of yourself. You never turned an eye back toward home when we left. I envied that, the way you said good-bye without even shedding a tear. It doesn't fit then, it seems to me, your needing Tyrell so much."

"None of your business neither," Tipton said. She gathered up her parasol and poked it on the ground before her.

"Now see, that's just what I mean. Put me in my place but then so...lost almost, as though you can't be your own post—you've got to lean on him. That can tire a man."

"Our love is a post. We're roped together around it. We don't intend to let it untangle loose after we say our vows, not Tyrellie and me, not the way some married folks do." Tipton stood then. "We're the same. We understand that being together isn't leaning at all. It's filling up. It's...tying up loose ends, now that we have each other." She eyed the woman chewing, still staring. "Maybe that's what you envy, ma'am."

"Just don't get so roped together you get hung up," Miz Bacon told her.

Tipton straightened the blue pleats of her skirt and opened the parasol. "I was not born in the woods to be scared by an owl," she said and swirled out across the circle toward the new wagons.

Tyrell hadn't soured on her. They did belong together. These six weeks had proved it. He'd been kind and good and gentle. It was how he proved his love, not coming back for Tipton after two years apart the way her mother wanted. The mere thought of two or three years without Tyrell took her breath away.

She let herself take in the sights and sounds around her. The smells of horses and men, of cooking and smoke all swirled about by her parasol. She walked past roped places; one held Marvel and another the Ayrshire cows, Jennifer and Mavis. People milled like water swirling in a bucket, more men, women, and children in one place than she'd seen in months back in Cassville, even dark-skinned people, and slender, bowing girls with ivory hairsticks and wearing what looked like trim silk dresses. She spied the boys who'd peeked in the wagon. They pushed hoop rings before them with sticks. She overheard one say, "You think she's blind?"

"Why else would she carry that stick?"

"To hit people with, she's so grumpy." The boys laughed.

A girl with short pigtails stuck straight out like thumbs ran between them, forcing wind through a sock attached to a stick.

Tipton spied a dozen dogs, some tied and barking, others lying about or marking their homes. She'd gotten used to the Bacons' dog. He was big and carried a deep bark, but he gentled when he knew a person. Other dogs proved more worrisome, and she made a wide berth around two snarling over a deer's leg bone beneath a wagon.

So much was worrisome. She tried not to think of it as she walked. But there was the river, the Missouri. Wide and gorged with rain, it was worth worrying over. People said lightning fires could race across the prairie and leave nothing but charred remains of wagons and people.

She could worry over that and over the Sioux, too, who could steal and kill stragglers, and the Pawnees who just harassed. She'd heard tales of messages left by travelers scraped onto human skulls warning of the dangers of sickness ahead. Everything was worrisome if she was honest, everything. Her mouth got dry with the thinking.

"You got to settle your thoughts," Tyrell told her nearly every day. "You can tell them, 'go straight away' and they will. It's the only thing we all control—our thoughts, our own actions. No one else's." But he helped control hers, when he was there to remind her to take deep breaths. She could bury the fears because Tyrell stood beside her.

He said he'd never leave her, sounding almost like the words in Scripture Mrs. Mueller read out loud before they went to bed. Because of that fine promise, she felt more confident now as she walked. Tyrell gave her that, and she took some small satisfaction in knowing that Miz Bacon, Mazy, a wiser, older woman, envied it.

Tipton meandered in her own world of thoughts and didn't notice the couple until she bumped into them.

The man apologized for not watching, then introduced himself as Bryce Cullver and his wife, Suzanne, who wore a bonnet so floppy it shadowed her face. She held in her hand a goading stick instead of a parasol. "She carries a pink parasol as pretty as the lady herself," the man said, apparently describing Tipton to the woman clinging to his arm. "She has blue eyes, dark as dusk. Quite a photograph she'd make," Bryce Cullver said, patting his wife's hand.

Tipton watched the woman tug awkwardly at him as though to move away. She swung the goad and Tipton jumped back.

"Suzanne," the man said. He shook his head, tipped his hat, his eyes saying "sorry" before they moved on.

Tipton watched them, then became distracted by a tall, well-dressed man who bent in attentive conversation to a bloomer-clad woman. He had the look of a white-collared man, a gambler, one Tipton knew best to shy away from.

At last, she spied Tyrell. Not in the circle of wagons but near the stock ropes, those reddish curls clustered around his head looking almost like spun sunrise. She smiled and took a deep, filling breath.

He bent beneath a gelding whose foreleg braced against the leather apron laid out on Tyrell's thigh. The whole weight of the animal leaned against the man though three legs held the big sorrel up. No wonder his back ached, with the constant bending and the leaning of horses against his frame. Tipton heard the familiar rasp of the file pressed into service to shape the horse's hoof. Clumps of nippered hoof littered the ground before him, giving up their pungent smell.

A woman—a pretty woman—held the horse by its halter.

Tipton felt her chest tighten.

The woman's face lit up when she talked. Tiny white lines made their way from her hazel eyes then disappeared like wisps into fawn-colored hair caught in a snood at her neck. She wore a faded calico dress, and what looked like men's boots poked out from beneath the hem. Judging from the color of her face, she seldom wore a bonnet and did not now. Leather gloved fingers pushed at a loose curl, folded it behind her ear. She nodded at something Tyrell said. He laughed.

Tipton clutched her parasol so tightly her fingers hurt.

Ruth Martin felt more than saw the parasol and girl approach. The closer she floated in her wide skirts, the straighter her back became. Ruth had seen the flash she guessed was fury cross the girl's face, replaced with a smile of white teeth.

"You must be Tipton," Ruth said in a gravelly voice. She cleared her throat. "Excuse me. This dust makes my throat thick."

"I don't believe we've met."

"I'm Ruth, Ruth Martin." She put her free hand out the way a man might. The girl stared, then touched it lightly with her fingers. "I'd know those 'startling blue eyes' and someone 'dressed like a china doll' anywhere. Your intended here has said few words, but most have been of you."

The girl's face relaxed a little, but Ruth recognized the anxiety in it, the fright folded into the fine-boned face.

"Thought you might do a painting for her," Tyrell offered, his voice spoken into his work.

"Of you, ma'am?"

"Me? Oh no," Ruth said. "I might like for you to draw my Koda here." Ruth nodded toward the horse. "He's a favorite of mine and getting on in years. Does a few tricks I've taught him. He counts and takes handkerchiefs from my sleeves sometimes when I'd rather he didn't." She patted the horse's nose, and he pulled his lips back as if he were laughing. "I'd like to have a keepsake of him. Do you do charcoals?"

Tyrell grunted with the horse's shift in weight.

"I'm sorry," Ruth said to Tyrell. "I'm not paying attention. Koda does have a nasty habit of leaning." She pulled the halter gently, spoke to the horse's nose, scratched it with her fingers, and the horse shifted its weight. "I shouldn't have let him go so long without a trim."

"Well spoken," Tyrell said, "though you have a gift for it, I'm seeing."

"Can't count on any but myself most times."

"Won't be needing to go so far for service this trip," he said. With the back of his arm, he wiped the sweat from his forehead, looked up at her, and smiled. He had an open, inviting face, Ruth thought. Kind.

"There'll be fair competition for your skills, Mr. Jenkins, on whichever train you join."

"You might loan your own trimming skills out," he said. "You did good."

"Oh, I doubt—"

"You and your husband are going west, then?" Tipton asked, interrupting. The girl fluttered her eyelashes and spun the umbrella. Koda's ears twitched at the movement, but Ruth had trained him well and the horse didn't jerk away.

"I'm driving my own wagon," Ruth said.

Tyrell lifted the horse's foreleg off his thigh and stood to stretch. "No husband or brother or teamster?" He laid the rasp in a wooden bucket and moved it and himself in one motion back toward the horse's hindquarters. "Could be risky."

"I have a brother," Ruth said. She heard the irritation in her own voice and made an effort to lighten her next words. "Though Jed and Betha and their crew're more likely to be needing taking care of than me."

"You don't share his wagon?" Tipton asked.

"Have my own. Bullwhack it fine. Jed does his. His wife, Betha, she has her hands full with their four little ones. They're around here somewhere." She looked around. "Pigtails, that's Sarah. One's chubby, Ned; the other, Jason's like a strip of bacon. Youngest is Jessie. My brother's a solicitor, or was, back in St. Louis. I'll help them with the children some, but he'll let me be 'responsible for my own lot,' as he said before we left. That suits me fine."

"What if something happens, who would handle your wagon?" Tipton asked.

"I believe what happens will, and having a man beside me won't stop any misery that might come." She knew that from experience. "Won't spur solutions into daylight, either."

"I didn't think women could go without a man's help assigned," Tipton said. "You wouldn't want to let your wagons get behind, not with children along. Mister Bacon would fairly sizzle at such an idea."

"Why is it people think only bad things can happen to women alone? If something happened to Jed, Betha would have to cover for him. I don't see the point of such thinking."

Tyrell picked up his nippers.

"Fine," Ruth said. She'd thought this out before, knew the subject would come up more than once, and she had to sound as confident and secure as she was but without challenging the men. They didn't like that, she'd found.

Ruth said, "I can take on a teamster at Fort Laramie if need be. Between here and there, the trail's easy enough. Don't see it'll be a problem. If I absolutely have to name someone wearing pants who'll walk beside me while I bullwhip, I'll find a kid. Someone fifteen or so, not otherwise committed. It's no small irritation though, for a kid to be considered more reliable than a woman who's already come alone all the way from Missouri."

Tyrell gazed at Ruth long enough that she felt uncomfortable. She turned to scratch the horse's nose. "We'll be just fine, won't we, Koda? You and me and Jumper and all the rest." The horse shifted weight again. "Whoa, now," Ruth cautioned.

"Don't let yourself get dirtied, Tip," Tyrell said, his hand urging the girl back. "You looking so pretty. Why don't you wait at the wagon? I'll find you later."

He'd patted the girl's head. Ruth saw her fury from the corner of her eye just before she swung her parasol and quick-walked away.

❧

Tipton didn't know when she'd felt more like a kite tail, up and down and swirled around. She'd felt so unburdened by the mere mention that Tyrell had held her in his mind and shared a pleasant thought about her with another—about her sketching and that she looked like a "china doll." Then she'd plummeted like a kite dropping in a dying wind when he'd dismissed her like a child.

She'd seen the way Tyrell looked at that Martin woman. Admiration. That's what she saw in his eyes. Admiration for Ruth Martin while his betrothed got a dog's pat to the head.

Her breathing tightened as she walked away, nodding and swirling her parasol at those who stood beside their wagons. She didn't hear them, just a buzz of words, harmonica music in the distance. What if Tyrell left the Bacon train, if he decided to go with a different group? He didn't need Mr. Bacon's money if what the Martin woman said was true about the demand for farriers, and of course it was. Tipton's worry raced on. *What if when we get to wherever we're going, he doesn't want to settle near the Bacons?* She hadn't thought of that before either. He'd have a dozen offers, and who wouldn't want to desert Mr. Bacon if the chance arose?

She shook her head, pasted on her smile, and headed back to the wagon to secure her pencils. Never let them see you fret, her mother always said. She'd pretend all was well. She'd get that look of admiration Tyrell had so easily given away.

❧

She spent the day with her stomach aching until Mrs. Mueller insisted they walk through the town, buying pins and palm-leaf sun hats and extra saleratus for keeping the biscuits raised. Mrs. Mueller traded plant cuttings, and they listened to rumors about the Missouri crossing. Then Miz Bacon sent them back to buy up matches corked in a bottle and another whetstone for honing the knives. Mrs. Mueller kept up a running chatter. "Talkful" was how Tipton thought of Mrs. Mueller, and she noticed with reluctance that the older woman's presence had kept her mind from Tyrell and his smiling at Ruth Martin.

In the evening, everyone in the vicinity was urged to attend a gathering to express their opinions about the upcoming journey. Dancing was said to follow.

"Not necessary," Mr. Bacon said over the meal that Tyrell missed.

"The meeting or the dancing?" Miz Bacon asked him.

"Only the meeting," Mrs. Mueller answered. "Dancing's required, I'm sure." Mr. Bacon scowled.

They'd wandered to the clustering, Mr. Bacon bringing coffee and a cold piece of pie. Across the circle, a round woman with a snow-white apron swept an area then laid a coverlet to sit on. Her skirts billowed out about her. *She must be Betha,* Tipton decided, as the woman waddled in, then urged Ruth Martin and an older, slender man wearing a monocle and smoking a clay pipe to sit beside her. Ruth had a whip coiled on her hip now. Tipton hadn't noticed that before. Four children whose heights were one step apart climbed around them. The slick-haired boy who'd peered into their wagon was one of them. The boys hid behind the man while they reached across to their sisters to grab at ears, pull hair, and squeal before running to hide behind their mother, who smiled, then spit on her handkerchief and wiped a smudge from one boy's face.

Ruth leaned to the youngest, a girl with deep dimples, who giggled and tumbled onto Ruth's lap. When Ruth pulled one of the boys toward her, she exposed dark brogan shoes beneath her skirts.

"Their papa must be deaf and dumb," Mrs. Mueller said, nodding their way.

"The Barnards?" Tipton said. "That's Jed and Betha from St. Louis and his sister Ruth Martin—she's a horsewoman. Jed used to be a solicitor."

Mrs. Mueller looked at her. "Aren't you the local paper."

"Tyrellie introduced us. He was telling her this afternoon about our impending marriage." Tipton patted the ribbon at the back of her neck, then lifted it to let the evening breeze lick at the moisture beneath it. She wouldn't let anyone know about the worms that twisted in her stomach. "She's asked me to draw her horse."

"I didn't know that you could make a likeness."

"Lots you don't know about me," Tipton said.

"That's only half that story," Mrs. Mueller said. She picked at her teeth with a thin little stick. "Other half is that I don't necessarily want to know more about you."

Tipton grunted. The woman could be so crude.

"So will you?"

"What?"

"Draw the woman's horse for her."

"I might."

"That should keep you out of trouble anyway," Mrs. Mueller said.

"As if I was in any."

"You haven't been trouble so far," Miz Bacon said, dropping down beside her, "much to my surprise." Mrs. Mueller had gathered her skirts and leaned over her crossed legs to pull at a grass stem she then blew between her palms. "Mother! That's a horrible sound. You're worse than the children!"

"Used to do this as a young'un. Makes quite a squawk, you think? Better than a tin whistle, if you don't have one."

Tipton turned away. At least here she could see that the Martin woman wasn't with Tyrell, wherever he was. She watched Ruth smooth her niece's braids. The child whispered something, and Ruth stood, walking with her, hand in hand, away from the circle.

Smoke from cooking fires drifted upward toward a sky that threatened more rain. Stock stomped in the distance, swished their tails at flies. Someone had hung a wind chime in a cottonwood, and its tinkling soothed the evening like fireflies in June. Tipton heard what sounded like a troubadour harp strumming and a throaty drum, then bursts of voice and laughter. There'd be dancing, and Tyrell could hold her clean and clear. She swallowed. Tipton just had to put any other thoughts away, the ones that threatened and strangled.

None of them had asked much of her, not really. It was a small price to pay for the freedom to be with Tyrell when she could, to have people see them as a pair. It was almost as though they were married.

"Got to have a little fun every day, I say," Mrs. Mueller said, breaking into her thoughts. "You're all so serious."

"This is serious business," Mr. Bacon said as he sat down beside his mother-in-law.

Tipton felt something shift in the air with his presence. He folded his long legs in front of him. His hands rested on both knees. It seemed to her that Miz Bacon sat a little straighter with him around. Mrs. Mueller stopped blowing the grass, just ran it through her fingers.

"You slept in this morning," Miz Bacon said. "The cow was a bit distressed."

"No one woke me! Mrs. Mueller, you said—"

"She's teasing you," Mrs. Mueller said, patting Tipton's hand. "You've done fine, child, just fine."

"I'm not a child." Tipton pulled her hand away, straightened her shoulders.

"Seems like you ought to be for a while yet." Mrs. Mueller blew her grass again.

Tipton started to stand up, to move away from this gathering where people treated her like a mindless doll.

Her heart skipped as Tyrell walked through the clusters of people toward her. She stood, lifted a hand to wave. Where had he been? Was that guilt on his face?

A stocky man signaled to a fiddler to stop tuning his instrument, then clapped his hands for attention as he stood in the center near the low fire. The faces around the circle faded into the dusk and people ceased their chatter. Tyrell stayed on the far side of the circle.

"Guess we may as well get this meetin' moving," the man said. "Gathered here to talk about some rules and such, and whether we should be teaming up. So I say—"

"There they are!" A woman's voice interrupted, carried across the crowd. Heads turned.

Tipton stiffened with recognition. Her breathing shallowed, and her fingers began to numb.

discovering home

"Adora? Adora Wilson? Is that really you?"

"In the flesh, Mazy Bacon. In the flesh." Adora bolted across the circle, a mother cow discovering her lost calf. She grabbed Tipton and wrapped her arms around her, rocking her, releasing and inhaling, then holding the girl at arm's length to gaze upon her child. "Oh, my baby looks so tired!"

Tipton's limbs, like rigid posts, bound her sides.

"Mama…?" Tipton's words slurred as though through cobwebs of confusion. "Why…? Did you come alone?"

"Course not, child." The older woman motioned behind her where a dusty-looking Hathaway Wilson wove his way through the neck-straining crowd that murmured over the commotion. His bigheaded son, Charles, followed. The men wore tired and resigned expressions in the dust of their faces.

Jeremy stood to shake Hathaway's hand, nod to Charles.

"Are you taking me back? You're not, are you?"

The man calling the meeting clapped his hands like an irritated teacher bringing in unruly students. "You folks catch up later, yah? We got business here. Act like a bunch of soaplocks," he said.

"We're not rowdies," Hathaway defended, "just late arrivals." He slipped to the ground on the other side of his daughter, who sank like a feather onto the blanket. Tipton sat pressed between her parents, rubbing absently at her right arm.

A fragment of home arriving in an unfamiliar place. All these people and sounds and smells and now the Wilsons' appearance made Mazy feel discombobulated. She couldn't imagine how Tipton felt.

Still, if the Wilsons had a change of heart and planned to take Tipton back, Tyrell would surely follow. Then the Bacons would have no teamster, no man to drive the second wagon, and perhaps that would be the sign Jeremy needed to turn back too. At the very least, they'd lose a few more days finding a replacement for Tyrell—if they could—and in the meantime, Mazy could make her case with renewed vigor. Going home pulled at her as Pig could when the dog wanted attention, nibbled at her fingers then tugged until he got his way.

"Yah, then. All set?" the self-appointed leader started over. "We're—"

"Don't you think we should begin with a moment of gratitude? We've all come so far." People turned to locate the source of the woman's voice, not unpleasant or strident, but clear. Mazy located her and noticed that in addition to a black wool dress, she wore a dark caplike hat that fit tightly over her ears and tied beneath her chin.

"Go ahead, then," the leader sighed.

"My intent was only to remind," the woman said. She stood stiff as an ivory comb, her hair pulled so tightly back into a bun it caused her eyes to look almost almond-shaped in the firelight. Mazy noted her bulbous nose, narrow lips, and tight collar held by a cameo pin. A cross on a chain around her neck flashed against the firelight. "Surely a man of the cloth is present?"

"Yah. Do we have a preacher, then?" Heads turned to look. In the more than a thousand wagons now gathered, there would be dozens, that's what Jeremy told Mazy when she'd asked about their spiritual "essentials." But apparently none gathered in this small cluster of wagons at this fire. Mazy wondered how they'd come to settle in a grouping without even one man of God to bless their efforts.

Music drifted across the gatherers. Many were already dancing beyond them. She could hear the calls and fiddle from the far reaches closer to the river.

The man spoke up. "Will you be leading us then…?"

"Sister Esther. And no, it is not my place."

The man shifted on his heels. "Yah, well." He said it with a kind of whine, as if annoyed by a problem brought to his attention without a ready solution. "There being no preacher present, I'll offer up. Let's bow." Mazy heard the hush of hats being removed as she closed her eyes. "Lord, we're glad you came to this meeting, then. Help us pay attention and not go off all bullheaded like I can…like we can." He coughed, as awkward as a schoolboy unpracticed in public praying. Mazy gave him credit for his effort. They might all be saying new prayers before this journey ended.

His "Amen. Name's Schmidtke," sounded like one word. Eyes lifted and he gazed across the group. "Antone Schmidtke. Late of New York. Got three wagons, a hundred head of cattle, four ox teams, some horses and mules, a boy, Matt, and one teamster, Joe Pepin. Good men, they are. Wave your hats, boys. Yah, then. Been farming my life long. Hope to keep doing it West. We're civilized folks, the Schmidtkes are. Know that men need rules to make it in a venture like this. Enforce 'em fair. I'd make you a good captain. My teamster's been this way once before so we've got trained eyes."

"Ya left out yer wife," someone yelled from beyond the firelight. "Ya got one a those, don't ya?"

"What? I did?" A few men chuckled. "Where you sitting then, Lura?" His eyes stopped at a small, straight-sitting woman quietly clicking knitting needles and wearing a lap of yarn. A slender lookalike girl sat beside her. "Wave then," he said and she did, a shy smile flashing across the woman's face before she dropped her eyes. The firelight flickered against her bodice laced with sewing needles and pins. She wore pearl combs in her hair and chewed on a smokeless clay pipe.

"Left out his daughter, too," Mazy whispered, leaning to her mother.

Ruth Martin returned, perched her nieces on her lap. "You have a daughter as well. What's her name?"

"I forgot my girl? Mariah, she is," Antone said, his thumb and finger massaging his chin, eyes scanning but not stopping. "If we can get past the ancestral count…now to business. Don't need to be blabbing all night, then."

"Looks like you're the only one blabbing," someone shouted—Mazy couldn't tell who—and the group burst into guffaws. The darkness offered protection so people didn't have to own their observations or ideas unless they stood closer to the light for recognition.

Antone Schmidtke opened one button of his high collar. He was a broad man, and the green striped vest he wore widened him like a watermelon. "Yah, yah," he said, irritated. "Is there any out there who thinks someone else should lead this group of ragamuffins west, then?"

Mazy felt Jeremy move to stand, and her mouth dropped open in surprise.

"Jeremy Bacon. Grant County, Wisconsin." He wiped at his nose with his ever-present handkerchief. "All due respect, Mr. Schmidtke—"

"Antone. First name's good enough."

"Harder for the law to catch you that way," someone shouted and people laughed. Mazy noticed that Ruth Martin didn't.

"If we need a leader at all," Jeremy said, "he needs to be someone who's reluctant, someone who wants to let folks do on their own as much as possible."

Mazy gazed up at her husband, wondering what he was truly thinking. They'd argued just hours before. He'd insisted they could go it alone, just the two wagons. Now he was describing what kind of leader their group ought to have?

"A fair number of us had no leader, yet here we are." He lifted his arms to take in the gathering. "Seems foolhardy to turn over our scheduling to someone who doesn't know each family's quirks and ways. Me, I can't see the benefit. All we need is folks willing to listen to each other. Ask for help and the rest of us give it."

Mazy's mouth dropped open, but she snapped it shut and

exchanged a look she couldn't name with Ruth Martin who stared at her from across the circle.

"Got what, fifteen, twenty wagons right here represented," Jeremy continued. "Now me, I've got Grant and MacDonald's guidebook that any who can read can look at with me. Just loosely head out in the same direction, stay on the North Platte road. Can't imagine we'd need anything more."

"Outdated, that book is," Antone said. He scratched a shaved cheek. "Lot's happened since '46. I tell you, we are all going to have situations where a firm hand is welcome as water. First time you decide to stop and I pass you by and take your grass, you'll be saying I should have listened to old Antone." People chuckled. "And there's Indian threats. Lone wagons, just one or two stopping to pick flowers'll make those folks think we're all daft. Can't risk vexing Indians, yah that's right." Mazy watched heads nod in private chatter across the circle. "Got to at least look like we defend ourselves, yah? Getting cattle across rivers, circling stock, would all be better with cooperation. Don't need lots of rules."

"We must decide about the Sabbath." It was Sister Esther. Mazy wondered who the woman traveled with. No one had come forth to claim her as kin, though two men sat on either side of her. Behind her clustered several young women whose faces were shadowed by straw-woven hats that looked liked mushrooms pulled to a point at the top.

"Best we decide on our own for that as well," Jeremy said, "about whether to stop or go on. We don't need rules for everything."

"But if Antone's cattle should go on ahead and I stay behind, then his cows'll get the goods." This from a ferret-faced man who had eased into the firelight.

"Push a little harder the next day. Pass him to get the better feed. Think for yourself, man," Jeremy said.

"Seems like it'd be better to have some rules we could vote on. Matt Schmidtke," the newest speaker said, introducing himself as he came to stand beside his father. His voice cracked in its youthfulness. "Be un-American to vote and not know what you're voting for." He had a streak of white in his hair though he couldn't have been more than fifteen. She guessed him to be the same age as Tipton. Mazy wondered if she noticed him. Mazy leaned forward to look at her, but the girl still sat staring without a flicker of recognition.

"What does Scripture say of it?" It was Sister Esther again.

"Are women going to be allowed to speak? I mean if women are, we'll be here all night." Another man's voice.

"We've been here long enough to be ate up by mosquitoes and bewitched by the dancing music with men doing most of the talking." It was a voice Mazy recognized well—her mother's.

"Guess we could vote on whether or not to have a leader at all. Bryce Cullver, here," the man said to introduce himself. He wore little wire-rim glasses. A shock of brown hair slipped over one lens. "Then let our chosen leader decide about women and dogs and the Sabbath stops and such after that."

"I ain't turning over my rights 'til I know who's voting. I won't follow someone I don't know," said the ferret-faced man, arms crossed over his chest.

"Who gets to vote on whether to vote?"

"You see the kettle of worms you've unleashed, Antone," Jeremy said. He sat back down. A few applauded. He shook his head, paused, and stood back up. "All right. I'm in for election. I stand for limited rules, independent thinking, and making decisions based on essentials. We stay together only so long as we agree. Disagree and we move out on our own, join up with others more to our liking." He sat back down, and Hathaway patted his back.

"Well, can women vote?" the ferret man persisted.

"Who'll stop us?" Ruth asked.

"I rest my case," Jeremy said. "We're all too independent to form up a kind of congress way out here."

"I rest mine, too," Antone said. He lifted both palms in the air as though to say, See? What did I tell you? "If we can't decide even who will vote, then how're we going to figure out how to cross a mountain together?"

"I suggest we take the matter up later, after people have had a time together. Once we cross the Missouri and see each other in action, we might know better who'll be a qualified captain or if we even need one at all."

"Whose wise counsel is that?" Jed Barnard, the former solicitor, spoke across the circle. Heads turned.

"Mazy Bacon, wife of Jeremy," Mazy said. She swallowed and didn't look at her husband, but she felt him turn to stare.

"All in favor of that sage advice say aye," Jed finished. The resounding response reminded Mazy of thunder.

"Good. Let's dance," shouted a youngish voice, and the crowd began taking sideboards from the wagons and laid them in the dirt. Several other people disappeared, walking toward distant fires. The Schmidtkes huddled near their wagons.

"You might have waited," Jeremy said. His voice was stiffer than a new leather stirrup, and he spoke low. "Could have had this decided tonight if you'd have kept your counsel to yourself."

"People need time to consider things, Jeremy. This gives it."

"Just because you can't make a decision until it's been wrestled to death, doesn't mean others can't and shouldn't."

His words stung. "Giving things a little time often reveals a right and perfect answer," she said.

"Or none at all," he said. "It's human nature to want to do things on our own. It's what this heading west is all about. Self-sufficiency. That's what's essential."

"Is it?" she said. "And here I thought marriage was a yoked team." She stood, turned her back to him, stared at the dancers beginning to assemble. She heard him blow his nose, stand up, and stomp away.

"I apologize for sounding critical of your care of our Tipton," Adora said, coming up behind Mazy who wondered how much she'd over-heard just now. "I remembered her with more flesh. But she says she's solid as an iron horse."

"Whatever made you decide to come?"

"I told Hathaway here," Adora poked a finger to her husband's chest, "I just could not take it, I just could not. Every night was a row up a salt river. I woke up more beaten than when I went to sleep."

Tyrell strode across the disbanding circle and faced Tipton, flanked by her parents. His hands gripped his suspenders; his eyes held Tipton's. Adora said, "Your daddy said if I was going to mourn you so, we'd best go west, too."

"All the way? To Oregon?"

"I believe our plans include California," Charles told his sister. He towered over the girl, tight curls around his head giving him a Roman look, even with his hat pushed high, exposing his smooth forehead. Mazy detected an edge to Charles's words. "More promise there, Papa says." He flipped coins, their clinking hitting Mazy's ear like an annoy-ing whistle.

"Figured you'd be grieving Tyrell if we took you home, so we'd only be exchanging one sad female for another," Hathaway said. His eyes looked tired and lacked their usual sparkle.

Mazy wondered at the finagling that had gone to bring them here. Their decision to leave Cassville would have followed within days of the Bacons' departure for them to have made it to Kanesville so quickly.

"Did you sell the store?" Tipton asked.

"Oh yes," Charles answered before his father could. "Nothing's too good for you, now is it, little Tipton."

"Aren't the men in our lives just too wonderful?" Adora gave her daughter a one-armed hug while she looked up into the eyes of her husband.

"So we're all going…west?"

"Looks like it, daughter," Adora said, high pitch to low. "Aren't you just pleased as pickles?"

～

It pressed against her chest, pulled then stretched until she thought she'd burst with the weight. Tipton thrashed about, strangled, gasping for breath. She heard sobs and Mrs. Mueller's voice calling her name and she wondered who was crying and then realized it was herself.

"A bad dream," Mrs. Mueller said in tones as soothing as a kitten's purr. "Just a dream, child." She untangled the light linen that had wrapped itself around the girl's thin chemise and laid it lightly over them both. "Mazy used to cry in her dreams."

"I don't dream, Mrs. Mueller," Tipton said and pulled away from the older woman. "I'd sleep better if I were outside where the air mills around instead of trapped in this wagon like a badger." She couldn't imagine how she'd survive these suffocating spaces when they reached the hot plains. "Men are so much wiser sleeping under the stars. We could drag the quilts out and—"

"Drier in here. Besides, Tyrell needs his rest," Mrs. Mueller said.

"Tyrellie never entered my mind," Tipton said. "It was a suggestion of comfort, yours and mine. A tent's a must, I'm thinking." She struck at the feather pillow, rolled it to fit beneath her neck. Her body dripped with perspiration.

"I've a suggestion for comfort," Mrs. Mueller said. "Would you please call me by my name? It's so formal to share a bed with someone who can't even say my name."

Tipton felt herself blush in the night. Silence hung like a sparking board between them.

"Care to speak about the dream, child?"

"I told you. It was the linen, that's all. I…don't like things tight around me. I'm fine now. I'm sure I'll sleep."

"Could always hightail it to your parents' wagon," Mrs. Mueller said. Tipton stayed silent.

"Guess you will after we cross the river. Rearrange everything after that. Course looks like you got rearranged as it is, I'll ponder that." The woman chuckled. "Look at it this way—you won't need to milk that cow no more."

After that, the wagon grew silent and Elizabeth's breathing changed. Tipton thought she might have fallen asleep. She could hear the pelt of raindrops against the canvas that stretched over the wagon top. "That Martin woman milked cows before, she tells me," Elizabeth said. "Interesting, that one. She doesn't say much to tell you who she is, though she lets on like she has. Gets you talking about yourself, and you forget she hasn't said anything about herself. She rolls that whip pretty good too, I hear tell. Got herself a fine herd of horses. Wonder myself how she did that."

Tipton turned over. If she didn't respond, Mrs. Mueller would eventually silence herself and fall back to sleep, which the woman soon did.

For Tipton, everything felt a muddle. She'd pretend she was composed, not left bereft by her parents' arrival. It felt good to hold them and yet she felt babied, stripped, and exposed. And Charles. Why had he come, wearing his usual dark and brooding face? Just to torment her, of course.

She couldn't tell anyone how she felt, not even Tyrell, who had tipped his hat early to say good night and then taken his bedroll to the fenced areas where the other teamsters slept. She longed to find a quiet place to talk with him, even though she knew that it was never wise to say out loud what made one worrisome or sad, never good to let people come too close. People took advantage. Tipton had found that out early.

What she felt for Tyrell at first surprised her. His very presence caused her to flutter and behave in jittery ways, but she kept her eye to the wheel hub. She thought of arms as thick as dock pilings, his chest that expanded as he worked beside the hot coals of the forge, and legs so powerful folks said he could outwalk a sturdy mule. Yet he was kind and quiet and kept kittens on an old pillow in a corner where he hung repaired harnesses. It was what had drawn her in at first, the sound of kittens mewing behind the wide opening of his shop.

He had not been in Cassville long, had planned to ride through and north, on to Prairie du Chien, then stayed. She sensed the safety of him, in the size of his arms and the breadth of his heart. And he extended that strength to her. It was the only time she felt powerful and truly safe. Tyrell made her more than what she was.

When he said he was heading west, she'd almost fainted. She'd taken huge breaths, couldn't get her air, her nose tingled at the tip, and she felt her hand go numb for the first time. She'd turned from him and saw tiny dots of light flicker before her eyes, but she hadn't fainted. He'd stepped behind her, had her drop her head and rubbed the back of her neck while he spoke in soothing tones, her ears hearing his words and the cries of the kittens. No one had seen the intimate exchange; she wouldn't have cared if they had.

As her breathing eased, he'd pressed her gently to his chest. In time, he declared himself to her. It was then that she'd made her plan. She would go with him, whatever it took, whatever the cost. He was the hub of her heart.

Mazy woke early, feeling nauseous. Maybe it was the Kanesville water. It tasted strong, not like the spring water they'd had in the barrels most of the journey so far. She slipped out of bed and found a basket with ash pone in it. She brushed the ashes from the corn meal and bit off a tiny portion to quell the bile building in her stomach. She'd never been sickly before. All the activity, the people and strangeness, it was probably that. And the longing to go home. She picked up her lead pencil and paper and small book of Scripture and slipped out of the wagon, darkness fanning a chill.

She wrote in the mornings, organized the feelings that didn't make sense in any other way. Sometimes she wrote about what she'd seen or heard, a phrase or two; sometimes of her feelings, the emptiness and longing; she wrote now of how Scripture nurtured in a distinctive way. Whatever it was, the very writing of a thing calmed her, gave her direction. Not feeling well had interfered with her writing of late. Perhaps the coarse corn bread would help.

She checked the tomato plant as she walked by, pressing her fingers into the earth at its base. At the sitting log beside the fire, she pulled her shawl around her and inhaled the morning. She looked up. The sky threatened rain once again. She began to write. *Met folk from Missouri yesterday, Suzanne Cullver and Bryce. Woman has no sight. Pig took a liking to her, licking at her fingers.* Mazy felt a little envy, remembering how the dog left her side to nudge the woman's hand stretched out into the air in front of her. The woman drew back with a start at the dog's brush of fur and said something with a snarl about "loose animals being kept at bay." Mazy'd felt her face turn pink and called the dog. He'd come reluctantly, apparently not sensing as Mazy had that the woman disliked his presence.

"I'm so sorry," Mazy told her, noting that she said those words often lately.

She began to write of that incident, of apologizing, when a soft light caught her eye. A shadow moved behind the canvas in a wagon. Another early riser. The light centered in front of the form, eased out of the wagon, then hesitated. It headed straight toward Mazy's low fire and became the woman Sister Esther. In her other hand, she carried an oak lap desk by its handle.

"You would probably prefer your time uninterrupted," the woman said, approaching. "Diary-keeping of this grand journey is a noble task. Others will read of our bringing these United States west."

"Nothing so grand as that," Mazy said, folding her paper. "Just ideas and impressions I have. And the mileage we make. I take it from the odometer." She nodded toward the gear wheel that counted the revolutions.

"I did not hear you out here or I would have chosen another path," the woman said. "It is not my intent to intrude."

"The night captures sound."

"So it does. You are the woman who suggested we wait to vote?"

Mazy hoped the heat of her face didn't show. "It's always good to have time to consider."

"Do you wish to avoid choosing a leader or traveling alone?"

"I think a captain's valuable if for nothing else than to settle disputes," Mazy said.

The woman nodded. She set down the lantern and then the writing desk. "A reason why the Israelites demanded judges—for when they failed to settle things among themselves."

"I wonder what difference there'd be now if God hadn't allowed that," Mazy said. "If the Israelites had been forced to learn to compromise, not to become dependent on a judge, but to work together toward a solution. Maybe we'd be better at that now, too."

"I have not thought of it that way," Esther said.

"I must say I like being heard in the deciding of a thing, though," Mazy said after a moment.

"A part of human nature," the woman said, finally unclasping her hands to brush at her dark skirts. She looked down at Mazy. "That is part of what I try to teach my charges." She nodded toward the wagon. "The importance of finding agreeable ways to live in close proximity. It is important that they remain clean and with the highest morals, to avoid sickness when there are so many people as we are here."

"Who do you travel with?"

"I am employed by the Caroline Fry Marriage Association. We bring young women to be joined in wedlock to deserving young men. Two of my brothers are with me, acting as teamsters. We'll deliver the young women to their new husbands in California."

"What after that?"

"Why, we'll head back for more."

"You'll return? People do that?"

"Many forty-niners came back, of course. Some in but two months' time—they claim—motivated by greed and the need to tell all of their exploits. But my brothers and I will return in an orderly, planned fashion."

"It would be so...dangerous, traveling back alone."

"Indeed. The newspapers do not mention the dangers of returning. They do not want to discuss the difficulties that would make souls turn around. But the fact is many do. How else would we have such guidebooks as your husband spoke of?" She lifted her eyes upward. "Others simply have a change of heart—the very meaning of conversion."

"I'd wager those are folks who didn't want to go in the first place," Mazy said. She tapped her pencil against her wool skirt.

Sister Esther looked at Mazy. "Perhaps something changed their mind." The woman's black eyes pierced like an eagle's. Mazy felt invaded. But the woman must have guessed that about herself as she turned away, looked as though to find a place to sit, then pushed with her foot at the end of the log feeding the fire.

"I didn't want to come," Mazy said, the thought of turning back gnawing. "So it's no change of heart that makes me think of going home again."

"That's what you pray for?" Sister Esther nodded to the Bible that rested on the log beside Mazy.

"For my husband to *want* to go back, before we go any farther," Mazy said, her words tentative, not accustomed to sharing intimacies with a stranger. "There's nothing waiting for us there except...uncertainty. We had this most wonderful farm in Wisconsin, along the Mississippi. Bluffs above a quiet valley. A pond lured ducks, thousands in the fall. Wildflowers everywhere, morel mushrooms. Good, rich soil. There was no place like it anywhere. I would have lived there forever."

"We are not yet where we will be," Sister Esther told her. "And not where we departed from, so all is strange. But we are not alone. The Psalm tells us nothing can separate us from the love of God."

"I know that verse." Mazy reached for a stick and poked at the fire. "I just can't believe God wanted me to leave home in the first place. That's what bothers me."

"He does not reveal all he has in store," Sister Esther said. She had a front tooth missing a piece and so her *S*'s whistled when she spoke. "But he's with us." She tapped at her heart. "Of that I am certain."

"Once I woke up with this phrase in my mind: 'Wisdom wears a dog's face, certainty, a cat's.' Strange, isn't it? I mean, I like dogs, their acceptance no matter what. Cats are so…"

"Self-centered, I find them," Esther said. "But being unwavering is appealing."

"But not always a sign of wisdom," Mazy said.

"Perhaps. I tell my little Celestials that we are never far from home as long as we have God in our hearts. This I believe is both certain and wise."

"Celestials? You call them Celestials."

"It's what their families name those who leave their homes to come to this continent as earthly angels, to rescue them. I suspect my future brides miss their homes too, though they have willingly come. They've already sent a portion of their contract money back to their families, so it is a matter of honor that they make their husbands happy. A new life they seek with a way to help their old."

"A little like slavery, I'll wager, with not even love to justify it."

"Certainly not!"

"But once they say the vows, do they understand what they've committed to?"

"The men they marry are worthy. There is a detective agency who helps us ensure that." She lowered her voice, became a teacher. "It is not unlike their own customs, where children are betrothed at birth. These young women had small dowries, and so their chance for marrying well at home proved limited. A path is always opened if one has faith, though it appear narrow indeed."

"You make it sound like a garden, all orderly and laid out," Mazy said, "but the seeds can get mussed up." She thought about Tipton's turn of fate with her mother's arrival and her own life now shattered and separated as old silk. "I wonder sometimes just how much of a say in her own future any woman ever really has."

"Oh, one always has one's outlook," Sister Esther said, deciding to sit at last. "That's certain wisdom. We can always control that."

❧

Tipton lay stiff as a bed slat, staring at the iron hoop that held the arcing canvas. California! They were taking her to California, all of them, Charles, too, while the Bacons and Tyrell headed north. How could her parents make a decision to follow her that quickly? Faster than a rabbit burrowing at an eagle's shadow. "To see the fashions of Sacramento," her mother'd said. "To try something new before my knees go," her father told her. "My cousin's been begging me since '49. I decided to listen. Be good for us, a family together." New clothes, new ideas. In California! Tears welled up in her eyes. She wiped at them, then stopped her hand midair: Coins clinked outside the wagon. Charles and the ca-chunk, ca-chunk of silver in the hands of a volatile man.

abiding

Their argument, spoken in hissed whispers to keep others from hearing, only brought Elizabeth closer to the wagon, a mother both curious and concerned.

"He's signed a contract with me," Jeremy told Mazy. "Nothing's changed with Hathaway's arrival except the girl will be needed to help her family now instead of us."

"And there goes the Tipton-watching money you said we badly needed. To pay Tyrell."

"Your arm's healing. You always said you like to keep busy. Weren't too crazy to take her on in the first place, if I recall."

"It's not my arm that troubles me. Milking Mavis and Jennifer'll be good for it, keep it limber, I imagine. It's what'll happen later. With the Wilsons arriving now, and the potential complication that causes and the delay at the crossing, these're all signs, Jeremy. Signs." Her hands dropped to her sides and she sat. "We've erred in coming. This isn't at all what we're supposed to be doing. We're not paying attention."

"Your worries are carried on frail legs," Jeremy said.

"We should go back. I feel it in my bones. Something's amiss, and this might be our last chance to turn around."

"You've got to let it go, Mazy, and just accept. There is nothing to go back to in Grant County, even if we did turn around, don't you see that? This, here and now, this is our opportunity."

"But with Tyrell gone—"

"He isn't gone, not yet, maybe won't be. I don't want to discuss it. No more, Mazy. No more!"

"They won't let us continue on without a teamster for mother's wagon."

He lifted his hand as though to stop her talking as a man might halt a horse with an upraised palm. Elizabeth gasped at the shadow, fearing he might strike Mazy. She thought to intervene when Jeremy dropped his hand, knelt down before his wife. "We'll go on our own, then, Maze. I've heard of plenty folks with one or two make it just fine."

Was that agony in the man's voice, such a drive to go west? Did Mazy hear it too? Elizabeth waited for her daughter's retort and found the silence deafening. She'd almost pulled at the puckering-string, to poke her head up under it and present herself a jolly interruption as though having approached just then.

"To go alone is witless, Jeremy. I will not be unattached. I'll—"

"What? Leave?" He snorted, stood. "Don't threaten, Mazy. It doesn't become you."

"We don't even have anything waiting for us at the end. Nothing. The starting over will just keep dragging on."

"Three hundred twenty acres await us. A new life awaits us. Let go, Maze. Move on."

Silence followed, then the sounds of people preparing for bed. Elizabeth decided not to enter that den of dissent and instead made her way back to her wagon.

This morning as Elizabeth recalled the argument, she wondered whether Jeremy'd have to give the "Tipton-watching money" back if Tipton traveled now with her family. He wouldn't part with that easily. He did tend to be tight-fisted when it came to money.

She rubbed her right hip and raised her leg to hear the "pop" that greased it, had ever since she'd broken it ice skating the year after she was married. The Wilson girl still slept beside her. Poor thing. Her free and frolicsome ways with the blacksmith were stopping quicker than a fast horse on a bridge-out road. Didn't seem fair, though the girl was but fifteen. She'd been good help. Might be her mother'd let her share this wagon still. Though it was not likely. Adora had a way of hoverin' a mite close and would want her daughter under her thumb, little doubt of that. Why else would she have come so far?

A blast of wind sucked the canvas sides out, followed by soft raindrops. They'd camped beneath a cottonwood, and Elizabeth hoped wet leaves and not a new storm accounted for the sound. She heard stirrings outside. Dawn seeped in through the thinner dots of canvas that arched over her. She smelled the mustiness of mildew where the water had surged in during a hailstorm not many days before. The strong scent bothered her as it pasted itself to the tie rounds. She rubbed her nose, wishing it were less sensitive but grateful she could smell. She'd give anything for a lemon slice to rub the canvas, salt the mildew down, then spread the covering in the sun to dry—if the sun came out while they waited their turn to cross. A square of Tipton's mirror reflected a shaft of sunlight—a hopeful sign.

Tipton groaned. Elizabeth would miss jawing with the girl when Adora took her back, even if she spoke little of what was ever on her mind.

A shout in the distance, the *gee*s and *haw*s and slaps of hats to thighs moving wagons to the river told her she'd best get up. Pulling or driving the herds of people and cattle across the Missouri was going to be quite an adventure, what with the river running so dirty and high. Jeremy said he didn't like the idea of paying the Mormons their ferrying fee. Well, she'd spend her own money on the ferry if need be—if she could find the bulk of it.

Her stomach hurt with that thought, and she hiccuped. How it came to be that her perished husband had created this new pressure before he died still rankled her. What was he thinking of, putting their home in Jeremy's name? And not telling her or him either, if she believed her son-in-law. As far as she was concerned, it was still her money. She'd think of it as a scavenger hunt, guessing what few places he really had to hide a sum of bills and coins between their two wagons. At least Jeremy hadn't argued about her need for a wagon. And he said he'd hold the remainder of the house-sale money for "safekeeping."

Today she'd check the flour barrel to see if what belonged to her lay buried deep beneath the grain. And once they crossed the river, she'd look to see how much of her money was left.

The girl beside her made soft sounds with her mouth, and Elizabeth smiled. It reminded her of Mazy making noises in her sleep. Mazy'd been an easy care, a baby sleeping through the night within the first month. Elizabeth had often lowered her face over the cradle to be sure she breathed, she had lain so still, her birth and life such a mystery. Then in the second or third month, as though to quiet her mother's fears, the child began making sounds, little mews and smacks in her sleep, so Elizabeth could lie beside her husband and listen and know the child lived. Mazy seemed early destined to be looking after others.

❧

Mazy didn't know when she'd begun talking more to the dog and the cow and even the brute than to her husband. She had always shared her thoughts with Pig, but the cow brute was new, and exchanging pleasantries with Mavis or Jennifer, as she'd named them, stretched her understanding. Her head bent into the hams of the cow, Mavis's tail swishing and catching in the braid of Mazy's hair. Agitated, the cow stepped from foot to foot.

"Oh, Mavis, now, let's calm, let's calm. No need to be sashaying without music."

The cow turned its head and stared at her, not chewing its cud.

"Wish we had a calf for you to be licking while I milk. That would settle you. Or maybe I should milk beside you." Mazy wondered how the cow would adjust to such a change. "At least I'd be less at risk of getting your hoof inside my mouth, right, Mavis, girl?"

The cow relaxed as Mazy spoke, chattered, and then hummed a lullaby. The wooden bucket filled, the cow's teat changing from firm to flaccid in her hand. Foam settled on the side, then disappeared into a pond of white, releasing with it a scent that usually gave no bother. This morning, however, it made her swallow, and she wondered if she'd be able to keep her breakfast down. She panted like a dog, as her mother had taught her. It kept the bile from rising. Then she pushed her shoulder over the bucket to keep Mavis's manure-clotted tail from dipping into it and ruining a morning's work.

Pig lay not far away, one eyebrow raised each time Mazy spoke. He'd always been a fine listener, following Mazy about or lying near her feet, so close she sometimes stumbled and found herself apologizing, or she would ask him if he wanted a scrap as though he could answer. Once or twice, Jeremy had even looked up from his paper, adjusted his glasses and said, "What is it? I didn't hear you," then adding "oh," before dropping his eyes, realizing her words had been for the dog.

As for the cow brute, even he seemed less lawless, though Mazy walked a wide berth around him as she did now. Jeremy'd kept him in a separate corral, not wanting him damaged by the horns of other cattle. It meant more care, but giving it made Jeremy's nose run and his head hurt, so Mazy took over the task.

Yesterday, she and Tyrell and Elizabeth had hitched up the wagon and driven to a green knoll. They'd cut and bound several bundles and brought them back for the stock. Fine stems of grass dribbled from her dress, still brushed along the wagon floor despite her sweeping. She couldn't imagine keeping the stock separated like that from those out grazing all the way west.

The brute's eyes followed her now as she headed back. She talked and he chewed his cud, his head like a heavy load being pulled up by his neck. It must have been the fright, Mazy thought, the newness of it all, that made him go daft upon their first meeting. She wasn't all that unlike him, wanting to lash out in uncertainty. He didn't seem that troubled now.

"You must have been frightened," she told him. "People do strange things when they are, and I suspect bovines do too."

"You don't look the part of someone knowledgeable of fright, nor that of a milkmaid either, though the scarf is becoming."

The man's words startled Mazy. "Pig, you didn't warn me." She turned to look into the open, tanned face of a man Jeremy'd pointed out to her during the dance, said it was the face of a "white-collared" man. He removed his hat, revealing hair parted in the center with gentle waves flowing out to either side. Mazy realized she had to look up to see into his eyes, something she seldom had the delight to do.

"I've been a milkmaid for some time now," she said.

"And the fright?"

"That's newly arrived, I'd say." She wondered at her own boldness in talking to a strange man, but she liked the quiet of his eyes, the forthrightness that pooled behind them. He must have used his shaving cup often as he wore no beard.

"I'm Seth Forrester. And you must be…?"

"Mazy Bacon. Mrs. Mazy Bacon."

"Ah, yes, the sage advisor of our meeting past."

Mazy blushed. "It was just an offer, a way around a thing."

"Admirable, though. I didn't relish sitting through a tedious discussion of the merits of men's leadership while a fiddle warmed up. I believe you're right, command reveals itself in action more than words, so perhaps today we'll see. You're planning to farm in California?"

"My husband wishes to build a dairy, but I believe he has his heart set on Oregon," she said.

"And your heart? Where is it set?"

The question came from a place of genuineness, the way her father might have spoken to her, helped her find her depth within a subject, urged her to risk searching deeper by his listening with his head and heart to what she had to say.

"Home, actually," she said before she could think. She looked away, took a deep breath. "I've thought we might do well in California, providing dairy for the mining camps, though I haven't a suggestion of how the land lays there, what it might be like for cows or families either. Ayrshires are said to be excellent grazers, though. They can survive where other breeds might not. We've read more of Oregon Territory, of course."

"They say there's a sign beyond Fort Laramie that points north with 'this way to Oregon' written on it, so those who can read end up there and the rest head into California." He smiled, and his thick eyebrows the color of clover honey lifted above amber eyes.

"They'll have to rely on their compass headings, the Californians, then, won't they?" Mazy said to Seth's laughter. "That's where you're going?" Mazy asked. "To California?"

"My kind of occupation thrives in places where people are willing to take risks. The territory is of little matter, though I do like to read."

"And that occupation is…?"

A flicker of disappointment crossed his face. "I suspect you know, Mrs. Bacon, as most people do."

Mazy dropped her eyes, not because she spoke with a gambler and a man who was not her husband but because he'd caught her being less than true.

"I do," she said and faced forward. "And it sorrows me a bit, to see so many people taking chances. Now I'm among them." She untied Mavis and slapped the cow's bony back. She'd be glad when Mavis came into her heat so she could be bred and the milking could stop for a time. "I'd best be heading back. We might cross today," she said, nodding toward the river.

"So we might." Seth reached to carry the bucket, and she let him take it, looking up again as he placed his black high top hat on his head.

"A beaverskin hat, isn't it?"

He nodded. "Got to have the trappings of the best," he said. "People like to play poker with someone they think is a worthy opponent. Makes them think they're special when they best me…in the early hands. I don't like to disappoint them."

"I imagine not."

Pig stood and trailed behind them. As they walked toward the wagons, they spoke of little things, the weather, she of her Wisconsin, he of Virginia, the state of his birth. It was a pleasant conversation between friends, more than talking to the dog. At the wagon, Seth handed her back the bucket. "Perhaps we'll chat again someday, Mrs. Bacon. It's been my pleasure. Pig," he said, and dipped his hat to the dog.

"Mine, too," she said as he tipped his fingers to the brim and strode away.

Mazy skimmed pans of milk, placed the cream into the churn. Then began the rhythm of the task, exchanging hands when her recovering one ached up to her elbow and her side began to throb.

Seth Forrester was an easy man to be around, she thought, the way that Jeremy had been those years before when her father had brought him home to recover from an injury suffered on the docks. They'd talked for hours as she cared for him, changed dressings, brought in food and fed him until his knife-gashed arm and broken ribs were healed enough to let him leave. Then Jeremy's absence had left a gnawing ache.

He had come back as though an answer to a prayer, and her father had permitted them to court though she was just sixteen. They'd walked arm in arm, Jeremy telling her of his travels, of his earlier immigration from New England back in '48. "Became a part of the greatest migration to the territory," he told her. "Every nationality and language one can imagine came to Wisconsin in '48. Helped make her a state." Mazy heard pride in his voice. "Want to save my money and then head east to St. John's College in Maryland, where George Washington's nephews went. Become a solicitor perhaps. Take up an essential occupation."

"Like my father's," she said.

He had scoffed at that, she just remembered. No, maybe he coughed. "Surgeons are well respected, Madison, but doctors can get their license in a month. Doesn't take much time to learn to bleed a person. Only remedy they seem to all have." He'd lifted her chin, stared into her eyes. "Your father's an exception. Good man. Could have been a surgeon, if he'd wanted, if he had the gall for slicing quick and sure."

The conversation had bothered her, but she didn't know why.

Jeremy had declared himself to her soon after, and she'd put the edge of uncertainty aside. Then before the marriage could take place, her father had been stricken by paralysis and everything changed. The doctor, her father, decomposed before her, went from round and robust to exposed bones as fragile as the future.

He could still talk with effort but mostly spelled words out on a makeshift alphabet board Jeremy had devised. As he grew weaker, he signed his wish to see his lawyer and that Mazy and Jeremy should marry.

The wedding ceremony itself on April 5, 1850, was a quiet one followed by a small gathering of friends with food and music but no high-stepping in their parlor. Her father lived to give his blessing. On the day they buried him, three weeks later, Jeremy learned of his own uncle's passing and that a farm in Grant County now belonged to him.

Mazy had thought they'd sell the land and head east.

"We'll live there," he said instead. He'd given her no reason except to say that improving the farm would be a good investment and that a change from working at the docks right then had become *essential*. They'd said good-bye to her mother, traveled several days west through dipping, rolling lands, and arrived in a green profusion of June. A stream pushed through it low, toward the Mississippi. Clamshells littered the shore. Mazy had christened the place by swimming in the river.

Now here she was, forced into another move driven by her husband.

"I suppose I shouldn't be surprised," she told Pig, who lifted her loose hand with his head as she considered and churned. She patted the silky fur and laced the dog's ear between her fingers. "It does seem to be the way he decides things—on his own, without counsel." She was left only to react. She remembered the simple interchange with Seth

Forrester and felt a longing for a man who would respect her and share in her desires.

"It doesn't have to be this way," she told the dog. Something needed to change—and soon. She called for Tipton to finish up the churning if she would, rinsed her hands in the water basin, then went in search of her husband.

~

"Come on ahead, man!" the ferrymaster shouted. Ruth Martin flicked the whip, and the heavy oxen team moved forward with a jolt. The wheels groaned, and the ferry lowered itself in the water with the weight. Once surrounded on three sides by the river as dark as Boston baked beans, Ruth had a temporary loss of direction, a feeling so strange she closed her eyes and shook her head then stared, attached to a point of land showing between the big oxen's ears.

A mist began dropping from a sky as gray as her broodmare. *Oh, fine. Just what we need. Rain on top of dirty water.* Well, she'd always liked a challenge. She took a deep breath and gripped the whip.

She'd wrapped her hair up high, stuffed it under the hat that had been her husband's, then pulled the felt down tighter toward her ears, the touch bringing back the memory and with it piercing pain. She shook her head, but she couldn't shake the feeling.

"Are you frightened?" Betha asked her from the seat above her.

Ruth shook her head and must have scowled because Betha said, "That's right—I'm not supposed to ask you questions."

"No one seems to care," Ruth said in a soft, low voice. She wore a pair of men's blue pants and boots and her brother's shirt with a bandanna at her neck she could pull up around her face to look more like a drover warding off dust. She stood hunched over to look wider and stockier. She didn't like being deceptive, though flouting convention by wearing a dress at the crossing hadn't seemed wise, either.

Jed's wagon rolled onto the ferry behind them. Ruth felt the water lift the ferry, which now began to turn downstream.

Her nieces squealed in the back. "Sit down!" Betha said, then to Ruth, "I think they're having fun, though I don't see ho-o-o-w!" Her words rang out as the ferry lifted on a push of wave, hesitated, then plunged, taking on splashing water over the oxen's wide feet.

Water lapped hard against the side of the flat-bottomed boat, sending another muddy splash over the side. Ruth swallowed. She didn't easily get seasick, but the rush of water and the twisting in the current threatened.

"Almost to the first island, kids. Hang on! Can you see your dad back there?"

"He's there, Mama," Jessie shouted. "Got's white eyes!"

"I'll bet he has! If he lives through this, I'll kill him," Betha said, "but don't you tell him." Ruth heard the girls giggle.

Beau, the right ox, bigger and less sure, bawled and raised the nose chain with a toss of his thick neck. The motion caused the wagon to roll back against the chock, and Jessie fell with a thump. Ruth heard Jed from behind them shout, "Whoa, now!" followed by the ferryman's orders.

"Keep 'em clear of each other! Keep 'em clear! Get 'em under control!"

"As though we had control," Ruth told Betha before she remembered to hold her own tongue.

They hit the island a few feet beyond where they'd expected. Another ferry waited on the far side to take them across the second fork if the wagons didn't sink too deep into the rain-soaked island soil. Ruth felt the jolt of the bow square against the land, signaling their arrival. The low gate dropped open. Six or seven men, some on horseback, shouted orders.

"Come ahead, then. Come on!"

Ruth cracked her whip above the oxen's heads, and the heavy animals lumbered forward, the yellowed wooden yokes about their necks revealing the calluses caused by the endless scraping of the oak.

"You kids doing all right?" Betha asked.

"Just chirk, Mommy," seven-year-old Sarah said, her eyes as big as cow pies.

Ruth tipped her hat with her leather-gloved hand as they passed by the ferryman who was too occupied with unloading to notice the smooth face of the bullwhacker.

She talked to the nigh oxen as they rolled across the strip of ground that marked the critical halfway point of the crossing. The ferry would head back, end up downstream from the crossing, and be towed by cable back up for another load. It was a long and tedious process.

When this was over, she'd rejoice. Then she'd have to stand and wait while wranglers drove her horses across. She would have preferred to be with them, but she had no other way to get her wagon here except to drive it. The horses were all branded and would be separated at the end so others could move them; but she was her own teamster when it came to the wagon.

Ruth just didn't want to bog down now, didn't want to make a mistake here or at the second boarding.

When the back wheel sank in almost to the hub, Ruth groaned. She shouted to the team, slapped their backs with her hands, snapped the air above their ears, all the while thinking maybe she should have taken the wheels off and paid the men to pull it with the ropes at the downriver crossing. Maybe she should have asked that Roman-looking man with the flawed ear who danced with her for help. Maybe she should have been where the oxen could swim instead of face this ferry contraption. She shook her head clear of the thoughts. Why did she always doubt herself halfway through a thing? It was her curse—one among many.

"Are we stuck, Auntie?"

Ruth caught her breath and followed the trail to the second ferry. "We can do it," Ruth said.

The children bounced happily in the back. As Ruth stared out at the even wider rush of water and what looked to her to be a much less sturdy craft they'd have to board, she wondered at the exuberance of children. What lay ahead felt more of faith than of assurance.

⁓

Tipton churned the milk, standing beside the Bacons' wagon, grateful for the task. She'd awoken with the heaviest of feelings in her stomach, and only when she heard her mother's singsong voice chatting with Elizabeth outside the wagon did she remember what had happened and how her life had abruptly changed.

Over the morning breaking of their fast, her father told of how they'd make this something grand, this going west. "I expect we can always head back next year if need be."

"Back to nothing," Charles said. He picked at his chin, pulling at the few hairs that threatened to require shaving.

"Now, Charles, you'll be tended to," her mother said. "Tipton, dear, tell me how you've spent your days? You're looking slender as a goose's neck. You've not been ill, have you?"

Charles glared, but not at his mother.

"Will I be—?"

"Going to California with us? I should say so," Adora answered.

"Remaining in the Bacons' wagon, is what I meant to say. Miz Bacon needs me."

"Why, after the crossing, when we make a few adjustments, your father and Charles plan to sleep beneath the tent, and you and I will share a bed of cornhusks."

"We can't sleep in the wagon?"

"Charles brought his photographic equipment with him, dear. It—"

"I had to get something out of this," Charles said. She expected to have words with Charles the first time they were alone. Fire had always flashed between them; and with him here against his will, he'd be slinging cutting words, and maybe more, straight in her direction.

"It just takes up a heap of room," Adora smoothed. "Mules are strong, of course, so we have an extra tent. What matters is that we're together now." She nuzzled her nose in her daughter's hair.

Later, before leaving to help with the crossings, Tyrell tried to settle her as they walked to the Bacons' wagon. "No need to be worrying," he said. "Your family came just to look after you, not to keep us from marrying."

"But I liked being with the Bacons."

"Don't always get what we like. Sometimes we got to like what we get."

"Didn't you like our times together, without someone hovering close?"

"Any time with you is pleasing," Tyrell told her. "We'll still have time together."

"Mother'll watch us like children." She turned to see Charles staring at them. "Charles could've had the store to work in for his life. Now he has nothing but uncertainty."

"Everything except eternity's uncertain. Charles could strike out on his own. He could have stayed there in town. I know lots of young men who've lived without their parents by the time they turned seventeen. Charles is already what, twenty-two, -three?"

"Twenty-five," she said. "An only child until he was ten."

"Your papa needed him. Being needed is a good thing, he'll come to find."

She kicked at a rock in the path with her slippered foot. She stopped and spoke to Tyrell's face. "What if my parents've changed their minds about allowing us to marry? Maybe they really intend to turn around. They didn't actually say they weren't going to turn back."

"Maybe, maybe." He drew his hand along the square line of her jaw. "Maybe they just wanted to be sure the folks they loved were all together in one place. Might have been willing to sacrifice what they had for that. You're climbing mountains of your own making, Tipton."

"When we get to the turnoff to California, what will you do? Go with the Bacons as you've contracted or with us to California?"

"I keep my word, Tipton."

He hadn't said to whom.

Tipton felt her fingers tingle. Tyrell bent to kiss her cheek. "I'll see you later. I've got work to do."

Her arm was numb by the time he was out of her sight.

She stood now, churning the Bacons' cream. She lifted and dropped the paddle, plunging the cream into butter, wondering when he'd be back. The rhythm of lifting and plunging, lifting and plunging, soothed her.

Matt Schmidtke interrupted the cadence. He rode beneath the fluff of cottonwood seeds drifting from the trees. Tipton watched the boy with that odd white streak in his hair ride over on a big sorrel horse, lean his arms across the pommel, and tip his hat to her.

"Guess you heard that this group of wagons won't be crossing until at least Thursday. Someone tried to cross on their own hook and failed. Caused some animals to bolt on the ferry. Now a wagon's hung up halfway on and halfway off, twisting around with the animals all unhashed. Quite a mess. But you girls'll have a few more days for churning and washing and such if the weather holds."

"And what will you boys be doing?"

"Tending stock's what I do, and well." He touched his finger to his hat and left.

He stopped at the Wilson wagon, and Tipton saw her mother stick her head out the oval puckered canvas. Adora nodded as she twisted a single long braid over her shoulder. Spying Tipton, she shouted, "I'll join you, baby."

"No need to hurry, Mother," Tipton sighed, her eyes still seeking Tyrell.

Mazy found Jeremy cleaning his Pennsylvania rifle not far from the river. He had a view of the Missouri, of water and wagons and scud clouds and sand. She thought he'd be with the others, helping push wheels at the ferry crossings, using what he saw and what others said as a way of gauging how many more days it would take for them to cross. But he had chosen a solitary spot, and she took it as God's working.

"You're not going to start up with me, are you?" he asked. His blue-striped shirt had smudges of mud on it, as did the cuffs of his yellowed pants.

"I came to see if you had things you wanted me to wash," Mazy said.

"Did you?" He gazed at her and she dropped her eyes.

"No, I didn't." She took a deep breath and sat beside him on the log, settling the wide skirts of her wrapper in a clump of cloth she stuffed down between her legs. Pig sniffed around at squirrels holding themselves still, then shifting their eyes in that quick way they had. "I came to talk, Jeremy."

"Lately, that means arguing."

She nodded in agreement. "What's happened between us...leaves more distance than I'm wanting." He turned his head to her but didn't stop the rifle barrel moving in the cloth he held in his hand. "Mostly my fault," she said. "I was just feeling so...betrayed."

"We've discussed this, Maze," Jeremy said. His voice held warning.

"I know, but not to decidedness. At least not to mine. I left so much behind."

"Took essentials with you. All one needs."

"Not the same. I have to grieve what isn't, before I can accept what is. What isn't anymore for me is having what we had before. We don't have the farm or furniture. But most of all, we don't have each other. It's the...friendship and comfort I miss more than the bluffs, more than anything, I'd say. And I wonder if you miss it too?"

He continued to rub, pushing his fingers into a circle now, against the bluing. She could smell the oil of the cloth.

"You don't have to be afraid to say one way or the other. I just need to know, to help me decide how to make this work or not."

"We haven't been beyond this much," he said.

"I know." She waited, wondering, aware of the throbbing in her throat, the breeze off the bluffs washing down on them. A red-tailed hawk cried in the distance.

Jeremy laid the gun down, braced it barrel up against the tree stump. He lifted her hand, kissed the palm. "I miss you," he said. "I'd give most anything to burn the thorns between us, but I won't change my mind about going. I don't want to talk further if that's where this is leaning."

"I've come to a conclusion," she said, "that if I'm ever to live again in some pleasant place, then being there with you would make it more so than lakes or trees or bluffs. I'd want my friends there. You're my best friend, Jeremy, or always were."

"You'll be able to go on without...holding the hammer over my head?"

"I believe I'm ready. I won't be all agreeable about the decisions we have to make along the way, but I've committed to the most important one and that's to be with you in a way that's...good. I could have stayed and I didn't. Maybe gotten a job as a day lady or something." He raised an eyebrow. "I could have. And I could turn back now, but I won't. I felt like a...casualty, until I realized that what mattered was you and being with you."

The dog stopped sniffing, turned to the shouts at the river some distance beyond. His ears pricked forward, and he barked once, low and short.

"I want that too," Jeremy said. He laid the rag down and pulled her to him, kissing the top of her head as his hand rubbed her shoulder. They stared out at the scene before them, of lives in a whirl as much as the water, of hopes borne on wheels so easily shattered. "A little less warring, a little more balance. I'd like that."

They sat there a long time, staring out at the river and the far side of the island, where the second ferry ventured out. Pig barked low again then stood and faced the Missouri.

"They haven't moved many wagons while I've been watching," Jeremy said, his eyes following the dog's stare.

"Maybe some sort of congestion."

Pig barked, a more insistent sound, his tail straight up and still.

"They'll work it out," Jeremy said and lifted her chin to him and kissed her, a warm and welcoming touch. More than the kiss of a friend.

Pig deserted them. He pushed past Mazy, knocking her over. "Hey!" she said as she caught herself, her fingers sinking into the dirt behind her. Pig barked a warning as his black paws grabbed at the hoof-hardened earth. He headed toward the river.

"What's startled him?" Jeremy said, helping Mazy up. "Must have gotten the scent of a rabbit or something."

"He's so purposeful," Mazy said. She watched the dog plunge into the swirling river, the brown wash bobbing him like a cottonwood branch. "Oh, Jeremy, he'll drown!"

"Not likely. Strong as an ox, that dog. Current's swift though. He'll end up at the low end of the island."

The dog's dark head bobbed like a burl before making its way toward the strip of land that sliced the river. Once there, a dash Mazy recognized as Pig sped toward the first ferry, weaving through the legs of oxen and horses and the arc of wagon wheels before disappearing into willows.

the pace of progress

Jeremy shaded his eyes. "Makes no sense, him rushing off like that." He reached a hand for Mazy, his rifle gripped in the other. "Crazy dog. Hope he doesn't frighten someone's team now." He shook his head. "More trouble than he's worth."

"Don't ever say that, not even in funning," Mazy said. People had gathered along the banks, pointing and stretching their necks to see through distant trees.

"Some wagon groups have a rule about dogs, that they be put down, so they don't alert Indians or upset the stock." Jeremy blew his nose.

"I've seen a greyhound and one of those pug dogs around. We'd leave any train that makes that rule," Mazy said. "Wouldn't you?"

"Faster than a ferret," Jeremy said.

"I do believe that is the nicest thing you've ever said about Pig. It's reassuring to know you'd never let them vote that way."

"Maybe I should encourage it," Jeremy said. He held her elbow now, to steady her as they moved toward the commotion along the bank. "That way we'd end up alone on the trail at last, just our wagons and Pig, and I could blame it on the dog."

Mazy looked at him from the side of her eye, wishing she could be more certain of when he jested.

Suzanne lived inside uncertainty. If someone touched her elbow, she startled. If she heard a swishing, she assessed: animal scratching or a man breathing? The wind sighing or water rushing? A dozen questions for every scent or touch or taste or sound. The effort fatigued her, and yet she needed the sounds, to tell her where she was. Now here she sat on a hard wagon seat, her son, Clayton, bouncing beside her, his soft fingers clinging to her neck. She could smell his diaper. It needed changing. Bryce stood below her. She could hear him talking to the ferryman, hear the rush of water splash against the logs that carried them farther and farther into uncertainty, deeper into her darkness. She had no "sentinel" as Cicero called them, no eyes to be her guide.

The cracking sound broke into her mind, then the shouts. "Hold it! Hold 'er back, man! Check the chock!"

It wasn't Bryce's voice. Her skin charged the silky hair on her arms as though she stood in a field during a lightning storm. Her husband's voice, raised to the oxen—she heard that next, then felt the vibration of the wagon moving and shifting. She grabbed for the sideboard, clutched for Clayton, his chubby knees poking her side with each half squat he made.

"Bryce? What's happening?" She started to stand.

"Oh, Lord," she heard him say, away, near the lead team. "Whoa, Breeze! What now, what now. My wife, Clayton! Someone, get them off there!"

She felt vibration, pitch, and yaw, someone wrenching Clayton from her side. She heard the child wail, smelled tobacco on whoever grabbed him, felt the weight of the wheels and wagon shift. "Clayton?" Strong fingers reaching for her, her dress tearing; then the splintering of wood, the heave of the wagon, shouts and cries and animals baying, her own body sliding and the smell of wetness and the flap of wind against canvas, her hands wet and slippery, and the putrid, cold water sucking, pulling her deeper into darkness.

Mazy and Jeremy counted. Their wagon was number eleven to roll onto the ferry the following Sunday morning, May 23. A makeshift rail had been pounded onto the side by the Mormon operator to repair the damage done when the load had shifted the day before. It was the Cullver wagon that had gone through and hung up, causing more delay.

Mazy shivered at the sight of the splintered section. The ferryman watched her and spoke out loud. "Their oxen startled and rolled right through it," he said. "That the dog, then? He's yours?"

"He is." The dog panted, sitting beside her, staring out at the water, turning to look up at her when she talked. Mazy scratched at Pig's ears.

"Headed from so far out. Think he heard that woman? Thought the whole ferry'd go. Her husband almost had her in, but the wagon went and threw her like a stone. Who'd a thought a dog could have dragged her?"

"Drowning people often bring their rescuers down, I've heard."

"Panic," the ferryman said, nodding his head. "Kills the same as a lead sinker."

"Pig's a strong swimmer," Mazy said.

"Don't envy any that'll be traveling with that man and his wife," the ferryman said. "Greenhorns. Oxen just two-year-olds. Shouldn't think about making this crossing with animals less than five. Too unruly." He slapped at a horsefly biting on his thigh. "Guess they got money to replace it, though a good hand with an ox'd be worth more." He held the rudder of the ferry against a blast of wind, settled it, then said, "Woman like that, pitiful. And her with a babe at her side. Bad omen, you ask me."

"Nonsense," Mazy told him. She pulled at the short jacket covering her bloomer costume. The wind whipped at the full pant legs that made her think of pictures she'd seen of Persians. "That's pure superstition. The woman has enough to worry over without carrying a belief that she's cursed in some way."

Mazy looked around. Jeremy stood beside the wagon, his eyes lifted often to the shoreline where their oxen waited. Since the accident, most were unhitching now and swimming the stock across, just using the ferry for wagons. It delayed things even further, but the risk of accident and injury lessened. The Cullver incident decided for several people that speed was less important than survival.

The ferryman grunted. "Women wearing pants don't bode well for river crossings neither," he said.

"These bloomers would keep me afloat if I fell in," Mazy laughed. "You might consider that, spending as much time on the water as you do."

He grunted. "No wonder the dog did what it did. Spent too much time with an addled woman."

Mazy waved at her mother perched high on the seat in her wagon behind theirs. She looked like a child, Mazy thought, her eyes sparking with excitement, pointing and twisting in her seat, calling down to Tyrell to draw his attention to some bird, some rush of water that raced past them. She looked younger, her eyes less tired. Mazy hadn't thought of it before, but her mother appeared inspired by the very excitement that pulled others under.

The river splashed up onto the decking over the logs. Mazy jumped back, but not before the water soaked her boots and darkened the crimson of her bloomers. They were her only pair. She'd seen a few other women wearing the practical garments, inviting a flutter of Jeremy's irritation.

The ferry bobbed, sloshing up more water. She bent to scratch Pig's neck, and the dog leaned into her leg.

Land jolted them. They rehitched their team as soon as the stock came over, water still pouring off the oxen's broad backs. The animals pulled the wagon to the far side, rolled onto the second ferry. They unhitched the team again. Jeremy did well with the detail of harnessing and unharnessing, checking the load of their wagon, conferring with Tyrell about Elizabeth's wagon. Both the brute and the cows had bobbed through the water along with the oxen and the Schmidtkes' cattle. Once on the far side, Jeremy and Tyrell headed back to push stock into the water for the next wagons, helping as others had for them.

It was nearly dark when the final wagon of their small grouping rolled off onto the west side of the Missouri. Men like shadows, their eyes adjusting to the dark, continued hitching and rolling the last of the wagons into a circle then unhitching again.

Mazy stood, exhausted from the watching and worry, from reshifting the loads. The guidebook had made the river fordings sound like an adventure with high drama ending in joy, not a day that strained. Someone like her mother must have written it. She noticed her mother reach into the flour barrel and started to ask her if she wanted to keep a piece of china safe there when she saw Pig's ears stand up at attention.

Pig trotted toward the woman, her arm gripping her husband's. A toddler preceded them, stooping to pick up pebbles as he walked. Suzanne Cullver's thick, straw-colored hair was tied back with a simple wine red ribbon. She wore a brown wrapper with buttons stretched across the bodice and a full skirt without an apron. She couldn't have been more than mid-twenties, Mazy guessed. A striking beauty. Round glasses covered her eyes, so dark Mazy couldn't see behind them.

"I'd like to thank you," Bryce Cullver said, "for your dog's quick…for saving Suzanne's life. Everything was so hurried…we didn't do it proper earlier. Don't know where he came from, but I couldn't be more grateful." He had a deep voice, resonant when he spoke though his speech was marked by caution. "Suzanne Jane would…she'd like to thank you too." He patted her fingers. "Careful, Clayton."

"Speak for yourself," the woman answered and pulled her arm free of him.

"Suzanne, please, these are nice folks. Their dog—"

"Didn't mind his own business," she finished for him. She had slender fingers though the nails were bitten to the quick. She fluttered them at her neck, and then she rested them around her throat above her white collar, as though to choke herself. "It would have settled many a question if I'd been left to be, to let the elements take me as they would. Drown or not, since fate made the ferry break. But no, he had to come and pull me free."

"I'm sure, in time she'll change her mind…be grateful for your dog's actions. This…it's been a hard year for us." Bryce shrugged his shoulders then, palms out in resignation. The child approached Pig.

"Don't think I don't know you're doing things with your face and your eyes to tell them to indulge me, pat me on my head," Suzanne said. She had a voice like a crosscut saw that didn't need sharpening. "I don't need anyone's pity. Had enough to last a lifetime, which would have been short enough but for your dog. Let's go, Bryce. See to Clayton."

Despite the rage of her words, her face looked blank. She thrust her hands out in front of herself then, stepped forward and stumbled, said something beneath her breath. Mazy surmised she had not been blinded long. She still used the tools of the sighted that no longer worked. Suzanne kicked at the sitting log and would have fallen but for Pig, who barked and set himself before her.

"You again," Suzanne said.

"Not the dog's fault, Suzanne."

"No, my own. That's what got me here in the first place. Isn't that what you're saying to yourself? Can we go now, Bryce? I've a headache." She pressed at her temples, all the color drained from her nails.

"I have some golden seal that might help," Mazy offered.

"Best not that," Bryce said. He shook his head and lowered his voice. "She's…we were worried she might have lost—"

"Tell everyone, Bryce, why don't you. Let them all know. So they can wonder all agog about how a stupid blind woman will birth and raise a baby along this wretched trail."

"Mint, then," Mazy said after a pause. "In a hot tea. That's good for headaches."

"I despise gentle people," Suzanne said, turning her body toward the direction of Mazy's voice.

"I'm sorry," Mazy said. "I'll just get the leaves from my herb box. When's your baby due?" Mazy reached for her mint at the wagon's side cupboard. "It was thoughtless of me not to notice. Your Clayton looks to be a pretty healthy soul. He's how old?"

"Bryce looks after him," Suzanne said. "I really do want to leave now. We've done our duty."

⸻

The next big river crossing would be the Platte according to the guidebook, but that was miles away. For days, they'd travel north beside it, in the valley it carved heading west. Mazy had the guidebook in her hand as they sat on the log, awaiting the meeting.

"Won't be needing that, now," Antone Schmidtke said as the group clustered around the fire. "My map's the recent one." He nodded toward her guidebook. "Will be sharing it after our vote. Hope you'll be joining up with us, Mrs. Bacon," he said and tipped his hat. "Got ourselves a regular town rolling out tomorrow. Like to have you. The dog, too."

Even in Kanesville, the women had found the evening gatherings strengthening, a word her mother used. "A place to share berries or biscuits and exchange information," she said. Tonight, Mazy heard voices speak of recipes and ways to add variety to the corn cakes or the tiresome wheat-berry coffee. Men boasted of the crossing and finally being on their way. She supposed these gathering times were important, to discover who had what tool, what supply might later be offered. But the conversations tired her, all the people, so constant.

They held the vote first at dusk, men only. Antone Schmidtke earned the honors as captain. The time they'd waited to take the vote hadn't given anyone but Mazy a chance to change her mind. Jeremy hadn't made a speech and in fact seemed indifferent to the proceedings.

A feeling like a spider crawling under her collar made Mazy wonder if they'd have another argument later about going on alone.

"You lost but won your independence. We Cassville folks ought to stick together," Hathaway Wilson told Jeremy after the group had begun to disperse.

"How many others are joining the Schmidtke train?" Mazy asked.

Hathaway combed his dark mustache with his fingers. "The Barnards, some Missouri folks, some others, can't remember their names. Oh, that Martin woman." Hathaway shook his head. "Determined one she is. The blind woman and her man, they'll go wherever your dog goes, I expect." Hathaway laughed. "Sister Esther and her Marriage Association girls agreed to travel along too, though she may change her mind if we decide to travel on the Sabbath."

"And will we?"

"Depends on the trials we face. Antone says if things go smooth, then we can rest. Trouble, and we've got to keep rolling even on a Sunday."

"I'd say resting a day could only gain us strength to live with the trials," Mazy offered. "And it sets a good example for the children, too."

"What about you, Jeremy?" Hathaway asked. "Still deciding?"

"You're heading to California. We aren't," Jeremy told him.

It was the first time Mazy knew for sure that her husband had chosen Oregon, and she felt a flash of irritation that she had to overhear it—where he'd set his sights.

"But until we turn south, it makes sense to have you with us," Hathaway told him. He pounded his clay pipe against his boot. "You started this, after all—this westering of the Wisconsin clan. And while Tipton's not needing to share your mother's wagon, Mazy, I believe she likes her company still."

"Tyrell's contract is to teamster my wagons, regardless of where they go."

"Don't doubt he'd like to keep his word," Hathaway said. "It'll create a wail from Tipton if he does." Hathaway cleared his throat. "I was hoping…haven't said, of course, that maybe in Laramie you could hire on another teamster. And that way, free Tyrell up." He pulled on his mustache that draped ragged edges over his upper lip. "Hope my not paying for Tipton's keep doesn't muddle this."

"I'm quite sure we can survive without the 'Tipton-watching money.' "

"That's what you called it?" Hathaway asked. "Guess it was, at that. She'll still need watching, but her mama likes that job."

Hathaway threw a few pebbles into the fire. "Think about freeing up Tyrell, will you? Could make my life…smoother." He clapped Jeremy's shoulder in that way men have of parting. Tired, Mazy thought, he's tired and defeated.

Jeremy helped Mazy step up into the wagon later and then lit a candle. He removed his glasses, splashed his eyes with water from the bowl, dabbing his long face dry before sitting on a plank chair. Without speaking, he lifted his foot to her, and she turned her back, reached between her knees and pulled at his boot. His other foot rested on her bloomered backside for added grip.

"It is the Lord's day," Mazy said. "We didn't keep it all that well." She grunted with exertion, set his boot down, and waited for him to lift his other foot. "Your feet are cold." She set the second boot beneath the narrow bed. "What are you thankful for?" Mazy asked, washing her hands now in the porcelain basin.

"Safe answer is to say I got a wife with warm feet and strong hands."

"No, really."

Jeremy sighed. "I'm thankful you've decided to come with me and that I'm out of the fire and back into the spider. And you?" He put his arms behind his head and looked at her. Drops of water from where he'd splashed his face glistened on his hair. Little red marks on his narrow nose told of glasses that didn't quite fit. A prickly chin hinted that he had begun to grow a beard.

"I'm thankful we'll be ended of this journey and in a new home before the New Year. Especially this year." She picked up his glasses and, with the edge of her bloomers, rubbed at the lenses.

He lifted an eyebrow. "Because?"

"It seems we'll be adding a Bacon to our family's frying pan."

<hr />

It reminded her of Indian country, this land beside the Platte. Ruth had seen plenty of Indians back in Kentucky. They'd been fierce at one time, warring, her father said, forcing her and her sisters to practice drills using a Kentucky long rifle. The drills were followed by a sneak and crawl on their bellies to the potato cellar dug out of the damp earth on their isolated farm. Ruth thought the snakes they had encountered in Kentucky much more dangerous than the Indians she saw once or twice through the door cracks. The Pawnee simply lifted a basket of apples or pulled at tobacco leaves hanging from the drying shed rafter or found a bolt of cloth they draped around them as they left.

None of the items taken seemed worth a life, though her father said what belonged to them was worth killing for.

Justice was a word her father used often. She wondered how his justice would fare in this place, with wagons owned by some and driven by others; with travel made without permission across uncharted lands; decisions made not by any standard law nor by the wisest, but by those who could convince the others of their certainty through the power of their words or might. Her father had been good at that, using words to convince. He had not convinced her, and that had been her loss.

Ruth slapped her hand on the shoulder of an ox. It was good to be on the trail, to be actually heading toward something instead of just running away. New sights and sounds and smells, that's what she needed to replace the past. She didn't mind a sky the color of pewter either, the way some did, or light misty rains that kept the dust down. Those kinds of days felt like quilts around her, comforting and close.

Zane had liked those heavy days too. It was just one of their many commonalities. She supposed that was what deluded her in the end, the belief that only those meant for each other could share so many finely tuned details like the rub of wool against skin or relishing the taste of caviar without it having to be acquired.

She shook her head. The neck string holding her hat pulled against her throat. He'd been a good man—hadn't he? She would not think further than that.

Ruth walked beside the last wagon. On either side and to the front rolled wagons hoping to avoid the puff and spurt of prairie dust by branching out at an angle from the other teams. She pulled the neckerchief up over her nose, straining the dusty air. Ruth would not rotate toward the front as the others would throughout the journey, a decision that had been voted on by men—and only men.

"A woman without a teamster ought not to place others in jeopardy," one man said.

"You have a breakdown and it will slow the rest of us, not having any man to help you right away like," Antone told her.

Even Jed had shrugged his shoulders as if to say, "What can I do?"

Well, what could he do or should he do? Nothing, she decided. She would keep to her own fire at night from here on in. She would cook for herself and not depend on Betha to feed her. She would handle the stock and harness and, yes, make repairs as well. She would be alone in her spirit. She needed no one. She'd already learned that by giving away all that she'd loved. She could even defend herself if necessary, though she doubted the attacks would come from Indians. That she had learned too.

Relief fluttered at Tipton's edges. That Martin woman had been told to bring up drag. Every day she'd bite the dust of others. The men assured the woman that they would not let any harm come to her, but they didn't want Ruth in the middle where her broken wheels or split tongue or lame animal would hold them up while they tried to find someone to make repairs.

"Got to hit Laramie by June 15. Can't afford delays."

That's what they always said. "Can't afford delays" as though speed were a commodity, something you could purchase at her father's Cassville store.

Ruth Martin in the back, isolated. That would keep that full smile of hers polished with dirt stuck between her teeth. It put one potential problem in its place, leaving Tipton free to work on the larger one: convincing her father of their need to head to Oregon since Tyrell was going there, or convincing Tyrell to head south—without the Bacons.

The men had determined Ruth *could* run her stock in with theirs. "That's only right," her brother defended. "She got this far with them. I'll call 'em mine if need be, 'til we get to Oregon. Horses are hers, though. If we have losses, stampedes and such, she can't gather up her own. Got to help each other when it comes to that. We'd do it for anyone."

Ruth hated accepting anything from them. But Jed was right. She wouldn't be able to herd them alone and bring the wagon too, and she needed the wagon for the grain. The horses couldn't make it without the grain. Mules, yes; fine horses, no.

Still, while she ate the dust of all the other emigrants, she wasn't far from the horses. Horses gave back what they got. Horses, like children, were just.

"At least you don't have to pretend anymore," Betha told her. "Don't have to keep my mouth shut or fib about you having a teamster waiting in Laramie."

"Right," Ruth said.

The wagon right in front of her today held the Marriage Association wives-to-be. The Association's wagons would choke on others' dust too. At the same meeting, Sister Esther had raised a ruckus about the Sabbath policy and their not stopping.

"Any who challenge tradition'll pay a price," Jed told her.

"Tradition! You call a group of total strangers making things up as they go tradition? It isn't as though we were a town. Not even a group. Where do they get their authority?"

"It's the way it is," Jed said, "and the sooner folks accept what is, well, the sooner we can solve problems."

Ruth cracked her whip over the head of the oxen—two-colored beasts, four strong—and forced herself to think of positive things.

A tiny-framed woman with almond eyes stared at her from the back of the wagon ahead of her. The girl kneeled, never changing the expression on her somber face though she shifted left to right with the road, her knees barely moving. She didn't seem at all a happy bride-to-be. More wisdom than age.

"Does that doll talk to people?" Jessie asked. The child walked beside Ruth.

"That's a girl, a woman actually," Ruth told her.

"Looks like a doll. One of Lisbeth's."

"Who's Lisbeth, one of your new friends?"

"She's big but she has a little girl named Mazy, and she still likes dolls. Like that one in the wagon. She says the doll in that wagon talks to bees, but she ain't ever talked to people."

The girl did look like a porcelain doll, perfect olive skin, high cheekbones, and dark eyes. Her hair was cut short against the nape of her neck, and beside her lay a pointy straw hat.

"Bees?" Ruth said.

"So would she talk?" Jessie asked.

"I don't know. You'll have to pay attention, and when we stop, if she looks willing, you might ask her."

If the beekeeper didn't talk much, it would add to her mystique, Ruth thought. Her silence already endeared her. Women's talk usually irritated Ruth. She'd heard Betha and that Wilson woman twitter and chatter over "Asians" and "savages." A silly waste, jabbering about subjects they knew nothing of. They spoke of rattlesnakes and rumors of cholera and musket accidents, but it was the talk of Indians that most incensed Ruth.

"Have you ever seen an Indian?" Ruth asked Adora once when the woman stopped talking long enough to take a breath.

"Indeed I have."

Several others hadn't, and the woman whispered tales that fed fears they'd be taken all the way to Cow Town. Ruth walked away, disgusted. Even Jessie acted scared when they saw a roll of dust off in the distance.

"Indians?" Jessie asked, eyes big as biscuits.

"No. The wind. Something you see every day just in a different way."

"Only new things're scary, huh, Auntie?"

Ruth considered the question as she watched the child smooth her little apron along her butternut-colored skirt, adjusting it at her hips. She'd seen Betha do that, often. Something in the gesture sent a sweet ache into Ruth's soul.

"Sometimes even what we're used to can be frightening, I guess, if it changes and isn't what it once was."

"Huh?" Jessie asked.

Ruth ran a gloved hand down the girl's bouncing sausage curls as they walked. "Fear just tells us that something is different. To deal with it, we just have to apply what we know, do our best in that new place."

"If that dust was a Indian, Papa might have to shoot him, huh?"

"Not you too, Jessie," Ruth moaned.

"What if they come and shooted at us and took Mommy away and—"

"It's a dust devil, just the wind making the dirt rise up like that. Don't get your imagination all worked up over nothing."

"What's 'magination?"

"Something you have in your mind, something you play like. A dream, sort of."

Jessie walked in silence. "But I'm awake, Auntie. I'm not sleeping."

"Strange thinking doesn't require sleeping, Jessie."

"Lisbeth says to dream all the time, so I know what to reach for when I'm big."

"That's more like hoping, having something to look forward to, to hang on to when you're…mixed up, when you're uncertain. So you have something to remind you of where you're going."

"Yup," Jessie said as though she understood completely.

Ruth cracked the whip over the ox's head to divert a shift to the left.

"Mommy says they'll steal food from us, the Indians will. Take your horses, too, she said."

"If you were hungry and someone had a picnic in your yard, wouldn't you want to join them?"

"We're in their yard?" Her brown eyes stared at Ruth in wonder, her face holding the awe of new insight.

"I'd say so."

"Wait 'til I tell Jason. He don't know they're coming to a picnic. Tell Lisbeth, too. I'm gonna tell 'em right away."

"Jason's pretty far ahead. Several wagons. You won't get lost?"

"I'm really fast." She started to bolt ahead.

"Wait a minute," Ruth said. The girl's skirt and apron billowed up around her like an upside-down tulip as she jumped up and down in her excitement to go. Her toes left small impressions in the soft dust.

Ruth looked behind her to see how closely the cattle and horses followed. She'd heard of accidents, wagons rolling over children, and didn't think she could live if something that dreadful happened to Jessie. Not Jessie. One lost child was enough.

"I believe the Bacons would release you from the contract if they could find another teamster at Laramie to take your place," Tipton suggested. She blinked her eyelashes. She gazed at Tyrell walking in the wagon's shadow.

"Not the point, Tip," Tyrell said. "I signed on to help the Bacons. They still need me."

"Maybe we should talk with my father about me heading on with them, then. I'll tell them that I'll follow the Bacons' wagon anyway if they don't agree. I threatened to do that before, and it got them to let me come here."

"Got them here too, Tip."

Her parasol shaded her eyes as she looked up at him. "Which means they know I'd make good on my threat."

"I wouldn't let you. Be too dangerous. The Bacons would send you back, and I'd honor that, you know I would. No, better we accept our disappointment and face what is. Set our sights on staying in touch so when you turn seventeen I'll know where to come in California to find you for my bride."

"Will you, though? Or maybe just choose another woman to share your life with in Oregon? Someone like Ruth Martin maybe." She twirled the parasol, the fringe flying almost horizontal.

"Tipton," he said.

"You never say," she said. "You never tell me really how you feel about that woman."

"There's nothing to tell. No reason to be jealous over her or any others."

"There are others?"

Tyrell shook his head.

"You never say you care most for me, you don't."

"I've said it so much the words start to sound hollow. A person can't make another person believe something. Either you trust it or you don't, Tip. It hasn't anything to do with me. It has to do with you, believing I could care for you, that you're worth caring for. Some things are taken on faith. I can't pour certainty into you."

"You could if you wanted, but you don't."

"Doubt's a poison taken from a snake, Tip. No call for it between us."

She could tell by the tone of his voice that he was irritated, so she stomped off, rubbing her arm as she did. She hoped he'd make her come back, but he didn't.

Alone, she breathed in short, quick gasps, the knoll she chose to climb higher than it looked from the wagons. Her hand tingled. Everything swirled, made her lightheaded.

She walked faster, her skirts catching on her legs. She could see the lines of wagons fanning out toward the west. Far behind moved the stock, grazing and allowed to meander rather than push. It seemed to her that they would be farther and farther behind that way, but so far they'd always caught up to the wagons by dusk.

The Bacons' brute and cows tugged behind their wagons; the spots of dogs sniffed in and out. A cluster of children leaned over some treasure that hovered in the shadow of emerald grass. White tabs of aprons ran down the front of little girls' dresses fluttering in the wind as the girls jumped back from something a boy said or were startled by the mouse they watched. Maybe she should sketch it. Her hand fumbled for the sewn-in pocket. She'd try to capture the smells of the grasses, the light on the knoll, the feel of the dust on the faces of children.

But her hands shook, and her fingers ached and tingled to numb.

patience

They made good progress, crossing the Platte no less than three times as it meandered and flattened out like an old brown snake. In places, it promised solid soil but didn't deliver. Maybe if it stopped flooding and flowing over its banks, if it ever stayed in a recognized channel, maybe then they'd see more solid ground, Elizabeth thought. Still these western expanses made her eyes sparkle with wonder beneath white clouds that fluffed against the sky like fresh feathers.

She'd met her limit of day-after-dayness. Antone telling everyone who'd be able to avoid the dust by being first in line—after him; who had to come last; his reminding everyone of the leaving time, no matter that they'd made twenty miles or only ten the day before. He wanted animals yoked, coffee downed, and morning fires out by an hour after sunrise. Dr. Masters always needed goading, Elizabeth noticed, not presenting the best side of a doctor's essential attention to detail. He was nothing like her husband.

Elizabeth bent and reached for her skirt hem between her legs, pulling the material up and tucking it into her belt in the front. She untied the reins and swung up onto her mule, Ink. Wouldn't Adora and Sister Esther have a calf if they saw her now? Let the ladies gasp if they must. Folks who farmed or lacked the luxury of carriages understood—sidesaddling just didn't work.

Everyone talked about getting to Oregon or California, getting somewhere they weren't, and all the while missing out on where they were. She pressed the reins against the mule's neck. Waiting until they arrived at their destination to experience joy was simply too long. The human spirit could not be so patient, could not hold on to the memory of happy moments as the only nurture. It needed feeding daily.

It was like the black pot she fixed the stew in: she could take venison and beans to feed a dozen, but unless she kept adding potatoes and onions and beef stock back, she'd eventually come up dry. No, to keep the stew always available with enough to give away, she had to keep adding to it. It was the same with merriment: better than a dose of laudanum, without the side effects.

She wished they'd traveled on the south side of the Platte so she could have seen the Mullalys' sod house that folks said served as a way station. She might like to run such a place someday. It would give her a chance to rub elbows with a whole range of personalities as people stepped off stagecoaches rolling from here to there. Her husband's habit of bringing people home for occasional recuperation had met a need she had, to be exposed to new and different. After he died and Mazy married and moved away, she'd missed that. The journey west pinched a flush back into her cheeks.

More people would be heading west. Something about the land lured, offered a promise that thrived in open spaces. People running as well as seeking came, and they all brought along their stories. She guessed that was what she'd missed most of all, living alone in the house after her husband died, no one to bring home a story and none to listen to hers.

Today, she was riding for stories, to see if one could be found where it looked like nothing could live. If she located mule deer or antelope for supper, she'd have added to the pot in more ways than one.

❧

"Pig! Stop barking," Mazy told the dog. His big head bunted at her, and he made slobbery noises. "Mother's right. You even sound like a pig.

Mother?" Now where had she gone off to? Pig barked, steady and high-pitched until she followed, finding herself shortly beside the Cullver wagon.

"I'm sorry," Mazy said. "The dog…"

"We're pleased," Bryce told her. Suzanne sat atop the wagon, Clayton bouncing on her lap. Bryce wiped his dusty face of sweat, and talked to the oxen as they walked. He had bushy eyebrows the color of cashews, and Mazy could see that Clayton had his blue eyes. "Aren't we glad to have a visitor? Suzanne, it's Mrs. Bacon."

"I heard the dog," Suzanne said. "Come to see how a blind woman raises a baby, have you?"

"Suzanne! " He spread his palms in surrender.

"In fact," Mazy said, "I've lain awake wondering how you do it. I can see, and I've got the jitters just thinking about how I'll manage."

"You're…?" Bryce asked.

Mazy nodded, then remembered Suzanne's limitations. "Haven't told many."

"Mrs. Bacon's…"

"Well, won't that be peachy, to have someone to trade baby stories with." Suzanne threw the words out, pelting each one against the air like hail. "We'll just all be one big happy family talking of napkins and messy bottoms."

"I'm sorry if this is a bad time. I hadn't planned to intrude," Mazy said, "but my dog likes you. And now that I'm here, I could take away some of Clayton's diapers, if you'd like. Scrape them when we stop."

Suzanne grunted, turned her head away.

"You're very kind. If you wouldn't mind," Bryce said. "I suspect his diaper rash grows from my poor handling of it."

"Oh, Bryce, please," Suzanne said. "Is there nothing you won't talk about?"

Before he could respond, Pig leaped into the wagon box, nudging Suzanne, who slapped at him. The dog merely moved beyond her reach, sat, and panted.

"He's never done that before, not even with my mother."

"Well, get him down."

"Come, Pig." Mazy slapped at her thigh. The dog whined but didn't move. Mazy stepped up onto the wagon to pull at him. As she did, she noticed a sewing machine in the wagon. It was a Howell, a luxury few had.

"Oh, you sew?" Mazy asked.

"Blindfolded," Suzanne answered, pushing at Pig. "About as well as you train dogs."

Elizabeth rode over a hill and spied a triangular shelter the color of faded mustard settled among waving grasses. It looked deserted, so she dismounted. Arriving around it, she startled a lone man. *Indian!* He turned and the sunlight glinted against the knife he held in his hand. This was more than a story.

"Quite ridiculous of him to write to you," Jeremy said, peering over his wife's shoulder. "Hardly necessary."

Mazy held the envelope delivered by some good-hearted soul heading west at a faster pace than the Bacons. She imagined it was meant to greet her at Fort Laramie, but the westbound rider had helped several letters find their way to the eager hands of those traveling with the Schmidtke train.

"He says his wife had begun the letter, to tell me how the lilacs bloomed, how the garden grew and all. How thoughtful," Mazy said. The script ran at diagonals over lines written one way with one person's pen then written across the lines by another's.

"Should have kept it to himself. It's past. Done." Jeremy checked the water bucket on the side of their wagon. "Saltbox is near empty. Can't get to Laramie soon enough," he said.

"I suppose it was his way of grieving her, finding an unfinished letter written in her hand and wanting to complete it. I might have been inclined to do it, to carry out someone's last intent."

"Then send it, don't add your own news, tell that the woman died. Or that you're alone now, with kids and the land, feeling oppressed."

"It might be hard to run the farm without her, go on, alone. Maybe we should—"

"Don't start again, Maze. It's not a sign of anything."

"I didn't say it was."

"You were thinking it. I could see it in your eyes."

"Now you read eyes," she said, "along with your books on Ayrshires and Oregon?"

⸺

Pawnee, Elizabeth guessed. She must have looked harmless in her dark dress because he merely grunted at her. Behind him, she could see a downed buffalo calf he'd been hacking on. Two rust-colored birds pecked at a pile of intestines pink as ripe watermelon mounded alongside. She rolled up her sleeves and motioned her intent. He turned back to his work.

Using his blood-stained fingers, the Indian lifted black strands of shiny hair hanging long, pushing them back behind his ears. A sage-scented breeze blew across his face. He wore a breechcloth; his chest was shiny with sweat.

Elizabeth noticed an obsidian knife lying in the grass. She picked it up and began cutting beside him, removing hide from neck and hams. He glanced at the knife in her hand once, then turned to his work. White globs of fat like Milwaukee winter snow stuck to the hide they peeled back. Several times they'd laid down their knives and shoulder to shoulder, with four hands, pulled, ripping it free of the muscle, the flesh still warm at their knuckles.

Elizabeth chatted about the calf, how big it was compared to a deer. In a pause, the man grunted.

"Can you hear us all rolling across the prairie like that?" Elizabeth went on. "Bet you can. Probably smell us, too." She sniffed herself, scowled. "Same old dress I started out with."

After a time, they worked in silence. Sweat dripped from her forehead. When the buffalo's brown, curly-hair hide with flecks of red lay in a heap beside the naked animal, a woman came out of the buckskin shelter.

"You been in there that whole time?" Elizabeth asked, standing. The woman's face looked pinched and drawn, and when she offered Elizabeth a gourd of water, Elizabeth noted tiny scabs on the back of her hand and others on her neck. A baby cried from inside the shelter.

❦

"Do you know what time my mother left or where she was going?" Mazy asked a weary-looking Tipton, putting away her pencils.

"We don't talk much. We *ponder* even less since my parents came. Whose diapers are you carrying?" Tipton curled up her nose.

"I'm helping Mrs. Cullver. Their poor child's bottom must be red as a radish. Thought mother'd have some ideas for chipping off what's dried."

"I haven't seen Tyrellie much, either," Tipton continued. "Have you given any thought to hiring a teamster at Laramie?"

"Doesn't Tyrell plan to go on with us?"

"Yes. I mean, no. Oh, you know what I mean."

"I know you're scared he will and you're not sure how to keep that from happening, right?"

Tipton nodded, and tears pooled in her eyes.

Elizabeth wiped her mouth of the sweet water and, at the woman's invitation, bent into the shadows of the shelter. A fluff of black peelings lay in a heap on the floor. The woman offered small, round roots with fingers stained dark.

"Good," Elizabeth said, chewing the white root and liking the pungent taste.

The woman motioned, and Elizabeth lifted the ends of her apron and spilled the roots into it, gathering the cloth like a pocket. She gazed around at the clean and simple larder of their shelter, the smell of burning sage heady from a clay pot nestled by what looked like bedding. She smelled meat cooking outside, and the man soon brought in a piece of backstrap. She was given a chunk, meat so tender when she tasted it, Elizabeth found she didn't need to chew.

"So you cook, too?" Elizabeth said to the man who just stared down at her, the way she often did when she offered up some new dish at a Christmas Eve supper, waiting for the nod of aye or nay. "Don't find too many men of my kind willing to work at the cooking fire," she said. She lifted the piece of meat up in her greasy fingers and smiled at him. "Just dandy." He nodded once, handed the woman a piece, and left.

Elizabeth studied her, a small-framed person with a heart-shaped face, wearing hides laced together with strings of gut and graced around the neck with what looked like yellowed elk's teeth. In the corner she saw a baby kick his feet. His mother lifted him from a bed of green moss and held him to her breast. The child appeared to be about ten months old. The woman didn't look to have an ounce to spare him. The man returned and brought a chunk of fat he'd sliced from the calf hide. The baby kicked his feet again, in excitement, smiled, and reached for it, laughing as he held the piece, then quieted into sucking sounds, content with the snow-white fat.

"That was good eating," Elizabeth said, wiping her hands on the dirt floor, then at her hips. She wasn't sure what the proper etiquette was when eating with a Pawnee, but appreciation must be universal.

What happened next surprised her. The woman set the child down, reached around her neck, and removed the string of teeth. She handed them to Elizabeth, motioning for Elizabeth to put them on.

Elizabeth started to protest, but something told her no, that the receiving of a thing became a gift in itself. The woman knelt behind her to put it on. She smelled of wood smoke and something sweet.

"It's just a jewel," Elizabeth said, patting the ivory teeth. "Wish I could give you something." She stood up then and rubbed her hip. As she did, she felt the pocket tied beneath her skirt. "Ah," she said. She undid the apron and set the roots down, then unhooked the skirt pulled between her legs. She reached up under the yards of material to untie the cloth pocket.

"*Godey's Lady's Magazine* won't approve the combination," she said, "you wearing skins and all. But I like to muddle up my fashion." From the pocket, Elizabeth handed the woman a pair of silver earrings. "My son-in-law would say these took up wasted space anyway," Elizabeth told her. "Go ahead, put them on."

Elizabeth held the earrings in her fingertips and heard the tinkling of the silver bells as she gestured for the woman to take them.

"Time I parted with them," Elizabeth said. "Bought 'em to please myself after my husband died. Thought they'd comfort, but they didn't. Only time and kind adventures do, I'd say. This afternoon here counts."

Silver Bells, as Elizabeth now thought of the woman, accepted the gift. The two women patted their exchanges. Elizabeth picked up her roots, and they stepped outside. The man still bent over the animal, cutting strips of meat and then poking the flesh onto sticks to dry by the fire.

Beneath an endless blue sky, Silver Bells walked with her a distance while Elizabeth's mule plodded behind them. The woman's rasping breath cut a slice against the prairie stillness. The baby'd been wrapped in a board the woman carried on her back. "Child's almost big enough to carry you," Elizabeth said. "How long you been sick?" Silver Bells merely smiled, then made a quick dart to touch a slender plant. She pointed to Elizabeth's apron full of roots. "I'll look for those," Elizabeth said. "Thank you for adding to my stew."

❧

"The scenery," Adora Wilson told Mazy as they walked beside each other the next morning, "takes a body's breath away, if truth be known. Just look at that pointy rock."

"It does look like a chimney," Mazy said. She shaded her eyes. The rock outcropping rose across the Platte, but those on the north Council Bluffs road could still see it. "Clouds look like fat egg noodles plumped in a string, don't they?"

"The river looks so soothing, truthfully."

"It does mesmerize, the way it meanders and yet keeps heading in one direction. Flowing back toward home."

"Hathaway says when we reach the Divide, the rivers all flow toward the Pacific. Imagine that! How does that work, water changing course, just like that?"

"Cross over a mountain and everything changes, I guess," Mazy said. "Have you thought any more about heading into Oregon?"

"Tipton won't let us not think of it. Hathaway seems sure we'd be better off south. He has a cousin came out in '49 on that horrible Pioneer Line. Survived to tell the tale. You'd have thought folks wouldn't talk about it, heading out as they did with that mountain man guide dying of cholera before they even left Independence! It'd be a sign for a body to stay home, I tell you, having so much trouble on a trail."

"Where's he live?"

"Sacramento area, his cousin is." She opened and closed the wrist purse she carried, a black beaded piece smaller than Mazy's palm. A habit, Mazy decided, the clasp clicking like knitting needles. "They correspond," Adora continued. "We sent a letter on so he knows we're coming. Hathaway's reluctant to say it outright to Tipton any sooner than he must. Besides, Charles has expressed little interest in Oregon. Even less in doing something Tipton might want." She sighed. "Don't know how some folks do it, raise children who like each other instead of being at odds."

"Might be an argument for having single children," Mazy said.

"Oh, birthing itself is as good an argument for that as there is, but we pay little attention. You won't either."

Somehow the word of Mazy's condition, her "feeling poorly," had spread. Perhaps Tipton had seen her ill that morning, or her mother had let word leak out. More like flood out, coming from her mother. Suzanne wouldn't have told a soul.

Mazy wiped the back of her neck with her handkerchief. "I feel so clammy," she said.

"Doesn't look like rain," Adora said, gazing up at the sky. Crows cawed and dipped above. A meadowlark warbled and landed on a single strand of leaning grass left behind by the ravenous stock of wagons gone before them.

"It never does, and then we find ourselves drenched. The mosquitoes are worse than I've ever seen too. Wish mother'd come up with a remedy for them."

"Your mother." Adora clucked her tongue. "I can't believe she entered that Indian's hovel. Disease and all? She's lucky she got out alive."

"She was invited," Mazy said.

"Still, I've heard their homes—if you can call them that—are so squalid."

"Mother described quite a pleasant—"

"Sister Esther's right," Adora continued. She swatted at horse flies then turned her head. Mazy could feel her staring. "Disease is a tool of correction among those with low morals. Your mother exposed all of us—"

"The roots made a nice addition to your stew."

"She put some of that woman's food in the stew?" Adora gasped.

"Just roots," Mazy said.

"Well. I think in the future we ought not to allow people to tramp off so far from the wagons," Adora said. "Indians could have killed her and us, too. She tells her stories so proud, but she invites danger, she does."

"Little scares mother," Mazy said. "She says she's too old to fight and too fat to run, so she just has to rely on her good nature to survive."

"I'd say your mother is having too much fun for a woman her age."

"I wonder how that's measured?" Mazy said and walked a little faster.

"I suggest you let me take the patent paper, Mei-Ling. I mean Deborah," Sister Esther said. They stood outside the wagon where the smaller woman tended her boxes of bees in the dusky light.

"It stay good in sleeve, Missy," the girl told her. "I keep good care." She showed Esther how the parchment folded into a square and slipped inside the sleeve pocket.

Esther pursed her lips, fingered the cross at her neck. "Very well," she said. "Be very careful. We would not want your dowry lost or damaged. Then you'd have nothing to give."

Tipton talked about Fort Laramie, of the adobe walls that harbored fresh cheese and a chance to feast at the "eating houses" well provisioned for both the soldiers and the overlanders by the sutler.

"I want a bath in a steamed tub," Tipton told Tyrell. "And dancing underneath a roof to real musicians and not just Mr. Cullver, who fancies himself a fiddler." She imagined a time when no one needed to be walking great distances or stepping away from the roll of the wagon or complaining about breakdowns or the dry weather shrinking wheels. People would nod and smile at the fort when they met her instead of wearing that scowl of hot faces with sweat streaks that Tipton thought contagious.

"I'll be pleased to have a hot forge to make some real repairs."

"Not a soul complains about your repairing, Tyrellie. I think they feel luxurious to have a farrier along." She cracked a walnut and dug the meat out for him, as his hands were occupied with a whip and dirty with grime. She looked up at his bearded face, popped the walnut meat into his mouth, his dry lips grazing her fingers.

"Then they'll be doubly pleased when I have real tools to do my work."

"It would be dreadful to be in a train without someone like you," she said. She brushed nutmeat from his beard. "I wonder if Papa has really thought this through, going on to California."

"Tip…"

"Oh, never you mind me. I'm just dazed from lack of a copper tub to lounge in. Mama says it'll cost, but be worth it after all we've been through."

"The folks crossing the South Platte have the dibs on tubs and complaints. We've been on a picnic by comparison."

"They have Ash Hollow to rest in, according to Mr. Bacon's guidebook. They say it's heaven there, all that lush grass and shade trees and pure water. Real trees to burn there, too, not those wretched buffalo chips we're stuck with."

"Better buffalo chips than a cold supper," Tyrell told her.

"Oh, Tyrellie. You're always seeing that things could be more foul."

"Like the chickens not laying eggs? Now that's foul."

She poked his shoulder. "That's a pun."

"A poor one, at that." The crunch of wheels scraping rocks and the jangle of harness, of chain against tongue, filled the silence as they walked.

"I like to imagine the tidiness and orderliness of the fort," Tipton went on. "All the uniformed men with polished buckles and boots."

"They don't appeal to me at all," Tyrell said.

"Well, I should hope not," Tipton said. "Say, can't a major or some-one like that act as an official, for court things and all?"

"You thinking of litigation?"

She pressed her head into his shoulder. "Weddings are official with-out being litigation."

"Tip, I don't think your father—"

"You always say I should think on pleasant things."

⌘

Patience, Mazy wrote the word in tiny script. *God is a loving sovereign who waits. He waits for his children. God waits for us to listen. He waits for me. I thank you for your patience and I seek it in my life. Amen.* She thought, tapping the pencil, then added, *Just don't give me too many opportunities to practice, please. Amen.*

She had taken to writing each day about a quality of God's charac-ter, to express gratitude for it, to consider the trait and its meanings, then ask forgiveness for its lacking in her life. Then throughout the following day, she visited that quality, nurturing it the way she had gentled her planting, prodding the soil, staking when needed, seeking the bloom it would bring.

Patience. This journey proved she lacked it. The vistas could not make up for the pervasive insects, the stifling heat, the dust ground into all the food. The doctor's loose shoats snorted and rummaged at any-thing in sight, and no amount of promised bacon by their owners made up for the disruption. Her tomato plant had taken on a dusty whiteness to its leaves that resembled a mold. Tiny stickers from plants she could not name attacked her bare toes and required patience to extract, despite Pig's effort to lick the stickers free. Even Jeremy's gnawing at her about her bloomers tried her patience. It was such a small exertion of independence.

"What difference does it make how I clothe myself?" Mazy told him as she picked at stickers after the cows were milked, the oxen fed, supper dishes wiped clean and stored.

"You tell him. I knew you was an adventurous one," Elizabeth said. The older woman sat, sewing a clamshell button onto one of Mazy's wrappers.

"Just draws attention to you," he said. "Gaudy."

"And having three animals of an unusual breed with strange markings and horns that arc up instead of out, that isn't drawing attention?"

"They weight the horns to get them like that. Did you know that? We'll have to do that too."

"Don't change the subject," Mazy said.

"You're not riding, you're walking. Skirts work as well as pants, and they define your dignity."

"I don't see no men wearing them," Elizabeth said.

"Actually, Scottish men do wear skirts, for the most dignified of occasions."

"Kilts," Mazy said. "You'd prefer I wear those instead of bloomers?"

He looked at her over the top of his glasses.

Mazy sighed. "I'll put them away once we reach the fort." It would cause too much commotion. And as she gained weight with the baby, the wrapper'd be more practical anyway, expanding with her. Meanwhile, why couldn't Jeremy just adjust?

Patience is understanding, being willing to sit beside another where they are without trying to push them this way or that. Calm endurance.

She'd been writing at night, after everyone was settled down, since the mornings now filled with gathering up, with getting on the way according to Antone Schmidtke's schedule. Traveling in this group meant adjusting, day in and day out, to the timing and events set by vote.

"I hate change," she complained, "but I'm not fond of this dust routine either."

"You just don't like other people choosing for you," Jeremy said.

"Human nature to resist change," her mother said, then she bit off the end of the thread. She folded the garment, stretched, and yawned.

"You don't seem to mind it, Mother."

"Learned long ago best way to get through the mud hole is to first admit you're in it, then decide how bad it is you want out and what you got to do to get there. Can always get clear-eyed and courageous about a thing, no matter what your troubles."

Get clear-eyed? How could Mazy do that? The effort of moving from place to place, never waking to familiar, tired her. She was impatient to nest. How could she expect to be happy or comfortable without certainty?

Even her body felt foreign, this carrying of another. A thickening here, a queasiness there—it all worked against her, a woman who liked the expected. Even her chickens protested change—they'd laid almost nothing since they'd left home.

"Are you coming to sleep, woman? Candle's burning down."

"I'll just finish and be in," she told Jeremy.

To be without a place of belonging is to starve the soul, Mazy wrote. She wondered how Mr. Malarky and his boys were managing their loss. At least she had her husband and her mother and this baby. She circled her stomach with the palm of her hand then wrote: *Made eighteen miles today. Saw four graves. At times, we can see the white dots of wagons on the south side of the Platte while we travel on the north. So many people disrupting their lives. Just days out of Laramie. I am impatient to see signs of civilization, the red, white, and blue flying overhead, to sit at a real table to eat once more, to smell the smells of a storehouse full. I am an unworthy waiter, impatient. Give me understanding for this changing time of my life.* She finished writing, entered the tent pitched beside the wagon, stubbed the wick with her fingers, and took herself to bed.

⁓

Jessie hadn't eaten much, though Betha fried up corn hash and eggs and sprinkled them with dried red peppers. After their fasting break, Jed patted his stomach while his plump little wife motioned that his beard still held breadcrumbs.

"Such a fine, fine cook you are, Betha," he said. "Wouldn't you say so, Ruthie?"

"I would," Ruth said. "And I'm glad it's you and not me doing the fixing. White tablecloth? And flowers? For breakfast? What's the occasion?"

"You've had your hands full, graining horses and whacking and all, and you don't join us in the evenings much. I could at least rinse out your clothes for you."

"I do fine back there. I can wander out and talk to Koda, keep my eye on the other horses. It's not all that bad. Do my laundry on days like today, when we stop."

"Jessie isn't a bother to you now, is she?" Betha's eyes looked anxious beneath her flounced cap "We can keep her up with us, you know."

"Never a bother."

"No, not now," Betha said, then dropped her eyes. "I'm sorry," she whispered.

Jed coughed. "Well, now. Looks like a good day. Not a cloud in the sky. A hill and valley or two, a river to cross and then we sight Fort Laramie not far ahead. Ladies, I do believe we are making progress."

"I'm glad to have a day to stop," Ruth said. They'd just completed a tedious section of trail that had required everyone's shoulders and effort to keep the unbending wagons upright on the steep and uneven prairie. They'd been rewarded for their efforts with a cluster of trees and a stream not mentioned in the guidebook. Here they'd stay a day, resting up the stock on good grass and giving the women time to dry and scrape the diapers and wash their meager wardrobes, bake up a pie or two.

"Wish Jessie'd eat up a bit more," Betha said. "Does she look poorly to you?"

"Just a child, Mother," Jed told her, pushing against his knees to stand. "Probably running on the newness of the day. Goes back and forth, visiting every wagon, I declare. Doesn't need much food. Come here then, Jessie girl. Let's see if you're approaching a fever state." He pulled the girl to him, and when Jed's smooth fingers reached around Jessie's wrist, Ruth thought the child's arm looked as thin as a chicken's leg. Jed touched his hand to Jessie's face and frowned.

"Is she feverish?" Ruth asked him. She set her tin cup of cooling coffee down and stood to feel the girl's forehead herself.

"Does seem a bit hot."

"Why don't you fetch that doctor?" Betha said. "What's his name…Masters, in that wagon with the bright green water bucket up ahead there. With the pigs about. Ned, see if you can find him."

"Do I gotta?" the boy complained. He and Jason held a handful of marbles. His brow furrowed beneath the center part of his slick, black hair.

"Your sister's ill," Jed told him. "Needs a doctor."

"You've got a lot more faith in those quacks than I do," Ruth said.

Ned squinted at Jessie. "She's just funning ya so she don't have to wash clothes."

"That is not the way we respond to our mother's request, now is it, Ned? You—"

"I'll go," Ruth said, a lump of worry growing in her throat.

What Tipton wanted was time with Tyrell. He'd shimmed wheel rims and checked ox hooves and hardly had a moment to rest on this day set aside for it.

"You might find some interests of your own," he told her when she pouted over his devotion to the forge.

"I have my drawing," she said.

"Then best you get to it," he said. "Waste a lot of energy trying to change my activities. You can't change folks, Tip. Only yourself."

"My parents are certainly changing me," she said. She flicked at a yellow jacket that tried to light on her bare arm.

"They want the best for you."

"We should be married," she said. "That would be best for me."

"You'd still be pouting about my working. And I'd still be telling you to occupy yourself with something worthwhile, like helping your mama today."

What Tipton wanted was assurance that, when they met the southern cutoff road, her father would have a change of heart. What she wanted was to be married so she wouldn't have to do the things her parents said. What she wanted was a child of her own so she would always have someone to love her, no matter what.

The air here felt too still, and she could not catch her breath. She needed to be *doing* something, making something happen. She could feel herself start to breathe with quick gasps.

"You need to be your own person, Tip," Tyrell said, patting the hand she rubbed against her elbow.

"Like that Ruth Martin, I suppose," she said. "What?"

Tyrell looked past her, his eyes attracted somewhere else.

Tipton turned.

Ruth Martin walked toward them. The woman caught Tyrell's gaze, then strode past, wordless.

riding the horse named loss

Mazy'd always been drawn to wounded things, as though she'd been born with salve enough to spread around for healing. Suzanne would have drawn her, whether Pig had noticed her or not. Maybe it was a gift she'd been given, so she could heal her own hurts through comforting the sorrows of others. Sister Esther said everyone had endowments.

"The talent of exhortation is one of the highest," the somber woman told Mazy as they hung washed clothes onto ropes they'd strung between their wagons.

"That might be yours," Mazy said. "But I doubt it's mine." She snapped her husband's wet shirt and laid it across the line. "Men get ready-made. We women have to sew our own."

"A benefit of war," Sister Esther announced, "men's clothing." They continued to work side by side. "We never know for sure," she said, "until we face a challenge what our gifts truly are. A great opportunity of life."

Mazy'd already faced her greatest challenge, leaving roots and home behind. She'd chosen her husband and the unknown he offered.

"Your women, how are they enduring the trip?" Mazy asked.

"They are committed," Esther said. "They are fine laundresses though they cannot reach these ropes. Their frames are diminished, and a tragedy has been afflicted on Deborah's feet, to make them so small. Their clothes are laid on bushes. Sun-dried," she said, the S's of her words zinging in the air.

Mazy looked over at the Celestials. One of the group in slender, narrow dresses darned socks, the yarn lacing in her lap. She looked pale, and sweat beaded on her forehead. The other three laid out dusk-colored dresses over blooming bushes. Mazy heard a low humming sound, frowned.

"Bees," Esther said in explanation. "Deborah sets out the six chests at dusk. Just every other week. As we've rested today, they are allowed to go out to get nectar to make honey for their queens. You've noticed?" Mazy nodded. "The bees are a part of her dowry." She leaned closer to Mazy. "She also brings special plans to enable her to gather honey without destroying the hives."

"I didn't think that was possible," Mazy said. She snapped her mother's butternut-colored wrapper and draped it over the line.

"It will be, if these colonies and the drawings survive. The plans are worth a fortune—and her future."

"Don't the girls like us? We never see them much, nor your brothers."

"They feel self-conscious with their English," Esther said. "My brothers and I instruct a small class for them. A few of the children join us. They're learning. My brothers are good men." She reached for a goad stick to bolster the line sagging with heavy clothes. "That white-collared man came by too, once." Her lips pursed as though sewn with tight thread. "He has a good ear for language and spoke some of their phrases. It pleased them. One of his gifts. I suspect he did not intend for God to use it in this way, but God does work in mystery."

Mazy said, "I never see him."

"God is seen in the everyday, by those who seek him, child."

Mazy smiled. "No, I mean Mr. Forrester."

"Yes. He stayed behind to 'work,' he said, at Kanesville and then moved forward on his own. Crossed back over at Fort Kearney. We moved too slowly for him and his mules, I suspect, and our little gathering lacked ample coinage for such a man's…work." After a pause she said, "I should not judge. His is a warm though wounded heart. One worth winning over with patience, before the devil takes his true gifts and gives him worldly riches."

❦

Elizabeth knew that laundry was important, but so was what she planned. And if she didn't do it now, they'd have traveled too far to go back. She studied her position in relation to the wagons, before she dropped down over a rise. A pair of hawks dipped and screeched above her. Her fingers rubbed the elk's teeth clasped at her throat. It amazed her how, faster than a ferret's run, she could feel alone. It would take most of the day, but the sun set so late, she could still see the river in a hazy light near ten o'clock at night. She wanted to find the Indian woman Silver Bells again, give her salve for the blisters and scabs, leave laudanum, maybe trade for meat or moccasins for Mazy's blistering feet. The train's hunters hadn't had too much luck. Even Charles had missed a deer, she heard, though he claimed to be quite a shot.

She'd taken the medicine, a meal of dried beef, a handful of hazelnuts, and a canteen of water and couldn't imagine she'd need any more. She thought of that later, of how little she'd taken, when she appeared over a rise and stared at the sight she faced down below.

❦

Mazy said later her mother's absence began the change for her. Up until then the journey had been tiring, dusty, and hot, unwanted. But not fearful. Before, waves of disappointment, unsettling rootlessness, and insecurity washed over her but not this heart-eclipsing woe.

Elizabeth's absence at nooning had not distressed Mazy either until Adora's clucking tongue began flapping. "She should be here with the rest of us, tending to laundry, if truth be known, taking care of you, with that arm of yours not fully healed and feeling poorly yourself. How's your side, anyway?"

"Mama likes to venture out," was all Mazy said as she scratched at Pig's neck, dabbed at her perspiring brow. A part of her agreed with Adora jabbing her finger in the air; another part of her wished to defend her mother's carefree ways even though she didn't understand them.

When she asked around later in the day, spending a few minutes in conversation with some women from a neighboring train scrubbing wool at rocks, one or two remembered seeing a woman in a blue felt hat disappear over a grassy knoll, riding a black mule. At least she'd ridden Ink, the surefooted mule. That was good.

During the day, the women decided to cook up a big stew with potatoes and beef. Mazy added what remained of the roots Elizabeth had shown them how to dig. They'd thicken it with buckwheat to be dippered over wild rice. One or two agreed to fix bread in Dutch ovens, enough for breaking open at the next day's stops.

"More of this sharing'd be good," Lura Schmidtke suggested. Mazy wondered if she still wore a corset beneath what looked like newly dyed wool. "Such a nice time to chat and plan together all day, too."

Mazy didn't join in the head nods of agreement. Now even family meals were being threatened as a place of refuge?

With Tipton's help, Mazy lifted the water bucket, and they carried it to the sinkhole Jeremy'd dug beside the Platte, dipping warm water from the hole into it. The girl looked thinner to Mazy, the fine squarish bones of her face sharp instead of striking. Tiny women's bodies had little room to absorb change, Mazy decided. She had that advantage, anyway.

Tipton stayed quiet, which suited Mazy fine.

Mazy gazed into the stream. It ran clearer as they'd had no recent rains. She wondered if river water rather than the water that leached up in the sinkholes would be better to drink even though Jeremy said not. She braided her wet fingers over the back of her neck, watched the reflection of a tired woman behind her, strain and dirt streaked across her face. She looked up to see who it was, winced with recognition.

Lura and her daughter Mariah, a noodle of a girl, walked toward them.

"Going to the necessary circle," Lura said. "Join us?"

"I'll take the bucket back," Tipton said. She nodded toward the circle forming and wrinkled up her straight-boned nose.

"I know what you mean," Mazy said. "But it is a natural thing."

"Truth be known, a nice grove of private trees would be a welcome sight," Adora said, setting the water bucket down as she approached. "But a woman makes do."

Mazy and the others stood not far from the sinkhole, hoping to catch breezes from the river. They were joined by two other women from wagons that had chosen the same grassy area to rest up their stock. The small cluster formed a now familiar circle, their backs to each other, their fingertips holding out their skirts wide to the wind. Mazy let herself be comforted by the gentle chatter about recipes and remedies, family and fate.

"If my mother were here, she'd have some story to make us laugh," Mazy said to murmurs of agreement.

"Aren't you worried?" Adora asked in a voice hungry for gossip.

"Not really," Mazy lied.

Finished, Mariah took her place in the circle of dark dresses tipped with white aprons while another woman squatted in the flattened grass inside the ring. Prairie breezes blew against the fabric fort, a protection all their own.

"I was just sure I saw your mama a bit ago," Lura said as she squatted behind her. Mazy could smell tobacco on Lura's clothes when she eased back into the circle. "You sure she's still adrift?"

"What's she look like?" asked one of the newer arrivals.

"Ample, darkish hair, going to gray," Adora said.

"A strong chin," Mazy said. "People say I have her nose." The breeze dried her sweaty face, and she felt refreshed just standing.

"Pulls her skirts up when she's riding. Imagine that," Adora said.

"Not the bloomer lady we've heard about?" This from a newcomer.

Mazy laughed. "That's me, I suspect, but I've had to give them up and wear this wrapper since I've been feeling poorly."

"When I carried my Ben," another began, a woman with a Kentucky lilt, "I couldn't fit a thing. Even my wrapper stretched tight. I just pooched out like a pumpkin. Babe was born big enough to vote." She called then to the tall toddler who wandered among the grasses, his head a fluff of yellow against fading green. She signaled him to stay close. "When'll your baby arrive?"

"In the new year," Mazy said. "When we're in our new place." The statement felt right, certain.

The conversation continued in a patter as gentle as spring rain against canvas until each woman had taken her turn behind the skirts. Mazy wondered about Suzanne and vowed to check on her, see how she managed her necessary time. Finished, they wandered back, not anxious to return to the work of washing and resettling supplies.

Mariah, her long braids dropping to the grasses, stooped to pick blue wildflowers. She stuck a blossom in her hair behind her ear and did a little dance. Sarah with the stiff braids and Jessie with the dimples joined her. The women applauded; the girls bowed low before all returned to their tasks of rudiment and routine.

By dusk, after the stew had been heated and thickened well past its prime and each family had consumed as much as they wished, Mazy's mother had still not returned.

It was then they discussed forming a search party.

Antone vetoed it. "Lose a bunch more in the dark night to snakes and stumbles too," he said. "We wait until morning, yah. That's the best way to work this. She may be back. She likes to wander?"

"She does that," Adora Wilson piped in. "An irresponsible sort." Mazy stared at her. "Well, she is, for her age."

"That's it, then," Antone said.

Lura, Antone's little wife, chewed her pipe, shrugged her shoulders at Mazy when her husband announced his decision. Her handsome children looked the other way as though accustomed to nonnegotiable pronouncements by their father.

"He's quite right, Maze," Jeremy said, lifting the bucket of milk from the stream to separate for cream. "Usually it's the children who wander off. If she'd stayed to help, this wouldn't have happened."

"I'm going to look for her," Mazy said, needing to take some action.

"Your mother's got a sound head. May well have decided to spend the night when she got so far out," Jeremy said.

"But she could be hurt, out there alone. You'd look for me, wouldn't you? Not just let me wander."

"You wouldn't be so foolish," Jeremy said. Mazy took in a deep breath to protest, but his upraised palms silenced her. "You do what you want. You always have," he said.

"I wouldn't be here if I'd done what I wanted," she said and turned toward the stock.

Crickets chirped louder than the frogs as she walked. A coyote called. Mazy's shoulders dropped, and she shook her head. When had her mother begun this behavior? Before this journey, had she pressed forward onto trails only the brave or foolhardy traveled? All she'd ever known for years was that house and the sick and needy people her father brought home.

"Careful now. Light's fading," Ruth Martin said from out of the darkness. "You're headed somewhere, hard."

"Oh! You startled me!" Mazy said. "I'm looking for my mother."

"The lady with the dolls?"

"I'm sure she didn't bring any of them along."

"Just what our Jessie calls her."

"I'm sorry. I never even asked," Mazy said. "Is Jessie better? Did Dr. Masters help?"

Ruth snorted. "Masters is a quack. Said he could bleed her or offer calomel or laudanum. Like most, he probably got his license in a week." Mazy watched a look of disgust flash across her face in the twilight. "The child's flush seems to come and go. Someone suggested mountain fever, but I don't think so. Maybe it's the climate change. At home, Betha used to bathe the children daily, odd as that sounds to some."

"I feel better after a bath," Mazy said.

"I think it kept them healthy. I'm hoping it's just an ague that'll disappear once we get to higher altitudes. Seems like she'd do better if we took the time to heat water and wash her clean regular."

It was the longest speech Mazy had heard Ruth make.

As though she noticed her exposure too, Ruth changed the subject by asking a question. "Has your mother ever gone off before?"

Mazy nodded. "Not for all night. I don't think she'd want to worry me. She knows I would. There's a moon coming up; at least I'll have some light."

"I admire your spirit," Ruth said. "But you won't do much good looking now." Her words lacked the clipped cadence of bristle she used when she talked about the doctor. "I think the men are right, much as it galls me. We might start a fire, though, burn it higher. It could offer a beacon to her. I'll go out with you in the morning if she's still not here, if you'd like."

Mazy sighed, allowing herself to feel the tiredness that always leaned on her shoulders now.

They built a fire, and Mazy sat caressing Pig's ears in her lap between adding buffalo chips to the flames. Several others came by to say good night. Even Charles made his way, his hat pushed back on his head, one foot up on their sitting log. He spoke mostly to Ruth about horses and such and offered to move out Ruth's wagon in the morning if she decided to help search for Mazy's mother.

"He didn't offer to search, though," Ruth said when he'd left.

"He'd have to find something in it for himself," Mazy said. "At least that's my view of Charles."

When the moon globed high, Jeremy brought the wedding-ring quilt out and draped it around Mazy's shoulders. He sat beside her for a time, his arm around her.

"Your mother's on a good mule. Ink hasn't come back without her."

"Maybe they're both dead, got in the way of Indians."

"More people have died falling off wagons or blowing against black powder than by Indians' hands out here," Ruth offered.

"My mother encountered Indians," Mazy challenged. "Maybe she went back. Got into trouble this time."

"You're not thinking logical," Jeremy told her. "You're tired."

"Why shouldn't I be?" she said. "Day after day of dust."

He kissed the soft place at the side of her face then, and she almost relented, almost allowed him to comfort her. His mustache prickled, and she brushed at her face. He stood, wiped at his nose, squeezed her shoulder with his well-tapered nails, then headed back to the wagon.

"You've been together a while," Ruth said after he'd left. She held a bridle and rubbed a salvelike substance into the cheek piece. The scent of it tickled Mazy's nose.

"Little over two years," Mazy said. "Known him longer. Nursed him back to health. At least my father did. Papa was a doctor. My mother did the nursing."

Ruth paused. "I meant no offense," she said, "About what I said earlier, about doctors."

"None taken."

"She'll know what to do then, if she's had a fall."

"Since we began this journey, she's been so much more…oh, unpredictable than I remember her being."

"I guess we're all a little different in unfamiliar places," Ruth said.

"She helped my father every day, and as a child she worked in the tobacco fields, she tells me. And as a cook in a Southern home."

"Maybe she sees this trip as a…pleasantry."

"One of the few who do, if that's so. Not very agreeable when the child has to worry over the adult." Mazy threw a broken piece of dried buffalo chip into the flames. "Turned around, I'd say."

"Your mother's an independent sort," Ruth said. "They sometimes get mistaken for being self-centered."

Ruth set the bridle to the side and began oiling the reins. A coyote barked in the distance, answered by several more. Pig gave a low *gruff, gruff* but didn't move from his place at Mazy's feet. The air chilled a bit, and Mazy pulled the quilt around her, gazing out at the moonlight reflecting against the cattle's horns like white dashes written on a dark slate.

"If you want to heat the water," Ruth offered, "I'd pitcher it over your hair. Always makes me feel better."

"I wouldn't want to be a bother."

"Wouldn't be. Pass the time."

The warm water felt good over Mazy's head. Ruth had strong hands and used something sweet-smelling with the henna she rubbed into Mazy's hair. Later, Mazy stood, her head bent to the fire, the heat and breeze brushing it dry.

"Can I return the favor?"

"Washed mine this morning, but thanks," Ruth said.

"I appreciate the company," Mazy said, surprised that she said it. "Think I'll get my book and write some. Maybe I can sleep. You should too."

"Never much got into writing," Ruth told her. She sipped a hot liquid. "Do most of my communicating with horses. Taught them lots but not how to read yet."

In a while, Mazy walked back to her wagon where she found a sleeping husband. She retrieved her writing book and returned to stare into the fire, smelling the oil Ruth's hand rubbed into leather. Through the evening as the moon rose and then set, the women disclosed a hope or two, expressed a worry, offered solace, just being there together giving comfort. It was how they fed the night.

〜

"Would you like a large family?" Tipton asked. Tyrell hung the heavy braces across the oxen's neck while dark still brushed against dawn. Tipton stood beside him, snatching up precious moments of his time. "A dozen or more?"

"Not so many," he said. "One or two would be fine."

"Boys or girls?"

"Not something we have a say about."

"A man always wants a son to carry on his name. That's what Charles tells me. To keep me in my place, I'd guess."

"Probably feels a bit uncertain of where he fits in your father's eyes," Tyrell said.

"Why should he? He's the oldest. The boy. He'll inherit whatever my father has. Charles'll be taken care of. And he knows how to take care of himself, I'd say."

"So will you," Tyrell said. "It's a father's job until his daughter marries. Then it's her husband's responsibility." He paused to lift her chin. "I'm not afraid of that task." He brushed her nose with his finger, then kissed it.

"You aren't?" She pressed her fingers on his arm, feeling the tensed muscles through the homespun shirt.

"But you need to eat better, Tip. A strong wind'll think you're a kite." Tyrell touched her hand as if patting a small child before lifting it from his arm, turning back to the yoke.

Tipton allowed her lower lip to pout out. She felt a desperation inside her, a clutching after clues of ways to make sure she and Tyrell were together, no matter where her family ended up. It took up so much of her thinking, she had no time to eat. She just nibbled at her bread and wouldn't touch the beans, ever, not with how they made her stomach feel, so large and protruding. Her hair felt brittle when she pulled it straight back from her face, and little clumps stayed in her combs when she removed them at night. Mrs. Mueller said it came from "poor feed," but it didn't matter. Some plans took great diligence before they ever met fruition.

⤝

At dawn, Ruth and Mazy saddled two of Ruth's mounts and prepared to look for Elizabeth and Ink's tracks. Antone said the wagons would have to move on. "We spend one day now, resting, so we need to go, yah. Even your husband thinks that."

"Your mother will likely ride in before long," Jeremy told her.

"The women should not go alone," Antone persisted. "We are not seeking a little child lost here but a grown-up woman. Only men should look for her if there be trouble."

"And we should just what, sit and wait?" Ruth said.

Jeremy started to agree, but his words stopped with the set jaw and piercing look that flashed across Mazy's face.

"All right," Antone said. "All right, then. We wait and start a little late."

"I'll ride a piece with you," Charles said. "Hunt some along the way. We'll head back by noon?"

"Agreed, Mazy?" Jeremy asked. Mazy nodded. "Stay within sight of me," Jeremy directed, and for once Mazy didn't protest his command.

They fanned out and rode over the first dip of land with pink light spilling onto the grasses and a rock formation in the far distance. Mazy tried not to think of the worst, of stumbling across her mother face-down in the grass; of seeing her injured, snakebitten perhaps, unable to move, maybe even captured, the victim of some dispute between warring factions. She might even have become ill. Elizabeth had described what sounded like measles scabs on the Indian woman's hands. Perhaps her mother had gotten their disease.

"Don't think about it," Jeremy said, riding closer to her on one of the mules. Mazy raised her eyebrows in question. "You're biting your lip. That's how I can tell," he said.

"You don't listen to my words, but you read my chewed lips," Mazy said and smiled but for a moment.

Pig ambled back and forth in front of them. Purple hills filled the distance. A herd of deer Charles pursued kicked up dust. The riders saw no signs of Mazy's mother. Time raced, and Mazy knew Jeremy would soon mention turning back, when Pig's short little ears alerted and he barked his low *gruff, gruff* warning.

"What is it, Pig?"

The dog stood planted, staring ahead. Mazy peered into the distance. Before long she saw a rider, maybe two, coming over a rise. Her heart pounded. Something didn't look right. There wasn't a second rider, but something being dragged and snubbed up tight to the mount. Mazy put her hand to her mouth.

"Let's take this slow," Jeremy said, pulling up next to her, "It's essential that we don't signal something that we don't intend."

∾

"Why have we stopped?" Tipton asked as Tyrell pulled at the lead oxen. The grinding and clattering of the wheels ceased. The wagons—minus the searchers—had moved out late and slow. They'd only gone five miles.

"Cullvers have stopped," Tyrell told her as he moved the wagons side by side. The oxen stood swishing tails at the flies. A pale and drawn Bryce Cullver crouched beside the nigh ox and grabbed at his stomach, beads of sweat dotted his face.

"Something you ate, man?" Tyrell asked.

Bryce shook his head. His felt hat shoved low toward his eyes made his whole face look square and squashed. An acrid, wary scent seeped from his skin.

"I …you'll have to go around me. Feeling…need to head out for a bit. Suzanne Jane," he called back over his shoulder. "You got to watch

Clayton." He turned toward Tyrell then, and Tipton caught her breath with the look of agony that crossed his face. Not waiting for his wife to answer, Bryce stood half-stooped and, still clutching his stomach, made toward the cover of the tall grass not far from the Platte where he collapsed on his knees.

"I'll check on Mrs. Cullver and the boy," Tyrell said to Tipton. "You run on ahead and fetch Dr. Masters. Get someone to tell Antone to pull up."

"I'll check on Mrs. Cullver," Tipton argued. "No need for you to."

"Tip." Tyrell had already lifted himself into their wagon. "I've got to see to Bryce next. He's not good. Go now. Do as you're told."

Tipton folded her arms across her breast and stared ahead. When Tyrell failed to plead, and instead stuck his head inside the canvas, Tipton thought better of it. She grabbed at her skirts and began to run.

"Mercy," she heard him say behind her. "Got two more sick ones in here."

❧

Something in the rider's pitch backwards in the saddle nudged at Mazy as she watched them approach.

"That's mother," Mazy said and lifted her arm above her head, brushing her bonnet back away from her face as she did. Pig started to bark and ran toward the rider, causing what moved beside the mule to jerk outward, then back to the withers of the animal as though a yo-yo on a rope.

Mazy's heart pounded as she kicked her mule forward.

"Wait," Jeremy said.

Mazy saw the rider wave in return; but she couldn't tell what was being dragged.

Jeremy signaled Charles with a shot from his cap-and-ball pistol, and Ruth and Charles moved toward them. Pig and Mazy reached her first with Ruth close behind.

"A welcoming party," Elizabeth said. "How thoughtful!" She sat astride Ink and looked fine.

"Mother! How could you?"

"Easy," she said. "Well, not so easy. Didn't have enough to eat to be out all night. But then I hadn't planned to sleep on rocks. Time just scattered. Almost as much as these antelope when they got my scent. You should have seen 'em! Must have been two hundred. But I got me one. Walked right up to it lying there in the grass. Shivered when I touched him. Now it thinks I'm his mother!"

"We thought you'd been lost," Jeremy said, his words clipped.

"I knew where I was. Kept that rock in sight and figured I'd catch up with you by evening."

"But what's the point, Mother?" Mazy asked. "Why spend a night out to bring back a what, an antelope?"

Elizabeth looked wounded, as if she were a child who'd offered up her precious drawing only to have an adult comment on how it might be improved. "Kids need a plaything," Elizabeth said. "Something to surprise their days. That little Jessie's one." Elizabeth nodded to Ruth. "She'll have a good time petting and tending it. All the kids will."

"A pet. You have chosen to delay us over a pet," Jeremy said. Pig sniffed at the antelope, circled around it.

"I don't see that I've dawdled anyone," Elizabeth said. "You were all washing and such. Calm down. I went to bring medicine to Silver Bells and get some moccasins for your wife's feet. "

"You might have spoken of it before departing," Jeremy said.

"People don't always say what they're planning now, do they?" Elizabeth said.

Mazy felt her face burn. "I sat up all night, worrying over you, imagining the worst kind of fate. And now we've been riding for hours and have more time yet to get back."

Elizabeth turned to her. "Sad you did, but I didn't ask it."

"We're responsible for what we do that affects others," Mazy insisted. "You can't just ride in with an antelope at your side and expect everyone to cheer because you invited kindness but worry arrived."

"She's right," Ruth offered.

"See," Mazy said.

"Elizabeth is. We made our own decision about staying up and riding out. Just as Elizabeth did."

"I wouldn't wish anyone to spend time in worrying, but I haven't caused anyone to do anything. I didn't bother anyone who didn't want to be bothered."

"You're not alone now, Mother. You are part of…us—this awkward dance we're doing with a dozen partners. And what you do does affect the rest of us." Her face felt hot, and she wondered if she felt embarrassment for her mother's lack of contrition or her own feeling of foolishness for worrying, for not trusting a simple answer. She'd wallowed in unpleasant places. "I'd be grateful if before you have another escapade you let the rest of us know about it in advance," Mazy said. "Some of us actually care about other people's feelings." She straightened her bonnet, yanked at the strings beneath her chin.

"Fair enough," Elizabeth said. "But it spoils the surprise."

At that moment, the small pronghorn jerked her arm and pulled Elizabeth from her mule. The woman landed on her bottom with a whoop, the rope still gripped in her hand. The small animal, not much bigger than Pig, nudged at her, made no attempt to run off. "See what fun'll it'll be?" she said, smiling up at them.

⟞⟝

The Schmidtkes' teamster, Joe Pepin, rode up to meet the returning group, eyeing the antelope that trailed behind Elizabeth like a dog. "Several cases of illness," he reported, his Adam's apple bobbing up and down. "One death. Antone says we're holding up. Glad you made your way back then, Mrs. Mueller." He tipped his hat at Elizabeth.

"Who died?" Mazy asked.

Ruth kicked Koda past them, not waiting for an answer, not wanting to be told, in truth, who had passed on.

Ruth headed first toward her brother's wagon. Cattle ripped at low grass, and she noted that the land look ravaged of good pasture. Signs of people already passed dotted the area: cold cooking circles, human excrement not far from the water, empty tins of alum and salt. *We're a dirty lot,* Ruth thought.

"How's Jessie?" She said, jumping off Koda and tying him to the side of the wagon as she spoke.

"Fine," Betha said. "She's doing fine." Betha pulled at her fingers, each one at a time. "One of the Celestials is down with something, though. And you might ask over your brother."

Relief, guilt, then worry churned in Ruth. "Is he affected?"

Betha nodded, her lip trembling. She pulled a handkerchief from up her sleeve and dabbed at her eyes. "Just started. He moans so. I've given him some laudanum. It may be what helped our Jessie. Someone in a new wagon saw me give it. Said I needed bismuth. Isn't that for cholera? This isn't cholera, surely. Is it, Ruthie?" She whispered the word. "We've no Asiatics here. Oh," she said looking up, her fingers pressed to her lips. "The Celestials." The last sounded like a wail.

"It'll be all right," Ruth said patting the woman's chubby shoulders. She looked around, still waiting to see the children.

Everything about Betha was soft and scented, Ruth decided, weaker than she'd hoped for.

"You think so?" Betha turned pooling eyes toward Ruth.

"We've got to keep our heads," Ruth said. "Let's go tend to my big brother."

❧

Bryce Cullver had died just after noon. They wrapped him in a blanket and dug a shallow grave in the roadbed after a short service at dusk.

Sister Esther's brothers commented on Bryce's kindness. Prayers were said. Then they drove wagons over the grave to keep the coyotes from digging—and any others that might think a treasure had been buried with this gentle man. Afterwards, people moved back to their wagons, the women avoiding each other's eyes.

Dr. Masters described it as most likely mountain fever.

"He was just fine this morning," Betha told Mazy. "He laughed and held his wife a moment before they rolled out. I saw them."

He lay dead just hours later.

⊷

Jed died that evening, followed by one of Sister Esther's brothers. The Celestial named Cynthia succumbed too. Antone announced that they'd move on in the morning soon after the burials. Then word came back they'd wait, allow a few already feeling ill to be treated and gain some strength. Then Matt, Antone and Lura's son, rode back telling them to be ready to leave at first light.

"He thinks something here might be causing it," Tipton told Elizabeth. The girl stopped by the wagon to look at the antelope, to reach out and touch the soft black nose and stare at the huge dark eyes with long lashes. She rubbed at her arm.

"Has eyes as big and deep as yours," Elizabeth said. "You eating enough, girl? Got some cornbread left. Mazy boiled up some jam. Smells good."

Tipton bristled. "I do not resemble an antelope, Mrs. Mueller."

"You'd be surprised how many different animal traits humans have. And please. Can't you call me Elizabeth?" Tipton nodded. "Good. Carry this for me, will you? Can't believe how my hip aches tonight and my back tooth, too."

She handed the girl an empty bucket off the side of the wagon, then with the dipper began filling it from their barrel. As it became heavier, Tipton set it down.

"You think it's something common?" Tipton asked.

Elizabeth turned to the tone in her voice. For once, she didn't chide the girl, actually heard the fear, saw it in the pinched look of Tipton's face.

"We don't know what it is. Getting muddled won't help us fight it. Got to keep calm, now. Keep breathing prayers. Where's your gumption?"

Tipton swallowed.

"Suzanne's still feverish, though Clayton's better, Mazy says. Must have been your quick help to them this morning, Tipton."

"I didn't do a thing. Tyrell did. I hope he doesn't get sick. He tended her an awful long time."

"I lived through the Asiatic cholera scare in '32," Elizabeth said. She shivered. "This acts a lot like that. Fast moving, that's for sure. Usually hit emigrants coming off a ship, though, or people living in filthy conditions, drinking dirty water. Not like here with the open spaces and fresh air, clean streams."

"But all those graves we passed…"

"Don't know what causes it, but we need to control the bowels. Oh, I know you do hate that topic. But we got to keep folks from drying from their insides out. Want to carry that to the Cullvers for me?" She pointed with her chin at the bucket, but then pulled it back and said, "Think I'll boil it first. Kill them swimming things."

"Cholera." Tipton whispered. "Can we do anything?"

"I'm fixing to reduce the woman's misery. Widowing ain't for wilting flowers."

⟿

"We'll have our man drive your wagon," Mazy told Suzanne. Mazy stood inside the wagon, waiting for her mother to bring back water. Funny how fast her self-righteous anger had dissipated—how silly she'd been to be so upset by the antelope adventure when they faced this greater grief. She wiped Suzanne's forehead with a cool cloth. Elizabeth stepped up onto the boards, carrying the bucket.

"Got to go again," Suzanne said, her throat sounding scratchy and parched. She pushed up onto her elbows, her straw-colored hair in tight, wet rings capped around her face. Even in the poor light, Mazy could see the puckered lines of scars that marked her damaged eyes without the dark glasses to protect them.

"The slop bucket's here," Mazy said, "on your left, next to your foot. Stand. That's good. Just bend if you can and I'll push it beneath you. Mother, hold up her skirts for her. We'll take them off, I think, keep her drawers on. Make it easier."

The scent of sickness filled the air. A small moan rose from the mattress behind Mazy. "It's going to be fine, Clayton. Mommy's going to be fine."

"Don't lie to the child," Suzanne said, her voice breathy. "I'm not now nor will I ever be *fine*." She spit the word, and a small amount of spittle glistened at the corner of her bluish lips. "You'll take him when I die."

"Shush now. Here you go, little one," Elizabeth said. She raised the toddler to her shoulder, folded him into her breast, rocking.

"Don't talk that way, Suzanne," Mazy said. "The sickness is slowing some. You're holding down the stew."

"But if I don't, you take him. Please," Suzanne said. Her fingers gripped Mazy's bad arm as though clinging to a cliff.

"If need be, I will," Mazy said and felt Suzanne's fingers weaken. "But he needs you most, he does. A child needs his mother most."

Mazy took a soft cloth and gently tended to Suzanne's backside. She felt the woman shiver and held her elbow to balance her when she realized the shivers carried tears, tears pressed out of scarred, unseeing eyes.

"Can't even wipe my own bottom," Suzanne said, her voice a wail, then a whisper. "Do you know how useless I am? How despicable a woman? I should have died in the river." Tears streamed down her face.

She brushed at them, hard, with her hands, her white cheeks stinging to pink. "It's wrong, just so wrong, that the last act between Bryce and me on the day he died should be tangled like this, with sickness, with being so needy, it's so, so—"

"Essential," Mazy said, wiping Suzanne's cheeks with her fingertips. "Needing is a part of being, just like loving is. So essential."

in this place

Something moved among them, a sharing of the grief and yet relief, a distance separating those now suffering from those not yet afflicted. It prickled the balmy air that fluttered freshly laundered aprons over wrappers worn by women bowed before shallow graves. Every adjustment, hardship, and disappointment that had gone before now paled in the piercing, exposing light of loss. The living threatened to pull apart, as stringed and shattered as old silk.

Ruth held her arms around Betha, her strong hands sinking into the soft flesh of her sister-in-law's shoulders. Jed, gone. Sarah leaned against her mother, silent while her brothers stood stone-faced, staring straight. Only Jessie spoke, though in a whisper loud enough to break Ruth's heart, "Why's Papa not paying attention? When's he coming to his senses, Mama?" She pulled on her mother's apron. "Isn't he coming with us?"

Betha stared, did not respond.

"Hush, child," Ruth said and brought the girl into the folds of her skirt while they listened to Sister Esther speak the blessing over Jed and one of her own brothers.

Ruth didn't even know the brother's name except in relation to his sister. She made a mental note to learn it, as though knowing that detail would somehow salt his once living presence in her mind, help sisters share their grief.

The wagons moved away from the morning burial site, dust whisked away by wind. The missing spaces the dead left filled up with reluctant shifting, the way an unborn baby forced all a woman's organs into places they would otherwise never go.

"Does Papa hurt?" Jessie asked.

"No more," Betha said. Jessie walked with her beside the oxen now, Ned on the other side. "Everything stops working when you die. You don't get hungry or sleepy and you don't hurt anymore. You're just…dead."

"Does he dream?"

"No. No dreaming. It's not like sleeping." The girl shivered against Betha.

"'Cuz I was bad?"

"You didn't do it, no, no." Betha knelt to Jessie's pinched face. "And we'll keep you safe." She pulled her close, looked up at Ruth. "Those who love you will keep you safe."

Betha would have left a marker of some kind on Jed's grave; Suzanne said she didn't care about marking Bryce's; but Sister Esther dissented, said hiding the graves proved a better testament to honoring the dead. So they left them, unmarked. But it still troubled Ruth. She noted the lay of the land, the sound of the river rush across rocks, and decided maybe someday she'd come back.

"It's not finished," Betha said. "When we passed all those other graves, I didn't realize. How hard it is to just…leave him there."

Ruth patted her pudgy shoulder. "It'll be better the farther away we go," she said. "Trust me, it's always better away."

Tyrell had hitched up Suzanne's wagon while Elizabeth hovered over the boy, chattering, letting the blind woman know without requiring the woman to ask. The baby, Clayton, showed no signs of illness now. Suzanne still looked pale and weak and needed help to walk. Odd, how the disease raged through some unharmed while inhaling others.

They rolled west, slowly. The "doll lady's" chatter lilted in the morning air. Had the antelope caper just happened yesterday? No, the day before.

Elizabeth's daughter lacked such daring, but the two shared a commodious heart. Despite her still healing arm, Mazy offered to drive her mother's wagon, freeing the farrier, Tyrell, to drive the Cullvers'.

"Just 'til Laramie, yah," Antone agreed. "We got to make other arrangements there." Charles condescended to drive Jed's wagon—for a fee Ruth paid. He had extracted a goodly sum from her, sentiment carrying no part in the bargain.

"It's a poor businessman who gives away what he's got," Charles said. He'd stood there slapping leather gloves against his smooth palms, the repetition an irritating rhythm against the background sobs of grieving women. Ruth had difficulty keeping her eyes from that missing chunk of his ear.

"And you're not a poor businessman," she said.

"I'm not a poor anything," Charles answered, a grin slithering onto the chiseled hardness of his face. Except for the ear notch, his face reflected perfect proportions, a masculine version of his sister's. "If you've the courage, you might want to test my veracity in that."

Ruth stared at him. "I've been challenged by better than you," she said, "and find I haven't time to waste on little men."

He'd reddened but pulled his gloves on with the slowness of a slug, tipped his hat, and stepped toward Betha's wagon.

She might have gone too far. Some men were piqued and not put off by a woman's retort. Unfortunately, she had a habit of mixing liberty with provocation when men sought to master her.

⸎

"If truth be known, I don't think Charles should have offered to drive that woman's wagon," Adora told her husband as they stopped for the noon break.

"He's not driving it," Hathaway said. "Walking beside it."

"You know what I mean. Disease there and all. And now Tipton and I are required to drive. That's not right."

"Do Tipton good to have a purpose," he said. "Mules aren't too hard to manage. I'll ask Antone if his boy can help some. Let Charles be. Does him good too, doing for someone else." He shook his head.

"You all right?" Adora looked at her husband's pale face.

"Fine. Just tired."

❧

Tipton chewed her bottom lip until it bled. Her hands ached from holding the reins. Tyrell said she could do this, but why did she have to? Four mules. How could someone handle four large, pushing animals? What if they took off? What if they refused to go? The dust gagged her. She couldn't even take a deep breath. Tyrell should have been driving *their* wagon, not Suzanne's. Charles should be serving his family, not that Martin woman.

"Think on the good things," Tyrell had said. "You'll do fine."

The good things. Charles stayed occupied some distance from her. Distance from him was good. He'd taught her that lesson when she was no older than that Jessie child, hanging on to dolls and being told by her mother that older brothers were protecting and kind. How blind her mother had been, blinder than Suzanne.

The color of his dark character had been unveiled that long-ago day.

"Got yourself a private place, hey, Tip," Charles had said, greeting her as she crawled inside a branch-and-leaf house she'd made in a dimple of Wisconsin forest floor. Tipton was six years old, and she had brought only one friend there, ever; Corinda, and no one else.

Now here lounged Charles, his lanky sixteen-year-old body smelling of tobacco and his boots muddying up her private place. Tipton shivered, remembering. *Think on good things.* But pleasant thoughts flitted like butterflies; awfuls and terribles rode in on fast horses.

Charles had followed her once, discovered what she'd tried so hard to hide. Her books and drawing pens Papa brought back from Chicago lay scattered like sticks. She couldn't see her doll. "What have you done with it?"

"Your precious gift from Mama and Papa? You can wheedle another from Pop. He'll give you anything."

His eyes had a glassy look, and he smelled of spirits. Her stomach lurched as he sat up, a ferret, quick and sure. He grabbed her hair, pulling her in, laughing.

"I want Mama! Let me go!"

"What's the matter, Tip? Afraid to fight for what you want?"

Her heart pounded; she smelled his sweat, her own. He pushed her back, throwing her hard, her head striking the ground. She smelled a burst of pine; a flash of pain like lightning shot behind her eyes. He forced his knee onto her chest, leaned over her so that she couldn't breathe. She gasped, her arm lay crooked, pinned behind her. She tried to tell him to stop, but he laughed.

Thinking, thinking, just surviving, she signaled to him to come closer, as though to speak.

"Got something to say?" he grinned. "Can't talk?" He bent his ear to her.

His first mistake.

She bit, hard and firm, the outer flesh like fish bones mixed with salty sea. He jerked back, his second mistake.

Her teeth held tight. She felt it rip, the petaled flesh of his ear threatening to choke her; that and the warmth of his blood.

He screamed and grabbed for his ear, surprise for the first time registering in his eyes. Blood spurted between his fingers. Gasping, she scampered backwards, her palms wet on the pine needles sticky with blood, throwing herself out through the side of her makeshift fort, gasping for air, rubbing her arm, her heart pounding, still clutching at breath. She spit out the knuckled flesh in her mouth. Sobbing and running and stumbling, branches caught at her face, her dress and her hair.

"I'll get you for this," he screamed.

She turned back, sickened by two things: his blood-streaked face; and her once friend, Corinda, now clutching the doll Tipton loved.

"You're gripping the reins too tight," Adora said. "Tipton?" She shook her. Tipton slowed her breathing. She was safe here.

Charles had told his father he'd caught his ear on a nail in the store-room while standing to stock the top shelf.

"Good lesson for you to learn, then. Pound those nails in firm," her father said.

"A lesson learned," Charles said, tossing coins in his palm, glaring at his sister.

"Betrayal is not the only ending to one's tendering of trust," Tyrell reminded her when she'd confided in him. "Your friend betrayed you. Charles betrayed you too, that once. But don't be seeking treachery everywhere with everyone or you'll likely find it."

⤙⤚

Betha must be trying to cool herself in the shade, Ruth thought, watching her sister-in-law walk beside the wagon. Betha's face blotched red, as dazed as if she'd been struck with a post. Perhaps she had been, a woman who lived her life as dependent on Jed as any grown woman could be on a man. "A marvel of a man," Betha repeated, "providing home and furnishings, even picking out the family linen. Jed handled all the details, Ruthie."

In return, Betha tended him, cooked and cleaned, gave him children, and covered for his lapses into drink by taking in laundry for small coinage, a fact she concealed from him so as "not to hurt his pride," she told Ruth, "when he comes to his senses, dear, which he always does."

It was odd the things coupling forced a person to do. And now here Betha was, on a journey she would never have chosen for herself, the anchor of her life no longer stabilizing her in unfamiliar waters.

"What'll I do now, Ruthie?" she asked later. "What would Jed want me to do?"

"Keep going. That's what he'd want."

"Think so? It was you I think Jed went west for."

Ruth swallowed. "Was it?"

They walked beside the wagon without talking for a time, Ruth checking back to see that her oxen plodded close behind. They lumbered past marked graves and even an abandoned wagon. Birds flitted in and out of the torn, silent canvas as through a dead man's opened mouth. A meadowlark warbled, landed on the broken wheel.

"What a story it could tell," Betha said out loud.

"What?" Ruth asked.

Betha nodded her head to the still wagon. A torn section of canvas swung in the breeze. Nothing inside marked it as unique. "Just wondering what happened there, to make them leave their things behind. Like us, you suppose?" Her eyes pooled with tears.

"Dropping excess," Ruth said.

"Perhaps it marks a grave," Betha said. She wiped at her eyes. "I wish we'd marked Jed's. I should have stayed there, to bring him flowers. Oh, will these tears ever stop?" She dabbed at her eyes with her handkerchief. "I think I'll lie down. I just can't think right."

"It won't be very comfortable in the wagon," Ruth said. "The road seems rougher here."

"Doesn't it," Betha said and sighed.

⤳

They stopped only briefly at noon. On their way again, Joe Pepin came back to say that a stream ahead dribbling into the Platte looked fresh and clear and that there were a few stands of good grass. He mentioned that a horse had died and lay rotting beside the trail with yellow jackets all over it.

Other wagons were moving on past them, people staring ahead. A rider approached from the west. He folded his hands across the saddle pommel on his mule, talked with Antone, looked back at the new widows, shook his head, and continued east.

The setting sun hurt their eyes with its brilliance. Elizabeth sat grateful at dusk after they'd circled the wagons, rubbing her bare feet, pulling stickers from the pads.

"Me and the dog," she said as Pig sat nibbling at his own paw.

Mazy urged Jeremy to join them as they ambled back toward Ruth and Betha, handing each a chunk of her Dutch oven bread.

Betha declined the food.

"You've got to keep your strength up," Mazy said. "For the children if no one else."

"For the children, then," Betha sighed, and nibbled at the brown crust with her tiny, even front teeth.

"You have so many good memories," Mazy said.

"I do." Betha's eyes watered.

"I don't even know Sister Esther's brother's name. And I hear her other brother's not feeling well now either." Mazy put her biscuit down, aware that she wasn't hungry herself. She rubbed at her temple.

"Harold," Betha said. "I believe his name was Harold. He and Jed shared a love of a certain tobacco." She leaned to whisper, "So does her brother Ferrel, but none are supposed to talk of it."

"I'm surprised that Sister Esther had a brother who smoked," Jeremy said.

"He imbibed a bit, too," Betha said, turning to see where the children sat. "I believe it's why he and Jed formed a friendship."

"We shoulda waited for Papa," Jessie said approaching the dog. "He won't like it we left him back there in the road."

"He ain't getting up, dummy," Ned told her. He threw a rock and it pinged against a pot.

"Is too!"

153

"No, he ain't. He's dead."

Jessie started to cry. "Ned, please," Ruth said. "She's young. She doesn't understand."

"You always take her side," Ned said. "Don't she, Mama? Ain't that what you told Papa?"

"I'm thirsty," Jason said. "I'm getting me a drink from the Platte, Mama, like Papa used to."

"Without my boiling it? Shame on you." To Mazy, Betha said, "I know it doesn't really matter if we drink the bugs, but the thought of live things squiggling in my throat..." She shivered.

Mazy nodded. "I hate that tepid water. Tastes funny."

"Not the temperature that matters," Jeremy told her. "Sinkholes we dig beside the Platte are as good as any to drink from."

"I'm with Betha," Elizabeth said. "If we can avoid the swimming tails sliding through the teeth by boiling 'em, all the better."

"Already drank from the stream," Jeremy told her. "Laid on my belly quite a while back. So did lots of others. Stream's clear as air. Don't think it's anything to worry over."

"Are you feeling well?" she asked. "Your pants look baggy."

"All this walking is firming me up," he told her.

❧

"There must have been some disease brought with us," Sister Esther said.

It was night. The moon had risen, just a swipe of silver in an ink sky. She'd come out to Mazy's campfire, carrying her desk, setting it down, just as Mazy wrote the word *keeper* and the accompanying thoughts in her book. *One who tends to things, like a beekeeper. God minds and ministers as a keeper. He has made the bee able to find a home in the most distant, ravaged places. He cares for the smallest of the universe and thus I thank thee, for finding me worthy of your keeping. Forgive me when I fail to keep the least within your world.*

"I'm sorry," Mazy said closing the book latch. "What did you say?"

"Someone carried it, delivered it here. The sickness." The Sister paced, a behavior that looked foreign to her usual rigid, wagon-tongue demeanor. Her words took flight too, so the sizzle of her S's cracked the air like heat lightning. Mazy watched her striding back and forth between the wagon and the fire, thought to interrupt, but lacked sureness.

"That child Jessie, she got ill first. Perhaps it is them, those people from St. Louis," Sister Esther said as she rubbed the cross at her neck.

"The child recovered."

"But her father died." Esther paced but kept her fingers clenched together before her apron. "We did not have illness until we began encountering those from the south Platte who crossed over. Perhaps they bring it."

"You're grieved, Sister, over your brother's loss."

"A victim of the baseness of those of poor and filthy rank."

"We've no way of knowing," Mazy said. She stood, touched the older woman's arm. "And there's no good in it, to blame and find fault." She reached into a basket attached to the side board, pulled up a platter covered with a stained double bag. "Come sit beside me," Mazy said, patting the ground. "Eat a bite of chicken. Focus on your brother who still lives, your charges who need you."

Sister Esther stared at her. "He sits silent as sage," she said, "my brother does."

"He misses him. Your Celestials may well too."

"The Celestials." Sister Esther spoke the name with numbness, and Mazy realized that her eyes showed no tears, weren't puffed the way Betha's or Suzanne's were. She was probably still shocked, still stunned more than angry. "Blame must be placed," Esther said. "Disease is God's way of correction."

Mazy swallowed. She didn't like disagreeing with older people. She considered them wiser, more experienced than herself. "I saw many ill in my father's house, and they were undeserving, fine men and women and even children. I don't think God uses disease and death that way, as punishment. He makes good come of all things. Like stinging involved with gathering honey. It's how I met my Jeremy."

"This cholera, if that is what it is, afflicts those with poor habits. Poor people have poor ways."

"But your brother—"

"Must have hidden something from me," she said with certainty. "A side of him I did not know." Her eyes held a glazed look. Mazy felt her face grow hot from the warmth of the fire. *Certainty wears a cat's face,* she thought, *wisdom wears a dog's.*

"I have bothered you," Sister Esther said, then retrieved her desk and turned toward the wagon, her straight back disappearing into the black.

≈

By noon the next day, several more members of their party carried the symptoms. They shook, complained of a looseness in their bowels, exhibited a putrid color to their skin. The afflicted lay confined, tightly holding themselves or being held by those who loved them, in stark contrast to their boundless surroundings beside a stream that flowed with freshness, in a land expansive and full of promise.

Antone called a meeting, but it did not materialize as he too turned ill along with Hathaway Wilson and Sister Esther's second brother. The emigrants helped each other and moved on. Adora now drove the Wilsons' wagon; one of the Celestials named Naomi drove the second brother's.

That evening, Jeremy bent over, dropped almost to his knees.

"Let me help," Mazy said. She set the butter churn down, dropped the glob of cream destined for a biscuit. "Tyrell!" she shouted. "Mother! Get the doctor!"

Dr. Masters, looking harried and rubbing the place on his nose where his glasses sat, suggested bismuth now, or acetate of lead. He shook his head and left.

"He hasn't any of that, a course," Elizabeth scowled as they laid Jeremy in the shade of the tent, pulled the flap back to offer breeze. "Used up our own laudanum too, almost. He said he could always bleed him."

"Not that, Mother."

"Course not. Barbarians, the lot, excepting your father."

"Someone wondered about the stew so many ate," Mazy said. She laid a cool, wet cloth on Jeremy's forehead, pushing back a shock of hair.

"Ate that myself. So did you," Elizabeth said. "Can't be that." She cleared her throat and spoke low. "It's cholera, that's sure. Try to keep liquids down him, and we'll restock the laudanum in Laramie—it's all we can do."

"I think we should stay here. The traveling's hard on people, confined in the wagons, then jostled about. That little girl, Jessie, she recovered when we stayed a day. The day you were off antelope gathering gave her a rest."

Jeremy groaned. "Keep going," he said.

"Your insides are coming out both ends," Mazy said. "You need tea. I can't keep it hot on the trail. I can't handle Mother's wagon and do that, too."

"I'll manage my wagon," Elizabeth said. "You worry over yours."

"That's what I'm doing," Mazy said, her voice raised. "We stay. So we can tend to Jeremy. Others might wish to stop too. Lura Schmidtke has her hands full with Antone, and Mariah's not doing well either. I heard a Celestial was ailing too. We can boil things, bathe Jeremy, have better food. He looks so…blue," Mazy said. Tears burned behind her nose. She swallowed and fought them back. "The only Wisconsin men who're well are Charles and Tyrell. They'll succumb to fatigue if we don't rest. He looks so blue."

Hadn't she just said that? Yes, she had. She could feel the repetition, the thing she did when fear settled on her neck. She repeated thoughts as though it sent her roots deeper against a prevailing wind. "We'll pray over everyone who's ill. That's what we need to do now. Not move. Stay here."

Elizabeth stared at her.

"Antone's in no shape to dictate. I'm stopping," Mazy said. "The water's good. Grass too. We'll get a decent amount of milk. That'll help. We'll stay and pray."

By morning few were better, but no more had died. Tipton brushed her hair over and over, a luxury. Her parents had decided to stay too, her mother a little weaker than usual, though showing no signs of what had claimed the others. Hathaway had taken a fever. Tipton looked in on her father, but his shaking had frightened her, so she sought refuge in Tyrell's presence.

"Papa's awful ill," she said. Tyrell bent beneath the Cullvers' wagon, checking the wagon reach. Finished, he stood, put one arm around Tipton, and pulled her to him, not saying anything, just holding her close.

"Help your mama, Tip. It'll help you too. Keeping busy, it's good for reducing a person's worrying." He smoothed her hair back from her face, tucked strands into a ribbon holding it at the back of her neck. She sunk into his chest, inhaled the scent of him, drinking in his comfort.

"Got to check the other wagons," he said. "Step careful now. Don't want you hurt." He eased her out of the way. "I don't ever want you hurt."

"Mrs. Cullver?" Tyrell said loud enough for someone inside the wagon to hear. "Folks are resting a day. Think that might be wise if you've no objection."

"And if I did?"

"Then I'd see if the Bacons wished to go forward today too, seeing as how I'm still driving under their canvas, so to speak."

"Mr. Bacon's taken ill himself," Tipton offered. "I think it's best to stop."

"Are you willing to drive me back, Mr. Jenkins?" Suzanne said, her head now out of the canvas opening, her chin lifted so her blank eyes looked up toward the sky. Tipton noticed she never looked in the direction people spoke. "I could pay well for the effort. It's clear I can't drive the thing myself." She made her way over the seat and, feeling along the side, stopped to suck at her hand as though she'd just picked up little slivers.

Tyrell reached up to her, said, "Put out your right hand. I'll help you down."

She had long fingers and wore a heavy ring with some kind of blue stone set in a twisting setting that covered the length between her knuckles. Suzanne put her hand into Tyrell's, and he closed his palm over hers to balance.

Tipton thought her heart would break with Tyrell's touch to the widow.

Funny how she'd begun to think of Suzanne as the widow already, the woman's status changing from "that blind woman" to "the widow" in an instant. In profile, the woman's roundness, the sign of her pregnancy, caused Tipton to turn away. What would it be like for her baby to be born without its father, to an unseeing mother?

Suzanne stood, brushed off her apron, and felt along the wagon side for the rope she tied around her waist. Tyrell left the oxen yoked but moved them inside the half circle of wagons, directing both women to stand back out of the way. "I've tied the rope to Clayton, missus," he said then, giving it a tug so she could feel the connection to her son.

"Puppy," Clayton squealed as Pig trotted over and pushed against Suzanne, causing her to stop.

"It looks like he doesn't want you to stumble into the fire," Tipton said.

Suzanne turned partway toward Tipton's voice.

"The dog stops just before you're about to step somewhere you shouldn't. Curious, if you ask me."

"No one has," Suzanne said. She turned back. As she did, the rope at her waist pulled slightly, tugging on Clayton. The toddler sat now, rope cinched around his middle, slapping at the dirt, his face smudged with the fruits of his effort.

"Since we're staying, believe I'll sneak away and see if I can't bring back some venison," Tyrell said. "Good meat'll be defense against this…whatever this is. Won't be able to hunt once we get closer to the fort."

"You're hunting for her?" Tipton asked.

Suzanne snorted. "I couldn't care less. I suspect it's for any who have need of it, girl. Mr. Jenkins is that kind."

Tipton was glad the widow couldn't see Tyrell blush. "You could use some meat on those bones, Tip." He winked, tipped his hat to her, said, "Ladies, see you later," and strode away.

"Tipton!" her mother wailed. "Come here this minute."

"Sorry I can't stay to help you," Tipton said to Suzanne.

"I've no need of anyone's help."

"That's what you'll likely get," Tipton said and hurried away.

❧

How long did it take to kill a deer, dress it out, and return? Tipton and Tyrell had seen a small herd last evening grazing at a distance. They would have bedded down, not moved far at all. Tyrell said deer rarely moved at night. He should have been back before midday. Charles had been gone most of the day too. The two of them wouldn't have hunted together, Tipton didn't think, but they'd left about the same time. Maybe he'd gotten a late start.

"What was the ruckus about?" Elizabeth said, falling in step beside her. "Between Charles and your Tyrell?"

"I didn't see anything," Tipton said.

"Must've heard it, words so hot they could have raised the dead. Oh, best I not say that."

"I've never heard Tyrell raise his voice."

"Looked to me like an argument over something in the Cullvers' wagon that showed up in your brother's sticky paws." Elizabeth clucked her tongue. "Everyone already so grieved, and he takes advantage. You didn't train him right, child."

"You can't train a snake," Tipton told her as she and Elizabeth approached the Wilsons' wagon.

"Your father's worse," Adora told them.

Tipton's mother pulled at her handkerchief in between trying to get him to sip water or hyssop tea as Tipton and Elizabeth stepped past her, inside the wagon. Hathaway shivered and shook, his eyes frightened almost, shifting. "Charles should have stayed to help," Tipton said, trying to get her father to take a drink.

❧

What Mazy planned didn't matter. All the green grasses, all the prayers, all the promise of this pleasant place did not forestall the losses.

Hathaway Wilson, the robust mercantile owner formerly of Cassville, Wisconsin, Adora's faithful husband, and Charles and Tipton's beloved father, died at noon.

His death was followed by Tyrell's.

# of longing and light

It was with Mazy's arm around her that Tipton gazed at last on her intended.

Together, they watched Charles ride in from a distance, leading a mule. Tipton stared at the familiar clothing, squinting, assessing what was out of place. Sunburst spurs hung from Charles's saddlehorn. Diggers, Tyrell called them, an old term he said was more descriptive than a spur. Then her fingers found their way into her mouth, pressed the flesh against her teeth until the pain exploded in her brain.

Mazy tried to pull her back while Matt Schmidtke and Joe Pepin lowered the body of Tyrell onto the grass, his face a distorted pulp of black powder and flesh.

"Took a shot at a buck," Charles said as though discussing a sudden change in the weather. He sat atop his horse, gloved hands loosely holding the reins, crossed and resting on the saddle pommel. His horse lifted a back leg to scratch at a fly, stomped back, and Charles settled, shifted without effort. "Blew in the barrel before reloading. Charge hadn't fired, and it discharged into his mouth. Stupid," Charles said.

"We all do it," Joe Pepin defended. "Have myself often enough with a flintlock."

"Still stupid. How's Father?" Charles asked then.

"Your pa went home this morning," Joe Pepin told him, Adam's apple bobbing. "Sorry, son."

Charles's face didn't change, but his words took on a swampy edge. "Your fault," he said. He blew air of disgust through his nostrils.

"Mine?" Joe said, his bushy eyebrows raised in question.

Tipton knew her brother spoke to her.

"Father would still be here. But no, you had to have your way, had to go with Tyrell. Now see what that's gotten you? You've killed him, too."

Tipton covered Tyrell's body with her own then, tried to pull him to her chest, rocking, moaning now, a haunting, distant wail. She stroked her beloved and sobbed.

"He was always looking after Tipton," Charles said. "Who's going to do that now?"

Tipton turned to her brother, watched the tensed shoulders, the bright red of his mottled skin, the throbbing of that vein in his short, tanned neck.

"Mother insisted Father find you, so she wouldn't be without her Tipton." He spit the word that was her name, a family name.

What would Tyrell do, what would Tyrell say to stop her thudding heart? Tipton didn't know and couldn't pull it forth.

"Tipton this, and Tipton that."

"Charles. Stop," Mazy said.

He continued his steely tirade, spittle forming at the corners of his mouth. Tipton could see his lips move, his eyes dark, hooded. The words ran together like thick cotton pressed into her ears. "No," she whispered, looking up into Mazy's eyes. "No." Mazy bent over her and loosened Tipton's distorted fingers from her intended's lifeless body.

"Tyrell neither!" Charles shouted, breaking through. "Went west to please you, make a life for you, Papa and Tyrell did. Always taking care of Tipton, that's what killed Papa."

"Charles," Mazy said, her arms wrapped around a wispy Tipton. "Enough."

Charles wiped the corner of his mouth with the back of his hand.

Tipton wanted him finished of saying out loud the painful words she said now to herself. "You'll pay for this someday. You will," he said.

"I already am," she whispered.

Mazy turned the girl toward the Wilson wagon. Tipton moved as though through mud, her feet heavy. She held her breath as Tyrell once told her to do. Still, her fingers contorted into a crone's hand, the thumb and index finger spread out, the others cupped and rigid. Her breath came short, and she felt the numbness creeping down her shoulder.

"I got his spurs," Charles said. "I'll take 'em in trade for bringing him back."

"Charles," Mazy said. "Please. It's all she's got left of him."

"Not much of him left," Charles said. "Like I said, stupid, in more ways than one."

Tipton moved in a nightmare. She saw Elizabeth striding toward her, arms outstretched. She searched for her mother, her father, then remembered. The silver rowels spun as Charles yanked on his horse's bit and trotted away. Tipton felt weightless, as if the wind could lift her. She prayed it would, lift her and take her away.

Help me, help me, help me.

Mazy held her up.

～❧～

"What's happening?" Jeremy asked her. "Why aren't we moving?"

Mazy wiped his forehead with a cool rag, ran it around his neck and over his chest. He shook, his teeth chattering even as his body oozed perspiration.

"We've decided to stop. Hathaway Wilson's died. Antone Schmidtke, too, and Mariah, their daughter's peaked." She busied herself with rinsing the rag, twisted the water out, letting her hands cool before turning back to her husband. "Tyrell's gone," she said. "Passed on."

"He was sick? I didn't…I've missed days?"

Mazy shook her head. "Not from this, whatever it is. An accident." Even as she told him, it made no sense—Tyrell was such a careful man, so methodical.

"Guidebook…"

"I know. More die of accidents than illness. Tipton's beside herself. Adora's of no help what with Hathaway gone too. Oh, Jeremy, you've just got to get better." She heard the desperation in her voice, vowed to change it. She took a deep breath to slow her words. "So we're staying, just for a day or two. I don't know what will happen now. I suppose someone will step forward to take Antone's place."

"Maybe…I'll improve." He grimaced.

"I'd not oppose it this time, that's sure."

"Timing's…essential," Jeremy said. He shook and sucked air in through his teeth.

She spooned soup into his mouth. His skin looked blue in the frangible light filtered through the canvas amber. She felt a tightness in her throat as she helped him lay his head down on the rolled blanket, settled it beneath his neck. He looked older than she remembered, and his skin puckered the color of her father's—just before he died.

She began to talk then, repeating and rapid, of the routine and everyday. She spoke of Sister Esther and the honeybees and the antelope's antics scattering pots and pans when it followed Elizabeth about, leaving her mother panting as she pounced on the animal's tether rope. She talked of the tomato, how her mother confessed that she'd sprinkled flour dust on it now and again when she made a pie, just to keep Mazy puzzling. Something to think about besides the blisters.

"One cow, Mavis," Mazy said, "I think she's been bred. She'll calve a month or two after our baby's born. Isn't that lovely? I think it's lovely. Do you want more soup? Oh, Jeremy, what can I do?" Her speech rushed as though utterance and disallowance could prevent from happening what she knew was now truth.

"When should I re-breed her, Jeremy? How many days after she calves?"

He answered with a thick tongue, and she knew when he did that he knew the inevitable too. "Breed her," he said, "so she conceives, seventy-five to one hundred days…after she calves. It will give"—he stopped to take a deeper breath—"the greatest milk. The eighty-fifth day it will be twelve months…between calves. Keep records, Mazy. Can't remember. Double the herd…still sell…milk."

"The eighty-fifth day. I'll remember," she said and felt the tears press against her nose and eyes.

The Lord knows my lot, the Lord knows my lot.

She wondered at what she chose to tell him, there was so little time. She couldn't say the words, didn't want to say out loud that this might be their last discussion over anything at all.

"Go on," Jeremy told her. He had thrown up the little soup she'd gotten down him, and now perspiration soaked him and the linens. "Donation Land Claim. You. Your mother…stay. Just three years. There's money. To prove up."

"Don't talk of that now."

"Money. In the wagon. False floor. A thousand dollars."

"Where did it come from? Jeremy?"

"Go on, Mazy. Don't turn back."

"But is it from the sale of the farm? Where?"

He shook his head, struggled to talk. "Just keep going, promise me."

She didn't want their last exchange to be of something so mundane as money, of calving and cows; she didn't want to make any promises she couldn't keep.

She squeezed the water from the rag, dipped it into fresh, and laid it back across his wide forehead. He looked stripped without his glasses, vulnerable and small. If she pretended not to hear him, then none of this would happen. She had to give God time to perform his miracle of healing. She prayed. She believed. All she wanted was her husband well and his arms around her heart.

Shadows flickered against the canvas that bounded them like a cave of thinnest bone. Candle wax smelled strong, his breathing raspy.

Suddenly, she had to know, had to find an answer to a question she had harbored in her heart.

"Would you have gone without me, Jeremy? If I hadn't agreed to leave the bluffs, the river, would you have gone on without me?"

"I am going on...without you, Maze," he said.

"But would you? If I had stood firm. I need to know, to know if I could have prevented this if I had just refused, been stubborn, and insisted that we stay home."

"I'm going home." He lifted his hand to her head, as gentle as a butterfly landing.

"Please, Jeremy, tell me."

"I would have left," he said then. "It was in my blood, to come. No regrets for leaving home; but for being willing...to leave you for it, for not loving you...enough to stay. For that I ask...forgiveness. Think God's given it."

He lifted her hand to his lips then, gazed at her. She thought she nodded to him. His eyes looked as though to sink inside hers. "You're...a big girl, Mazy," he rattled from his chest. "You can do this." He took one, then two last halting breaths before his labored breathing ended.

❧

It could be sliced with an icicle, Ruth thought, as the emptiness of death settled on them, heavy as any snowfall back in the States. This time of grieving brought all that back, that winter past when she couldn't lift her legs without them aching, pushing against the wet and heavy drifts to feed the horses. The next day she'd done it all again, not because she wanted to or thought her body could, but because to succumb meant a loss too great to imagine; animals down or dead, her own desire defeated.

This time shadowed that. Her brother, gone. Her gentle, caring brother, dead, and now others, people new to her but somehow connected like the spokes of a wheel all bound to a hub. What Ruth could offer was a push to action. That was what countered grief.

Tomorrow, they'd get through the burials. So many. Sister Esther's second brother dead too. Ferrel, his name was. The Sister's face carried the look of a frustrated cat about to pounce on something. Antone, Tyrell, Hathaway, and Jeremy.

Then Ruth would press to convene a meeting, provide relief with the presentation of a plan. Move forward. They'd slip through the grip of grief as long as they headed on. She was as sure of that as she was that the Platte harbored quicksand.

She'd talk with Matt and that Pepin man about taking the cattle ahead, to make faster time to Fort Laramie. Some of her horses could go too, send packs full of grain from her wagon. She'd bring Jed and Betha's and meet up with them later. Maybe the Bacon bull could go with them, be less of a trouble for them. They'd have to combine wagons.

Ruth made her way past Suzanne's wagon, surprised to see the Bacons' dog lying there, what with Jeremy passed on. She checked on Betha, brushed the hair from her nephew's puffed eyes, let the children cling to her. She looked for Sarah, who asked for so little, and held her, too. Jessie had begged to come with her for the night, and she'd agreed. She liked the action of tucking the coverlet around the child as she crawled into the bed. She'd pulled the flannel up to the girl's chin. Jessie flipped it back. "Too hot," she said, then closed her eyes to sleep.

In her bedroll, Ruth listened to the crickets and swatted at the buzzing of mosquitoes, wanting to drown out the sounds of sadness she heard from wagons beyond. Jessie slept beside her. She'd concentrate on the child's safe, even breathing. A tiny island of joy in this sea of frozen grief.

~~~

Mazy had seen people die before, her father's patients. But those were distant people, men most often, people she knew had families, parents, sometimes wives and children to mourn them. But she hadn't inter-twined her life with theirs. She'd never felt love's other side—great loss, betrayal, even dark anger—when they died. She had not hung grief on her shoulders and worn it like a cloak.

They'd been gone but two months on this trail, and yet her world had changed beyond any power she had to change it back.

"Good to see you're up, child," Elizabeth told her.

Mazy stared at her, sorting the words. She barely remembered the night.

"Lura's boy, Matt, and their teamster, Joe Pepin, are helping folks get their wagons hitched. Charles might help too, though I have my doubts about that one. We'll have the service for Antone and Hathaway and Jeremy, that Ferrel fellow. Then be on our way."

"Go somewhere?"

"You'll have to handle a wagon, Mazy. Madison? You think you can?"

"But there's no reason to keep going," Mazy said. She heard her voice as though weighted, carrying rocks from a long way off.

"No reason not to. Almost halfway." Elizabeth's voice softened. "Not even June 15. Making good time."

Mazy's mind moved over to the cold places death left behind. "How could he do this? Let this happen?"

"Wasn't Jeremy's fault he took sick."

"I promised and prayed, Mother. How could he?"

"Madison, we're gonna bury these good men, and then we're head-ing on to Laramie. No sense blaming. Don't remember anywhere it says if we keep our promises God'll be forced into something he might not have in mind."

She looked up at her mother, stared at the soft waves of gray-streaked brown that made her mother's eyes look exceedingly blue. "God loves obedience. I obeyed. I came as Jeremy asked me. He told me, Mother, that he would have come without me. It would have torn our marriage apart if I had stayed at home." Her eyes watered, and she brushed at the tears. "But maybe he wouldn't have come, maybe I could have saved him then, from this…horrible death. Or if I'd stayed, he could have moved faster, gone on ahead, missed this disease."

Elizabeth picked up the ivory-handled hairbrush and began undoing the twist of her daughter's heavy chestnut hair. "You're torturing yourself, Madison. No need for it." She laid the combs aside and drew the bristles through natural waves that expanded with the brushing. "He didn't promise us a smooth ride, darling," Elizabeth said. "Just that he'd be there with us through it, that he'd never leave us nor desert us. So I 'spect he's here still, making plans. He knows our lot."

"I had good boundaries and I left them. For this, this godforsaken land without a tree for miles except beside a stream."

"We just can't always see what lays ahead, Madison, and we sure can't let the past alone be creatin' our present. Got to see it for what it is and let us find the pleasant places wherever we are, wherever we're planted. It don't seem like it now, but you'll come through this, you will." She retwisted the hair into a soft roll that rose up from the back of Mazy's neck to crown her head. "Come now, let's get your face washed and put on a fresh wrapper. Unless you want your bloomers."

Elizabeth lifted loose wisps of hair with the backs of her fingers and caught them into the roll. Mazy felt the tears press against her nose and pool inside her eyes. She leaned her head into her mother's skirts and wept.

Suzanne opened her eyes, expecting to see light. She was disappointed, once again. How many more years would she be sightless before she opened her eyes and did not experience that split second of hope, the belief that she would not only feel the warmth of light but see it before the darkness came upon her like a mud slide. Perhaps forever. At least now she noticed the warmth. And she saw the colors.

It had taken her awhile to discover swirls of stain in reds and yellows and whites and blues. She could remember as a child—a seeing child in Michigan—that if she closed her eyes and pressed her fingers against them, she would see tints and hues of soft light beneath her lids, not unlike the northern lights. Something about the pressure against her eyes brought out the color, that's what Franklin had told her. He was a wise older brother, and she loved that she could see something he could not, but that he still believed in what she said.

"Like the aurora borealis, Coot," he teased.

"Boars aren't roaring," she'd said, taking her fingers from her eyes. She turned toward the pens where their father kept the large hogs they raised. She could see plainly then, the big shoats snorting. "I can't hear them roaring, anyway."

Franklin laughed and tousled her hair.

"Aurora borealis," he said, enunciating. "It's the name of the bouncing lights you've seen against the horizon. Remember? I think that's what pressing against your eyes is like."

She did remember the northern lights at home. Home, in the Upper Peninsula of Michigan; home, where she'd first learned to love. She'd seen them in a night sky as black as her world was now but for the strings of color that shot through it, flickering, glowing green and yellow off the far horizon.

"How did they get there?" she asked Franklin.

"It's where they were put," he said, providing as good an answer as any she'd ever heard. "Just like us."

Years later, after the accident, when they'd removed the bandages from her eyes, and she opened them with all the hope she dared, she remembered Franklin's words. She'd been dropped like a shooting star crashing to a dark earth. Not even the soft hues; nothing but blackness. That's where she'd been put.

She didn't have to like it.

Weeks later she became aware of the colors, soft swirls of egg and strawberry jam creamed into a cocoa-floured cake. Small consolation, she thought, dribbles of yellow and red when once she had known an artist's palette of paint.

Once she had seen the blond head of her child bobbing in a bassinet, smiling and kicking his feet as he cooed; once she had looked through a camera's lens, seen the image of a wedded couple upside down but known that it would appear perfectly on the glass plates. She had once sewn intricate garments fit for senators' wives on a sewing machine Bryce purchased when they married, an extravagance her cousins had marveled about.

Little good the thing did now. She hated that Bryce insisted they buy a new one just before this journey.

"What, you think I can thread a needle?" She'd asked him.

"Your fingers…I could do that part if you would let me."

"And then what? Turn the wheel and stitch my hand into the cloth? That's what I'd do and be even more crippled than I am. I can no longer sew, Bryce. No longer do anything that matters, don't you see? Leave it here, that machine. Leave me here! Take Clayton and go."

But he'd taken it anyway, and he'd brought her, too, to a place "where no one will expect you to do what you did before," he said. "Where you can…we can start new."

"I'll know what I could do before," she'd shouted at him, tears burning against the scarred eyes that looked out on nothing. "I'll be with myself. I'm not allowed to leave that behind."

What did it matter now? Bryce was dead and here she sat with Clayton, alone, another child on the way, a child whose light she'd never see. The scent of bacon being fried reached her, was strong enough to push through the mildew smell of the canvas and the pungent scent of Clayton's scraped but as yet unwashed diaper covering his bottom.

She needed to change him. She turned her face in the pillow, her hand patting for her child. Instead, the scent of Bryce greeted her from the down, along with a dozen memories. The world of the past was stored within scents and sounds and proved more powerful than any book of old photographs.

She heard the sounds of birds coming alive just before dawn. She made out the soft stomping of oxen, the heavier beast that didn't like the yoke. Men from a distant camp shouted. Dogs barked. The black dog who had taken to her barked back. He must have stood close below the wagon. Why the dog had chosen her to spend his nights with she did not know. She had kicked at it, though she probably missed, and she scolded it, but for some reason it kept coming back.

Bryce had been like that. After the accident, she pushed him away, disgusted with her stupidity. He wouldn't leave. She would have gone if he had been the one who was blind. She never would have allowed herself to be boarded in by a cripple held hostage by darkness.

"I think of you as having limits, that's true," Bryce told her once, "but not a cripple. You have so much to offer, Suzanne, to me, our son, to the future."

"Are you up?" It was the woman Elizabeth, the good-natured one who smelled of lavender and leather, an oddly comforting combination.

"Why should I be?" Suzanne said. "Nothing to rise for."

"That boy of yours'll be howling 'fore long. May as well get yourself around. We've burials to attend to, then we're heading on to Laramie. You up to that?"

"Just leave me. Take Clayton and let the buzzards feed."

"You think I'm that cruel? You'd probably give 'em indigestion." Suzanne snorted. "No, we'll get your wagon hitched. Take a few of us to do it 'til we get the hang of it. We'll move slow 'til we get our rhythm. Let's get you dressed and fed first."

"I'm quite capable of dressing myself," she said.

"Thought you might be. We'll head out to the circle for our privates when you're ready, 'less you want to use the slop jar. I'll stand right here and pat Mazy's lazy dog 'til you're about. Or let me come get the boy and help you down."

"Just…leave."

"I'll be back with bacon." The woman almost chirped as she left.

Suzanne laid the covers back, patted the bed for her wrapper, fingered the buttons on the front that expanded to give her more room as the baby grew. This one was larger than Clayton. She pulled the wrapper over her head, combed her hair with her fingers and braided the strands into a tight knot at the base of her neck. Bryce had said her hair looked like spun gold.

"Spun straw is more like it," she said out loud, yanking at the strands coarse in her hands. She pulled until tears stung at her nose. "Mommy? My mommy?" Clayton jabbered, pulled at her hair.

"Oh!" she said. But like the color that appeared when she pressed against her eyes, the pain demanded she think of it instead of what was missing.

⬲

"You hurt?" Naomi asked Sister Esther.

The sturdier of the three surviving Asian women opened wide her almond-shaped eyes. She had called herself Passion Flower, but Esther had renamed each of the girls. "Missy Esther, you burn finger on spider pan?"

"I'm fine, Naomi," Esther said. She smiled at the round face with skin the color of millet. The girl looked healthy now, but so had Cynthia and then she'd died.

"I get grease?" Deborah asked.

"Not necessary," Sister Esther said. The girl shrank. "I did not mean to upset you." Esther sighed. "Water will do if you care to bring me a dipper. I shall drink it and also soothe the burn." She ran her long fingers to tuck gray hair beneath the black mesh cap she wore, patted the bun at her neck beneath it, folded her hands in front of her apron as though about to make a speech, but took a deep breath instead. Such a tightness she felt, even to breathe.

"I help, Missy," Deborah said, taking labored steps to the water barrel. She was always the eager one, the beekeeper who knew how to tend, but her damaged feet interfered with her willingness. Esther watched the girl check the six white squares that lined the side of the wagon, their little platforms folding down to permit bee flights every other week. Deborah made sure the ventilation door with tiny holes opened to give them air. Daily, she lifted the feeder lid at the top, renewed the water supply, made sure the larva and brood stayed protected.

Esther was glad Deborah checked the bees often. They were said to be a gentle strain, but Sister Esther did not want them to break free, pour out into the wild land they moved through when they gathered up their juices from the plants and not come back. "Bees come back for queen," Deborah had told her once, but Esther wasn't sure if such rules applied in this territory beyond the States.

The bees were Deborah's future. It was the bees her contract husband purchased more than the "damaged goods" of a woman whose feet kept her in constant pain, though the girl never complained. Well, the paper plans, Langstroth's patent for the new kind of hives, that was the real wealth. Harold said once that Deborah had been "thrown in just to sweeten the bargain."

"We go back? Brothers all gone?" Deborah asked, breaking into Esther's thoughts.

"No! I...perhaps it should be considered. But if we continue through the alkali country to Laramie we'll be, as they say, 'a third of the way to heaven.' Perhaps closer, as I believe the term refers to those going on to Oregon territory while we will head on south. Thank you, dear," she said lifting the water dipper.

Sister Esther swallowed, then stuck her burned finger inside the wooden cup. "Can you girls yoke Harold's wagon? Perhaps we should stay here a day or so." She twisted her hands together, rubbed at the knuckles. "I will go now to check on Zilah. Don't leave the wagon."

"Yes, Missy," Deborah and Naomi said in unison, bowing their heads.

Esther knew they wouldn't leave. They were like children, dependent, despite the time they'd had to get acquainted. Only Harold and Ferrel had spoken to them. Now her brothers were dead. She couldn't make sense of the illness, why it affected their wagons when they'd been pure, faithful. How would she tell Cynthia's intended of the girl's death? Explain to her parents? She forced herself to straighten her shoulders. Well, it was her penance, this additional load, for insisting her brothers come with her.

Tipton lay in Elizabeth's wagon, her hands tingling and numb but less contorted now, less like a crone's. Something blotted out the light. Tipton shifted in the bed. "Time you were getting up, child," Elizabeth's words were soft when she spoke. "Just got the Cullvers up. We all got to be moving on. Your mama needs you now."

Tipton turned to her. "We can't go anywhere." Tipton's words sounded slurred even to herself. Probably the laudanum. Or maybe that whiskey she'd found. It helped her disappear, took the edge off things. She wanted no edges now, not with Tyrell gone.

"We'll have the final burials and head on. It's what we have to do," Elizabeth told her.

"Papa and Tyrell—"

"Can't do nothing for them," Elizabeth said. She sat on the bed, and Tipton rolled toward her, her body a fragile stick tumbling toward a stone. "What's done is done."

"I can't."

"Truth is, you're needed. To drive this wagon."

"No, I—"

"This one or the Cullvers'. Which do you want?"

"But that can't be. Charles can drive this; Mama, the other. I can't." She could feel her heart pounding. "Let me be. Please." She took short, shallow breaths.

Sprigs of lavender hanging from the top ring of the wagon mixed with dried peppermint brought a sweetness to the painful place. Tipton smelled it and squeezed her eyes tight against it.

"Lots you haven't never done before. Never been fifteen and never lost someone you loved." She brushed the tears at Tipton's cheeks, her fingers callused but kind. "Never drove a wagon west, neither. First two you're surviving; last one you will too."

"But my…hands. See how they get." Tipton held up the already contorting fingers, using her left hand to steady the right.

Elizabeth looked at her. "You do that to yourself," she said quietly.

"How dare you!"

"You're not taking in good breaths. I seen it before."

"I lose my father and my intended and my hands twist against me and you say it's me?" Tipton sat up in bed, glared.

"Not saying you don't have pain, child. Just suggesting that a useless hand of yours serves a purpose. Your mind knows you need protection from something, so it lets your hands go numb, look all strange like the roots of an old tree." She cupped the girl's contorted fingers in her own. Tipton let her.

"It keeps you from thinking of something else. Or doing something else, I'll ponder. Least it did. Won't save you from missing your papa or Tyrell, though. Won't keep you from that. And it won't keep you from driving a wagon. If you don't, what Tyrell did to get us all this far will be for nothing. That ain't the legacy he meant to leave you."

The woman came too close, pierced too deep.

"You don't want a legacy, either, that says Tipton Wilson might've come through but didn't. You think on it, child," Elizabeth said. " I need to talk to Mazy." She patted the girl's hand, stood to leave, then said,

"She's a widow and a mother-to-be. Be grateful at least you ain't bringing a baby into the world without its papa being about."

Tipton lay on after she left, staring at the twisted hand attached to her wrist. She lifted the limb to her eyes, moved it this way and that in a kind of slow and mournful dance.

Bearing Tyrell's baby would have been a reason to live. Now she had none. Tears pressed against her eyes. What were you thinking of, Tyrell? To die so uselessly, so unfulfilled. She sat up in bed, her heart pounding. It hadn't been his fault, the accident, but hers! She had sent him away, clinging to him as she did. He went to hunt to get away from her! Tyrell's death was her fault. She'd killed him as sure as if she'd blasted the cap; and she'd sent her father with him.

She reached for the bottle, pulled the glass stopper from the laudanum, and placed her mouth over the opening. Then she tipped her head back and swallowed. The warmth rushed through her just before she stuffed the stopper back and sank into the pillow.

⌘

Esther lifted the tent flap, relieved to see Zilah sitting up.

"I better, Sister," Zilah said. "I leave Ferrel's tobacco, not chew."

"What?"

The girl dropped her narrow eyes. "Ferrel say make me feel better some."

"I did not know he…imbibed." Esther yanked on the bow beneath her own chin, pulling the tight cap so the outside ribbing pressed against her bony cheeks. "It is not good for you. Now you know. Are you up to helping hitch ol' Snoz?"

The girl nodded. "He walk to not trouble bees."

"My favorite as well," Esther said. "The bees are bothered by steps?"

The girl reached for the bag of buckwheat kernels and popped a palmful into her mouth, chewing with motions like a mouse nibbling.

"Mei-Ling—Deborah," she corrected, "she say bees tell voice and know name of thumping feet. If they unhappy, they fly away." She munched. Her lips formed an upturned smile in her oval face. Her skin bore the color of soft dust, marked with pocks from a previous illness, long before they began this journey west. She was not a pretty girl, but stout and until now sturdy, and her contract husband had written enthusiastically about the match after he'd seen the photographic likeness the girl had sent.

"I strong like ox," Zilah said, unwrapping her legs from beneath her. She burped the buckwheat kernel, pressed tiny fingers to her lips. "Do what we do not before. That where courage live. My grandmother say this long time ago."

"Best we believe her," Esther said and helped the girl from the tent.

❧

Mazy's eyes hurt, she couldn't think straight. She wanted to comfort the others but had nothing to give, anger and loss, leaving her as drained as a shattered pitcher.

"I'd give anything for you not to be feeling this, darlin'," Elizabeth said. "Losing someone you love, it's the worst ache known to humans, worse than being cut on or suffering from sin." She hesitated. "Maybe not worse than suffering sin, but we all got to live through that. When your father died, I thought I'd die too. But then your heart keeps beating, you keep taking breaths and getting hungry and needing sleep, so you know you're not dead. One day, something makes you laugh and you're ripped with guilt because you can. A month passes and then a year, and you've gone on with your life even knowing you couldn't, but you do.

"A morning comes and you wake up and the sky is blue and you smell flowers you'd forgotten you liked and the dog bumps his head beneath your hand and you take him for a brisk walk beneath budding oak and maple. It's like a garden coming back in spring after a long,

179

tough winter." She lifted her daughter's arms. "You're like a rag doll," she whispered then pulled her daughter to her breast.

They held each other for a time, then Elizabeth removed her daughter's wrapper and replaced it with a laundered one.

Mazy smelled the lye soap and river water on her dress as it slid over her head, brushed against her face. "It seems so long ago we were stopped, doing laundry, and I was irritated with you for leaving."

"I didn't leave you," Elizabeth said She placed the combs back into Mazy's hair and found the splinter of mirror and held it before her daughter. "I think Jeremy'd want you to keep going on. For you and his baby. Don't imagine he'd want you to just sit here and waste away."

"I'm already holding water," Mazy said, taking the mirror from her mother and laying it down.

"Got to stay healthy. Come along now, Mazy. Let's see if the two of us can yoke the oxen by ourselves. Give this grief train some direction."

"I don't know if I want to, Mother," Mazy said as she let Elizabeth help her down the wagon stairs. She looked around at the stream and the cattle and horses clustered toward the back. Ruth already at work. The cows and cow brute lay chewing their cud. "What would be wrong with our staying right here?"

"Ain't our place, for one," Elizabeth said. "Indian Territory. Don't think the Pawnee nor the Sioux'd take our being here as some kind of pleasant party. This ain't even the States. We're in a foreign country. Besides, what'd we do if we stayed?"

"Raise a garden, sell the vegetables to people coming across, people like us. We've bought up a thing or two along the way. Sell them milk and cheese and eggs. Do like the Mormons have, run ferries and such. Buy time; then turn back."

Elizabeth said, "I say we go on to Oregon, get the land Jeremy spoke of. Three hundred twenty acres each. Can't hardly beat that."

Mazy turned, taking in the stream and the Platte and the folding slopes and the rich loam of the earth. "I think there are better choices than simply going on."

～

They gathered around the bodies wrapped in blankets, Antone's in what must have been the extension boards from the Schmidtkes' table. A survivor of her first night as a widow, Mazy leaned against her mother. Mazy had insisted that they dig graves and mark them with rocks and wooden crosses. "I don't see any sign of Indians or coyotes or anything else interested in digging up old bones," Mazy said. "Someday I'll make a marker, a real one, and come back here, to this place. I'll need to know exactly where they are."

Sister Esther spoke the words, about dust to dust and ashes to ashes.

They heard the clatter of a wagon, and the group turned to see Dr. Masters rolling out, his shoats squealing after. That left the women and a few sons to lay their men to rest.

"He's leaving?" Adora wailed, leaning against Charles, who stiffened at his mother's touch. "Now?"

"Didn't do anything for us," Ruth said. "Good to see him go."

Following the prayers, Mazy pounded the simple cross between the rocks she'd carried to cover the grave. She thought of what she'd come through, where she'd been, and what the future held. Then she made up her mind.

～

Lura Schmidtke hadn't spoken since they'd prayed over Antone's grave. For more than twenty years, she had not moved until her husband told her, had not fixed a breakfast without him saying first that he preferred buckwheat pancakes that morning rather than a mess of eggs. She was what, forty-five years old, forty-six? Yet she felt older than her grandmother who had died the day she turned seventy-nine.

For twenty years, Lura had seen the world before her always filtered through the shadow Antone cast. Yet here she sat. She knew she should move. The rest of the women had.

"Mama?" Mariah said. The child's voice still sounded weak. "It's time to go now."

Lura sighed. She let herself be lifted by the shoulders, her short cape sliding upward along thin arms. Her legs ached from the sitting. Mariah picked up the high-back chair and scooped it to her elbow while, with her other arm, she helped her mother balance as their toes scuffed up loose dirt.

"Where's Matt?" Lura asked, looking around. Her voice sounded flat like a piano key out of tune.

"He's back checking cattle. Likely Joe Pepin needs a little help. He'll be back to drive Pa's wagon. I can do the other. Joe'll have to take the stock alone. Don't see how he'll handle that many," Mariah said.

"Is that what Matt thinks best?"

"Just what needs doing."

"You're a good girl," Lura said and patted her daughter's hand. "But I'm so tired now. Just so tired."

"Pa said walking's good for the back."

"Yes. He knew everything important," Lura said.

"Sometimes I worry that I gave it to Pa," Mariah said, no longer sounding like a competent young woman looking after her mother but as the thirteen-year-old she really was. "I drank from the river, on my belly, just like Pa. I heard someone say that's where the sickness came from. I had it."

"I think I'd do best if we just rested a day or so right here. We need to know what Matt thinks we should do." Then she remembered something. "It was likely those Asians," Lura said, her voice lowered, "not you. Likely them what caused it."

~⟐~

From her position beside the oxen, Mazy watched her mother feed the antelope, a last task, she said, before they started out. The little black nose jabbed for milk, pushed against the rubber bottle her mother had fashioned from the rain gear sleeve. Fip, they'd named it, for its small size. Even Pig joined the act, barking his *gruff, gruff* sound, his tail wagging the whole time. A simple, everyday thing that seemed out of place.

Everything felt uprooted: the antelope, a child laughing, Suzanne standing beside her with lips pursed as tight as machine-stitched seams even while her son giggled. What good were psalms that said God guided everywhere if Mazy couldn't feel him? What good did it do to write praises in her book when beside it she wrote of graves passed and lives changed forever? She had followed God's plan, and he had promised to take her to pleasant places. She looked around. There was nothing pleasant here.

She was a needle on a compass, just bobbing forward and back, seeking direction. She scanned the low hills, the grasses, the Platte wide and shallow as it headed east toward where they'd come from, through what was familiar. That was it, then, to find direction. Her mother was certainly clear about the importance of such a thing. Jeremy had changed his whole life and then lost it because of his passion for a single thing. Well, she could be determined too. Some would call it obstinate, stubborn, headstrong. Whatever the term, it had served her well once or twice in her life, and Mazy decided it could cut through the haze of her confusion now.

She strode to the back of the wagon, her dress flapping between her legs with the speed and length of her stride. First, she would get their attention. Then she would advocate for a bearing, her bearing. She reached for a heavy kettle tied on the wagon's back and, with an iron spoon, began clanging her way through her losses.

sustenance

Mazy's clanging on the kettle startled Suzanne, intersecting her sorrow with vibration and sound. Most of the teams, already hitched, shifted with the unexpected noise, their heavy oxen hooves moving from side to side, tails flicking at flies. Wheels groaned forward and Suzanne heard only women's voices talking to animals as they stood by their sides, urging them to stillness. The pain of the sounds both pierced and angered.

"Stop that!" Suzanne called from beside her wagon. "You'll cause a stampede." Both hands cupped over her ears.

"Whoa, whoa," Naomi said, speaking with words that sounded like chirps. "What are names, Missy Suzie?"

"It's Suzanne. Suzanne, not Suzie." The clanging stopped.

"You name the oxen as yourself?"

"No. I am Suzanne. No Suzie or 'Missy Sue.' Can you remember that?" She sighed. "Bryce named the oxen Breeze and Blow—the lead team. It doesn't matter."

"That Missy Mazy. Okay I call her Mazy?"

"What's wrong?" Betha asked.

"I'm sorry," Mazy said. "But I want us to gather. For just a moment."

"A prayer for our journey would be welcomed." Sister Esther nodded sagely.

"Can't a meeting wait until evening?" Ruth said. "Better we get rolling. Need to take advantage of this weather and good grass while we can. Chimney Rock." She nodded to a site across the river. "There marks the beginning of rougher terrain."

Mazy lowered her voice. "Unless we meet now, I won't be at an evening gathering."

"What'd she say?" Lura asked Mariah.

"You're not thinking of leaving us?"

"I am thinking, Ruth." Mazy turned to her. "I'm thinking of what's essential. I have determined something. Some of you might want to determine it too."

"This really ain't a good time, child," Elizabeth said. "Not for you or any of us. Not good to be making some rash kind of decision. We just need to keep going."

"Things have changed, Mother. What kind of reasonable people would we be if we didn't take into account a change in circumstance, look at new information before moving on. If the cows stampeded, we'd stop to collect them after they scattered, we wouldn't just pretend it hadn't happened and try to keep on going."

"There's been no stampede," Suzanne said. "I know that much."

"In a way there has," Mazy said. "We've all been trampled. But we could be in worse shape."

"Now what could you be imagining, Mrs. Bacon?" It was Charles Wilson asking.

He'd ridden up on the far side while they'd been yoking. He sat there now, a used ember hanging on, challenging wind, threatening to burst into flame. He wore Tyrell's spurs. Mazy looked to the women instead.

"What's happening, Mama?" Tipton asked. She stuck her head outside of the wagon, her eyes dreamy as though she still slept.

"Mazy wants to discuss something. I don't know. I think we should get moving."

Tipton sighed. "It's fine with me."

Mazy thought the girl looked more hollow, wizened than when they'd headed west. Adora, too, had aged since the day she'd appeared in Kanesville full of the delight of catching up with her daughter. They were all changed.

"My head's in a swirl," Adora said. Her fingers rubbed little circles against her temples.

"I'm sure Tipton can settle you, Mother," Charles said. He spit.

"I say we move on," Ruth Martin offered. "Seems to me—"

"I agree. You was just trying to buy time, right, child?"

"We have a long distance to make and have not yet encountered the mountains," Esther said. "But the Lord will see us through."

"What do you think, Matt?" Lura Schmidtke turned to ask her son who had just ridden up.

"I have a proposal," Mazy said. She set the kettle down and stepped up into the box of her wagon to give herself additional height. She wanted to see everyone, evaluate their faces and their posture in addition to their words.

She drew deep for the will to make something happen, to be determined. There was a power in that word *determined,* even a conviction. It overcame the heavy sighs of resignation that formed a carapace of sadness over these people and this place.

"We are now an unlikely group of overlanders," Mazy began. "Some of us did not want to leave our homes at all. None of us chose this time when disease or accident—chance—permitted some of us to live and some to die. Who knows who'll be ill this evening—or dead by morning? I can't see a way to change that. But there are some things we can control."

"What's your point?" Suzanne said. She'd lowered Clayton to the ground but kept the rope tied to his middle and to hers. He tugged against her, and she jerked forward slightly as she talked. "Naomi, can you see him? Is he too close to the ox?"

"He fine, Missy Sue—Suzanne. I watch him good."

"This many wagons without a teamster," Mazy said, "if we have a breakage or if we lose an ox, or you there, Adora, if you should lose a mule, will be disastrous. The single men, Matt and Joe Pepin and Charles, you'll be needed with the stock." She glanced at Charles when he shot a blast of air through his nose.

"We'll be at Fort Laramie soon," Sister Esther said.

"And what will that gain us?" Mazy asked.

"The Lord will provide for us there, in ways we have not yet imagined."

"I'm not prepared to stake my future on that," Mazy said. "Not anymore. Who're we going to find to help us drive our wagons or stock? The people there, trappers, traders, soldiers? None of them are likely to want to sign on with women."

"We could join up with some of the groups across the Platte," Betha said. Her voice was tentative with its little-girl breathy sound. "Couldn't we, Ruthie? I see across there. Lots of dust so must be lots of wagons."

Adora said, "I just want to rest."

"No matter if we tried to join up with folks even on this side or at Laramie. They'll take one look at us and know that our eleven wagons joining in will put their own at risk."

"What I'd like is to go back to Jed's grave. I should have marked it like you did Jeremy's, Mazy. And Antone and Hathaway. Theirs are marked," Betha said.

"Am I allowed to talk?" It was Mariah. Mazy nodded. "Could we just split up? Trail along with one or two groups that might take us in?"

"That presents the same problem, as I see it. Who will want to be saddled with us?" Mazy said. "Wagons without teamsters."

"You're acting like we're…lepers or something," Ruth said, her words sharp.

"Join up," Suzanne said. "We're all cripples, with no guide, no leader."

"I am no kind of cripple," Ruth said. "We're capable, all of us, just been given a hot pan to hold with the deaths. It'll cool. We just need to head west. Quit jawing about it."

"People get blinded in all kinds of ways," Suzanne told her.

"Death confuses," Ruth responded. "We should go forward, stay our course. I've driven this far alone. If I can, the rest of you women can."

"But this is the easiest part," Lura said. "I know I shouldn't be speaking; I didn't ask permission. But I remember Antone said that. He said, 'Mama, once we pass Laramie, the hills get higher and the mountains're bad. We got to stick together, yah, that's the answer. Need all hands then and a good captain.'"

"So that's a yes?" Ruth snapped.

"Well, yes, I think it's a yes to stay together," Lura said. "Or maybe a no, to going on."

"I do believe Lura has made good points about the rigors of continuing," Esther said. "But what are you actually suggesting, Mazy?"

Mazy took a deep breath. "I'm determined to go home."

There. She'd said it and the world had not stopped turning, but her compass needle had.

"I never wanted to be here," Mazy continued. "I want to go back to Wisconsin, to what's familiar, to what I know. It's what I want my child to know, the things I knew first, the breeze off the bluffs."

"You learned that later, Mazy," Elizabeth reminded her. Mazy scowled at her. "Just want to keep this discussion honest. You met those bluffs after you stepped out in a new life with your husband. This is a new life he wanted for you too. And another waits in Oregon."

"But it won't be his life, will it, Mother? And it won't be one I chose. He won't be there to bring me to it. So I've got to tend to my own life, my own way. I never wanted to be here. I have a choice now, and I'm going to make it for me and my child. You can come along, or you can head on and hope someone takes pity on you and helps you through. Me, I'm going home."

Mazy heard her own heart beat with the sureness of what she wanted. She wondered if she would turn back all alone if no one chose to go back with her. Well, she decided, she could. Silence cloaked the group.

"I don't have much say in all of this," Suzanne said, breaking the silence first. "But if you want to know about being trapped where you don't want to be, ask me. No wolverine caught could feel more violated for all the good it does her. So I guess I need to ask you, Naomi, since you're doing the driving of my oxen. Which way are you heading? East or west?"

"She'll go where I decide," Sister Esther said.

Naomi continued to rub at the big ox's shoulder, calming the animal as she did. She talked low to Breeze, scratching the animal behind his ears, avoiding the long horns that extended out toward the sides. Mazy watched her. She seemed disinterested in the conversation, so Mazy found herself surprised with the girl's insightful response. "Plants grow best in same soil. Grow close, offer—safe house—from winds. They are of same place, grow best not alone."

"Trees seldom grow alone," Elizabeth said.

"Meaning?" Suzanne said.

"Whatever we do, we should do it as one," Betha said.

"All together, in one place," Mazy said. "Exactly."

"But we have obligations," Sister Esther protested. "People waiting for us in California."

"What's the likelihood you'll be able to deliver?" Mazy said. "You'd be better off to turn back, find new drivers or bull-whackers and start again next year. You have three other lives you're responsible for, and even with two men, you were taking a chance going overland."

Sister Esther sank to the chair she had not yet loaded back onto her wagon. "But to have come so far already and turn back..."

"There is strength together, Missy Esther," Deborah said, patting the woman's bony shoulder. "The bees make way. Know duty."

"To take care of the queen, isn't it?" Charles said.

It startled Mazy to hear him enter this women's circle.

"A group of drones looking after a queen," Charles continued. "Fortunately, Mrs. Bacon has excluded the men from this discussion. But then, I wasn't planning to be in one place with any of you for long."

"Charles!" Adora gasped. "What are you thinking of? You've got to drive us, me! You can't leave us!"

"I've got to do nothing, woman. Mrs. Bacon's right on that one thing: It's a choice. You made yours when you made Father follow Tipton. See what it got him? I'm sure you two'll do well together as you always have. If I were you, I'd head back. They know you there, and someone's likely to take pity on you until you can find a suitable bene-factor for dear Tipton."

He finished his speech and slipped inside the wagon. Adora stood, her mouth open. When he stepped back out and onto his horse, she grabbed at his gartered sleeve. He leaned across her, as though to snap at Tipton inside the wagon. "What've you got in your vest?" Adora asked, reaching to touch his pocket.

"None of your business," he said, grabbing her wrist, tossing it back to her hard enough to make her stumble.

"Charles!" Mazy said, "Your own mother—"

"Can take care of herself." He jerked the reins, and the horse stepped back, twisting. He gouged the animal with the sunburst spurs, the horse barely missing Adora as man and animal shot past.

"Mama?" Tipton stuck her head out of the wagon back.

"He's leaving us." Adora chewed her lower lip, rubbed at her temples.

"But, Charles, we're your family," Tipton said, her words slurred.

Charles pulled the reins and turned back. "You never gave me any-thing I'd want to claim as mine."

"Just Papa's good money," Tipton said, cutting through her fog. "You'd take that with no hard feelings."

The vein in Charles's neck became suddenly thick and pulsating. His hazel eyes hardened to ice. "I earned every eagle putting up with you, sister," he said. "I've paid my dues. Paid them well and with interest." He started to turn his mount. "Something more you should know before you get too high on your horse, little sister." Spittle gathered at his mouth again. "Your intended had other plans than marrying you. He told me so the day he died. Said he'd had enough with sniveling females and that he was glad as glad could be he'd be heading north to Oregon while all the Wilson clan went south."

"That's not true," she gasped. "He would have told me if he'd changed his mind."

"Why tell you?" Charles said. "He didn't have to. Once we hit Casper country, you'd be out of sight, out of mind. Just as you are now for him. Just as you're going to be for me."

He pressed the reins to the horse's neck then and gave the animal a sharp kick with Tyrell's spurs that sent it into a trot.

Birds twittered into the silence. Tipton looked as though she'd just awoken, her hair and clothes disheveled, like someone drifting into distance.

Grief is as singular as a snowflake, Mazy thought, *and just as algid*.

"I think Mazy's right, Ruthie." They all turned at once to Betha. "I know this'll be hard for you to hear, dear, but I want to go back to Jed's grave. Couldn't we? I could decide better about what to do there, I could. Talk it over with him. You could go on without me."

Ruth stared at her.

"Well, I don't suppose you could." Betha looked away. "I need to go back, though. I do. Go with me. Please."

"Esther, do you wish to do the same? We could pray again over Harold's grave. And Cynthia's," Mazy said.

The woman nodded. "Just for a short good-bye."

Ruth sighed, resigned. "How about if Matt and Joe take the cattle and the horses on, pack some of my grain. They'd find better grazing west without us. The rest of you could head west while I take Betha back. Collect ourselves."

"We all stick together," Adora said. "I can't imagine going on without you and Mazy both."

"For the children's sake. I just want to take a little time to mourn at the grave," Betha said.

"Matt?" Lura asked her son. "What's your pleasure?"

"I been thinking while you all been talking, that we should do that. Take your cow brute too, if you want, Mrs. Bacon. Meet up at Laramie or keep going. Applegate's route goes south, then on into Oregon on the California Pack Trail. If we drive your horses north there, Miss Martin, you won't have to worry over the Columbia River crossing."

"Oh, we'll be caught up with you long before then," Ruth said. "You want your brute to go, Mazy?"

Mazy didn't want that; but if it meant the others would turn back with her, it would be worth the loss of the brute. What did she care about it anyway? She had the cows. And if they turned back all together, if only on the pretense of stopping a day or two at the graves, it would be worth it. Turning around was the hard part. Longing for home would keep them facing east.

"Take the brute," Mazy said. "We'll go back, rest at the graves."

"Yes, rest," Lura said. "That sounds so good."

"I go back with Missy Esther," Naomi said. "Take Missy Sue— Suzanne."

"And you...others traveling with Sister Esther?" Mazy realized she did not know one of them, had only heard Naomi's name because Suzanne used it.

"They'll do as I bid them," Sister Esther.

Mazy didn't think Esther noticed the looks the Asian girls exchanged.

"To get our rhythm and rest ourselves is a good idea," Elizabeth said. "Practice helping each other through."

Mazy didn't know when she'd been more grateful to her mother.

A silence followed, broken when Mazy said, "It's decided, then. We turn east. All together."

"For now," Ruth said. "All together for now."

Before they left, Matt showed his mother and Mariah how to lift the heavy yokes off their oxen and where to place them beside the wheels.

"You set 'em the same place every night, you'll know where to find 'em in the morning," he told them. "Got to watch and make sure Boo is always on the left, smaller means left. Minnie on the right. Hitch up Minnie first, otherwise she thinks she's being left behind and gets unruly. Same goes for your team, Mariah. Baxter left, Cow Chip right."

"Cow Chip. On the right. Yes. I'll remember," Mariah said. She hugged her brother good-bye.

"I'll see you in a few days," he said.

Lura hugged him tight. The boy stepped back and thumbed his eyes. He put his hat on and scanned the circle of wagons and women. He looked as though he might propose another plan, consider staying with them. Lura could see the confusion, the compassion in his young face, that streak of white hair yellowed by the sun. She started to speak, but Mariah said it for her.

"You go on, Mattie. We're Schmidtkes too, remember? We'll keep going where we're pointed, and we'll meet up again."

"Lord willing," he said. Then he mounted up, and he and Joe Pepin headed west.

Mazy noticed the ache, how her shoulders, breast, and breathing pressed against her heart as heavily as stone. Her arm throbbed from the constant cracking of the whip, of pushing with her shoulder against the oxen when they moved too far right or left, of bending to check the wagon tongues and heavy iron chains that held the animals to the wagon. She hadn't realized how diligent one needed to be to keep them heading the right direction. Had Jeremy ever complained of it? But she couldn't let the knowledge penetrate her senses, scratch against the surface of her skin.

"Least we ain't got the sun in our eyes in the afternoon," Elizabeth said. "Feel sorry for them boys having to head back into it."

"We haven't come all that far today," Mazy said. She checked the odometer on the wheel. "Only ten point five miles once we got turned around. We'll do better tomorrow."

"Assuming we don't have a tongue break or lose an ox," Elizabeth said. "And we find decent grazing."

That first night headed east, they'd circled the wagons not for protection from any kind of threat but to contain the oxen, the Bacons' cows, the one or two riding stock they trailed, and the Wilsons' mules. The antelope trailed around bumping its nose without invitation into pots until Pig barked at it, sending it scurrying under a wagon.

"You just tie him up," Adora told Elizabeth from across the circle. "He's worse than a dog."

"We don't have enough dogs," Elizabeth said. "Can't have enough. Good for guarding, good for fun."

"If food is ever short, I do suppose they can be eaten," Adora said. She bent back to lift the water bucket off the side of the wagon. Elizabeth opened her mouth to speak, but at that moment Adora spilled the bucket of water down the front of her dress.

"Oh no," Adora wailed. "Now we'll have to drink that alkali tasting stuff. This was such good water too."

Something about her wet dress, the fatigue of the day, the strain of Hathaway's death, all the deaths, even Tipton's empty distance—all of it came together, flooding her as the bucket had surely soaked her dress. She looked down at her feet. They were drenched too, her last pair of shoes without holes in them. It was too much, all too much. Adora leaned her head against the wagon and wept.

Elizabeth waited a moment for Tipton to hear her mother crying, to go and comfort her. When she didn't, Elizabeth finished tying Fip to the wheel and walked over to Adora. She touched her back. "These first days are always tough."

Adora turned to the comfort offered and sobbed, the cries of a woman lost, a woman coming to terms with herself as a widow.

"It's like my arm's been cut off, a side of my heart ripped out." Adora dried her face on her apron, touched its wetness, and let it drop. "I must have thought of him fifty times today, wondering what he wanted for supper, had he tightened that hitch he said needed it, how far did he think we'd come. Each time stopping myself. He's gone. Hathaway is gone." She dabbed at her eyes. "Not that I listened to him all the time. No, I surely did not. But I needed to hear what *he* said to know what I wanted."

She shook her head, wiped her eyes. Elizabeth patted her back.

"Did I tell you that once he told me he thought we should hire someone to make up women's clothes to sell, the way we had men's available in the mercantile. I told him no woman would want to come into a store and buy something not made just for her. A ridiculous thing. I talked him out of it. I didn't even have an opinion about it until he brought up his." She hiccuped from the crying and gathering air.

"I'm sure he knew that about you," Elizabeth offered. "Loved you for it."

"It wasn't endearing to him, I'm sure of that." She took in a deep breath, looked at Elizabeth now. "I feel like a paddlewheel hitting a rock and stopping every time it turns."

"Hard to make progress with that kind of bumping."

"Isn't it."

"You're movin' through it."

"Moving but not well, if truth be known. Hathaway didn't want to come, you know? He liked the mercantile. He had plans for Charles there, he did. Charles was so impatient, always. Troubling, if truth be known. Charles was right to be fussed with me." She wiped at her nose with the edge of her apron again. "Oh, this thing is all wet. I'm getting you all wet!" She dropped her hands and stepped back as though burned, looked at the wet stain against Elizabeth's apron. The observation began a new wail of tears, her hands pressed against her temples. "I can't seem to do anything that doesn't hurt someone else. Maybe if we had put our foot down with Tipton earlier, she wouldn't have turned so headstrong. Maybe she wouldn't have run off after all. But I knew she planned to. That wasn't just a threat. Do you think it was?"

"Your daughter is a strong-willed one."

"Not a bad quality, though," she defended. "My family has it. But if she'd been a little less so, maybe we wouldn't have come, Hathaway wouldn't have…nor Charles. Could we have avoided it all, Elizabeth? You knew Hathaway some, and you know my Tipton. Did I tell you that people often thought of us as sisters? Sisters! Oh, that child. What am I to do?"

"I don't know, Adora."

Elizabeth knew it would be useless to try to tell her what to do. The best consolation came from faith and friends, but only when one was ready to let that loving in. Once opened up for healing, a person could mine the past until the rich, sustaining ore was found. All in good time. Tonight, Elizabeth simply listened to the telling of the stories that would unearth where Adora had been, tell who she might become.

Elizabeth held her, let her cry, gave her the food of being present, the sustenance of love.

coming to their senses

She should eat but she wasn't hungry. Mazy couldn't remember if lack of appetite was a sign of cholera, or if Jeremy's first sign had been fatigue. Had he drunk something he shouldn't have? Eaten something? Was it in the air floating and settling on them like the ever-present dust? They had no protection except to get out of its way. That's what they were doing, heading back, away.

"Sarah complained some of stomach cramps today," Ruth told her as they set in for the night. "She's some better this evening."

"Clayton's recovered too," Mazy said. "Children are more resilient than their elders. And so few women have died. The grave markers we've seen with names are mostly men, a few babies. Losing a baby would be even harder way out here."

"Wouldn't it," Ruth said. She had a tone in her voice that raised a question in Mazy's mind, but Ruth walked on, and the moment to wonder passed.

Mazy pulled a high-back chair from its side board hook. She sat, lifted her feet, rested them on the wooden spokes of the wagon. The position took the pressure off her legs. She would sit here for a time, then milk the cows and turn in. She would go to bed without Jeremy, again, turn over and feel the cool, empty space beside her. She shook her head to toss away the image. A surge of air cooled her hot face.

"I fixed us some dried beef and beans," her mother said, coming up behind her. "Best you keep your energy up. Here. Brought some bread, too."

Mazy took the wooden bowl handed her, too tired to resist. She soaked the bread in the juice and sucked at it. She ate more for the baby than because hunger called. She hadn't been hungry since Jeremy became ill. Had that only been two days before? How could so much happen in so short a time?

"Have you seen Pig?" Mazy asked, looking about. "I know he was here earlier."

"Off with Suzanne, " Elizabeth said. She nodded with her firm, square chin toward the Cullver wagon. "Seems to have taken a liking to her."

"I'm to travel on alone, it seems."

"Dog has your eye for the needy," she said. "Besides, you got lots of human company," Elizabeth said, "if you want it." Her mother squeezed Mazy's shoulder, and she winced.

"What's wrong, Madison?"

"Just sore," she said. "I'm fine. I'll be fine."

Mazy lowered her face to her mother's callused fingers still resting on her shoulder. The roughness felt good against her aching skin. Elizabeth stroked her daughter's face as though she were a baby.

"I'm tired enough tonight that nothing matters," Mazy said, breaking her vow to not complain.

"Suspect it's not the journey," Elizabeth told her. "Being wore out seems to fester in the missing places. It's temporary, though."

Without interruption from Mazy, her mother chattered on about the mosquitoes and what they fed on when people and stock didn't wander by. She commented on the pink of the sunset and how fortunate they were to find fuel for the fires without having to walk far for it. Mazy wondered where her mother got her verve, her curiosity about things, her appetite for gratitude dressed in the ordinary life.

"Don't you miss him?" Mazy asked.

Elizabeth stopped midsentence. "Of course I miss the man," she said. "The others too, but Jeremy for sure. He was kin, after all."

"You seem so…accepting of everything that's happened."

"Can't do much else."

"You could grieve his going."

Elizabeth was thoughtful. "Yes," she said. "And I am. I'll remember his ways, what he wanted for you and his child, his letting me come along, letting me be closer to you and that grandbaby. But I'm a sober soul and won't pretend to feel what I don't. Jeremy didn't easily warm to people. He was more practical than that, I'd say. Always worried me a bit about the two of you."

"Jeremy loved me," Mazy said.

"Not protesting that. Just always thought you was needing someone who was more cherishing, who'd bring out the passion and kindness of your heart, someone who'd make you feel at home no matter where you was. A friend, kind of."

"We were close, Mother."

Elizabeth sucked on her piece of bread and stared at her daughter for a time before saying anything more. "Hate to see you be one of them people who in death pretends everything was dandy in life when it wasn't. Wouldn't take away from the person to be honest with yourself," she said.

"Aren't you always saying people grieve in their own way?"

Elizabeth nodded. "Some folks get mad, or go mad; others go so deep inside we never see 'em again. Don't go to those places, Mazy, please. For me, I just try to keep the person in a corner of my heart and make them comfortable there, call on them now and then. Try to be honest with them in death as I was in livin'. Doesn't mean I don't mourn them. Sorrow doesn't look the same to everyone."

Elizabeth had taken bites in between her words, and now her bowl, too, was empty. Mazy looked at the lines in her mother's face, the tiny crow's-feet that flowed out from her eyes, the deeper impressions that bordered her mouth. Where had she acquired that warmth and composure? *Wisdom wears a dog's face,* she thought. *One of acceptance, selfless generosity.* What had happened to make her mother, like the surface of the lake on a quiet summer afternoon, carry that calmness that ran deep and threatened no great turmoil beneath?

"Why don't you just take some time tonight to write in your book?" Elizabeth suggested. "Might soothe you."

"I doubt I'll be doing that anytime soon."

"You always got enthusiasm from your writing," Elizabeth said, surprise in her voice.

"I'm done with that," Mazy said.

"Now that does grieve me," Elizabeth said. "That you've chosen not to let your gift and faith feed your soul. Let grieving change you in a good way. It's—"

"What's he barking about?" Mazy asked, turning to the sound of the dog. "I don't see him half the day, and then he shows up troubled."

Her eyes found Pig, nose pointed beneath the Cullver wagon where Clayton sat. The child wailed, and Pig's tail stood up in warning.

~

Away from the activities of the women, Ruth brushed Koda. Hand over hand, she brushed, the rhythm familiar and comforting. Here at least with the smell of hay, manure, and cooling horse, her life made sense.

Everything else did not. Matt Schmidtke was young and inexperienced even with Joe Pepin riding beside him. They were honest enough, but Charles was a question. It'd be like him to lay back, join up with them. He didn't seem the kind to want to be too far from places where he could take advantage. She wished she'd gone with them. Why hadn't she pushed Betha harder to go forward? You couldn't ever put the past behind if you kept turning back to it. Ruth knew about that; her life was written in afflicted ink.

She hadn't thought that six years ago. She was happier than she believed possible then, happier than she deserved. She brushed Koda, remembering how the horses had nurtured her then, too. She should have known it wouldn't last. Happiness flitted into her life like a hummingbird, startling and bright and tasting of succulence just before it flew away. Her two-year engagement to a young banker originally from Indiana was about to end—joyously, with the wedding of the summer.

They'd met while Ruth worked as a lithographer at the Columbus paper, taking the drawings the men brought in of fires and celebrations and such, and engraving them backwards onto the limestone plates with detail so precise her skills were often asked for, so the designs could be printed perfectly against the paper. It was a gift not many had, and she took pride in the accomplishment, though in the West she'd never use it. It would make her too easy for Zane to find, even with her last name now changed. And he must never find her.

❧

Tipton lay on her mother's bed, her eyes staring at the canvas canopy overhead. What had awoken her? She tried to judge the time, how long she'd been inside this cluttered space. Her mother must have saved everything from carpet tacks to balls of string to crock jars full of buttons. Her collection of "things" left little room to even stand. What had awoken her?

Maybe she'd heard Zilah about outside. Tipton thought herself a genius for soliciting the Celestial to drive her wagon. It was true the Asian had been sick, but she looked recovered. And she spent her days kneeling in the Sister's wagon in that way they all had, or quickstepping beside it with no real purpose that Tipton could see. Oh, they held the strings on the chickens' legs, let them pluck at bugs for a time each day before placing them back in their cages, but that was a mindless task, one that took little effort.

Someone shouted again, but it sounded far away. Tipton thought it a fine bargain she'd struck, if she could just remember what she'd promised the girl for handling the mules. Something to do with making her a pandowdy, that was it! It was reassuring that the girl could be gotten to through her stomach.

Tipton turned to her side. The effort of remembering made her head ache. It throbbed at her temples and she itched. She could smell herself. Not pleasant. The wheels had hit a hundred rocks during the day, each one thumping her head into the board. Her head throbbed now, though the wagon wasn't moving. Any minute she would rouse herself, use the chamber pot and slop it. Yes, any minute. As soon as the dog stopped barking, that would be her sign. Or she heard a child laugh, yes, that would be the signal to stir—unless she could get that girl to slop the pot. Perhaps offer her walnuts.

The thought of food made Tipton wonder when she'd eaten last. Was she hungry for one of Betha's pies? No, no craving for food. It would make her fat, the food would. She must not get fat, but she couldn't remember why. Something gnawed inside her, something just below her heart.

She shivered and rolled over, her hand slipping under the pillow to pull it to her face, to muffle the longing and the canyon of ache. Her fingers touched the cool bottle. She pulled them back as though burned. No, she needed to save it for when they were ill, when any of them were sick. She rolled back over, her hands knotted like a crone's over her stomach. She stared up at the mottled canvas arched over her. Her breathing shifted, she had trouble taking in air. She heard the cool of the laudanum calling her name, and she answered.

~⊱~

Ruth finished with Koda, hobbled him, then began brushing Jumper. The stallion nickered. "Yes, you're my friend," she said. "Horses are more reliable than men." Men like Z. D. Randolph had taught her that. Back in Ohio, he'd breezed through the door, ducking his head as he came through, the bell jingling above the jamb, black cape and cane swinging out from his vested black suit. A sweet scent of his cologne drifted into the cavernous space known for its odor of oil, wet paper, and ink. Somehow, he filled the room, made everything else fade away.

She'd looked up from her work, to see what the freshness was and the cause of the bell and the breeze swirling the scents, and stared into the brown eyes of the man she would marry.

"I am in awe," he said, "to find great beauty in such an unlikely place." Ruth blushed. "I'm seeking a lithographer to characterize Columbus," he said. "I've people in St. Louis I'm wishing to send it to. Do you know of someone?"

"I have family there," Ruth said. "And I do lithograph work." He cocked his head to the side and wore a half grin that made his sculpted face all the more intriguing.

"Do you? Well, now, you'll know precisely what I need to make my family wish to join me." He nodded at the limestone bar she held firmly in one palm, her fingers holding the engraving knife in the other. "Such lovely hands," he said, "ought to be holding more than stone."

"A wise woman holds on to what she needs to," Ruth said.

He arched a thick eyebrow. "Again, I stand in awe," he said, revealing a single dimple when his mouth slid into a smile. He removed his dark hat, reached out his hand. She set the limestone down, touched his hand, and shook it. Her action interrupted his lips on their way to the back of her palm, but he smiled, squeezed her palm like a man's handshake. "I like that," he said.

They began a long and leisurely courting, of strolls and picnics and attendance at the theater. He bought her small gifts, then more extravagant ones. It pleased Zane to see earrings dangling from her ears, necklaces sparkling against her olive skin. She asked him once not to spend so freely on her, tried to tell him her tastes were simple ones.

He'd frowned like a boy told he had to put his toy up for the night.

She shouldn't be so direct, she decided. She didn't really mind making small adjustments in what she packed for picnics or wearing the jewelry he sent that was not fully to her liking.

He told her of his family, his banking interests. She told him of her love of horses, her joy in practicing with a whip. He'd frowned, but just slightly. She'd noticed, though, and didn't mention those subjects—and many others—that mattered to her, again.

"That was my downfall, Koda," Ruth said, finishing. "I gave myself up for someone else. Never again," she told the horse. Koda hobbled over at the sound of her voice, pulled at the kerchief tucked at her waist. "Except this short turnaround for Betha," she said. "And the children."

⚒

Pig's barking brought them all. Sister Esther, Naomi, Deborah, Lura, Mariah, and Zilah were walking slowly back toward the circle of wagons, having completed their necessary time together. When they heard the child wail, the dog bark, and Suzanne's yelp for help, they picked up their pace.

"Clayton's there," Sister Esther said, able to see better than the other, shorter women. The S sizzled in her teeth. She pointed. "Beneath the wagon."

They hoisted up their skirts and stepped through the grass and small yellow flowers that sprinkled the ground like sparse confetti.

"What is it? Clayton?" Suzanne said, her chin up, her neck stretched out like a chicken's, hands flailing before her. The rope, she felt for it at her waist. There was no resistance—he'd come untied. She had gotten down from the wagon box, her hands swinging in a wide arc in front of her as though washing off a lengthy table pushed heavily before her. Where was that goading stick Naomi used for the oxen? "Clayton? Where are you? What's wrong?"

~

Mazy roused at Pig's bark. Stung from her grogginess, she took long strides toward the boy, watched the child start to stand as though to wobble toward his mother's voice when Pig's *gruff-gruff* bark grew louder, more insistent, hair standing up at his neck. Mazy suddenly understood and shouted, stern and sharp. "Clayton! Suzanne! Stop! Tell him not to move!"

"What is it? What do you see?" Suzanne said.

"Rattler, between Pig and your boy."

Mazy heard her mother run up beside her. "Get me a hay fork," Mazy told her. "Just stay, Clayton. We'll play a game. Just sit now. Tell him to sit, Suzanne."

Elizabeth jerked at the fork attached to Betha's wagon. She was joined by Sister Esther and the others.

Behind her, Mazy heard a small wail. She looked to see Mariah, fist to her mouth, her eyes wide. "Kill it! Kill it!" she said.

"Sit still, Clayton," Mazy ordered, turning back. "Your mama's here. Sit still, now." Mazy stretched the fork out toward the snake. "He's paying more attention to the dog than Clayton at this moment. Pig, don't get too close."

She jabbed at the reptile, the buzz of its rattles zinging in the dusk. It struck at the fork, slithered past to the left, coiled again. "Soon as it's out of striking range, Mother, grab the boy."

The snake swayed its head like a compass needle. Mazy jabbed and poked again, then heard the sting of a whip snap past her head. It connected between her and Pig, the lick of the leather beheading the snake.

Mazy turned to see Ruth a step behind her, turned back to see her mother grab the child and hand him to Suzanne, who smothered him in kisses. The snake's body continued to wind back and forth in the flattened grass.

"He don't know he's dead yet," Elizabeth said.

"We need to bury the head," Ruth said. "Keep the yellow jackets from feasting. Make their stinging worse."

"Don't want no one stepping on it either," Ned said, still agog.

"It could poison ya even after it's dead?" Sarah asked. She held Jessie's hand tight.

Ruth nodded. "Should beat around the grass good before we turn in, try to discourage as many others as we can."

"I can't stand them, I just can't," Mariah repeated. "Snakes and spiders." She shivered. "Spiders most."

"Provides a little something extra for dinner," Elizabeth said.

Mazy rubbed at the dog's ears. Pig still barked at the slithering snake but not as loud or with as much aggression. "It's all right," Mazy said. "Good job, Pig."

"Thank you," Suzanne said, her chin resting on her child's head. "To whichever of you. I couldn't see. The dog…I'm just not able to look after Clayton." She shook her head, brushed at tears, rubbing against her cheek.

"There, there," Betha said. "Toddlers are hard to keep track of for everyone."

"Look how long it is," Mariah said. With the fork, Mazy lifted the form from beneath the wagon and turned toward the fire with it while Ruth dug a hole with her heel and pushed the head in with her boot. "We aren't really going to eat it, are we?"

"Enough there for each to have a taste," Elizabeth said.

"How would we fix it?" Lura asked.

"Ma!"

"The way you want to eat rattlesnake," Elizabeth said, "is to be real hungry. You don't want to have breakfast or nooning, not eat all day long on a day you're going to have rattler for supper."

"I believe we can forgo that delicacy, then," Sister Esther said, tying and retying the black ribbon at her throat. "Seeing as how the Lord has provided us with two meals already this day."

The women decided to sleep inside wagons that evening, instead of set-ting up tents. Perhaps they were all as tired as she was, Mazy thought, and it was easier to sink into the cornhusks in the narrow wagons than it was to set the tents and then wonder through the night if they'd be waking in the morning with a snake beside their heads. Mazy heard sounds outside by the low fire. She guessed Sister Esther hadn't yet turned in.

Tired as she was, Mazy hadn't slept. She allowed her mind to chew once again on the day. She had to make everything go without a hitch, be responsible for the ease of their turnaround. They'd have to find some way to keep closer watch on Clayton, assign someone to watch him all the time. Then she thought of the old sleighbells in her mother's wagon—she could attach them to the boy's shoes. That would help.

Had it been her imagination, or had Suzanne been less like a wasp? No, Mazy just hadn't been tending to her; her mother had. She needed to change that. She must think of a task for Suzanne, something valued, not just meant to keep her occupied. She knew little of Suzanne's inter-ests except for the sewing machine she'd seen. The Cullvers had musical instruments along, but she'd only seen Bryce play the violin. A stack of muslin and what looked like carpeting rolled into a cylinder were snugged along the wagon's sidewalls. Mazy had tripped over them a dozen times while looking after Suzanne when she'd been so ill. She wondered how it was Suzanne didn't stumble on them.

Sister Esther coughed. Mazy imagined her beside the fire, writing.

Mazy tossed again, pounded the feather pillow. She should write of that, write down what she experienced in this place so foreign without her husband now, without any sense that God still walked beside her. Her mind, her body, her emotions, her life of prayer were all disrupted. Writing gave her words to frame the feelings that tumbled and tossed, bumped against memory and mourning, wondering and will. The act of putting lead to paper by itself had comforted even before she focused on the words of praise, placed prayer notes on the pages. But no more.

She couldn't bring herself to write, to use it as a healing gift. For that would mean she'd have to think of prayer, and prayer was lost, as lost as Jeremy. What was the feeling? She wasn't sure. Confusion? No, betrayal. Not from Jeremy; he was mortal, after all, someone entitled to human error. But God permitted this to happen, allowed the deaths and disappointments. What part of perfection required such disasters? What part of her had failed in prayer? She didn't know, and now she could not ask.

She just wanted to be refreshed, to start over again without losing her place.

Sister Esther began singing, the low song they had sung at the gravesite.

"O Beulah Land, sweet Beulah Land!
As on thy highest mount I stand,
I look away across the sea
Where mansions are prepared for me,
And view the shining glory shore—
My heav'n, my home, forevermore."

Home. The thought of it pulled at Mazy. Home held her happiness, it always had. Happiness settled on some pleasant place, now lost. Tears pooled at her eyes. She blinked them away.

Ruth lay on the ground near the stock. She stared up at the stars, so grateful nothing had happened to Clayton. Children were precious, treasured, and fragile. Her own loss came back to her. She sighed. She'd pulled blinders on herself, the same kind she used with the horses to keep them from becoming distracted.

What began with Zane as a courtship of joy had moved into pauses: pauses in her conversations, pauses that drifted in like flotsam on the

Ohio River after a summer storm. Pauses she avoided acknowledging. She hadn't wanted to see the bursts of temper her fiancé displayed with a dog who chewed on his shoe or with a green-broke horse that failed to respond to the quick confusion of the big man's instruction.

"He's just a fervent man—intense," was how she responded to her father's concern. "He's just nervous about the wedding, the responsibilities," Ruth told him and believed it herself.

"There's something not right there, Ruth. You're deceiving yourself," her father said. "Yes, yes, he can keep you in good stead financially. But that's not all there is in a marriage. Little of it, to be exact. Will he be kind, fair, just? Can he be counted on? Those are the questions worth asking."

It was the first of many insights she discounted from those she loved.

She'd planned for Zane's family and her brother, Jed, and his wife, Betha, and their children to arrive for the ceremony; the rush of wedding plans would pass and then all would be well with her and her new husband.

Ruth's family arrived. "My parents send their regrets," Zane told her. "Illness. My father's sister. They extend their blessing."

So Zane and Ruth did marry, but all was not well.

When the babies came, then it would be better, when they were settled in, she told herself.

She'd been careful not to voice her worries, not with anyone at all, and when they rose as troubling thoughts and not just anxious irritations, she rubbed them out as carefully as she used the abrasive to correct drawing errors made on the expensive limestone plates. In fact, she no longer drew the pictures that illustrated the news accounts of fires or celebrations. Z. D. Randolph suggested she find other pursuits for such pretty hands.

"It reflects on me, Ruth, that you're not happy as my wife."

"But I am happy. I love the lithography."

"Others don't understand," he said. "And being with all those men all day, you might find someone more enchanting." He'd grinned, and she'd been charmed at his insecurity.

Never mind that her days dragged without human bond. Never mind that Zane worked long hours and couldn't often be with her. Never mind that she saw more of the stablehand and housemaids than her husband. When she told him she carried his child, all that changed. His attention to her was complete. "I'm in awe," he said, rubbing his hands across her abdomen. "And I created it." He relished her, savored her, spoke of her beauty, her grace as a mother-to-be. Then the babies had come. Twins. Ruth turned over and looked at the stars, blinked back the tears of remembrance.

It was afterward that Ruth indulged her love for horses, found them safe and willing listeners. Their discretion unimpeachable, their constancy never failing.

Koda stomped close to her. She heard Jumper nicker and was glad she'd kept the two back. Horses. They'd kept her from insanity after the twins were born. After she came too late to her senses and slept through her young son's death.

❦

The hitching up in the morning took four hours. Tempers and time tangled, and midmorning arrived before the wagons began lumbering east. Two parties heading west had already passed by them on the trail while the women struggled with the heavy neck yokes, moving oxen into place and then losing one or two, having to bring them back into the lumbering arc. The animals stomped impatiently; tails swatted at flies as the women took so long to hook the braces shaped liked a smoothed-out letter *U*. Help was offered and they'd accepted it, but then those in the westward parties moved on.

In the past, the women had helped husbands or sons, but the men had always assumed the lead, been the ones to give the orders, anticipate the difficulties with the animals or tack.

Adora felt a flash of anger at her husband for having left her. How dare he die and leave her here with these beasts and bugs! She pushed the thought away to concentrate on the mules.

She and Tipton had the only wagons pulled by mules. They were sturdy and made better time than the oxen, which was how she, Hathaway, and Charles had caught up with Tipton and Tyrell. A pang of guilt punched her stomach. Adora grabbed herself and rocked a bit, closing her eyes. She was not a strong person. Others thought she was, but they did not know she played a part. She had always had a leading man to play against; standing alone on life's stage made her feel exposed, as if she were undressing in front of a night candle.

The mid-June morning hung hot and humid, and with the extra effort of harnessing, sweat dribbled down the inside of Adora's corset, dampened her chemise, and wet the drawstrings of her drawers. She dabbed at her forehead with her apron, took a deep breath, then stuck her head in the back of her daughter's wagon.

"Tipton, you have got to get up here and help. I can't do this all alone. Zilah is just too inept."

"I lift harness, Missy Adora," the girl said, straightening her pointed bamboo hat.

"Yes, you're doing your best, but we need extra hands. To hold the mules steady until we get everything settled. Tipton!"

"I'll be there, Mother." Her daughter's voice sounded dreamy and soft.

"She's had a terrible time, losing two she loved so," Adora said, then clucked at herself for explaining anything personal to this foreign child. "Perhaps you could drive that wagon again today? I can pay you."

"In pandowdy like Missy Tipton say, or coin?" Zilah asked.

"Why, whichever one you prefer."

❧

Suzanne held her son close while she listened to the grunts and heavy breathing of Naomi working beside Mazy to lift the yokes onto Breeze and Blow. She could hear the clank of wood, the creak of wheels and wagon tongue as all got pulled together and held by smoothed leather.

She could smell everything, hear everything, even imagine how it would feel to touch the leather, the cold, forged rings that kept the oxen attached to the tongue. These were all familiar things, things she'd known, had seen through clear and studied eyes. Bryce had been her guide. He'd described life to her, wind in a hawk's wing, the Missouri River, the look of red bloomers. He used references to objects and events, sights and sounds that she had known before. That was a rare gift in a person, to take something unique and unusual and give it depth and texture for someone who had never been there, never visited in that place. It took away the fear.

She heard the bells jingle on Clayton's feet. She tugged on the rope. He was close. Still, fear wormed back. Even worse were the other feelings that fluttered to the surface, those old songs of incompetence that Bryce had silenced were now given new voice.

"Anger usually isn't the real emotion," Bryce told her after she'd screamed at him about something. "It comes...it's second, I think. First...there is something else...a loss, some feeling of incompetence. A harsh judgment...we make about ourselves. The loss is too much to bear so we...skip over it...go directly to...outrage."

"Such a philosopher," she had spit at him. "One who stutters."

But she had remembered what he said and considered it. So much loss pushed her into anger. And here she sat, while others did her work, chords of unworthiness clanging against the dark.

That's what she was—unworthy. She had been since the day she'd spilled the mercuric chloride in the developing room, had sloshed, slipping and falling, the liquid splashing into her eyes. It had startled her more than pained her at first, then stung. It was useful as an antiseptic, she had heard, so she didn't expect it to really harm. But she couldn't see through it, couldn't find water to rinse her eyes. She expected no one to hear her shouting. She and the baby were alone in their studio, Bryce having gone out to photograph funeral flowers.

Funeral flowers. How ironic. She had photographed and developed hundreds of them for the fine people of Cape Girardeau, but none for her own husband's death.

At Bryce's funeral, she'd been led by someone she barely knew, told where to stand so as not to slip inside the hollow, and laid yellow larkspurs on his body, taking someone else's word that those were what she held.

She remembered holding Bryce alive, the smell of soap, the way his beard cradled the scent of sweet mown hay in the summer, the warmth of his hands as he held her face within them then bent to kiss her lips. When had he kissed her last? She couldn't remember. A deep sob reached up to choke her.

"Mama sad?" Clayton said, touching his soft hand to her cheek.

"I'm fine," she said, taking him into her arms, burying her face in his sweet-smelling hair. She could hold her child, but she could not protect him. She could give him half a family, half a life. But he would be better off with someone else, someone sighted. So would this baby that moved inside her now.

"I think we're ready," Mazy said. She stuck her head into the back of the wagon. "I'm sorry it's taken so long. You and the Wilsons were last to hitch, but we'll move out now. Naomi's going to follow Mother. Maybe later in the week, your wagon can lead. We'll rotate, as we did before, but include Ruth now."

"Ruth wasn't in the line before?"

"Because she was a woman and had no teamster with her or male driver, Antone insisted she stay back. Now here we all are, just women looking after each other."

"I failed to thank you for your help with Clayton and that snake. I'll do my best to keep Clayton occupied. You have things to do."

"I've had some thoughts, if you really want to be more independent."

Suzanne stayed silent, not sure why.

"But that can wait," Mazy said. "Until after we reach the graves."

She couldn't see what Mazy did, just heard her labored breathing.

Before her losses, Suzanne would have asked after the woman's health, said something about what they now shared. But there was no sense in forming up friendships that required the dance of give and take. All Suzanne had on her dance card now spelled *take*. Who would want to partner up with that?

※

Tipton wondered what day it was. Had she eaten? What was the rub of pain against her hip? Her mouth tasted like the bottom of the hen's cage. She wondered if she should get up. Disappearing would take time, time that kept reminding her of Tyrell's death, of her being alone and unworthy to live. She pulled silver hair combs from the knot of tangled hair. Chunks of blond came with it. It did not matter. Nothing did, or ever would again.

※

As they approached the terrain that meant they'd soon come upon the graves, Mazy felt each woman tending to the tightness of her own wounds. They'd met westbound wagons, and sometimes those they encountered already knew of the reason for their silence, having greeted others heading east who carried the message that behind them came a widow's party of eleven wagons.

How incongruous, Mazy thought, that the words *widow* and *party* should be found in the same sentence.

Sometimes, the westward wagons they met pulled aside, left the trail to let them pass, and Mazy could tell by the looks on their faces that they knew. Westward travelers dropped their eyes when they caught the gaze of Mazy or Elizabeth, stared at the blank face and dark glasses of Suzanne or the still-tear-streaked face of Betha, who was walking stoop-shouldered, her calico cap with wide ruffle sagging in the heat. It was as if to look these turnaround women in the eye would somehow mark those heading west as casualties too, curse the hopes and dreams they left home for, make a mockery of the risk they'd already taken by leaving all they knew.

Mazy wanted to stop and shake their shoulders, shout at them that turning back was no evidence of error. Nothing criminal lived in starting out, then later, coming to one's senses, throwing off the harness of routine and turning back. Hadn't hundreds of forty-niners been turnarounds? Hadn't a stagecoach passed them by just a day before carrying people to the east as well as letters any might send? Lewis and Clark had come back home; they hadn't chosen to stay in lands that lacked the boundaries of familiar.

These women had no reason to apologize for traveling an eastward trail. Mazy wanted to scream it at those west-facing souls who stood there, allowing them to pass, their faces reflecting the sorrow the women carried in their wagons.

A man, no, rather a boy who said his name was Ezra Meeker had looked almost stricken with disease himself as they wove their way through that group of wagons. He'd introduced himself, asked if there was any way he could help.

"No," Mazy told him. "We'll be fine, just fine."

What could he offer? A young woman who must have been his wife held an infant to her breast. She cooed at the baby, lifted her hand over its face to shield it from the sun and the dust kicked up by their wagons.

Perhaps, Mazy supposed, she chose to shield the child from even the look of them, protecting her baby from having to view the grimness of their faces, lest he come too early to recognize the other side of hope.

sudden rush

They stopped when they sighted the hills that overlooked the graves. The grass proved inferior, and they drove a distance off the trail, ending up at the base of a ravine that made a perfect *V* between two treeless mounds. They carried water to the oxen and mules before unhitching, which put them late again into unharnessing.

"I'll take the riding stock down to the river to water," Ruth offered. She walked toward the animals, passed almost by Betha's wagon, her mind on Koda, when she heard sounds beside her.

"I wanna go along," Jessie said.

Ruth paused. "What do you think, Betha?"

"It'll be dark before you get back," Betha said. "And you're bound to get dirty. I don't know." Betha's head shifted from left to right like a chicken's pecking and stretching. Had it always done that or was this something new? Ruth wondered.

"Auntie Ruth will watch me. And I'll stay very, very clean."

"Yes, that's true, but…"

"Can't we all go?" Ned asked. "A fellow'd like to go to the river." He looked around. "This place looks like a river ran right through it once, right out of those hills."

Ruth looked in the direction the boy pointed. "Just a dry ravine," she said.

"Don't let nobody go but me," Jessie said. Her lower lip pouted out.

"She always gets to. You let her ride Koda when Papa died, and—"

"Now, Ned," his mother said and patted his head. "You and Jason are the men in the family now. Ruth'll have her hands full with more than one along." She sighed. "I need to cut your hair anyway. Getting so it turns up at your collar."

Jessie grabbed Ruth's hand and skipped, her brown curls bouncing.

Behind them, they heard a ruckus. Ruth thought it might be Ned kicking up a fuss and decided she could just as well take the boy. But when she turned, she saw Fip being chased by Pig and Clayton. Antelope, children, and dogs toppled the iron bracket that held Betha's, Ruth's, and the children's supper.

"You catch that thing," Betha shouted. "Go along, Ned. You help, Jason. You boys wanted something to do. Grab that overgrown goat, and we might just eat it for supper."

Ruth turned back, shortened her stride to allow Jessie to keep up. "You've got to stay off to the side," Ruth told the child, "where you can see me, but out of the way in case one of the mules decides to jump ahead. I don't want you to get hurt."

"I know," she said. "I know everything, Auntie." She looked up at her with eyes so wise. Ruth swallowed

"About horses and mules and all such things?"

"That too. But I know 'bout you."

The skin at Ruth's neck prickled. "I'm sure your papa and mama have talked about your auntie. I came from far away, in Ohio."

Jessie kicked at a rock, skipped backwards in front of Ruth and the animals she led. "I know things I 'member hearing. But Papa said I couldn't."

Ruth heard her own heart thud in her chest.

"Sometimes we dream things but they aren't real, Jessie," Ruth told her. She watched Jesse's eyes squint in concentration. Her little brow tensed, but the skin, so young and supple, did not furrow, so she looked distant more than troubled.

"It was like a dream, but different, Auntie," she decided after a pause. "And Papa said I could only know if I had been there. Want me to tell you?"

"No!" Then more gentle, "I'm sure it was a dream, and I don't wish to honor such fragmented thinking by listening to you recite it. Let's concentrate on the stock, Jessie, taking care of them."

This time Jesse's face did expose a pinch as she turned and stomped off toward the river.

❦

Elizabeth bent under the wagon, luring the antelope, her skirts hiked up so she could crawl. "Come on, now, you little thing. Let's get you outta there." She reached for the rope attached to the halter she'd had Ruth manufacture. Fip was slippery as an eel. Her fingers grazed the rope. She almost had him when something cold and wet butted against her backside. She jerked up, and when she did, she knocked herself cold beneath the wagon.

❦

Betha just wanted to be alone, to tidy up the area around the wagon and then to walk the distance to where she thought Jed's grave would be. "Why'd you have to leave me," she told him, "tending kids and cooking in a faraway place and you just hang up your hat! After all I did for you too."

"You talking to us, Ma?" Jason asked, looking back over his shoulder. His hair was slicked tight to his head, folded behind ears that stuck out from his head like open barn doors.

At least she had good children, Betha thought. At least he left her with fine, healthy children.

❦

Elizabeth came to in seconds, Mazy hovering over her. "Are you all right? I couldn't find a drop of anything, not smelling salts, nothing."

"Need something for the lump on my head," Elizabeth said, rubbing it as she sat in the dirt. "Ain't nothing to give me for my stupidity."

"Pig came by."

"Well, I know that. He's what knocked me out. Silly thing. Just surprised me."

"Ned caught Fip, and I've resettled the cauldron, cut up new potatoes, and added beans and water to the pot."

"Go lie down," her mother said. "I'll finish getting supper."

Mazy shook her head. "I'll eat something cold later if I feel like it. Otherwise in the morning. Sure you're all right?"

"Just give me some stew," Elizabeth said, standing. "Lucky Fip's not in it!"

∽

Mazy dozed inside the wagon, tossing and turning in the twisted sleep of discomfort and disillusion. She woke to a gush of wind that billowed out the canvas. She wondered if she should lower it, heard it settle down with a sigh. Sister Esther and her mother talked low outside.

"We have every reason to honor the Lord's day," Sister Esther said.

Mazy heard a wooden spoon clink against a tin cup and knew her mother had brewed tea and stirred honey in it. She could smell the sweetness.

The Sabbath? Which day was that? Had it been that long they'd traveled? Yes, tomorrow.

"Mazy's the one you'll have to ponder with over that, I imagine," Elizabeth said.

"And it does make one consider why your daughter is the one to establish rules," Sister Esther said.

"Nothing written says she does. You got something you itch to say, just say it. Call a meeting same as any."

"Well, I believe I'll do that, then," Sister Esther said. "Now that we have come this way, had some time to gather up our thoughts. But I believe it was wise to return to the graves."

Mazy smiled.

"And thus refreshed, we can turn again west. On Monday."

No! Mazy's mind reeled. They couldn't go west. They were going home. That's what Mazy needed to remind them of, the importance of going home. She should get up and tell the Sister now, not wait, tell her that home was where nurture lived, where strength thrived. Home was that place that fed the soul, healed the broken pieces of a life. Home was where she'd find what she was seeking, had been seeking when she passed it by to go with Jeremy.

Mazy started to get up but felt dizzy. She lay back down, trying to regain her equilibrium. It would have to wait. She would talk of it in the morning. She listened for the sounds of Ruth rejoining the circle, of the children quieting, of Adora calling loud for Tipton to please have something to eat. She smelled the tobacco smoke of Lura's pipe. They would all rest, yes. Tomorrow they would pray at the graves, and then she would convince them to go home.

❧

Disaster struck at dawn.

The shout woke Mazy, and she sat up, breathing hard. Who had yelled? What was it she heard? Wind howled and the wagon shook, but no human sounds broke through.

She decided it must have been inside her dream. Yes, she'd heard the words within her sleep. What was it? *You don't listen to me! You don't listen to me!* She'd been home in her dream, screaming those words at Jeremy. She leaned back into the pillow, recalling the detail, the fury in the words, the frustration.

The wagon shook, resisted a blast of wind.

He'd had his back to her in their bed, his face to the chinks of their cabin that had been tight and white in her dream. She'd shouted at him, crying in desperation to have him hear her, to know that she spoke, not to feign indifference. At least she hoped he pretended it, she prayed that his apathy hadn't been real.

He had not turned over. She willed herself to see movement in his shoulders, willed them to announce that Jeremy would be turning over so they could talk, so she could look into his eyes and know he loved and listened and lived. He had not moved.

In her dream she had shrieked at him, *You don't listen to me! You don't listen to me!* Then she woke, all sweaty and scared.

Her heart stopped pounding. It had been a dream. And what had she always found about her dreams, vivid and colorful as they were? That she always spoke to herself within them, regardless of who or what character called out. Sometimes objects had voices, sometimes it was a feeling that would stay after she woke, like the residue of milk on an unwashed mug.

"I must have shouted out loud," she said. "Woke myself up."

Mazy lay back down, pulled the quilt up to her chin. What wasn't she listening to? Who wasn't she listening to? Maybe this was about Jeremy after all. She'd been so frustrated with him, so angry when he failed to include her in his silences. She'd begged him to share her hopes; at times, she believed he had. They'd cleared trees and burned the stumps and made the place for her garden. She had loved the days they spent working side by side with the promise of something tangible waiting at the end.

She recalled a fallen tree near the garden plot; it held a swarm of bees. "You have to destroy it to get the honey out," Jeremy told her.

"There ought to be some way to leave their home intact," she told him.

"'Less you're willing to tear it up, you're stuck without honey."

"I'll wait, then," she said and plotted the garden so the bees would flourish beside it.

No, the voice wasn't about her and Jeremy. It had cried with too much desperation, a voice squelched for so long that it had screamed to make sure it could be heard at all.

It was her own voice. She wasn't listening to herself.

The skin at her ankles chafed, and she threw the covers back and reached for the glycerin to spread on them, to stop the itching that plagued her. Her face had broken out too with tiny bumps. Her mother said it was the pregnancy, that everything inside changed to make room for this new and ever-changing being. "It's what life's about, girl, all the change. Starts with the first seed planted. We live and breathe it our whole life through."

Mazy rubbed her ankles. The glycerin intensified the cold of the wagon box. It had been so hot yesterday as they traveled, but now the air harbored hidden snow.

She heard a horse neigh, a mule answer, and a blast of wind hit again, this time shaking the wagon. Something about the fierceness of it frightened her. She grabbed the side board, balancing herself against the blast of wind. Pig barked close outside. A pan tossed by the wind rattled and clanked against the wheel. She was about to get up and call Pig in, check the flaps to see if they were secured, when the first shower of hail pounded the canvas, ripping the top, shredding it in seconds. Ice pitted against her like rocks thrown by an army of bullies.

Mazy put one arm over her head, her elbow tight against her ear, the other arm over her stomach. She tried to remember in the darkness if she had anything hard she could put over her, a board from a table, a bureau drawer she could lift out and get under. Then she decided the wagon would be the safest spot. She should get under it.

She grabbed for a shawl and scrambled in the dark. Lightning lit the rubble around her. She started to cry out to her mother. The wind blasted and shook the wagon, which pitched as though at sea, lifted up on two wheels, paused for what seemed a lifetime, and then...the wagon dropped back. With a gust of wind so brutal it took her breath with it, the wagon rolled and pitched on over.

Esther heard the howling of the wind and then hard chunks of ice pitted against her skin. At first she thought the bees had somehow gotten free and were stinging, but they only did such things if the hive was threatened or if they'd been hurt. Had they been either? She looked for the lantern. Sleet struck the side of her head. For an instant, she floated. Something sticky as the propolis of the bees oozed beside her eyes.

"Missy Esther? Missy Esther?"

Esther moaned as the soft hands of Deborah pushed against her, the rough rub of the tiny callus of her fingers pressed against her arms.

"Go under wagon. Storm very bad!"

The girl tugged at Esther, who moved like thick batter on a sloped bowl while she let herself be lowered down the ladder. Cold rain and hail pounded their backs even as they knelt in the mud, hunched and shivering beneath the wagon box. The sound of the wind roared in her ears, roared like a storm she remembered as a child, huddled in a potato cellar with her brothers and parents.

"Move, Missy," Deborah said, pressing her knees against Esther. "Make room for friends."

Esther thought she heard the Bacons' cows mooing, maybe ol' Snoz with his high-pitched bellowing. She could hear the black dog barking. She didn't feel well. Her head throbbed like a drum. Deborah's paper! Where was it? She heard loud cracks of thunder. Voices shouted, and though the hours promised dawn, the night was as black and slimy as seaweed coughed up from the depths of sea.

"Ay-ee!" Naomi said, pushing Deborah closer to Esther. "Rain sting! Sky burn fire." White marbles of ice covered the ground around them.

In a flash of lightning, they watched one of the Schmidtkes' wagons tip and topple.

"Sister's God leave?" Deborah asked Esther.

"He already gone," Naomi answered.

~❧~

Ruth heard the sounds of Koda in distress before she realized her bedroll and clothing were soaked. The hail battered apart the end of her wagon's canvas, exposing the dresser that had been her mother's and the trunk that held the baby clothes that had been worn by her twins. Inside was something else, something that had once belonged to Zane. She had wondered why she'd bothered to bring it, but tonight it might prove useful.

She climbed to the wagon then flung open the trunk. She grabbed up the pair of men's pants with double rows of buttons and the heavy leather boots. Her fingers were cold, and the wet buttons resisted being pushed through the woolen, machine-made holes. She settled for two buttons on each side, stuffed a shirt beneath the wide waistband, pulled on his boots, and pushed the felt hat on her head. She'd packed a rubber slicker of Zane's too, packed way back in Ohio on a hot summer's night when everything that mattered had been stripped from her. The rubber might be hard and brittle now, but against this wind and rain, it could keep her from becoming chilled until she found Betha and the children.

Ruth jumped down, startled by the urgency of the wind. She splashed mud, her boots sunk almost to the tops. Had it rained that much? Hard enough that water rushed beneath the wagons as though they camped inside a stream? She steadied herself and reached for the lantern, but the wind and rain frustrated the lighting. Ruth so concentrated on finding light that she failed to hear the shifting sounds of oxen groaning from uncomfortable to fretted, working into rushed.

~❧~

"Tipton, wake up. Get dressed." Adora's voice grew frantic. "Right now. Please, get up!"

"Mother?" The girl's voice was dreamy with deep sleep.

"Can't you hear it? There's a terrible storm. The oxen, they'll push right through this ring of wagons, not a thing to stop them, and you can bet the mules will go with them unless we get out there and hold them back."

"It's windy?"

"What has become of you?" Adora shouted to her. "Where have you gone? Wake up!" Adora shook her daughter's shoulders again.

"That hurts!" Tipton's head lolled back, and for the first time, Adora let something unknown creep up her neck, enter at the base and tingle at her hair. *Dear God, what has happened to this child?* She pulled her daughter's soft-doll body to her, then wept for her daughter and for herself.

~

Clayton wailed. The buckets on the side of the wagon lifted and pounded against the wooden box with the gusts of wind that swallowed up the air between. Thunder made hearing him almost impossible. "Mommy's here," Suzanne shouted to him. "I'm here."

Thunder! She reached for her son, rubbed his wet arms and drenched nightshirt. His napkins were soaked both inside and out. "Mommy's wet too," she said, her hands feeling for a blanket that might not be saturated. Finding one, she wrapped the boy in it and laid him on the bed. She stood, raised her arms up over her head, waving them like a palm tree, for the moment unafraid of spiders or wasps or other unsuspected things that might drop from above. She shivered. So cold and so wet. Thunder. A flash? Or did she just remember one went with the other?

She searched the air with her fingers, seeking information. The canvas was intact though wet, so the soaking rain had to be coming in through the end opening. She felt Clayton moving out of the blanket

225

behind her. He would crawl to the wetter end of their bed unless she stopped him. She tore at the quilt, found the part that was dry and wrapped it around her son again, swaddled him, then held him close.

"Just a bad storm," she said, smelling the wetness on his hair, hearing the rain pelt down hard and some odd sound coming from outside.

⁓

Sister Esther prayed. She prayed that the storm would move on. She prayed that the wagons would stand upright. She prayed that death would pass by. And she prayed for courage for herself and for the others. She wanted to dwell on that which was worthy and of the Lord, but the howl of the wind pressed against her like a tree fallen on her chest.

It was weakness she perspired, feebleness her heart pounded, fear more forceful than her faith she breathed out into the air.

The life-changing storm when she was eight—this was like that one. They waited beside the squash and beets in her family's storm cellar, waited for the howling winds to pass. If their faith had been enough, wouldn't they have stayed inside the comfort of their beds, confident the Lord would protect? She tried to explore this thinking with her father, but he had silenced her, said she ought to pray, that was what they did inside the cellar, offered prayers of thanksgiving and praise.

But Esther defied her father that night—in the silence of her heart she prayed for safety, prayed that the storm would pass them without harm.

One of the huge trees uprooted and crashed across the cellar. It was her grandmother who had reached out to her, brought her close until the wind had stopped and the driving rain no longer pounded against the door. When the winds had hushed, they pushed against the wooden brace and the door opened to a crack large enough for Esther to crawl through, the branches of the fallen tree entombing the others with the potatoes.

Full of scratches and scrapes, Esther took in the devastation and destruction of the wind. Their house, gone; the roof of the barn, curled up at one end, exposing the rafters inside; trees now just circles of tangled roots.

"Run, get Brother Conrad," her father shouted through the crack. "Tell him to bring rope and mules to move the tree. Go now!"

And she had gone, racing through the dawn hours, slipping on the wet mud, crying as she ran the two or more miles to the Conrad farm. She brought back help and freed her family from the cellar, and she should have been so glad for what she'd done. But her disobedience, her prayers said not for praise and glory but for safety, spoken out of self-ishness instead of faith, they had caused her grandmother's last breaths.

Even now, as a wiser adult, the storm brought fresh regret. She was still not perfected in her faith, still harbored fear, and still prayed from that selfish place in her heart. Who knew what devastation she could bring?

⁓

Cattle bellowed and shifted. Suzanne's skin tingled though she could neither see nor touch them. But she heard them, felt their hooves move against the soggy ground. She smelled their fear. They thumped against the wagon tongue, bumped it, jerking it sideways. The wagon shifted. A throbbing came up through the floor, through her feet. The dampness smelled of mud and rain, manure. She thought again that she saw light. A terrible crack of thunder followed, another change in the darkness of her eyes, and then a low and thundering beat.

Oh, no, please, no! Should she leave, take Clayton…where? Get behind the heavy sewing machine? Bryce's camera? If it fell on them, what then? The harp, the boudrah drum, the violin? How could she protect them? No, think. Got to think. Stay inside or get out, get under?

Suzanne heard the dog bark, then felt his bulk enter the back of the wagon that shifted, not forward and back, but rocking on two wheels. "Pig, no," she said.

The dog didn't tug at her or push until she moved toward the opening to leave. Then she felt his body against her knees, his head pushing her back. She smelled his wetness. He almost tripped her—with his insistence that she stay.

She shouted, but he stood his ground in the narrow wagon, taking up space. Suzanne eased back toward the bed, holding Clayton close, wishing her body were smaller, her pregnancy not so prominent.

Another clap of thunder and blast of wind, this one knocking her onto the bed. She cried out, felt the dog's body roll against her as vibration shook the wagon and it teetered on two wheels. This time it tipped.

Suzanne felt herself falling, the dog slipping beneath her, her arms wrapped around a blanket that held her living son, her body big and bulky falling, falling forward. Then her face splattered into cold, wet mud.

⤜⤏

Ruth thought it couldn't have lasted longer than eight minutes. In that time, forty or so oxen, the mules, the Bacons' cows, all seeking in their confusion to be outside the confines of the circle, rushed and rumbled through wagons, jumping on and over tongues, driving against ropes once set to keep them from the eating areas. They'd butted their way through, as frightened in their movement as Ruth had been just watching, catching flashes of their growing agitation each time the lightning sliced across the sky to reveal horns and driving rain and hail on the backs of animals.

She'd run to Betha, found her safe beneath the farthest wagon, the children huddled. She ran back, swung a leg over Koda, held the horse firm with her knees, his body shivering. She held Jumper by a rope, the animal pulling until she had him snubbed up close to Koda. She thought to sing. She knew the wranglers did that, sang to quiet cattle, but the animals would never hear her against the storm. If she yelled or slapped her hat, snapped the whip, could she turn them into themselves if they started to stampede? She'd heard that could be done.

She didn't do it. Instead, she stayed on the edge when the next crack of thunder and the flash of lightning so close began the racing of the heavy animals, the flesh of her cheeks vibrating as they thundered by.

⁓

The rain still fell like pitchered water and the wind howled, but light seeped through the morning and with it came a modicum of hope. Daylight shed itself on five wagons still standing, though with gaps of shredded canvas, bent tongues, twisted braces, rims separated from wheel hubs. The other six wagons lay on their sides, some dragged by the disappearing stock, others crashed together, spewing out their trunks and barrels, petticoats and pans, slick and blackened, given up to gushing water.

Elizabeth knelt in the mud beside her wagon, crying.

Betha, a blanket wrapped around her shoulders and over her head, made her way to the woman kneeling beside her daughter, who was lying silent, her lips faintly blue.

"She's not movin'," Elizabeth said, looking up, rain streaking down her face. "I've got to get her out of all this wet."

Betha held the blanket out like the wings of an eagle, out and over Elizabeth, over Mazy and herself. "Bring her to ours. Ned and I've got the tent canvas pulled over the torn parts. It's partial dry in there."

Together the two tried to pick Mazy up, but the slickness of her skin and her weight and wet clothing foiled them.

"We need help here," Elizabeth shouted, bringing Zilah from where she tended Sister Esther's bruised head. Naomi followed when Esther motioned she was fine. The four working together lifted Mazy, gentling her onto a blanket they held at each corner, carrying her like a cradle to what was left of Betha's wagon.

"Check on the others, Betha," Elizabeth said. "See how many more we got that's hurtin' bad. Haven't seen anything of Lura or Adora's clan." She turned back to Mazy, wiping her daughter's face with her rain-soaked skirt. "I'm here, child. I'm here."

Elizabeth could hear the cries of others, some muffled, others clear. But it was Mazy's cry she longed for. She couldn't tell for all the mud and the rain, but she thought blood had oozed from beneath Mazy when they'd picked her up.

Inside the wagon, she unbuttoned her daughter's wrapper, loosened the collar, stripped her of the wet.

Ruth appeared at the Barnard wagon greeted by the wide eyes of children huddled in the corner, silently watching Elizabeth tend Mazy.

"You rub Mazy's legs," Ruth told Jessie and Sarah. "You'll keep yourselves warmer that way too."

The girls scrambled forward on hands and knees. Each stared at a leg and Mazy's ankles, narrow and white, sticking out from the blanket. "Don't be embarrassed," Ruth told them. "Rub."

"What about us?" Ned asked. He and Jason sat still huddled.

"Come with me," Ruth said. "I'll see if I can set a lean-to up, with one of the dumped wagons. Get a fire started. We're all going to need warmth and hot food."

"Is anyone else hurt?" Elizabeth asked.

Ruth stepped back out, and the boys leaped out behind her. "Sister Esther's at the Cullver wagon now. I don't see Suzanne or Clayton yet, nor the Wilsons or the Schmidtkes. All the oxen are gone. Guess you know that. Mules too. I believe the Asians have survived without a scratch. Tough little things. I'll find out about Tipton," she added. "We'll make a final assessment. You look after Mazy. Oh, look, here comes your dog."

Pig limped toward the Barnard wagon, a large gouge of flesh hanging in a flap from his shoulder. He stood, tongue hanging out.

"The inside of his mouth's white," Ruth said, touching the dog's mouth.

"Lift him up if he'll let you. They can warm each other," Elizabeth said, slapping her knee to urge the dog upward. The boys pulled on the dog, and he allowed it. He panted inside the wagon, and his wet body brought one more scent to the already rain-drenched odors permeating the space inside. Elizabeth slapped the bed, looked up seeking permission from Betha's eyes.

The squatty woman shrugged her shoulders and said, "It'll wash," as Pig jumped up, turned around once, then dropped to Mazy's side.

Elizabeth swallowed a sob. Mazy hadn't even moaned.

14

turnaround women

For several hours, Mazy moved in and out of being present. She recalled sounds and smells and voices and tried to enter into conversation, but then she'd disappear again, slither down a rock slide of the mind, puddle at the bottom. She heard people speak of water, that what gushed down the ravine lessened. She thought she heard Ruth's low voice, something about her boots being soaked, and her mother saying she'd paw through the trunk of her own tumbled wagon to find dry moccasins.

Still later, she heard Lura tell Ruth, "Be careful."

Mariah had spoken into the veil of sensation that was Mazy's foggy life, said something about herself and Ruth riding off to see what, if any, hope they had of rounding up the stock. She thought at one point she heard Lura come in, talk about her hair being soaked and flattened on her head. She'd brought dry blankets, said their wagon's canvas had endured.

It was nearly noon when Mazy made a sound. She heard it herself and knew it not to be a dream but the croaking of her voice. The sound brought with it something so sharp and scorching, a pain so piercing it forced her back to arch. In an instant she knew. The baby! She'd lost her baby!

Was it the tightness of the blankets wrapped close around her? Maybe it was the dog pressed to her side. Her body hurt so. No, the baby's leaving had forced this new and wrenching grieving.

"What is it, child? Where does it hurt?"

"I just—" Mazy thrashed her arms, sending Pig to the floor. She twisted, gulping for breath. In between, she panted, but the pain like a poker seared through her skin. Something deep and precious pressed against her heart. "Mama?" she said as she felt a wetness where it shouldn't be.

"Shush, now. I know, I know," Elizabeth said, her voice choking. "But you're still with us, that's what matters. You're still here. We're all still together."

"No more, Mama. No more."

Elizabeth drew her fingers across her daughter's forehead, pulled tendrils of hair behind Mazy's ears. Mazy could feel the tears pool there, deafening the sounds of rain and gushing water. For the first time, she felt that she was truly letting go of all that she had lost.

"I'm so sorry," Mazy said, her voice a whisper. "So very sorry."

"Hush, now. Nothing for you to be sorry over. Just rest. When the rain stops, we'll fill you in on what we've got and take a gander at what's to be. It's the Sabbath, and Sister Esther says it's best we send up words of thanks, and I agree."

"Laudanum?" Adora said, sticking her head inside the Barnard wagon. "Does anyone have laudanum?"

"You need it for yourself?" Elizabeth asked.

"Tipton. She's hurting bad," Adora said. "A cut, on her arm. Skin's like parchment. She's so fragile, truth be known." Adora dropped her eyes and fussed with the parasol handle.

"Need some to sew the dog up, too," Elizabeth said, "if you find any."

The last thing Mazy remembered before falling back into her fitful sleep was Betha's apron, white as snow, leaning over her. How did she keep it so clean and tidy when all about her chaos dyed everything with ever-darkening smears?

❧

It was late afternoon when Mazy learned how Suzanne fared. The widow with the striking face entered the Barnard wagon. Zilah had Clayton in tow, bells ringing behind her.

"Your dog's responsible for saving me again," she told Mazy. "Why, I don't know. This time he helped Clayton, too. I don't know what to say." Mazy didn't hear complaint in Suzanne's voice this time. She wasn't angry with Pig—grateful, it sounded like. Maybe she understood that she was all her young son had. And accepting that gave her a reason to live.

Clayton played with a wooden top painted with stripes of burgundy and black. He rolled it along the bed covers to Mazy, who used the pads of her fingers to roll it back to him. The boy smiled, grabbed the top, and waved it toward his mother.

Mazy stroked the dog, who lay as close to her as she allowed. His sides showed thick white threads stitched by Lura's hand.

"I wasn't sure what to do in the storm, whether to leave the wagon or stay. I…it…I thought the cattle might be rushed by the wind and the hail," Suzanne said.

"Could a warned us," Elizabeth said.

Suzanne actually laughed. "I predict nothing," she said. "But Pig seems to have that ability. When the wagon tipped, your dog was there. I landed on him. My shoulder too, but he broke my fall. He must have. Is he wounded bad?"

"We've stitched a good flap of skin back together, much as he'd let us. Looked for laudanum, but can't seem to find enough to even help out Mazy. You got any?" Elizabeth asked.

Suzanne shook her head. "Bryce may have put some somewhere. What did you hurt?" she asked. Mazy noted it was the first time—other than about Pig just now— she'd ever heard the woman ask after the welfare of another.

"She lost her baby," Elizabeth said, choking in the telling.

"Oh." Suzanne said. "Oh—maybe if the dog had been here, he would have broken your fall instead of mine. You might have saved—"

234

"He wasn't," Mazy said.

"And me, not able to keep one child safe. I'm not deserving of two."

Elizabeth told her, "Not good for a baby to hear such thinking."

"No sense lying about the kind of life he'll be born into."

"Don't you have family back east where you come from?" Elizabeth asked. She watched Zilah roll the striped top now to Clayton, who giggled.

"Those ties were severed," Suzanne said. She hesitated before continuing. "Bryce had opportunities with his father in Missouri." She pronounced it with the gentle *ah* sound at the end. "When Bryce chose to take us west, his father said to not expect him to be part of our future. He said his son had died to him. I don't even know how to tell him his son is truly gone. Or if I even should."

At least she didn't have that task facing her, Mazy thought. Jeremy had no family, none she knew of. His family grieved him here.

"And your own kin?" Elizabeth asked.

Suzanne took a long time to answer. "I've a brother in Michigan. He has eight children and an overburdened wife who I'm quite sure would not open her door easily if at all. Our parents are both dead. Cholera. Isn't that ironic? Epidemic of '32."

~⚮~

They had been riding for several hours, Ruth on Koda and Mariah sitting high on Jumper, Ruth's stallion. Low, scudding clouds brushed the sky above them, cast gray shadows over ground already darkened by the rain. The wind had lessened but struck them with little blasts as a reminder of its power.

Mariah grinned. She looked over at Ruth and sat straighter, as the woman did, moved the reins so she held them just like Ruth. She adjusted her hat.

"Feels more like October upstate than June," Mariah said.

"At least it's stopped raining," Ruth said. She reined up, scanned the horizon for the tenth time.

"I didn't remember seeing so many ravines and knolls and hills when we came through here before. I must not have paid attention," Mariah said.

"I rode out this way looking for Elizabeth," Ruth said, "and it looks different to me too."

"There were places on our farm like this, where cows could hunker down and we'd ride right by 'em," Mariah said. "Had to almost go over them to get them to move."

"That's when a good horse is worth his weight. Some of them can almost smell cows out. We need that now—if we're to get out of this mess intact."

Mariah kept her eyes on the ground as she talked. "We relied on old Buck for help lots," she said. "Pa's dog. He passed on just before we started west or we'd have brought him with us."

Ruth's horse slipped on the slickened earth, recovered. "I know this ground lets us track good, but I'll be glad when it dries up some."

Mariah nodded. She rode astride as Ruth did, her knees pressed tightly against the horse's withers, giving him direction with her legs, her weight, and position as well as with reins. "I've ridden since I was old enough to walk," she told Ruth, who guessed she just wanted to keep the conversation going. "Mattie helped me."

"You miss your brother already, don't you?"

Mariah nodded. "Almost more than Pa." She bit her lip as it trembled.

"I miss Jed, too, though my brother drove me crazy sometimes," Ruth said. She straightened, scanned the hills poking over the low, stringy fog. "He was a comfort for me, though…" Her words trailed off before she changed subjects. "If we find one or two cows, we're sure to find more."

Mariah's hair was held back with a blue ribbon. Ruth thought she'd never seen her without braids before and smiled when she realized Mariah had done her hair up like her own.

"They might try to find where they last fed. That'd be back our way," the girl said. Mariah pointed to the ground. "See there," she said. They rode several more minutes on either side of what looked like the tracks of three or four oxen before Mariah pointed out a change. "Looks like mules have joined in."

"Good. The Wilsons' wagon still stands, so if we get their mules, that'll be one complete unit at least. It'll be a miracle if we get all of the stock back."

From the advantage of the higher hill and distance, Ruth could see wagons heading west like dots and dashes beside the Platte, even on the south side. The river ran dark and muddy as barley coffee what with the rain and the wind to stir it. She shook her head. The cold air pushed against her yellow slicker. The air smelled fresh of wet sage.

"Looks like those tracks over that way; they go into that ravine with the trees," Mariah said. "I'll roust them out if they're there. You keep following these, all right?"

"I won't separate," Ruth said.

"Aw, there's nothing to worry over," Mariah said. "I'm a good rider."

Ruth assessed the source of her reluctance. "It's not your skill I'm concerned about," Ruth said. "Or the horses. It's just...if something goes wrong, this is a disorienting place. One of us could get turned around and lost worse than the oxen. No, we need to stick together."

They altered course and rode together up, then down a tree-pocked ravine toward a cluster of cottonwoods, hoping to find the familiar cattle bedded down inside.

It wasn't what they found.

She would have to stop pretending, tell someone what was happening with Tipton, then ask for help. But who? They'd surely judge her, Adora Wilson, from then on, judge how poorly she had provided for her daughter getting skinny as a stick, how deplorable her own morals must have been to have raised up a child so selfish and self-indulgent. A flash of anger coursed up through her, heated her face. *That child! How could she do this to me?*

She'd said those exact words the day Tipton informed her they were heading west, that it was all arranged between her papa and the Bacons.

"How could you?" Adora had screamed, losing her composure.

"Because I want to and because Tyrell wants me to and because we're going to marry someday. We would marry right now if—"

"Over my dead body!" Adora shouted.

She should have let it happen; then she'd have detoured around this.

She found the empty laudanum bottle beneath Tipton's pillow. Another hidden in the girl's folded parasol and still another in between the layers of lace they'd so carefully laid in her own mother's dresser drawer. What would people say when they found out? Hopefully, Mazy would recover without need before they were back in Laramie or Kanesville or wherever they were going and could buy whatever was needed.

She hadn't found her wrist purse, even with all the looking for laudanum. It wasn't where she'd left it. In the chaos of the storm, Hathaway's death, and Charles's untimely departure, she'd misplaced it. Maybe Tipton stumbled onto it and put it somewhere for safekeeping, away from prying eyes. Those foreign girls might not speak much English, but she guessed they knew what currency and coins were good for. Zilah'd spent a fair amount of time with access to the inside of their wagon. Perhaps she should refuse the girl's help, make Tipton come around and drive the mules. Though now, they had no mules.

She'd have to ask Tipton about the missing purse when her mind was clear, when she was…present. That was what she was trying to accomplish, bringing Tipton back to the present, whether she found it inviting or not.

So who could she talk with about all this? That Betha woman might know. She was neat and tidy and seemingly kind. She had two daughters and might understand a mother's dilemma. Perhaps she could begin the subject somewhat hypothetical so Betha wouldn't know exactly what worried her. Yes, that was a plan, and so much better than just coming right out and saying that her daughter had developed some problems and, lacking a resident doctor, had begun to treat herself.

Adora caught a glimpse of her face in the oval of mirror. She looked gaunt and uncared for. Well, that was understandable what with the storm, but she'd have to correct that, put glycerin on the wrinkles of her neck and around her eyes. She pressed her fingers on the newly lined skin beside her mouth. This so-called dry country sucked up moisture from her skin, then suddenly drowned a soul in its downpour. She'd have to find her powder and fill the wrinkles in.

⌒

"Missy Esther wish to know you come to meeting?" Naomi asked. "She say come. We decide next things."

"Let's wait until Ruth and Mariah return," Mazy said. She felt achy and warm. There'd be no purpose in sitting and talking until they knew if they'd have stock or not. The thought of others' pitying eyes on her, futile efforts to salve her new loss was too much. She felt tired and empty and alone.

"She probably just wants to see how everyone's doing," Elizabeth suggested.

"We're not doing well," Mazy said.

"You're always good at assessing things. We can take a gander at what's left." Elizabeth turned to Naomi. "Tell her we'll be there."

"Missy Mazy not good?" the girl asked. Elizabeth noticed that Naomi had darker skin than the other girls she traveled with. The sun had blistered lines at her higher cheekbones, and she had straight, even teeth.

"She's not, but we'll be there. You tell Esther."

The girl stepped off Betha's wagon box so lightly Elizabeth continued to talk to her until Mazy motioned that she was no longer there.

"You have to go."

"Why? What difference does it make?"

"Because you insisted on your meeting at a time that did not seem convenient for others, child. Now it's turnabout, and that's fair." Her voice softened. "A little fellowship and faith will be healing. Let's get you settled in a chair looking out, at least."

"There's no reason until the girls get back. We don't even know whether we'll be driving oxen or walking with packs on our backs until we know if there are oxen."

"Or leadin' or drivin' those Ayrshires," Elizabeth said.

"Those Ayrshires," Mazy said. "We're here because of them."

"Because you did what you thought was best. Now things've changed. It's part of living." Elizabeth stopped herself. "Well, those cows know where their stomachs got filled last, so I'm countin' on 'em to just amble on in here come feedin' time. Might just lead the rest back."

"If they're still in the country."

"Mazy, it don't do no good to dwell on the possible worst. We are still alive, and there's something to be said for that."

"Not all of us," Mazy said. She spoke so low her mother had to lean in. She started to ask her to repeat it, then knew what she'd said.

"I know, I know. It's a grievous loss you've been handed. But handed it you have. Staying in here, waiting and wondering, won't make any of it come back. Might as well try to sit a spell in the chair. We'll face it looking out of the wagon, so if you want to say somethin' you can. See everythin' that way," Elizabeth said, already moving one of Betha's highback chairs toward the wagon opening. She reached for a feather pillow, felt its dampness, set it aside. She found a fat picture album, placed it on the chair, wrapped one of Betha's sweet-smelling quilts over it then wiggled her fingers at Mazy. Putting her arm around her daughter's ribs, she pulled Mazy up and helped her to the chair.

⤖

They heard the gunshot from a distance. A repeat, and then it seemed as though they listened to a war.

"Get down!" Ruth said, pulling Mariah from the horse. They'd brought the animals into the thick growth around a spring that accounted for the cottonwoods and huckleberries. Wild roses grew among the mix, and though they were beautiful and fragrant, Ruth would have preferred they'd found trees instead. Koda already had one long scratch where he'd stepped within the roses' grasp and jerked back. Then they'd heard the shots.

"Who are they?" Mariah hissed.

"Pawnee, most likely from their dress. The others—not many of them, are there?—must be Sioux. We just best stay right here as quiet as we can 'til this is over."

And they had stayed, watching the bloodshed, the screams, and the men felled like rootless trees from their horses, their bodies splayed across the ground. Mariah had her fist in her mouth as though what she watched were more frightening than snakes, though the skirmish did not involve her. They crouched and watched, listened to gunpowder exploding and the whoosh of arrows through air. Each woman held her horse's nose and hoped the sounds and cries of death around them would cover any cough or whinny they might put forth.

Ruth tried to remember if the woman who had befriended Elizabeth was Pawnee. Ruth thought she was. And while there were more Pawnee, they appeared to be losing. The Sioux had many rifles and better ponies, and the Pawnee swung hatchets, the crunch of blade to body causing Ruth to cringe.

Deaths. Destruction. Murders. Was there no end to the madness humans inflicted on each other and themselves? Ruth didn't think there was, and now here, in this land of vast and natural beauty, as far from conflict as one would hope to be, she'd stumbled onto it again. This time between two groups she would have expected to be allies if not friends.

What could these Indians possibly hope for with this battle?

The noise, the cries of people dying, powder exploding, horses thundering and smashing to the ground pressed against her. She reached an arm around Mariah, pulled her close, feeling guilty for not protecting her from witnessing such horror. "I'm sorry," she whispered. Mariah nodded, and then her eyes enlarged in terror. "What is it?" Ruth said and turned to where the girl pointed.

⤙

Lura pawed through her trunk. She knew she'd put those pearl combs there after Matthew left. No, she'd put them there *before* he left, before he and Joe Pepin took the cattle west. She'd given them each coins, packed food for them, seen the combs, the expensive gifts Antone had given her, and put them inside the folds of her good silk dress inside this trunk. She must have put them somewhere new and forgotten. She did do that sort of thing, more so in recent years. But she had never forgotten anything so important.

"Are you joining us?" Sister Esther called out.

"Yes, yes. I'm on my way. Just wanted to check on something." Lura reminded herself to ask Mariah just as soon as the girl returned. She crawled out of the wagon, such as it was, and walked to the cooking area Ruth and Betha had set up before she and Mariah left. "Is that gunfire I hear?" Suzanne asked.

The group stood silent. "Don't hear a thing, child," Elizabeth said.

"Oh, it's there, all right," Suzanne said. Pig barked then, as though to confirm it. "Lots of gunfire, horses."

"Oh, pooh," Adora said walking out from behind their wagon. She had Tipton in tow, a parasol twirling over the two of them. "I don't hear anything." They walked near Suzanne, Tipton almost stumbling on her. "You must be daydreaming," Adora told Suzanne.

"Not something I do, actually," Suzanne said, "though others here might recognize the syndrome."

Lura shrank from the heat of the blind woman's tongue even though she was sure it wasn't directed at her. She surprised herself by speaking up. "Now, we just don't know what others can hear. I have the worst hearing, for example," Lura said. "Oh, I can hear sounds all right, but I run them together. Why, one time I remember someone handed me a bowl of black-eyed peas and they looked me in the eye and said, 'Pat it.' Well, I did wonder why anyone would want to pat a pan of peas, but I tried to oblige. I patted the sides of that tin treating it like a baby's bottom 'til they looked at me as though I was a worm and said clear as could be that time: 'I said pass it, not pat it.' So Suzanne just might hear what others of us can't."

She'd never spoken so much at once in her whole life, she didn't think. And about what? Nonsense. Antone would have said it was all nonsense. He said that often, now that she recalled. It may have been why she had stopped talking and just started knitting. And forgetting. Her lip trembled but she didn't cry.

❧

Swipes of black and white and red streaked across the Indian's face. His eyes, vacant and moist, stared up at them. A dark patch of red oozed from behind his throat. The body lay twisted and still glistening from the sweat his fear and anguish had produced just moments before his death. The skirmish raged around him, but for this man, this warrior, it had ended.

Ruth put her finger up to her mouth to signal silence to Mariah.

How she wished the girl had not been here! Ruth held Koda, brushing his soft nose as a reminder to be still, but he stood uneasily, the smell of blood and death and uncertainty moving in the muscles of his chest, in the tilt of his ears, and the rolling of his eyes.

The dead man's horse had found him.

They'll come for the horse and see us, hear us, Ruth thought. Ruth noticed a rider approaching. Arrows whizzed by before him. He ducked, his head dropped to the side of the pony he rode. He started down the hillside toward Mariah and Ruth.

Better here than at the wagons. She didn't think the wagons were in danger. What did they have that anyone would want? The stock was most desirable, and it had vanished, scattered, except for these two they held. These might be of value, but not likely. Emigrant horses didn't acclimate well to this prairie grass.

What did it matter now? He was on his way to where they hunkered down.

The man's black hair flowed out behind him as he rode hard toward the cluster of brambles and roses then slipped off his pony in one fluid motion. One hand held a long knife, and with the other he lifted the dead man's head, prepared to cut the scalp with a quick slice.

Mariah whimpered, her fist tight inside her mouth. She almost swooned. Ruth stepped in front of Mariah to shield her from the slaughter. Then the man looked up.

⮥

"We shall begin in prayer," Sister Esther announced, louder than she needed, Mazy thought. Who would protest? It did no harm; just did no helping either.

The women in the circle, arms around children loosely laid, bowed their heads. They had not prayed as a group since they had placed their loved ones in the ground.

"Heavenly Father, we thank thee for your many blessings on our days. We thank thee for permitting us to gather here, for all thou hast provided. We ask thee to provide safekeeping for your servants Ruth and Mariah. Please return them with our stock as many as thou feelest we need. We pray thee send thy Spirit to reside among us as we gather here. Help us put our own small needs aside and allow us to be stretched to fill the plans thou placest before us. Thou knowest our lot. Thou makest our boundaries fall on pleasant places, Lord. Amen."

Their heads came up all together, and something in the movement, something in the unison of it, the simplicity and grace, made Mazy ache in longing, blink back burning tears.

"Six wagons are no longer in service," Sister Esther announced. "It appears that the wagons still able to move out belong to me, Betha, and Ruth. Both of the Wilsons' and one of the Schmidtkes' are all right." She nodded toward Deborah. "The bees, miraculously, survived. Currently, we have no stock, but I am prayerful that Ruth and Mariah will return with answered prayers pushed before them."

"This could be beneficial," Mazy offered, surprising herself by talking. "It will allow us to move faster with fewer wagons to tend to."

"Truth be known, we should have done that when we first turned back," Adora offered. "Tipton, sit up, dear. Take this all in. It affects you. However, ours are the only wagons with mules, assuming we get a span back."

"What difference does that make?" Lura asked.

"The difference," Adora said, "is that mules travel faster and can't be teamed with oxen, of course. So we'd either trail them, or ride them if our wagons had been destroyed. This way, we can keep going, regardless. If we get mules back." She twirled her parasol. Setting sun broke through a low cloud, casting a spiraling shadow off the parasol's top. "That would be more difficult for those with oxen. They cannot be ridden."

"We all keep going, yes, Missy Esther?"

Sister Esther turned to Deborah. "Yes. I believe we are all together in this. That has not changed."

Something subtle had changed, Mazy realized, in the Sister's allowing the Association girls to have their say.

"What if some wish…change?" Zilah asked. Her face looked less pocked in the fading light. A patch of skin stretched out from her nose and made her face seem wide and flat, her eyes far apart.

"We will all be forced to alter where we have been riding or keeping our things or walking," Sister Esther said. "The storm has seen to that."

"What if some wish sun finds us in new place?" Zilah persisted, looking over at Naomi.

Mazy felt her heart begin to pound. It was as though her body knew before her mind when fright or flight demanded choice.

"Now, that'd be crazy," Adora said. "Can't change the direction the sun comes up."

"Some would turn again, west," Deborah said. She lowered her head. "Change the sun's direction."

"Well, of course, we're going back west," Adora said. "We just come here to tend the graves."

⇜

Ruth had not prayed for many years, not since John's death, not since she had faced the trial and her greatest agony, the deepest betrayal that any woman could endure. Afterward, she had struggled to understand the kind of woman she'd become: a woman who could still love a man who had harmed her child.

She prayed now, a silent prayer that they be made invisible, that the man who stared into her face would be struck blind, not see Mariah, not see her own form stiff before him, not smell their fear nor taste the fruit of victory by carrying off the downed man's scalp. Or worse, take their horses or their lives. *Make him deaf and blind, Lord, if only for the moment.*

246

Her prayers were seldom answered, and this one was wrought with selfishness and a lack of gratitude, but it was fervent and, she hoped, heard.

Time drifted over them on the scent of wild roses.

The warrior turned, confusion on his face. He looked straight at Ruth, into her hazel eyes, into her soul. He did not move. She could not breathe. But she knew she lived because she could still hear her heart; knew he lived, too, because his heavy breathing broke the silence, breathing from the effort of his wars.

The dead man's pony stomped behind him. The warrior turned to look at it, shook his head as though to ward off a pesky fly, then dropped the dead man's head, scalp still intact. He reached for the pony instead, swung up, and whistled a plaintive call through his fingers. He turned, his own horse followed him up the hill, kicking out little clumps of mud as they cleared the mound and disappeared beyond it.

Ruth's heart rejoiced, sang inside with gratitude for grace!

⟳

Mazy's words sounded defeated, even to herself. "Turn west? For what? We haven't far back to go to Kanesville. We can walk it if we have to. Hitch up with others heading back."

"Lura, what's your opinion on the matter?" It was Elizabeth asking.

"Oh, well, I think it's too soon to know. We can't decide anything until we find out whether we're walking or not. Our cattle are heading west, Mazy. You remember that? Your cow brute too. Still, I don't relish walking east or west though I've heard some have done it."

"You've been walking," Ned said. "Every day beside the oxen. I'd like going on, Ma," Ned said. "It's what Pa wanted, something new for us in Oregon. And Auntie Ruth, she wanted it too. She'd say so if she was here to speak it."

"I want what Auntie wants," Jessie said.

"Of course. We know that, Worm." It was Jason, but his chide to his sister held gentleness instead of whine. He'd found string and wound it into a cat's cradle for Jessie and Sarah to watch while the women talked. Sarah tired of it, stood to check her partially finished sampler spread on a line to dry.

"It frightens me to go west," Betha said. She sighed. "But encourages, too. I spent some time today at Jed's grave. It was peaceful. It is here now too, with all of you."

"This is insane," Suzanne said, "but—"

"Thank you," Mazy interrupted. "I couldn't agree more. We've been through this. We know what to expect heading east."

"Didn't know this was coming," Lura said.

"Actually, you might not like what I have to say," Suzanne said. "I'm going to…there'll be another member of the party before long—"

"Which means getting back to civilization, people, doctors, midwives. That's what's important," Mazy said.

"Oh, I can midwife just fine," Elizabeth said, "when it comes to that."

"Mother!"

"I mean I can't be doing it alone," Suzanne said. "I'm like a turtle turned upside down, and my child, my Clayton, he's needing all of you, every one of you. There's nothing in the direction we're headed now. The world as I knew it there ended when we left. The world with Bryce ended a week ago. It did end. For all of us. No amount of turning will bring that back."

The intensity of her voice, the wavering of the final sentence forced a thinking.

"Start again in Kanesville," Mazy said to Suzanne. "No one knows you there."

"But there's no vision there," Suzanne said. "Imagine me, speaking of something visionary, the one among us who can't see." She breathed air out through her nose, a short sound of disdain.

"Tipton? We haven't heard from you," Mazy said.

They turned their heads as one to face the girl who had said almost nothing for four days now. Her face was hollowed out at the cheeks, her eyes red. She looked up at the sound of her name.

"What's your desire, dear?" Elizabeth said.

"To die." Tipton turned empty eyes to gaze around the circle. "And I surely don't care where or how that happens."

keeping

Something in Tipton's voice, something beyond the hardness of the words, the sureness of intent, sounded to Mazy like the bleat of a lost fawn. She wore the weariness that warned of giving up. The girl's need reached inside Mazy's own layer of distance and disappointment, and she turned toward Tipton, reached out a hand, her fingers pricking the air between them.

Tipton stayed still, but Mazy thought she saw a flicker of recognition in the blue eyes as dark as a snow-filled sky.

"I am so sorry, Tipton," Mazy said, dropping her hand back into her own lap. The flicker in Tipton's eyes closed over, blocked her out. Mazy chided herself. She'd done it again, expressed her "sorry-ness," apologized but did nothing to touch the sentiment of sorrow. She tried again. "Is there anything I can…?" The offer sounded shallow and insignificant.

Mazy sighed. She was useless. This effort was useless. Maybe Tipton was right. They may as well stay where they were and just die, let these broken wagons be their markers. But there was something inside her that insisted upon life, even though her own baby had lost its life that very day. No. She had to go on.

"I think we've all thought of dying, Tipton," Mazy said then. "None of us seems able to stretch past our own weariness."

A silence broken only by meadowlarks descended on the group.

For a moment, Mazy feared the burden was all that they'd been left with, these widows, these survivors through no effort of their own. Perhaps they'd wear the cape of guilt for simply living, for death having stepped over them and plucked the ones they loved.

She looked around. Her head felt thick, her courage smothered by an old and matted quilt. She wished to push the weight aside, to invite hope inside the circle, give meaning to the losses. She opened up her mouth to speak, willing something wise to find its way into the world.

A shout in the distance interrupted, brought all their heads about.

"It's the girls," Lura said, standing.

"They've got ol' Snoz and Snuff," Sister Esther said, *S*'s of their names singing through her lips. "Yours are there, too, Betha. And, Suzanne, I see Boo, at least. Oh, thank you, God, thank you, thank you!"

"Not to mention mules," Elizabeth said. "Tipton, look! How many do you see? Oh—" She squinted her eyes at the riders following and added, "I see someone else I know."

Mazy welcomed the shift, rescuing them from decision. She kept an eye on Tipton. The girl stood, at Adora's prodding, but her shoulders sloped, her mouth stayed drawn and tight. Even before the storm, before the illnesses and deaths, Mazy'd paid scant attention to the girl. Her mind fastened on her own needs, on pushing down her disappointment with Jeremy, then her loss of him, on trying harder to get home. Had it been Tipton in Mazy's dream seeking a compassionate listener?

"You want to stay sitting here?" Mazy's mother asked her.

"I'll help you back inside," Esther said. "You go greet them, Elizabeth."

"Isn't it grand?" Elizabeth said, watching the stock move closer. "What a gift." A grin as wide as a johnnycake spread across her face. Elizabeth crawled inside the back of her broken-down wagon, pawed about, then came out, a necklace in her fist. She waved at the riders and headed toward them.

"Just help me down," Mazy said to Esther. When the older women left, Mazy said, "Tipton? Please? I could use your company."

Tipton shrugged her shoulders, slouched her way toward Mazy. They leaned a bit against each other, the two like old stovepipes, tired and used up.

"Bet we look as weary as those wagons," Mazy told Tipton. "And just as in need of keeping."

⌁

Ruth beamed. She cast a glance at Mariah, and while grit darkened the teeth of the girl, smudged her narrow face, she sat straight-backed in her saddle. They herded hope, at least that's how Ruth saw it. Hope. That the women would survive, that they could endure, and maybe, if she admitted it, that they weren't alone. She hadn't even considered yet how to explain the incident at the battle. Neither she nor Mariah had spoken of it yet. It was as though it hadn't happened, except it had.

When the warrior rode off, she and Mariah had stared at the grassy slope, empty of life. They led their horses out of the foliage, away from the arrow-laden body that lay fallen before them. Then Ruth spied two horses riding fast from the opposite direction.

"Mariah! Wait!" she whispered, but too late.

At first, Ruth thought the two were in pursuit of the Sioux, but the Pawnee pulled up their horses when they spied the women. They stared, spoke to each other, then turned around.

Mariah looked to Ruth. "Should we go? Stay?" Ruth was responsible, she was the adult, she was the one to protect a child.

Then she'd felt the vibration at her feet. Thirty, maybe forty head of stock, including the Wilsons' mules, lumbered up and over the rise. Behind them rode the two Pawnee, their stocky ponies pushing the herd before them. The afternoon light caught something shiny at the woman's face, glittered like a spark as they watched the glorious sight of faithful oxen rumbling over the rise. Silver earrings? Out here?

As pleased as they'd been to see the stock, nothing compared to the spirits they lifted when they rode back into camp. The Marriage Association women clapped their tiny hands and bobbed their heads, their pointy hats bending to each other like sunflowers bobbing to the sun. Betha wiped at her eyes with her apron. The children ran out and to either side. Jessie reached to be pulled up by Ruth, and the child rode sitting before her, waving as though she herself had accomplished the task. *Why not?* Ruth thought. *We all need to celebrate.* Jed would have celebrated. She shook her head, missing him, missing him so.

As she watched that crazy antelope follow Elizabeth out toward them, Ruth tried to remember when she had felt such joy as in this moment, when people that she cared for had found reason to rejoice. Perhaps at her wedding years ago; all but her father had rejoiced then. But this was surely different. This was a fuller time, because they'd been so low, and now together—at least for the moment—they were divorced from their despair.

Elizabeth had hiked her skirts up between her legs the way she did to move faster. She strode toward them, waving. Behind her, Ruth watched a scurry of activity.

Lura and Adora, Esther and Betha, rolled barrels, helped lift boxes; the boys dragged broken wagon tongues, hoisting them onto the barrels to serve as a kind of corral, incorporating the broken wagons to make the circle larger. It looked as though even Tipton had been enlisted, helping her mother shove a trunk into line. Suzanne stood off to the side holding Clayton near a campfire, the black dog panting at her feet. Mazy held Sarah by the hand.

Into this makeshift boundary, the oxen moved with additional speed as though happy to be home.

"Would you look at this!" Elizabeth said, breathless beside the riders. The Indian woman Elizabeth had befriended smiled down at her from the pony, the silver bell earrings shimmering. Her man lifted his chin with a nod of recognition from the far side of their herd. "Isn't this a sight? You girls did real good," Elizabeth said. "Just real good."

"We're only short a few," Mariah said. "Who would have thought? We even got your cows!"

"Did you find 'em all in the same place?" Elizabeth asked, wanting to hear the details of the story.

"Guess you could say that," Ruth said. "It was your friends that located them. They could have kept them for themselves, but didn't. Not even the mules. I think all eight are here."

Elizabeth shook her head, patting the withers of Silver Bells' horse as they walked. "Ain't this just a moment for rejoicin'," she said.

Ruth beamed. "My thoughts exactly."

⁓

Outside the circle, cooking fires started. Mazy made an effort to help Ruth by putting grain in a bucket for the two horses and threw in a couple handfuls extra. Ruth picked up the buckets, one in each hand. "I'd carry," Mazy said, "but—"

"No matter." They walked quiet for a time. "You'll get back to where you were. I'm sorry, though. About the baby," Ruth said. "Your mother told me."

"I'll never be back to where I was," Mazy said. She took a deep breath. "Even though we'll eventually reach Wisconsin."

Wisconsin? Ruth did not respond, outwardly. Inside, her stomach lurched. They had to turn back west, and soon.

Mazy's breathing sounded labored. Animals stood drinking from puddles of standing water. The mules were hobbled now. Ruth bent to check the iron links at their front legs.

"They should have been hobbled last night—they wouldn't have been lost to the storm," Mazy said. "I was just so tired, not thinking clearly. Should have checked with Adora and reminded her."

"They weren't your responsibility," Ruth said. "They belong to the Wilsons."

"Adora's had her hands full. And Zilah's too new to it to know what's right or wrong. Besides, I think if we're to make it, we've got to pay attention to each other, take notice and walk beside each other a little more. At least I need to be less...pampering of myself."

Ruth laughed. "Not a term I'd use to describe you, Mazy Bacon. Pampering?"

"I am, though. Thinking about how I feel, my loss, my...disappointments and not even noticing what others need for keeping. We might have staked the wagons too, when the wind came up. I just wasn't thinking. Now I'm even more addled."

"You've had lots to think about and lost more than most," Ruth said.

"How can you compare?" Mazy said. "I mean, I know so little of what others face, what pool they draw from to see them through. They're so peculiar—troubles and loss. They hit us like a cold. We think we know how others are affected because it seems so common, something we've all faced. But something can be just a sniffle to one soul and to another, it's pneumonia."

"Just seems to me we have to take responsibility for ourselves," Ruth said. "We can't rely on others to see us through." They stood quietly listening to the horses crunch against the grain. "People fail us," she said. "Not good to put too much stock in them."

"You didn't fail us," Mazy said.

Mazy turned back to look at the oxen and her cows. They were lying down, chewing their cud in the fading light. She brushed the air against the insects buzzing and hovering. For Ruth, it was a miracle those stock were back, an absolute miracle. What on earth did it mean?

~⁓~

"Get back! Get back!" Tipton's words cut through the evening air, but still the flames licked up against Suzanne's skirt, finding fuel in the petticoat, smoldering putrid smoke against the damp wool of the woman's skirt.

Tipton pushed against her, toppling Suzanne from the flames, throwing dirt on the butternut-colored dress. She used her own hands to pound against the flames.

"What are you doing?" Suzanne screamed at her. "Let me be!"

"You're burning up! Don't fight me at it!"

It had happened so quickly that others barely turned to the shouting before the flames were out, the smoldering smell of wet wool now filling their heads.

"I've wanted to do this," Mazy said, walking to help Suzanne up, touching her arms, "but I got distracted."

"Burn me up?" Suzanne asked, though Mazy thought her usual acid tongue had been slightly diluted.

"No, try out an idea." She and Tipton brushed Suzanne off. Then Elizabeth checked over Tipton's hands to examine her burns while Deborah brought over a bowl of honey she spread on Tipton's fingers. "Using Ruth's skills," Mazy said, turning back to Suzanne. "At converting a harness into something that'll fit Pig. With a handle you can hang onto. I think he'd keep you from getting too close to things, lead you around danger. If you'd let him. Maybe even warn you of Clayton's whereabouts."

"He'd get distracted," Suzanne said. "Like you. By the children or Fip or whatever."

"Might be worth a try, though, don't you think? Give you more of that…independence you're always saying you want."

"Where's Clayton?" Suzanne snapped.

"Growing up," Mazy said, adding with kindness, "now, how about you?"

They had agreed to continue their gathering in the morning and had retired with full stomachs and hopeful hearts, sure medicine for untroubled sleep. Silver Bells and her man spent the evening outside the circle where the others slept too now, mostly on the ground that had begun to dry quickly with a strong west wind.

The Pawnee braced some cottonwood branches at an angle into the earth, covered them with a buffalo hide, and shortly had a lean-to, windless and warm. Elizabeth thought it a pretty fancy abode and altered the makeshift lean-to she'd prepared for herself and Mazy to a similar configuration. She returned Betha's wagon to her and her children.

She wished Mazy had agreed to spend one more night on the mattress at Betha's, but Mazy had insisted she share Elizabeth's space. Both of their wagons were mangled beyond repair, making them the only family—as Mazy put it—to be homeless.

Gusts of wind struck the wagon canvases, cracked them like wet sheets. Elizabeth lay where she could see the stars poking through the windswept clouds, feet first inside the blanket-covered lean-to. Same sky that arched over her back in Milwaukee, that she and her Hans had looked up to as they stood on the porch steps. He taught her the constellations' names, reminded her how thousands before them had studied the heavens and they had not changed, had not failed to disclose the north star where it belonged, night after night, the lip of the dipper marking its path.

"Few things are steady as stars," he told her.

She loved the hint of Germany that sifted through his English. He always said her speech brought Kentucky back country to his old ears. His old ears. Why, he was younger than she was now when he'd said that, and she felt young as Fip. Life had too much to offer to be speaking of age. This whole journey just proved it, offering up daily doses of delight, even in the midst of misery.

Elizabeth sighed and rolled over, her bulk not enough to keep the cold from seeping into her hips. Sometimes it was as though Hans still lived. Not the way he looked, so much. That had oddly faded. But he came to her in a voice, a choice of words, a moment in time, in the little mannerisms she noticed in Mazy, like her tendency to hold her chin in her hand while she thought deeply on some subject or the way she rubbed the back of her neck to buy time.

Mazy had his slender form, too, though the girl seemed to think she was big as a house.

"Have to find a way to let her see herself as others do," Elizabeth said out loud.

"Hmm?" Mazy said, tossing, then resumed her sleep.

"Your father would have loved this place," Elizabeth whispered. Mazy didn't answer. "Well, good, you're resting." She inhaled the night air, spoke a prayer for her child, that in her grief for the baby she'd lost Mazy would find healing. Who knew what tomorrow would bring, what new way they'd discover to wash away the little chunks of dying daily that came along with living?

"I'm awake," Mazy said.

"Are you?" She turned to face her daughter, stroked the curls in Mazy's hair.

"There's nothing left of him now, is there, Mama? Nothing. Just physical things, his eyeglasses, his clothes, a book or two his fingers have touched. But no…baby. Nothing that was a part of his living is left in me or anywhere on this earth. Nothing."

"Memories, Mazy. That's all we ever get to hang on to when we lose someone we love. Just the give and take of memories, living inside our hearts."

"It isn't fair," Mazy said. "We'd just begun. Our baby…"

"I know it. It's just what is. Got the memories. That's what'll warm us on the journey back."

"So you think we should keep going back home too?"

"I meant in our journey back to where we began, where God sent us out from." She said it softly, hating to disappoint the longing she heard in her daughter's voice. "He makes us new and different people here, stretches us, some beyond what we can even recollect. But he's always with us, Mazy, always gives us just what we need no matter where our feet might land. It's how he fills us up."

"So there's nothing there then, at home. That's what you're saying. Back in Wisconsin. Just the memories of what was."

"Memories you carry with you. You don't need to go back for them. I'd say you got to long for something different, to recognize the new trail God's put you on—then you'll be truly headed home."

In the morning, Adora awoke to see that the Pawnee family had departed. Just as well. She didn't want to seem ungrateful, but there was still that question in her mind of where the disease had come from, the disease that had taken her Hathaway and the rest. The Pawnee woman had funny marks on her hands and face, scabs almost. And she'd given the roots to Elizabeth. After that, the sickness had begun.

It was never wise to mingle with other races. Those little women with Sister Esther presented enough of a strain. She made sure she didn't sit too close to them either. It was probably good also that she couldn't smell much anymore.

Adora stood, stretched, and arched her back against the morning. She looked at the corset and cast it aside; slipped on her dress and apron, splashed water onto her face. Tipton seemed to have slept better, even with her burnt hands. She'd seen no evidence that her daughter had imbibed laudanum or whiskey lately. Couldn't find any, even to relieve the pain of Suzanne's legs, which had turned red as beets after the flame. She didn't hold with that honey, but Tipton said her hands didn't sting.

Adora noticed the Pawnee had left behind their buffalo hide laid gently over the lean-to Elizabeth had crafted. Hairy old thing. She stuck her head out of the wagon back and scanned the stock. The Bacons' riding mules were there. She looked for her eight. She could only count six.

❧

"You had no right to let them have my mules," Adora said. Her shrill voice left no late sleepers, though Elizabeth was surprised to see that she and Mazy were the last to rise.

"There's no way you could keep your two wagons going. You were depending on Zilah to drive one as it was," Ruth said. The younger woman poked at the fire, requiring Adora to talk to her back. "And we wouldn't have gotten any of the animals back without their help."

"I'd have found those mules," Adora said. "They'd have come home."

Ruth scoffed. "Not without the herd. At least I know few mules likely to come back to a spot they'd only barely been to except to join up with a bell horse. Which we don't have."

"Mules are smarter than some people, if truth be known. You overstepped your boundaries, Ruth Martin," Adora said.

"I'll pay you for them if it comes to that. But you won't even need them, probably."

"Money doesn't settle things," Adora said. She slammed her tin cup against her plate, spilling her coffee down her apron. "There, now see what you've done?" She spoke louder. "They weren't yours to give away. You should have handed over one of your fine horses if you wanted to be generous. Why didn't you do that?"

"Because my horses aren't worth much out here. They wouldn't survive without grain the way Pawnee ponies do. But mules will."

"She is right, though," Elizabeth said. She sat on a wagon tongue, watching Clayton play hide-and-seek with Jessie and Sarah around the wounded wagons. "It wasn't your decision to make without conferring.

You robbed Adora of the opportunity to be generous instead of quarrelsome."

"I fail to see what's quarrelsome about defending my rights," Adora said.

"You might have agreed if you'd been allowed to have a say. Wouldn't you, Adora?"

"Almost nothing worse than having someone take away your choice," Mazy added.

"Both of our wagons are intact," Adora whined, "and we had all our mules back."

Ruth said, "I just know other Pawnee have come begging, and some Sioux have harassed wagons. Remember hearing about that? We witnessed a major battle…" She paused. "They'd could've just taken what they wanted, maybe all of the mules. Those two did nothing but help, and they deserved something for it."

"Give them beads then, or baubles or something, but not my mules!"

"Do you want Ruthie to go get them back?" Betha asked, patting Adora's hand. "I'm sure she could."

Ruth frowned at her sister-in-law.

"What do the rest of you think?" Mazy asked.

"So we vote?" Ruth asked. She spit the words out. She stomped toward the cooking fire, pulled off her neckerchief and picked up the coffeepot with it, poured herself a cup.

"It's no one else's decision but mine," Adora said. "They were my mules."

"You might be right, Adora," Mazy said. She tied her thick hair back with a piece of rawhide. "But it's been done now. We have to decide what to do from here, maybe learn from this about talking with each other before we just act."

"So we don't let you push us into things?" Ruth asked, addressing Mazy. "Maybe we wouldn't be in this fix now if we hadn't turned around."

"Didn't see anyone doing what they didn't want," Elizabeth defended.

"I just wanted a marker for Jed's grave. That's why I came back," Betha said.

"They were my mules," Adora whimpered.

"But they were a part of this gathering," Mazy said. "And things are different now. Our decisions may look like they're drawn individually, but they're colored by each other."

Esther and Betha walked on either side of Suzanne to the place in the road where their men were buried. A hundred or more wagons had rolled across the site since the graves had been dug.

"I hate leaving him here," Betha said. "But it does ease me some that your brothers lie here too. And Bryce."

"And Cynthia," Esther reminded her.

"I'd just like to leave something here, maybe a rock we could scratch their names on or—"

"I can smell the cottonwood trees," Suzanne said. "And is that columbine?"

"Yes," Esther said. "We will memorize the hills and the river and the sounds of wind in the trees and the scents in the air. And when we reach the West, we will set a marker in a place to remind us of them. It will be better."

"Mazy says that *columbine* means 'I will not give thee up,'" Betha said. "It's good for Jed to know that, that he won't be given up." Betha sighed. The wind whipped at her flounced hat. She pushed it down with one hand; the other still held Suzanne's elbow. "So you plan to head west?"

Esther nodded. "It was to comfort you and Mazy, too, that I turned around. The girl seemed so…needful of securing her purpose. But our future is west, not east. It will be different without my brothers, without Cynthia. But it will still be what I believe I'm called to do. If I just listen."

"And you, Suzanne?" Betha was never sure if the woman would stay silent, bark back, or bite, but it was rude to talk around her, as though she wasn't there.

"I don't have the luxury of a calling."

"Oh, but you do," Esther insisted. "We all have such a plan. We must just be open to seeing what it is."

"Seeing. Well then, there's the problem."

Something made Betha risk. She lifted Suzanne's hand and leaned into the taller woman, not meaning to touch her, but when she did she felt Suzanne's stance first stiffen and then soften. "I'll help you see it," she said. "We all will. That's what friends are for." Betha felt her own tears come again and watched two others ache down Suzanne's cheeks, too. Esther put her arm around Suzanne's shoulder, and the three stood together overlooking what some might say was only an empty stretch of trail but which Betha would always remember as the place of cottonwood and columbine, a place where Jed—and Bryce and the others— would not be given up.

❦

"I don't see why we have to leave one of our good wagons behind," Adora complained. "First you give away my mules, and then you say I get only one wagon."

"Because we're all leavin' something behind," Ruth said. "We didn't get all of the stock back."

"I got all of mine."

"If we were part of that Rough and Ready Company or the Spring Rangers group, we'd have been forced already to pair up in fours and fives. They would have fined us if we hadn't," Betha told her.

"That wasn't Antone's way. He didn't want so many rules," Lura said. She'd found her clay pipe and had taken to chewing on it without tobacco.

"We don't need many rules, either," Ruth said. "But some." She looked at Mazy. "Like hobbling the mules and horses when we camp. Might have saved ourselves this stampede if we'd done that. We'll make better time with fewer wagons."

"Some have either stock or wagons, is that right?" Suzanne asked.

Mazy felt her heart start to pound. She'd known the group had been circling around a western tent. And she knew within that moment she was too tired, too beaten and defeated to talk them into going east. If only she had the courage to go that way herself.

"In addition to beginning all our gatherings with prayer," Sister Esther announced, "we must stop on the Sabbath and rest ten minutes of every hour we travel, to preserve the animals."

"I don't mind prayer and preservation," Elizabeth said.

"While heading west," Ruth said.

Elizabeth looked out of the corner of her eye at her daughter, expecting protest.

"Setting aside an entire day each week when we're already so far behind seems a little risky," Ruth said. "Let's rest when the terrain permits."

"Oxen work hard with rest. We too," Naomi said. "Mei-Ling—Deborah's bees fly out without fear of being lost."

"It will be a part of our witness to God's wonderful provision," Sister Esther said, clasping her hands in a ball before her, "if we can say we arrived safely and still we rested each Sabbath."

"Do we vote?" Lura asked. "What did we decide about that?"

"I'd still like an explanation about why we can't take our two perfectly good wagons with us," Adora said. She chewed her lower lip, and her voice had risen an octave.

"Because the wagons we brought are not as sturdy, Mother." Tipton sighed when she said it, as though the words were as weighty as the wheel she and Mariah had been struggling to pull off of one of the Bacons' wagons. Grease smudges streaked both girls' faces. They'd hang the good wheel underneath the box of someone's wagon as a spare.

"They survived the thrashing taken by the rest of the wagons," Adora argued. "Seem pretty sturdy to me."

"Only because they were on the near side, opposite where the animals bolted," Tipton said, "Otherwise—"

"Fine. Fine," Ruth said. "Let's just decide what we're taking and who's going with us."

"So we're not voting," Lura said, almost to herself.

Something in the bickering, the quarreling in circles, each person clinging to her own ways, to what she knew best, pressed against Mazy's temples, ached at the back of her neck. She searched for something to say that would get at what they were struggling with, tried to identify the feelings that were bouncing off the arguments like water on a hot three-legged spider frying pan. It wasn't the words they were saying; it was what wasn't being spoken of that drove the dissension; she wished she could grasp the meaning. Perhaps make sense of it for herself.

"I know you'd like to take everything you brought along, Adora," Mazy said. "We all would. The thought of leaving a chest of drawers or the dishes that were my grandmother's is—"

"Or Hathaway's picture," Adora wailed. "How can I leave any of the little I have left of him? You tell me that." The last words had come out shattered, splintered. "You tell me how I'm to live without my son, gone off to who knows where. With a child that's aching and so far away I never will get her back. I can't..." She dropped her hands to her sides, the palms up in defeat. "I just can't. The wagons and mules were the last thing Hathaway bought."

She turned aside, reached for her apron, and held it with both hands to her face. She stood alone, her shoulders shaking, speaking grief, catapulting them back to their own.

Betha stepped beside her, put an arm out to reel her in. The woman allowed it, sank into Betha's arms and, with the movement, gave permission to release the hard, racking sobs of powerlessness, of mourning what was no more, pushing the world away while reaching for connection, begging not to grieve alone.

Like an eagle comforting its young, Elizabeth pressed against them both, her face to their backs. "So hard," she whispered. "So hard." Soon Lura moved across the circle, eyes glistening. Tipton, too, pricked out of her sighs, stepped before her mother, and the two held each other. Mazy reached for Suzanne's hand.

"What's happening?" Suzanne asked.

"They're overpowering pain," Mazy said. "And it's time we joined them."

Mazy led the string of clasped hands, Clayton now on Ruth's hip. The Celestials and children joining in, the women circled Adora and Tipton, Betha and Elizabeth. It occurred to Mazy that these women wept over the lost leaves of their lives, leaves that had dropped never to be recovered; not yet believing those leaves could nurture life.

"We've lost our bearings," Mazy said. "We've been too busy pushing. My pushing as much as anyone's. We never took the time to give our loss its due."

Sister Esther sniffed, and tears dampened her large nose. "We've acted selfish and quarrelsome. Shame on us."

Mazy put her hand on the woman's shoulder. "No, Esther." She spoke without scolding, with a gentleness Mazy knew she seldom used within herself and whose tenderness she suspected might be foreign to Sister Esther, too. "This is no place to find fault. Don't let blame live here, not between us and not inside ourselves. We might wish that we had done something differently, lament the mistakes, but then we have to forgive ourselves, accept what's happened, and move on."

Suzanne's hands were cool inside Mazy's palms, but the woman didn't jerk away.

"I don't think of anyone here as cruel or shameful because the wounds are so deep and we stopped to tend them, or because we needed others to help. We are just women, after all, just human. Our being together can be a place where we can cry and remember and take care of each other."

Adora dabbed at her eyes, moved into the wider circle. "I'm making such a fuss."

"Thank goodness," Betha said. "I've craved a good cry with someone who wouldn't tell me how to fix it." A few of the women ventured a chuckle.

"We do not hold hands this way before," Deborah said. "It is nice thing. I will tell bees. They like to know family secrets."

"So we are, now. Family. Thank you for that, Deborah. And, Adora," Mazy said, "for helping us remember that we have so much: our lives, each other, and a warm place to be."

Suzanne squeezed her hand. Mazy looked at each woman and each child around the circle and thought she recognized something in their faces. A look of profound loss and trauma faced, but of compassion and determination too. They were more than a group of surviving women; they were stronger people because they stood beside each other, all together and no longer alone.

16

flux

Betha stood not far from Ruth with red eyes, staring at the ground, Ruth's arms around her sister-in-law. The boys placed an old picture frame, gilded and gold, and leaned it on a pile of rocks and greasewood branches off from the trail. Esther thought the photograph of the somber family a fitting memoir to the way they clustered now, the breeze blowing Betha's apron corners out from her dress, her children clustered at her knees.

"Someone'll come along and pick that up," Ruth told them. "It's a good frame." Ruth fidgeted with her whip.

"No matter," Betha said. "I like Jed knowing we left a bit of ourselves here."

"Jed, yes, but others—someone might recognize you all," Ruth said.

"Wouldn't that be a miracle, to meet up with old friends from home through the photograph? I should write on the back of it, where we're headed."

"No!" Ruth said. Betha stared at her. "Someone could use that later to take advantage of you," Ruth offered an explanation, "a widow…"

"I don't see—"

"Can I leave my wind sock?" Jessie held a mud-caked toy she'd raced with the wind on a stick. "So Papa can run wind through it up in the stars?"

Betha nodded, distracted, now not able to speak.

It bothered Ruth all day. It wasn't like her to be impulsive or disrespectful, and yet she had not hesitated to give Adora's mules away. It came to her that they would be the best gift, and she couldn't imagine the group not being so grateful to get the oxen back that anyone would object. Still, Elizabeth was right—her arbitrary decision robbed others of being generous, especially Adora and Tipton.

It had robbed her, too. She'd been so happy to be spared by the Sioux warrior, to have her fumbling prayer answered. People sang her praises, had been grateful to her and Mariah, and she felt that way herself: so powerful, so giving.

Then she gave away what wasn't hers, and now instead of carrying with her the memory of doing something wonderful and wise, she bent here over Koda's foot, digging out the small stones and caked mud, feeling empty and alone. She'd been given a lovely moment in life, and she had robbed herself of it by doing something stupid. It was the story of her life.

"Do you want to keep these things?" Betha asked her, holding up the pair of Zane's pants she'd worn riding the day before. "Seems like something we could leave behind."

Ruth stood and stared. "No. I'm going to wear them instead of this dress."

"Oh, Ruthie. Do you think you should? People will…point their fingers at you."

"What people? Why should I care, anyway?"

"If you want to call attention to yourself, I'm sure these should do it." Betha handed her the folded pants, arching her pinkie finger to avoid touching the mud caked on the legs.

"The pants are convenient, that's why I prefer them."

"Oh, well, whatever you tell yourself," Betha said.

The cleanup began. At last, Betha thought. Daily cleaning was to her as necessary as eating, as invigorating as singing. Scrubbing, wiping, polishing always sang for her, called to her almost the way some people like her Jed had felt called to read the law. She couldn't understand people who found tidying up a troublesome chore. For her, the sight of polished chimney lamps, well-beaten carpets, and the smell of lye soap left on the floor were as rapturous as worship.

"Two moves are as good as a fire," her mother had told her as she tossed out anything she thought useless before beginning each of the sixteen moves she'd taken Betha and her brother on before Betha turned ten.

Through it all, she and Betha tidied up, which wasn't always easy in a dusty wagon, wearing the same faded clothes that ripped if you rubbed them too hard at the wash. She scrubbed the rough boards of each new shack they found for shelter and looked for herbs and spices to trick the mold and mildew smell from the walls. Each time they transformed something that looked forgotten and forlorn and turned it into a warm and welcoming home, Betha experienced the greatest satisfaction.

She expected the same pleasure when she completed this task of stripping wrecked wagons of salvageable canvas or muslin, righting barrels that had fallen, and sweeping out field mice already making their homes in the wagon remains. Broken wheels on good wagons had to be replaced with good wheels left over from wrecked wagons. Tongues, too, had to be salvaged and attached as spares. The whole effort consumed her. Perhaps that's just what she needed with Jed lying so cold and so close.

"Woman, you are devoted to this orderliness," Jed had said once. Then he'd teased her about how lovely she looked with the flounces of her cap streaked with dust, her face wet with perspiration, cheeks pink with the warmth of washed floors, and her eyes sparkling with accomplishment.

"Nonsense," she told him, looking up from her knees where she scrubbed.

"Look at yourself," he said. "You're positively beaming."

"I'll beam you, you don't get out of my way, you old goat," she told him and laughed.

He stuck his feet straight out, and she scrubbed the floor beneath them. But when she stood, he grabbed her hand and pulled her to his lap. "Jed, please. The children," she said glancing toward Sarah and the boys watching from the far side of the room. Jessie had not yet arrived.

"What better gift can we give our children than the joy of watching their parents in joint adoration?" he said and kissed her soundly. "Wish you were as devoted to me as to your cleaning, woman," he whispered.

"Oh, but I am, Jed. I am!" Betha kissed his already balding head and returned to her work.

She remembered that day. She regretted not taking the time to hold him a little closer, to be a little less busy with her need for order. She wondered if everything she did now would bring back a memory of regret. At least she'd held her tongue. Truth was, if she hadn't been so devoted to him, she could never have stayed with him the days he came home having indulged too heavily in spirits, nor forgiven him the times he missed the chamber pot and relieved himself in the bedroom corner.

It would take the better part of the day to do this work, Betha decided. Her own wagon would be relatively easy, but then she'd need to help Suzanne, if the woman would consent. She seemed more interested in the harness contraption Ruth and Mazy were concocting for that big dog than in tidying up. The Celestials seemed to tend to their own, and if Betha was honest, she'd say those Asian girls were as neat and orderly as she was. Yes, it would be interesting to see how this chaotic mess turned into harmony. She, for one, expected both to be tired and, for the first time since Jed died, beginning to feel contented.

Lura suggested they draw lots for riding in the good wagons. The owners of the usable wagons could then get compensation from the riders, so much per woman, with credits applied against any spare parts taken from the rider's wagon. Wheels would be worth so much, tongues perhaps more. Taking turns in bull-whacking or cooking could help wipe out the debt by the time they reached their destination. Then the profits of the sale of the wagons could be split accordingly. She thought Antone would've been proud of the intricacies of the business venture. No one took up her idea.

"We have to decide what's essential," Mazy said.

"Water," Betha said. "I believe we must take as many water barrels as we can. We need to be healthy and to stay clean."

"A clean and sober soul is blessed by the Lord," Sister Esther agreed.

"Oh, isn't that just so!" Betha said.

"We can have some barrels empty while the Platte is good, but in the alkaline country we need fresh water, my Antone said," Lura said. "And shelter. He insisted we have tents and wagons to protect us. Then worry over food."

"I could live a week off the fat of my hips," Betha said.

"A family of four could live off mine," Elizabeth said, and the group laughed. It was a full laugh, Mazy realized, a welcome sound, like wind chimes in a cooling breeze after days of stifling heat.

Someone had tied a ribbon around Fip's neck with a small bell attached to it. They heard its tinkling as Fip pulled at the grass, then bounced back and came trotting over to Elizabeth who stood next to Adora. Elizabeth bent to scratch the soft place behind the antelope's ears.

"Is that bell going to confuse us about Clayton?" Mariah asked.

"I do not believe that animal's essential," Adora said. She crossed her arms over her chest, looked around, then lowered them.

"Unless we find ourselves hungry," Ruth said over her shoulder.

"Not my pet, you don't," Elizabeth said.

"You've got those hips to rely on," Tipton said. "The rest of us are on our own."

"How nice to have you with us, Tipton," Elizabeth said, looking kindly at the girl. "And no, Clayton's bells are sleighbells. I don't think we'll be confused."

Adora tapped her fingers against her thighs. "Well, Tipton daughter, we're about to have more togetherness than you've ever tolerated before in a little space. I hope you can endure it."

In the end, they decided on four wagons. Ruth said she might hang on to some of her things, if room existed. Otherwise, she would sleep under a tent, drover the relief oxen and mules, tend to her two horses, and keep just what her bedroll would hold.

Six oxen each were needed for the three wagons, four mules for the Wilsons' transport. That left ten oxen, the Bacons' two cows, Ruth's two horses, the Bacons' riding mules, and Adora's extra mules to travel behind.

Having decided on accommodations, as Sister Esther called it, they then finished the work so each rig carried a spare wheel and tongue. The extra weight meant fewer personal "essentials."

"This is worse than when we left home," Mazy told her mother. "I thought we'd gone through what I could stand to leave. But now, to sort even more…"

"Think of the joy we'll have replacing things when we arrive."

"It'll cost us a fortune with the prices they'll ask," Mazy said. A marsh hawk swooped low, the white stripe of his wing clearly visible. "With luck, the stock'll make it with some meat on so we can sell them."

Elizabeth touched her daughter's hand as it reached for a handful of linens. They exchanged glances. "The cow brute, too."

"At least Jeremy saved some money for us to use," Mazy said, turning back to her work.

"You know where it is?" Elizabeth said. "Or should we look in the flour barrel?"

"There's nothing in there but some mice droppings by now. Mostly tumbled out with the stampede."

"No. Down in the bottom. That's where he'd have my money, I think."

"You gave him money? For safekeeping?"

" I didn't *give* it to him," Elizabeth said. "He refused to give it to me after the house sold. Your father put our home in Jeremy's name."

Mazy looked at her. "You never told me that."

"Didn't seem to matter much once I got used to the idea myself. Your father wanted to protect me, I guess. Us. So when it sold, the money was to be handled by Jeremy but to come to me. He did buy my wagon with it. Said the rest was safe. Didn't feel the need to find it right off. He wasn't going anywhere, I didn't think, and neither was the wagon."

"He had money left over from the sale of our place. He told me he did. And what was left over when he bought the brute and the cows," Mazy said. Her heart began that quickened beating that told her this was something she should pay attention to. "He told me he left it in a satchel beneath the wagon boards. Maybe I got it confused," Mazy said.

"I'm not confused about his having money," Elizabeth said. "And now I've a strong hankerin' to tear up the floor boards of our old wagon to get to the bottom."

⊰⊱

Deborah said, "We go mountain?"

It was the evening of the "tidying up" day, as Betha dubbed it. Coffee was served, along with a shared pot of wild rice, beans, and dried beef. The evening air had not yet attracted the swarms of mosquitoes that would send them all scurrying under cover.

"Tipton," Betha said, "have some beans, honey?" She handed the plate to Tipton, who shook her head. "We wouldn't want to decide something without asking everyone's opinion. Getting it said out loud, final-like."

"Before we discuss anything further on this journey, I believe the first rule of any real importance is this," Sister Esther said. "It always amazed me when I was a child at how we would begin our family gatherings sometimes with problems so complex we could not conceive a human solution. But we would bow our heads and somehow, miraculously, before we closed our time, a resolution would appear as if from God himself. I see no reason not to invoke such a tradition now, in this family. Could we agree?"

Betha glanced at Ruth, and when she didn't protest, Betha said, "All in favor? Opposed? None. Good."

"Now, that's a vote," Jason said.

Sister Esther prayed, then Ruth said, "Let's settle this direction question."

"Some not want—" Deborah began.

"Going back west'll honor what our men hoped for," Ruth interrupted. "It's easier to dream in a place where everything is new and different instead of trying to shoehorn ourselves back into an old high-button slipper back home. Our feet may have grown on this journey, and that old boot, comfortable as it might have been, could be a tight fit."

"What we're seeking may well be back where we started from, at home or what we remember of it or believe is there," Mazy said.

Suzanne cleared her throat. "The vision...what calls to me is what spoke to Bryce: to smell new air, new trees, new earth." There was something different in her tone, something less biting. She held on to Pig's harness. "When the wagon tipped and I survived, again...I believed I'd rather fail trying to climb the mountains in the West than to wallow in familiar foothills."

"You've had a change of heart," Elizabeth said.

"Aye-ee," Zilah said. "Not climb mountain, not climb."

Naomi spoke next. "Happiness live inside, same like joy," she said, patting her heart. "Where house built, no matter."

"So who's right?" Ned asked.

"No one," Mazy said. "And all of us. It isn't a 'right' kind of decision. More of a 'what's good for us' kind of choice."

"We have new information now," Betha said. "Even before you brought the oxen back, Ruth." She used her fingers to list: "We've survived the worst we could imagine, living on after the deaths of our kin. We figured out the hitching and got the wagons to go morning and night without a breakdown—'til the storm."

"We even forgave those who went on without us—at least I'm trying to forgive that doctor and folks who passed us by," Lura said. "That was so distressful for that man to leave us, like we all had a sickness ourselves." She lit her clay pipe and blew smoke out in little puffs.

"Even endured the strange looks from those we met acting like we had horns growing out of our heads," Elizabeth said. "That's a feather in our caps that we faced them and still kept going'"

Suzanne said. "And we survived the storm—almost all."

The women turned inward, the slurp of coffee and the sounds of the oxen tearing at grass an accompaniment like a softly strummed harp to a song.

"Now it's how to decide," Ruth said.

"I always hated voting," Lura said.

"Because you always lost, Ma," Mariah noted. "Matt and me and Pa outvoted you."

"Someone has to lose," Adora said. "We cannot all have our own way."

"Yes, but you had whiplash over losing your mules. If it'd been your idea or you'd agreed it was the thing to do, you'd be feelin' fine," Elizabeth said.

"I never would have agreed. Those were fine mules, some of the best in Grant County. Why, Hathaway raised—"

"So what happens if we don't vote?" Ned asked. "Do we just stay here forever?"

No one spoke for a time, and then Mazy said, "We listen to each other, until we understand, to see if there is some shared way to solve the problem."

"We'd have a better chance of things working if we all agreed rather than just be outvoted," Betha said. "It'd feel more grownup-like to have the choice."

"Are we still talking about my mules?" Adora asked.

"Not really," Elizabeth said.

"It will take too long, deciding that way," Sister Esther said. "See how long we're here discussing? We need a leader."

Ned said to his brother, "Want to flip an eagle for it? We're the men in camp."

"I say head west," Ruth said. "I never did see how to look forward while heading back. What we're doing now, trying to work out the differences in a just way, simply makes the possibility that we could reach Oregon or California that much stronger."

Deborah swallowed after she spoke. "It please me to bring bees to new husband."

"Zilah?" Mazy asked.

"I not good choose," the chubby girl said. Her eyes dropped as though the prairie ground held more safety than the faces of these women. "I go where taken."

"That makes two of us," Suzanne said.

Mazy wanted to say something to the soft-faced girl, to Suzanne too, something to help them understand that accepting help didn't have to mean giving up their independence; it didn't have to mean saying good-bye to all they knew. The thought crossed her mind that she might be speaking to herself.

"Mariah?" Mazy asked.

"Golly, no one's asked me before," Mariah said. Her thin little back sat up straight on the broken wheel she perched on. "I guess I'd like to find Matt."

"Before they get too far ahead," Ruth said.

"We could do it, Ma, if we stuck together," Mariah said.

"Naomi?"

"Some not go here, there." She nodded east, then west. "Feet stick in sand."

"I thought you were satisfied with the marriage choices," Sister Esther said. She turned her stiff upper body toward Naomi. "The man's letters have been most kind, most respectable. Surely you don't want to break the contract?"

"Zilah believes he will break it," Deborah offered.

"Why would he? I think you worry overmuch. I regret that—"

"So where are we?" Adora interrupted. "Does everyone get to have a say here?"

A chorus of "yes," "go ahead," "speak your mind" urged Adora on.

"If truth be known, I am not looking forward to facing people back in Cassville, the ones who'll say how silly we were to have left in the first place. Hathaway...dying. Charles...even though I know he left in a fuss, well, he is still my son..."

"It will be harder to pretend everything is fine back home, won't it, Mother?" Tipton said.

"Yes, it will," she said, in the high to low tone that marked her speech.

"So. Tipton," Suzanne said, summarizing.

"I really don't care," Tipton said.

"It's finding something to go to that matters," Elizabeth said, "finding a thing to believe in, that's what'll get us through. Hard parts'll show up either direction, and we got to have something bigger than a river to ford to keep our eyes on."

"I want to go where Ruth goes," Jessie said. "Are you going to feed Koda now?"

"In a minute," Ruth said and smiled at the girl.

"Sarah? Boys?" Betha asked.

"Hey, Papa thought Oregon or California was what would be good for us, so I'd like that," Ned said. Jason nodded his head.

"Do we have enough supplies?" Betha asked.

"If we share and share alike," Lura said.

Suzanne said, "I don't hear that all have said their preference yet."

They calculated, and then eyes turned to Mazy.

Elizabeth reached her hand and placed it on Mazy's as it rested over the tin cup. Her mother's hands felt warm against her cool ones. "What would you need, child, to go west? What would make it your own choice and not because you had to, or because someone made you, or because not going would mean you'd broken up a family?"

Mazy heard her heart beating. Their looks frightened, the way they put such weight in what she'd say. She wanted to do what would make them all happy, wanted to please them so. She recognized the feeling. It was who she was, giving up her wishes, lacking courage to stand firm.

"A little time," Mazy said. "That used to drive my husband crazy, how long it took for me to decide a thing. But I still wonder if we could finish this discussion first thing in the morning?"

❧

The women turned in for the night in their tents. Tomorrow would be soon enough to settle into the new wagons, say one last good-bye to the treasures and trunks they were leaving behind.

Tipton pulled a muslin sheet over her shoulder, her back to the side of the wagon. No one was all that interested in her. She could tell. They talked around her as though she wasn't there. Maybe she wasn't. Maybe the laudanum had transformed her into a wagon tongue, something still and straight that could be sat on, stood on, made to drag around, but could break under pressure.

She hadn't found any more laudanum. Her mother must have hidden it. The whiskey, too. Not that she needed them. They took the edge off her hunger was all, and she liked knowing she was in control. Ignoring the gnawing in her stomach encouraged her, even if she did have to rely on the laudanum to do it. And the lightness in her head? A sign she could disappear even in the center of the women's circle. She could go where nothing could touch her. No pain, not ever again. Deep inside she went, refusing to feed the knot of fear that made her stomach puff out like a pumpkin. Still, she'd have to get spare laudanum laid up somewhere; that was just planning ahead.

They carried spares of wagon tongues. Her mother could even get a spare daughter. What would it take? Mariah was about her age. Her mother could hover and worry over her if she chose, or even Miz Bacon. She wasn't that much older than Tipton herself. She'd make a much better daughter for her mother. So much brighter, so much kinder, so much less likely to make mistakes, less likely to hurt others. She was more lovable, that was the truth of the matter. And in California or Oregon, Tipton's mother would have lots of motherless daughters to choose from, lots of spares to make everything work the right way.

Her arm ached. It had been numbing up less with the laudanum. Lura kept a whiskey bottle for medication. Tipton hadn't tapped that yet, but the aching might demand it. *Breathe, hold your breath when you're frightened,* that's what Tyrell had told her. The very thought of him gone made her swoon.

"What?" Tipton said.

Someone had called her name. She sat up. "I didn't hear what you said."

"I wondered what it would take for you to agree to stay with us each day, be around?" Mazy asked. "Not go away in your mind quite so much."

"What difference does it make?"

"It matters to me," Mazy said. "We've both lost something, Tip. Something important and someone essential too. Now we have to find a way through the empty spaces. I'd feel better, if I knew that before you did anything foolish, went any farther away, that you'd come to me, as someone winding my way through it too. At least tell me…if you just can't stand it any longer."

"So you could talk me out of it?"

"So you could know that someone cares. And because you're a good person, one Tyrell loved dearly. He believed in you. And I believe you'd keep a commitment to someone else almost easier than to yourself." Tipton stared, surprised that she didn't turn aside. "So what would it take for you just to stay?"

"Someone wanting me to," Tipton heard herself say.

⌒≈⌒

Mazy had never been good at decisions. She tried to think of those she had made for herself, made without pressure or thinking of others, to please her father or her mother. Had she ever made any just because it was what she wanted? There hadn't been many. She had expressed an opinion about the log home, a piece of furniture they might make, where it should sit in the main room. Jeremy had such strong opinions on everything that hers came out as tentative, frivolous almost.

One evening, Jeremy suggested that the quilt she'd gotten for their bed might be better replaced with another or filled with less down; or that the amount of water she'd added to the venison stew could be cut back—though when she did that, he complained that she had too many added for the volume of liquid or shouldn't have added the potatoes at all. She began to question everything she did, even when he wasn't near her, to anticipate what objection he might make to whatever she chose to do. Sometimes, when she was tired or felt as large and as lumbering as a cow, she failed to act at all, certain of her incompetence, certain of his chastisement. Gentle chastisement, of course; he never struck her, never shouted at her. But still her decisions felt awkward under his scrutiny, and so did she herself.

Then after, she made biting comments even when he sounded pleased and nice. She didn't know why she did that, but she did, snapping about the fence not getting finished or his constantly running nose. She wanted to see herself as kind, but the price she paid for harmony was the tension inside herself.

Mazy tried to remember something she had decided without giving in to Jeremy's wishes. She wanted the garden plot made, she had pushed for that. And when he traveled to Milwaukee to get the brute, she had insisted on staying home. Looking back, he had agreed without effort. Still, he must have approved of both of those decisions, or they wouldn't have happened.

If she was honest, she would have to admit that at some moment— she didn't know when—she had been sucked into the cool place of the river and had stopped deciding for herself. She didn't ask what the right thing to do was, the best thing, or even what God would wish. She didn't decide because something would make her happy or more content or because it would give her new information or make her feel stronger or even more sure of who she was. No, she simply made her best guess at what Jeremy would want—or anyone else involved in the matter—and then chose that. Harmony. Then sometime later she made them pay for stripping her of her wishes.

Perhaps her insistence on going back to Wisconsin was because she had said she'd return, said she'd "make Jeremy pay" for making her leave. Hadn't the voice in her dream demanded that she listen to herself? But not if she headed back just to spite someone else. Mazy shook her head. She didn't do well with choices.

Bacon sizzled, the coffee perked in the old pot. Everyone gathered around the fire and commented on the glorious morning, the eerie music of the coyotes that had serenaded them in the night. They enjoyed light talk and chatter. Pig chased the boys and barked until

Betha urged them to stop. She shook her head when Sarah gave her tin plate to the dog to lick. Fip's bell tinkled as he ripped at the stiff grass. Then a silence cloaked the group, and Mazy knew it was time to answer the question put to her the night before—in some ways, to answer the very question she had put to Tipton too.

"Shall we bow our heads?" Mazy asked.

"I'll say a prayer," Mariah said. Mazy tried to organize what she'd be saying and didn't listen, but Elizabeth said it was "so loverly" that several asked Mariah to repeat it.

"'Tis a gift to be simple,
'Tis a gift to be free,
'Tis a gift to come down
Where we ought to be
And when we find ourselves
In the place that's right
'Twill be in the valley
Of love and delight."

Mazy inhaled a deep breath, the phrase "find ourselves where we ought to be" still ringing in her head. Longing overwhelmed Mazy in an instant. She wanted to go back, more than anything, to what was, to what had been. But it was not there. It no longer existed.

"I said I'd go back, even if no one else wanted to. But some new dream," Mazy said, "digging into some new plot of life rather than attempting to retill the old one, I think that's what we're all wanting. I saw the brightness in your eyes last night when you talked. A kind of passion filled your face, Mother. It washed away that blank and empty look that's clouded our eyes like an old dog's. Maybe it's what we need to wash away the tedium of greasing the wheels or ease our aching arms and backs from cracking whips. Maybe it's the inspiration of going toward something, of doing something that seems right regardless of how it comes out, that's what'll keep the ache in our hearts at bay."

If she told them no, that she wouldn't go west with them, would they all turn back with her? Was she prepared to deprive them? She liked these women. They were good people, enduring. And they'd been kind to her. She wanted to please them, hoped it would also please herself.

She took a deep breath. "I can plant a garden in Oregon or California," she said. "Or places in between, I'd guess. I never wanted to come at all, not ever; and what would please me most would be to have what I left at home, do what I wanted back there with the husband I loved. But that's gone. It will never be."

Her stomach hurt, and she wished Jeremy were there beside her so she could tell him of the trap she'd closed over her soul, blame him for what was. But he wasn't, and blame wasn't hers to deliver. It was a lesson she was coming to learn. Blaming just got in the way of her seeking what she wanted.

"So you'll go west with us?" Mariah asked.

"Yes," Mazy said, "I'll go. I'm sorry it isn't with more joy, but I'll do everything I can to get us all there together. So we'll find that place for all of us that's a valley of love and delight."

being guided

Sister Esther had insisted that her brothers come with her, badgered them both into submission. They'd obliged, the younger following their elders' lead, done as she bid, until dead. Now she stood alone, staring at the place that marked her second brother's grave. After two days of travel the women were back where they'd started, back by the stream where her brother, Jeremy, Antone, Hathaway, and Tyrell were buried.

The boy Clayton giggled and chased that antelope near Jeremy's grave. Sarah and her brothers followed close behind. Had they no respect for the dead? There was something incongruous in laughter beside these lonely graves. Yet what was disrespectful about loving life, celebrating the end of earthly disappointment and betrayal? Esther watched Mazy standing beside her husband's marker of stones. Mazy motioned to the child as he passed Jeremy's grave, called out his name. He waddled toward her, and she swung him upward and around, then pulled him to her breast. It looked as though she wept on the child's blond head.

Esther shook her head, unclasped her hands. Grieving. Done in so many different ways. She took long strides back toward her wagon, her skirts swishing limp around her aching knees. She wished she knew for certain, when bad things happened, whether it was part of God's guidance or just a consequence of one's own will.

Ducking inside her wagon, she dampened a handkerchief with

warm water and dabbed it on the back of her neck. Rested, she stepped out into the sunlight looking back toward the graves. What she witnessed soothed her aging eyes. Adora walked with Tipton. Mariah bent to her mother's head, too. And there stood Zilah, the sunlight fading the depressions on her cheeks so that her face looked almost smooth. She leaned over the area where Ferrel would have lain. When she walked away, wildflowers bobbed inside a mint green vase. Esther recognized it as one of the Asian girl's few possessions.

❧

"First real grieving you've had," Mazy told Tipton later. They stood alone at the pile of rocks. She rubbed circles with her palm on Tipton's shoulder, talked as though soothing a child. The two leaned into each other. "It's easier to go away, I know, but it keeps coming back unless we look it in the face."

"Are you?" Tipton asked between shuddered breaths.

"Facing things? I turned west. My life has changed. Me, who likes everything to stay the same." She sighed. "Like Suzanne said, life as we knew it ended. All we have left are the things we choose to remember."

"Yeah," Tipton said, pulling away. "And the misery of learning to accept what is."

❧

Life moved into routine, the physical movements of milking the cows, hitching the oxen, bringing the mules to harness became familiar as pulling water from a well at home. Who did what at dawn, which oxen snubbed behind which wagon at noon, who hobbled the horses at night, all became expected.

Pig walked beside Suzanne, who gripped hard leather that stood up like an upside-down letter *U* from his harness. Deborah rubbed honey onto Suzanne's burned legs once when they stopped. Mazy even heard Suzanne say "thanks" and saw her touch the girl's arm with tenderness. Over the sounds of the mules and oxen, she heard Adora's voice rise as if meant to rouse her daughter, who rode, eyes glazed, beside her. Mazy tried to memorize the landscape and in her mind imagined a grassy mound made in the shape of a bird over Jeremy's grave.

The routine fed their need for familiar in a foreign land.

And while the patterns gave them confidence, recognition of their bent, they also gifted them with time: time to think and remember, reevaluate and wonder. Time to live with the loss birthed by long hours of lament.

They were a few days out of Laramie—again—by Mazy's calculations when they pulled up earlier than usual for the evening. Deborah made her way in her quick-quick steps to the wagon Mazy walked beside.

"Clover good for stopping," she said. "For bees. It is time."

"I'd forgotten," Mazy said. "I'm sorry."

"No need," the tiny woman said. "Twice each moon enough, but they have changed their songs. One colony very quiet. The queen dead, maybe. Bees dance out. They bring harmony back for others."

The women circled the wagons up, and Deborah and Naomi set out the six boxes of bees a few feet away. The buzzing picked up so that even to Mazy's untrained ear, she could hear the change.

The two small women donned mesh draped from their hats and over their faces. Then they pulled back the tin that gave the insects ventilation but kept them securely inside. Once released, the tiny black dots lighted on the girls' jade-colored dresses, then rose and fluttered, almost dancing, lifting amidst a soft humming song.

"What are they doing?" Betha asked. She'd come by and stood beside Sister Esther a good distance away.

"I am told that they are cleansing themselves," Sister Esther said.

"Tidying up?" Betha asked. "Well, I'll be."

"Perhaps. They clean their hives this way. They will seek out nectar and pollen of plants and what else they need to make honey. And when the night cools, they will return. This is an experiment, taking larvae and queens across the land, as we are."

Betha fanned herself. "Feels pretty hot to me. I hope it cools down before it gets too dark for them. What keeps them coming back?"

Deborah approached the women and answered Betha. "The queen remains. She is what they live for. They see nothing else, just one thing."

"Just feed and protect. Seems a dull life."

"It is a...rewarded life," Deborah insisted. "They are certain of what is needed and they do these things. It is a remembrance for me."

"A reminder," Sister Esther corrected. "I believe the word you wish is *reminder*."

Deborah bowed her head, accepting the correction. "A reminder," she said. "I make duty good, day fill with sweet honey."

~⁓~

Mazy actually looked forward to the necessary circle in the evening when the chores were finished, before they quieted their thoughts and slipped under their tents for the night.

"We need to be laughing some," Elizabeth said. She held her skirt out and fluttered it to create a breeze against her legs.

"Laughing? I'm too tired at night to eat, let alone laugh," Betha said.

"But that's what'll keep us going," Elizabeth said, "Got to tend to business, take care of each other, and then we got to laugh."

"How do you propose to do it, Mother?"

"I'm pondering that."

An owl hooted in the distance, and they could hear the buzz of insects, the low hum of returned bees mixing with the whine of mosquitoes. The women made their way back to the tents. The air felt cooler outside of the wagon box, and allowing Suzanne and Clayton to stay inside kept the child from wandering off should he wake in the night. Elizabeth pulled the muslin sheet over her head. "Maybe we should borrow some of those tin coverings that keep the bees in," she said. "Might keep the mosquiters out."

Evening scents of dying embers drifted around them in the dark.

"Best laugh I've had is finding that money," Mazy said into the quiet.

Elizabeth chuckled. "Guess we can laugh at old things if we can't think of anything new. Still surprises me that it was so much."

"The Malarkys didn't strike me as people who could cash us out."

"And what was left over from the wagons and the brute and cows purchase, it shouldn't have been that much."

"Something doesn't seem right about it," Mazy said.

"Jeremy did want to provide for you. Maybe he just planned to surprise you when you reached Oregon. Me too."

"He knew I didn't like surprises."

⚬⚬⚬

Several wagons passed them going east; riders, too. Ruth tipped her hat to men leading packed mules. They rode fine ponies, sturdy, short-bodied animals. They'd be good to mix with her horses, give their animals a little more size and, in her breed, bring in more stockiness, the toughness needed for these prairies. Maybe today they'd catch up with her small herd, find Matt and Joe Pepin and travel with them. Ruth wished they had split up the wagons right away, never turned back at all, not waited for a disaster to set them back on course. She'd be farther from Zane if they had. They'd be in Laramie by now if they hadn't. But that, too, had been her story: hindsight, doubling back.

Families in wagons hauled by mules stared as they passed Ruth on the left, the side toward the Platte. Well, let them. She guessed the men's pants and the floppy hat might have thrown them off, made them wonder. But she'd seen a few women wearing bloomer costumes—hers wasn't much stranger than those. Most didn't speak to her or to anyone as far as she could tell from her view back at the end of the line. At least they weren't attempting small talk, and so she needn't worry that anyone would remember later who she was.

"We need help with one of Betha's oxen," Mariah said. She'd ridden up on Jumper, the girls and the horse having the task of patrolling along the four wagons, passing messages back and forth, checking on yokes and mules. "His foot is bad, I think. His shoe come off."

"We knew that would happen," Ruth said. "Just not when. Feet should have been tough enough by now. You stay back here. Will you be all right?"

"Sure. Me and Jump can handle it."

Ruth trotted forward to Betha's wagon, which was always second so that Zilah could be called to assist Mazy and Elizabeth if needed. She reined up next to Betha's team.

"It's Cicero," Betha said, wringing her hands. "He's just the best one, don't you know."

Ruth called for a halt, dismounted, then ran her hand down the ox's leg. "This one?" she asked Betha.

The big ox objected to her touch, and he shifted his weight, putting more of it on the sore hoof, which made him bellow and slip his other hoof from her hand. It landed, solid as a tree trunk. He fluttered his skin against a fly and switched his tail toward Ruth's bent face.

"Have you done this sort of thing before?" Lura asked.

"Just seen it done," Ruth said. "I've helped throw a horse, get it on its side to geld, but I don't know that that same procedure would work here."

"Oh, he's already a steer, dear, I'm sure of that," Lura said.

"I know that," Ruth said, the only one of the group who didn't laugh. "I wasn't talking about gelding him, but throwing him."

The ox let Ruth lift his foot when she tried again, but when she touched the tender spot beneath, he leaned in to her and dropped his hoof to the ground, barely missing her toes as she jumped back.

"Maybe we can use a rope just to hold him off balance," Tipton said.

Ruth turned to look at her. "Have you seen that done?"

Tipton shrugged her shoulders.

They talked of digging a trench and tipping him in it, upside down.

"That seems dreadful," Betha said.

"Grease his foot maybe," Mazy offered. She swatted at flies circling her bonnet.

"We might try that first," Tipton said. "See if he'd step into a bucket. Make up a temporary shoe with some buffalo hide, until we reach Laramie and can have a farrier look at him."

"All that tar and tallow? That's so dirty."

Ruth ran a rope she secured from Betha's wagon, reaching it over the big animal's shoulder. She drew it across his back and over and tied to a back hock, then around so it could be pulled to keep him off balance if he tried to lean in to her when she lifted his front leg.

"Pour all but an inch or so out of it, into someone else's grease bucket," Ruth ordered. Her voice came out sharp. She didn't care. "Put it right beside me, Tipton. You control it. Elizabeth, when I lift on his leg, you pull on the rope to keep him off balance, so he doesn't crowd me. Tell me when you're ready."

Tipton filled a bucket almost to the top. Then she set the nearly empty bucket where Ruth directed. "Ready," she said.

Elizabeth tugged slightly on the rope, the ox being used as its own pulley, and when Ruth lifted the big foot, Elizabeth pulled the rope, holding it.

"Let it down!" Ruth said, sliding the bucket under as she did.

Cicero lifted his heavy foot again, out of the bucket, just as Mazy handed Ruth a large square of buffalo hide cut from the Pawnee gift. Ruth dropped the hide, and Cicero put his greased foot square in the middle. Ruth shouted, "Rawhide!" and Naomi handed her the twists that Ruth used to tie the buffalo hide around his hoof.

But something about the rawhide bothered Cicero. He shifted his weight now, bellowed and lumbered his body side to side, moving the wagon forward and back.

"Pull the rope, Elizabeth," Ruth yelled. "Chock the wheel! He's not liking all this. Everyone step back."

What happened next came quickly.

Cicero yanked Plato, his yoke mate, distressing the four oxen behind them. Mazy struggled to set the wheel chock. Shouted orders drifted back. Then from the side came Pig chasing Fip.

Little black nubbins like buttons on Fip's head could be seen like snake eyes by the women as the two made straight for the wagon. They ran under the oxen, Fip squeezing beneath the oxen's bellies, Pig panting and bounding over the tongue.

Betha, who'd climbed up onto the wagon stood, yelled, "No, Pig!" just as she lost her balance, toppled over the side onto Lura, who'd been standing too close to the grease bucket—the full one—which spilled over them both.

Women, grease, dirt, and skirts rolled together just beyond the oxen's feet while Ruth steadied the team on one side and Mazy at the other.

"Whoa, Cicero. Whoa, now," Ruth cautioned. The ox bellowed, shook his head and long horns. "Get over here, Betha," Ruth shouted. "He knows you. Help settle him."

"He won't know her now," Mariah said.

Black tar and resin, thick tallow and dirt covered both Betha and Lura, who pulled each other up. Betha laughed first, pointing a filthy finger at Lura.

"Do I look as bad as you?" she said.

"Much worse," Lura told her. "I always wanted a cocoa-colored apron. Just didn't want it sticking to me!"

Cicero calmed with Betha's chuckling. Ruth shook her head and snickered, the rest joining her in relief. The laughter started as a ripple and grew until even Sister Esther's stiff shoulders shook. The Celestials smiled and waved their arms in excitement. They ducked their heads beneath their mushroom-shaped hats. Deborah's wide sleeves collected the breeze as she pointed and laughed.

"What is it?" Suzanne said. "What's so funny?"

"Kind of hard to describe," Mazy said. "Two pretty dirty women."

"Try to describe it," Suzanne said, and Ruth heard a pleading in her voice, a wish to join in such as Ruth had never heard from her before.

It was Tipton who described it.

"Pig chased the antelope that startled Cicero, who jerked the wagon that discombobulated Betha, who toppled onto Lura, and both splattered on top of the full bucket of grease that I filled. Both are sitting in the dirt, spitting up grease."

A smile moved across Suzanne's face. "I'm trying to picture it," she said.

"Good thing I had padding to land on," Betha said, shaking her hands as if the muck would flick off.

"Are you talking about me or something else?" Lura asked, attempting to stand. Her tight little curls of brown hair wore splattered grease that spread as her fingers forgot and scratched at her nose. "How can such a little amount of grease go so far?"

"That blasted Fip," Betha said.

"Elizabeth?" The women said in chorus.

"I know, I know," Elizabeth said coming from around the other side. "I've a heap of cleaning to do, maybe all the way to the Pacific. But Pig helped."

"Pig, how could you!" Mazy said, but she was laughing.

"Oh, let's blame the ox," Elizabeth said. "Our wagon shouldn't bear the full brunt. We'll be cleaning in heaven if we have to make amends for everything."

"Why, that'd be a joy," Betha told her.

Tears rolled down their faces, and Mazy thought how odd tears were—that they arrived looking alike whether worn by grief or relief. "At least Cicero survived," she said.

"And Clayton didn't cause this," Suzanne said. "I'm glad of that."

"Nope, the kids are out of this one," Mazy said, wiping her eyes with her thumbs.

"Where are they, anyway?" Betha asked. They all turned to search.

At that moment they heard Mariah's cry.

~≈~

Behind the wagon, Sarah spied something white. The breeze lifted it, but she caught and unfolded it. She tried to read the big words, wishing they still had the classes studying letters and such. There were lots of numbers and lines and rectangles. She thought she read the word *propolis* and maybe *frames*. The paper had some weight to it, perfect for folding into a kite. She creased it and threw it. It lifted, rose, and then dropped. She skipped after it, refolded it, and this time sent it soaring, somewhere far behind the last wagon toward the stock. It caught in a bramble of greasewood and sage. She had started toward it when she heard Mariah's cry and rushed back to that excitement instead.

~≈~

Mariah carried the small boy. She cried as she handed him off to Mazy's outstretched arms. He was wailing, and Mazy was grateful.

"I didn't mean to," Mariah said. "I mean Jumper didn't. He just showed up. I never saw him."

"Where're the others?" Elizabeth said.

"I haven't seen them. I didn't see Clayton. I was just sitting on Jumper, shoving the mules off. They was circling like they do sometimes, and pushing, and then I heard this sound. Clayton musta walked behind us, just walked right there."

Her description seemed to make Clayton's crying more frantic.

"Give him to me," Suzanne demanded. She'd stumbled her way behind them, the dog close at her side.

Mazy handed her the child.

"You did all right, girl," Elizabeth told Mariah, crying herself. "The cobweb you stuffed on the cut stopped the bleeding pretty good. Head wounds always bleed a stream. He's breathing."

"Someone, put your hand on my shoulders and move us to the wagon," Suzanne said. "Help me, please! I'm ready to be guided."

⁂

Naomi had preceded them into the wagon. And when Suzanne arrived with her son, Naomi's strong hands took the boy from his mother. "I put him here," she said, pressing the boy to her silk-covered breast while Mazy helped Suzanne climb inside.

Her amber fingers dipped a soft cloth into a basin of water and dabbed at the boy's face.

"Not deep," she said. "It bleed and dirt and grass mix not so bad." He began to calm and take in huge gulps of air.

"We need to keep it clean," Mazy said. "Doesn't look like it hurt his eye. Just above it, Suzanne."

"What does he look like?" Suzanne asked. "Tell me."

How hard to not know, Mazy thought, to never know, to never see, to sometimes touch their faces, to hear only rustles in a room, to smell only sweetness of fragrances.

Naomi pulled the web free, pressing it back when the bleeding began again.

"He looks fine but for the dirty face," Elizabeth said gently. "And Naomi's a whiz with plants and such."

"I find Mei-Ling," Naomi said. "Back soon, Missy Sue." She turned to leave, but Deborah stepped up to the canvas opening and handed a jar to Naomi. Immediately, Naomi pressed her fingers inside and then spread the clear substance onto Clayton's wound.

"I smell honey," Suzanne said.

"Not honey, Missy Sue," Naomi assured her. "Same like. Bees make at home. Heal good. Make better smell. Help bone, too."

"What if he's...? Is it safe?"

"So safe, Missy Sue. New things not always bad."

❧

"We need a plan," Mazy said over supper. People turned to her but kept chewing.

"For what?" Betha asked. Her face looked scrubbed pink—the butter supply had been depleted, used to remove the resin and tallow from her and Lura's hair. Lura had thrown her apron away; Betha planned on a major cleaning once they reach Laramie.

"For making sure that someone watches Clayton every day."

"It's my fault," Sarah said. "I got to writing my letters in the sand with a stick and forgot about him."

"No one's fault but mine," Mariah said.

"No sense in blaming," Mazy said. "We need to ask what to do next time, to prevent the problem. Tipton, perhaps you—"

"I'm not good with children," Tipton said.

"You were wanting your own bad enough," her mother said to Tipton's scowl.

"I should have watched the mules closer," Mariah said.

"They were just being mules," Adora said. "They don't like little things much, like children and dogs."

"It's no one's fault but mine," Suzanne said. "I just can't watch him. Can't *watch* anything."

"There has to be a way," Mazy said. "Our losses should weave us together, not tear us apart."

❧

Koda shied as Ruth rode him past the sagebrush once they got underway. "What is it?" Ruth asked, then noticed the white kite. "Get it," she said, and the gelding shook his head, jangling the steel bit. He arched his long neck and with his lips tugged at the paper. "Good boy!" Ruth told him, patting his neck as she leaned to take the kite from his mouth. She unfolded the parchment and read.

❧

While others commented on the fascinating rock formations that marked their way, the glow of the sunsets, the occasional glimpse of the patches of white that belonged to wagons on the south side of the Platte, Suzanne lived on in darkness. She could not take away the bleakness that Clayton's accident brought back. Her blackness, a reminder of her incompetence.

"I've an idea," Mazy said.

"About Clayton's care?" Betha asked.

Mazy shook her head. "No. Something to lighten our days and evenings, which my mother says is so critical. A game, sort of."

"Oh, good," Elizabeth said. "I was hoping you'd come through."

"Each of us should think of a truth and a fiction," Mazy said. "Something no one would know of us just by looking at us or our having said it before. In our evening circle, one of us will tell the two things and the rest will guess which is the true thing."

"Make up lies?" Sister Esther said stiffly.

"Just for a game," Elizabeth said.

"I like it," Mariah said.

"A lie. We get to tell a lie?" Jason said.

"You have to tell something truthful, too," Betha said. She stood, thinking. "So here's my lie. I left four pairs of shoes back home that I never wore." She paused. "No, that's true." She thought again. "This'll be something to consider. It's hard to say what I'm not."

"Somewhat…exposing," Ruth said. "Or could be."

"Good then. We'll start tomorrow after our necessary circle."

Suzanne listened to the muffled voices of women readying for bed. She fought back tears. She had a truth and a lie she could share. Truth—she was unable to care adequately for her child. Lie—anyone would offer to help. Truth—she would surely fail her other child on its way. Lie—she couldn't give away either child.

⊸

"I so sorry, Missy Esther, so sorry." Deborah's face pinched in humiliation as Esther shook the parchment at her like a shaming finger.

"You simply cannot be trusted with something so important. I will take responsibility for it now as I should have before. It goes inside my writing desk," she said, showing the shivering girl, whose fingers pressed against white lips.

"You take better care, Miss," Deborah said.

"We will lay it between linens and hope the creases will ease out so the plans can be read. You owe your future to Ruth," she said.

"A new debt," Deborah said as tears pooled in her eyes.

⊸

They made Fort Laramie on July the first. They'd crossed the North Platte, using the rickety public ferry found in working order, though requiring exorbitant prices. At least that's what Sister Esther thought.

Still, it was either stay on the north side, bypass the fort, and roust a sol-dier to operate the ferry, or, as Ruth suggested, run it themselves. The women decided to pool their resources, though Adora and Tipton were busily looking for something in their wagon when the dollar demanded was paid.

"Koda's foot isn't good," Ruth said. "He'll need a bar shoe. Can you take him, Tipton?"

"Don't you want to go?" Mariah asked.

"No!" Then with less force she said, "Someone needs to stay with the stock. Tipton? You've been around farriers. Could you do it?"

"I stay help with oxen," Naomi said, an offer Ruth accepted.

"Make a list of what we need," Betha said. "I want to check the reg-ister to see when the boys went through."

"And maybe Charles," Adora said, her face brightening.

"Thanks, Tipton," Ruth said as the women moved out. And to Betha she whispered, "Don't register. I don't want to give Zane any help."

"You think he's following, Ruthie? There've been no signs."

"Trust me, Betha. It's the one thing I'm certain of."

❦

The adobe buildings set in a square, some two-story, with a thatch of green and raised from the treeless banks of the Laramie River, perked the women up. This was a place of ceremony—they were halfway to their destination.

Mazy said, "I almost said out loud that we were 'halfway home.'"

"You did say it out loud, girl!" her mother said. "And right you are."

"How many of you are there?" the sutler asked when they'd come into the storehouse, the group of them too many for the size of the room.

"A few weeks ago we were eleven wagons, twelve women, seven children," Mazy said. "Now we're four wagons, all on the north bank, and just one large gathering."

"And we're all filthy," Betha said.

"Speak for yourself," Elizabeth chided her.

"Baths are a twenty-five-cent piece each. You got that?"

"The baths are on us," Mazy said. "My mother and me. For everyone. Our gift."

"Nonsense," Sister Esther said. "Each can pay their own way."

"Each can, but each can also accept a gift," Elizabeth told her. "Want to keep me cleaning through Eden's Gate for what my Fip did? I'm needing ways to find redemption."

Sister Esther pursed her lips and nodded, conceding.

"All right," the little man said, his white mustache like a sleepy caterpillar beneath his bulbous nose. "Who's first?"

"We are," Adora said. "We look a fright, my daughter and I. She's been ill, and on the trail it's just so difficult, truth be known."

"Costs extra if someone else hauls your water," he said.

"I'll pay the extra," Adora said. "Tipton, you did find my purse?"

Tipton stared at her. "I haven't done anything with your purse. Haven't even seen it."

"Weren't you looking for it? Where could it be, then? You're so addled these days you could have put it somewhere and not even known."

"Did you have it before we went back to the graves?" Elizabeth asked.

Adora thought. "I think so. Oh, my. I can't exactly remember." Her eyes looked pinched. "There was so much to think about. Hathaway's dying…if it got lost in the storm…maybe my other wagon." Her eyes opened wide. "Tipton, are you sure you didn't just misplace it? What'll we do without money?"

"Nothing you can do now. We can check in the wagon—"

"You ladies bathing or not?"

"I carry water for you," Deborah offered.

"Why thank you, dear," Adora said, accepting. "Lord knows I'm in need of pampering."

She didn't notice Tipton roll her eyes.

The world did look better after a bath, Elizabeth decided. And tonight they'd sleep on a regular bed following a meal that included fruit and whipped, sweetened cream. This was quite a place what with all the folks who'd arrived a few days before still staying on, resting up animals and all. Wagons coming in after them. The register included Charles's name a good two weeks ahead of them, the little weasel. Good news for Ruth, too. The boys had been here, resupplied and headed out, leaving a note for Ruth and Lura, assuring them they'd meet up in Oregon City if they didn't catch up before then.

One night here and they'd move on. The boys and the stock weren't too far ahead. Elizabeth heard music, a fiddle and harmonica. The sutler said there'd be a dance later. Elizabeth thought that she might go, not to dance so much as to people-watch, catch the glances from one to the other that said more than words could ever, watch skirts swirl, and feed on fun. They could all use a little dancing to push the losses away, have fonder memories, though she didn't expect to see anyone else she knew there.

Tipton stood before the sign that read *Blacksmith Shoppe*. Earlier in the day, she'd helped Betha bring Cicero and Koda here, one leading the horse by a halter and the other prodding the ox gently with a goad, both talking as they moved.

"Got the foot in time," the blacksmith said. "Greased it when you shoulda. Nice work, whoever did it."

"It was all of us," Tipton said, liking the truth of it.

"Horse needs a bar shoe, all right," he said. "I'll put a little vee-bar on it. Marks my style."

"Look at you," Adora told Tipton when she got back. "Already dirtied up after your first bath in months. We've no money for another, not until we search for my purse again."

"I just wanted to help the farrier," she'd told her.

She'd come back that night. She felt a closeness to Tyrell here as she stood beneath the sign, watching the blacksmith work. It was how she'd met Tyrell those months ago back in Wisconsin. This was where Tyrell would have spent his day, fanning the big bellows, bending and shaping the iron, forming and tapping it across the anvil. Tipton rubbed at her arm, willed herself to breathe evenly, without quickened breaths.

They'd kept the anvil and the tongs and the hammer, some iron shoes, too. Tipton had been unable to part with them. Everything here was twice as large as what they carried, twice as hot with the coals burning red. The steady clank of a hammer reached her ears, the clink of a tong each time the blacksmith shifted the shoe. She loved the sound, the smells of hot metal, and the sizzle of steam when the blacksmith stuffed the shaped iron into water to cool it down, turn it, and clank again.

Timing and shaping. Tyrell had been shaping her, too, though he would have said it wasn't him at all, but God's work with Tyrell as the tool. She wondered, for just a moment, what all the hammering and shaping would force her to become.

⌁

Elizabeth led Suzanne to a covered porch surrounding the largest building of the fort. The older woman insisted that she come inside, but Suzanne drew the line at the porch.

"I'd prefer to be here," she said. "I can hear the music and listen to the laughter without having to negotiate being a part of it." She patted her stomach. "Negotiating is no easy task these days. Besides, Pig would be hard to manage. I can smell the food they have in there spread on a table I'm assuming is just that dog's height."

"You'll miss so much by not being inside," Elizabeth told her.

"I can't see people, I can't read their lips, so listening is what I have. And the scents of things and the vibration of their feet on the floor. And

I can feel the shaded area we just stepped up on, and that's bound to mean a bench."

"There's one here, all right," Elizabeth told her. "Suit yourself."

She'd settled herself on the wooden slats, which felt cool against her cotton wrapper. Suzanne found her fan and waved the air before her face. "I'm leavin' ya," Elizabeth said. "You want to join me later, just follow your nose." She stuck her head inside, then stepped back out. "You're right. There's plenty of food covering the side tables."

The cooler night air drifted around her, joining the vibrations of the dancing feet, the clapping. She'd never spent much time on those sensations until she lost her sight. She'd paid attention to what she could see; that's what a photographer did. One looked for the subtleties of light and shadow, of shapes and angles. There were no angles in sound, no shapes wrapped in scents.

She could smell yeast coming from the bakery. She listened and thought she detected someone walking across the square. Pig growled low. She heard the shuffle of leather against the worn Spanish brick steps and then a quietness broken by breathing.

"I am in awe of your beauty, good woman," a man's voice said, deep, controlled. She smelled cologne and something antiseptic. She gripped the leather handle on Pig.

Suzanne smelled the sweet scent come closer. She stiffened. Pig barked once, stood, and lunged against her hand. *Pig didn't like him!* A wash of cold swept down her spine.

volition

The thump of a Virginia Reel with hands clapping and whoops and hollers drew Tipton, not that she planned to go inside. That would be disrespectful to Tyrell's memory and to her dream, one they'd shared of how they'd dance together when they reached Fort Laramie. She did not believe she would ever dance again.

Above the music, Tipton heard Pig barking and Suzanne's protest and a man's melodramatic cajoling. And while Tipton couldn't see Suzanne, she knew the sound and conversation came from somewhere near the well-dressed man on the porch.

"Is something wrong? Suzanne?" Tipton asked.

The man turned. "I meant no harm," he said. Light from inside the paned windows flickered against a diamond stickpin in his neck scarf. He wore a white suit that deepened the bronze of a face furrowed with what looked like concern.

White. White hat, white hair—in all this dust, he wears white.

"I merely wished to introduce myself." He wore a short beard, cropped around a firm chin. It, too, looked white, with black streaks.

"Oh, Tipton. Good. Pig, it's all right," Suzanne said.

"Pig?" the man said.

"Tipton. Could you walk me back?"

"I'd be pleased to perform that task," the man told her, "if your dog allows. To amend myself for having startled you, Madam…"

"Tipton?" Suzanne ignored the man.

"I'm right here," the girl told her. She stepped onto the porch, put Suzanne's arm through hers, and said, "If you'll excuse us."

Suzanne's hand trembled. Pig growled low.

"Please," the man said. He swept his tall hat off and bowed at the waist to them both. "Could I start again. I'm—"

"She has no interest, and I'm sure that neither do I," Tipton said. She twirled her skirt wide with her right hand, leading Suzanne out with her left. "There're steps here. Two," she told Suzanne. "We're walking straight away." Tipton looked back over her shoulder to see the man still staring, hat in hand. "Did he hurt you?"

"He assumed I wanted my glasses off and didn't bother to ask if that was so," she said. "And his words, how 'awesome' I was. It was…seductive, almost. I hadn't thought about anyone…about even a gentleman approaching…I…it was frightening." She swallowed. "I'm not wanting…how will I…?"

"You're pretty," Tipton told her.

"Big as a barn, too," Suzanne said.

"Say, big women are pretty," Tipton told her. "Look at Miz Bacon. Oh, sorry. Guess you can't."

"Describe her, Tipton." Suzanne breathed deeply, and Tipton sensed a calm she was pleased to be a part of.

"She's taller than most. Has lots of hair, kind of tilled earth colored. Eyes like emeralds, green and real round, that peer into you."

"She doesn't strike me as invasive," Suzanne said.

"Invasive? I wouldn't say that. Those eyes let you sink inside them, too. Her mouth turns up so you think she's smiling even when she isn't. Her forehead's wide. My mother says that's a sign of intelligence."

"Is yours wide?"

"Ha!" Tipton said. "Not mine. Anyway, Miz Bacon has this habit. She rubs the back of her neck when she's thinking. She walks real determined, never meanders the way my mother says I do. She has a little waist. Smaller than mine, I think. When she wears bloomers they show her shape real fine."

"You've a photographer's eye for detail, Tipton."

The sunset sprayed pale light behind distant mountain peaks. It lingered like a woman's longing.

"My baby's due near August first," Suzanne said. Tipton swallowed. Such a personal thing to say. "I thought earlier after the storm…but the pains didn't last. I don't know what I'll do without Bryce."

"I don't know what I'll do without Tyrell, if truth be known."

"That sounds like your mama, now," Suzanne said.

"It's a step up to your room." Tipton released Suzanne's hand. "She says that often, doesn't she, my mother? 'If truth be known,' like it was something that could be."

"And wouldn't we all like to have truths known and be known for who we are?" Suzanne said. "Thank you, for helping just now, not trying to tell me how I ought to…feel, earlier. I get so tired of that, people treating me like I was a child who didn't know what she wanted."

"It's all right," Tipton said and shrugged.

"Bryce used to say that was what all humans long for, to be known, truly known and just accepted by another."

"Can't say I ever wanted that," Tipton said.

"Oh?" Suzanne said. "Now would that be one of your truths, or a lie?"

⤿

Ruth bent beneath one of the Bacons' cows and checked the bag. "Good work, Naomi. Do you want to do the other or feed Fip?"

"Milk Mavis," she said.

"I don't blame you," Ruth laughed. "That pet of Elizabeth's is more work than it's worth. The children love the thing, though. Don't know what she'll do when it gets big." Ruth listened to the antelope's bell, located it, and shook grain in a bucket to gather its attention. It came running, and she fed it warm milk, dribbling some from her fingers into the soft mouth. She wished Jessie had decided to stay back with them instead of going to the fort. She would have liked the quieter time with the child. Jessie would have enjoyed seeing the Indians camped not far away too.

She wasn't sure how Betha did it, cooking and tending and still mediating the children's squabbles with fairness.

"Do her eyes work?" Jessie had asked her one day, pointing at Suzanne.

"She's blind, dummy," Ned said.

Jessie handed Betha the dreaded buffalo chips to be added to the cooking fire. "Then why does she have eyes that open and close?"

Betha scowled at Ned and said to Jessie, "There was a time that she could see by looking out through them, just like we do," Betha told her. "But then something happened, and now she sees through her fingers and her ears and through what she can smell. Here"—Betha put her spoon down and took the chips from Jessie's hand—"close your eyes. We'll play a game. What do you hear?"

"Birds," Jessie said.

"Anything else?"

"Horses dancing their feet. Cows spittin'. Wind. Going in and out my nose."

"Breathing, yes, the sound of your breath. It's restful, isn't it, to see with your ears? Anytime you're feeling scared, you can listen for your breath and make it come slowly in and out. Now keep your eyes closed, but tell me what you taste. Just trust me now," Betha'd said. "I won't hurt you. Open wide." She placed something on Jessie's tongue.

"I know that. It's a berry," she said. "Huckleberry."

"Look again," Betha said, "no, no. Not with your eyes."

"Oh, currant."

Jessie beamed when Betha announced her correct. "See how much you can see without looking? But you have to pay attention, not let your mind wander too far. And find people you can trust. That's what Mrs. Cullver does, and it's not always easy when we are here in a place none of us has ever been before. She's got to learn to trust her little Clayton, too."

"Can she see buffalo chips?" Ned asked.

Betha laughed. "They do still have a bit of scent, but I suspect you children are going to have to pick at them for your supper, even if Suzanne could spot them."

Ruth had listened to the interchange first with curiosity but finally with admiration. Ruth tended to be stiff with the child, and often found Jessie's questions annoying, distracting even, taking her from her chores. But then chastising herself was nothing new to Ruth.

Ruth brushed Koda, looked at her hands. The nails were broken, and she had blisters and calluses too. It was almost as she was when the twins came. She hadn't tended herself, after. Her hair wasn't done in the upsweep Zane liked so well; the house wasn't the welcoming home he had come to expect. He hadn't an inkling of the work two small babies took, to keep them fed and bathed and diapered—she never told him, of course, and he'd pressed her for another right away. "As majestic as a Madonna," he'd said.

Then John had taken sick, his three-month-old body turning wrinkled and pinched. Ruth took in a deep breath as she remembered. The horse nickered as if in comfort, twisted his neck to tug at her light-colored neckerchief stuffed in her waistband. "Not now, Koda," she said and wondered how he knew when her thoughts turned to that time so frazzled of hope. She had hoped the child would eat and drink that night, fall asleep as she paced; that she could quiet the crying baby arching away from her breast; that she could give him all he needed. No one had told her it could be like this, that a mother could not soothe her own child.

But he had cried for no reason, nothing the doctor could find. Once or twice his piercing sobs drove her to want to shake him, to startle him into quieting, and one desperate day she'd laid him down abruptly, terrified that her fingernails had sunk into his skin. Terror flashed across his eyes for just a moment before his shrieking escalated, and she had shoved him back into the cradle and rushed from the room, holding her ears and sobbing.

She told no one. How could she?

That evening, Zane had looked at her and said, "You're ill. Don't expose the children."

And while a still, small voice told her Zane too lacked patience, her fatigue shamefully asked if he could tend John if he cried in the night.

"Of course," he'd said. "It will be magnificent to spend time with my son."

Ruth checked the hobbles on the horses. Walked out among the oxen lying and chewing in the distant twilight. Naomi made up their bedrolls in the grass, first beating the ground to ward off snakes. A coyote howled, and the long and plaintive wail reminded her of what became a blur of agony and loss.

From the nursery, John crying, crying; her own body so tired she could not lift her head, the baby screaming then, high-pitched and frantic, hour after hour. She'd buried her head under the pillow, didn't want to hear Zane's words sounding sharp and short. She should get up, relieve him. It was so hard, the boy's crying.

And then quiet, the eerie, welcome quiet. Zane had comforted him.

Everyone does it better than me. Those had been her last thoughts before she'd fallen into a fitful sleep. She'd awakened to a nightmare.

In the morning, the women bought up a few supplies at the fort, purchased maple candy for the two left behind. Lura had taken extra beans in and exchanged them for flour. Adora asked Mazy for a loan to purchase laudanum and whiskey for medicinal purposes, then asked, her eyes darting to where Tipton stood out of hearing, if Mazy would be sure to keep them with her as "we Wilsons and Schmidtkes have a few too many baubles taking up space."

When she saw the supply of tobacco, even at the outrageous price of a dollar a pound, Lura reached into her wrist bag for her coin purse. "Mariah, did you put my pearl combs somewhere? I declare I'm getting addled in my old age. Or do you remember me telling you what I did with them?"

Mariah looked confused.

"I was sure I put them in the dresser drawer, before your father...passed on." Lura shook her head. "I know I had them when I passed money to the boys. This is so distressing." She patted her hips, checking her sewn-in pocket.

"You want the tobacco?" the sutler asked.

"No. Just thinking about those missing combs takes away my appetite for luxury," Lura said. "They were so special."

"Perhaps it is the Lord's way of urging you to put aside that demon," Esther told her.

"Tobacco? Demon? Why, it keeps the mosquitoes down."

❧

Just before crossing back over the Platte to where Ruth and Naomi and the stock waited, they pawed through the bushelbasket of letters at the end of the store counter. They didn't really expect to find any mail for themselves, but it was what emigrants did, register their presence at one end of the sutler's store and press their fingers against pages at the other end.

Mazy read the addresses, pronounced the names out loud, and imagined the writers sending thoughts all these miles hoping to catch some loved one, someone held dear, to let them know they were thought of even though they weren't near.

She nearly choked, then stumbled over the words: "Sister Esther Maeves."

"You have a letter, Sister Esther!" Mariah squealed.

"Nonsense." The woman bent at her waist to secure the missive from where Mazy squatted at the basket's edge.

"Oh, it isn't bad news, is it?" Adora said.

Esther turned the battered envelope over in her long, bony fingers.

"Open it," Mariah said.

"Is there one for me in there?" Jessie asked. "Is there a letter for me?"

"Hush, child," Betha told her. "It's for big people."

Betha lifted the quill pen to register, then became distracted by the discovery of letters. Jessie slipped her lower lip out, looked around for Clayton and Zilah, then headed off toward the ferry.

Sister Esther stared into pairs of expectant eyes. "I'll review it later," she said.

"Oh, drats," Lura said. "I was hoping for something exciting."

"Just getting a message way out here's that," Elizabeth said, "no matter who it's from. Let me paw through that basket some more."

"Here's one," Mazy said, standing, her voice distant to her own ears. "For Jeremy. From California." She held the envelope in her hand. It was fat and looked official. Her heart began to pound and her fingers shook.

❧

Betha bought a bushel of dried apples for twelve and a half cents, and all agreed she'd made the best bargain. "Good for you," Ruth said.

"They weren't grown local," Elizabeth said. "Looks like nothing grows here."

"They must have some fresh vegetables," Mazy said. "See that plowed field above the fort?" She pointed.

"Some rosy-eyed thinker living there," her mother said. "Thank goodness the world seems full of 'em."

311

"The soldiers looked kind of puny, if truth be known," Adora said.

"That man who bothered you last evening, Suzanne, he said that scurvy is a problem here. It's hard to get fruits or things like that to grow. He said California was the place for good health. He was from the Ohio Valley himself, looking for cropland."

"You returned to the dance, Tipton?" Suzanne asked, surprise in her voice.

"No. That man, he had a mule to be reshod, and I was, well, watching the blacksmith work just before we left. He seemed nice enough, when he wasn't accosting ladies," she added.

"You met someone?" Mazy asked.

"Pig didn't like him," Suzanne said. "Maybe Pig needs his vocabulary expanded," she said scratching at the dog's neck. "Probably doesn't understand things like 'I am in awe' or 'majestic Madonna.'"

"In reference to other than the Virgin Mary that would be a sacrilege," Esther said, lips pursed.

"Did he wear black?" Ruth said, rising from where she checked Koda's new shoe.

"No, all in white," Tipton told her. "Even his cape and his cane."

Back across the river they held a discussion that resulted not in a vote but in an agreement.

"We've done well, just us," Lura said. "And most folks I talked with at the fort said their groups have grown and shrunk like women with child finally giving birth. So we could join up with someone but then have a falling out. I like it that we've got ourselves a group we trust already."

"Seems chirk that we're women, mostly," Mariah said. "Gives us something dandy."

"A dandy headache," Adora said, "if we find ourselves in trouble and wish we had some men around to help us out."

"That Pawnee that helped return the oxen was a man," Jason noted.

Betha ruffled his hair. "So he was. And you boys fit that model, don't you now? I say let's head out with what we got. Stay on this Council Bluffs road to South Pass."

"I agree," Ruth said. "Let's push a bit more. Longer days would be good."

"I should stay here then," Suzanne said, "Have the baby where there's a doctor and all, not hold you back."

"You making the offer to be kind?" Elizabeth asked. "Or because you want out of this clan?"

Mazy scanned the group that lounged around the wagons, some sitting, some kicking feet on a box, some standing with coffee in hand. Tiny strings of smoke from Indian camps lifted to the sky against rock formations both vivid and bold.

Suzanne took in a big breath. "I worry that keeping track of Clayton will be a strain on everyone. You have to watch out for both of us. And then there'll be the baby. It's too much to ask of family, let alone total strangers."

"Total strangers?" Mazy said. "Is that how you see us?"

"You're not family," Suzanne said.

"We're all you got," Elizabeth said. "All any of us has, here."

"People who recognize each other as they are and still can love, that is a community not unlike a family," Sister Esther said.

"Well spoke," Elizabeth told her. "And unless you're planning to divorce us all between here and the ocean, you're coming with us."

"But we've got to settle on Clayton's care," Mazy said. "To reduce Suzanne's worrying, if nothing else. Mine, too."

"Zilah would care for child," Deborah said. "But she is necessary for help as Sister Esther is alone, with only me and bees if Zilah leaves."

"I would make the exchange," Naomi offered. "Zilah for me until Oregon."

Oregon. Hadn't the Celestials planned to head for California? Mazy thought. It was Ruth and Betha, she and her mother who spoke of the

Donation Land Claims, the 320 acres Oregon promised to any soul hardy enough to stay. They could deal with that later, Mazy decided. What mattered now was settling Suzanne's mind.

"Looks like we have a plan," Mazy said. "That covers all the essentials."

❧

"You would have loved the stables," Mariah told Ruth when they were underway again. "They had lots of nice horses. Could you see anything except the wall of the fort from here?"

"Enough," Ruth said. "We could hear the artillery drilling this morning, early. Watched the stars and stripes go up. They must have dragged that pole all the way from Laramie Peak since there's no timber in these parts. We did fine. Naomi let the bees out an hour or so before dusk, and they came back as planned."

The girl beamed. "Now I learn to churn cream."

"You didn't register, did you, Betha? At the fort?"

"Oh no," Betha told her. "But Mattie did. Left word saying when he hoped to see you too! Such a thoughtful boy."

❧

Snow covered Laramie Peak in the distance. The women moved in that direction, still following the Platte, the wagons lumbering to a rhythm of familiar creak and crunch. They were truly emigrants now, among the best who came west and, having reached Laramie alive, could "spit in the elephant's eye," Elizabeth said. The West—the elephant. Hung over, hung on to, and hugely expanding a dream, a dream to include this grand adventure of all who sought to cross the Great Divide, a dream to make anything that mattered, happen.

They made a good two days, twenty miles each on the odometer.

This day began with new sounds and shouts from distant wagons. It had taken a minute of beating hearts before Suzanne explained it, "It's the Fourth of July. They're celebrating Independence Day outside of the States."

Pig's ears stiffened, and he barked his warning bark but settled back when Suzanne reached up her sleeve and brought out some beef jerky for him. Soon the distant *pop-pop* became routine.

The dog and the woman were one, it seemed, and Suzanne actually had taken to practicing commands to get the dog to stop, come, lie down, wait. He panted happily and, even when off the harness, never strayed far from Suzanne's side.

Mazy wondered how she'd give the dog up when Suzanne went south with him. She shook her head, the thought too painful and narrow to move through, like the rock walls of reds with streaks of butternut and black they had woven through that day.

⁓

How close would Zane be? Would Matt's note to her signal her presence, even though she used a false last name? She should have changed Ruth into Zipporah, not just turned "Randolph" into "Martin." *Maybe he's still at the Fort, wining and dining Madonnas,* she thought.

If only Matt hadn't mentioned the horses in his note; but Betha said he had. Ruth shook her head as she walked beside the horse, giving his foot a good rest. "Your foot! Did he recognize you, Koda, when Tipton got your foot fixed? Oh, Koda, what are we going to do?"

She bent her head to the horse's side. *Are you there, Zane? All dressed in awe that I've made it this far?* Ruth shivered. He had no way of knowing her name. He might still be waiting at the fort or headed south. Her heart hammered against the anvil of her spirit.

⁓

They stood at a rounded rock the guidebook called "Independence," which rose up from the desert floor. "Too bad we weren't here on the Fourth," Jason said, running his hands over the carved initials of so many who passed before them.

"Well, go ahead with your knife," Betha said. "Your initials probably won't last that long anyway. Put your JB in it."

The boys entertained themselves, and even Tipton and Mariah acted like the children they were, scampering at the base of the rock, climbing and shouting down from what looked like the back of a giant sleeping mole. They'd spent only twenty minutes climbing to the top with Sarah and Jessie following them up.

Sister Esther considered reading the letter while they climbed—but waited.

She didn't read it when they turned south around the great bend of the Platte nor when the oxen's feet pushed rocks that echoed to the Sweet Water River below. She still hadn't read it in the shadow of the Rockies on the way to South Pass, where the terrain proved more gentle than her thoughts. They neared the Great Divide, that place where water turned around, ran west and east, two hundred miles or more beyond Laramie. They were awakened one morning to low clouds that lifted like gossamer to reveal the shadow and valleys below. Esther picked that moment to know.

Seven thousand feet she sat at, her shawl pulled around her bony shoulders, her black cap tied beneath her chin. The slope was gentle there, rising to a long, wide flat of sandy, sagebrush country, and at first she did not believe this could be the place where the waters divided, where everything changed. It wasn't dramatic enough. The climb so gradual, she barely noticed. But once there, she could see that the headwaters of two rivers ran in opposite directions. *A paradox,* Sister Esther thought. *Right here in the middle of nowhere.*

That's what her letter was as well. Perhaps the altitude addled her brain, perhaps she didn't understand what it meant.

We regret to inform you that two of the assigned contracts have been dissolved. It will not be necessary for your charges to repay the expenses of their journey. However, at your earliest convenience, please proceed with negotiating the repayment of the contract portions advanced to the women's families. The Association assumes no responsibility for this unfortunate event.

Please respond at your earliest convenience regarding the matter of your success.

Respectfully I remain,
Benjamin Furnas, Esquire,
Caroline Fry Marriage Association, Inc.

At her earliest convenience? What was convenient? To not be told why or which ones? To be given no names as though the women all ran together? Esther shook her head, fanned herself with the thin pages. She hadn't told the Association that one of the women had died. That was an error. So was not reading this letter until now. She should have written to get clarification before they reached California. Delaying did not increase one's control.

She would have to pray to make sense of this, find a way to protect her charges, and still meet her obligations.

No one asked her about the letter's contents. She kept it in her pocket when they'd crossed Dry Sandy Creek, the wheels finally tightening up against the iron rims after several days of dry heat. The soaking kept the wheels on her wagon from shrinking further. Afterwards, she and Naomi packed the space between the shrinking wheels and the rims with strips of Elizabeth's soaked buffalo hide to keep the wheel tight against the iron. She did not want the wheels to break, the wagon to drop, or anything to happen that might upset Deborah's bees.

The insects had taken extra tending through the driest areas. One day they had gone thirty-six miles, Mazy said, because there were no water holes between. The bees had become agitated, and when Deborah lifted the lid to add more water, she heard their angry tone rise an octave.

"It is the warning!" Deborah shouted. "They will sting. Back away, Missy Esther. Away!"

As she tried to lower the lid, Deborah struck some of the bees. They stung her close to her eyes, then another at her wrist, the soft spot at her ear, the warning already sent to the others, frantic now, being caught up as she tried to secure the lid. Deborah slammed it now and struck at the loose bees flying and darting, knowing those who stung her would die an agonizing death unless she could kill them. Esther sat splayed against the side of the wagon, her heart pounding, while Deborah rescued the bees and her future.

Perhaps losing the bees would be a penance for her delaying, for not being truthful with the Association about Cynthia's death. But perhaps it didn't matter, if what was in the letter was a truth and not a lie.

❧

Tipton couldn't get the blacksmith from her mind. The tools he used, pounding hot iron, making something useful out of nothing, discarding bits and pieces that didn't fit. Was she just a bit and piece? Did she belong on the scrap pile of things no longer needed? Or was Elizabeth right? And the aching and numbing of her hand resulted from resistance. Maybe she was being pounded into something she could not yet imagine. She tightened the strings of her drawers, wrapping the excess into the waistband. She put little in her mouth—that was her agreement with herself, to eat only the food on one side of her plate. She didn't want anyone to notice how her belly pooched out. Yet her drawers fairly hung at her hips. How could she be so fat and yet her clothes get bigger?

❧

They took the Sublette Cutoff rather than head south to Fort Bridger. The discussion had been amiable among the women, the decision easily come to. Sister Esther had only half heard it. Once they reached South Pass, the air had become cooler and the bees more restful. They'd stopped early to let them fly. But she felt there was no point now.

She watched the Celestials. Each had revealed unique skills along this journey, though they still had much to learn.

Naomi had fine, strong arms. Her silky dress no longer stretched across her body, now turning from soft to lean. She kept herbs in her pottery pots, seasonings that scented the quilts and the clothes. She said fond things too, offering cheerfulness especially to Tipton or Suzanne when clouds marked their days. Her herbs healed cuts and scrapes, and she'd actually rescued one of the Barnards' oxen by giving it salt pork and vinegar after it drank the alkali water. Who would have thought of that?

Zilah did not look down so much either, or cast her eyes as though in shame as she had before they began. She tended Clayton, and since she'd taken on this task, the child lacked even a scratch on his face except for the scar near his eye from the mule incident. She played with him, making little circles out of colored papers, folding them until she could blow into them and they would puff up. She was not a pretty girl, with pockmarks and lacking the delicate features of Deborah, but she smiled easily around children, and they transformed her into something of joy.

And Deborah, so delicate with those tiny, damaged feet. She proved tireless, if a bit irresponsible. She did remember details not only of what the bees needed but of people as well, keeping the wagon orderly and anticipating what Sister Esther wished, often before she said the words.

But none of the women had resources, except for Deborah's bees and the paper patent she'd nearly lost. Sister Esther felt tears come to her eyes. What would become of them once they discovered they were on their own, without husbands to provide for them?

❧

"I'll go first," Lura said. They stood in the necessary circle. "Here are my truths and lies." She cleared her throat. "I can play the harp. That's one.

And I have always wanted to run a sutler's store." She grinned. "Mariah, if you know, don't say."

"Oh, the harp. I think you can play that," Adora said. "I heard that sound the night we made Kanesville, so pretty. Didn't know it was you playing."

"You carry a tune well," Suzanne agreed.

"Not so good with valuables, though," Adora said.

"Mother!" Tipton scolded.

"Well, she lost those pearl combs and all, Tipton."

"You've lost your purse, Mother."

"Well, I'd say that one about the store's your lie, Lura, if truth be known."

"The store's the truer," Ruth said. "Your wagon is well organized. Boxes in little places. A sutler would have that skill, shelving and stacking and keeping products from shifting."

A few others made their guess, and Lura took in the kindnesses expressed within the guesses, knitted them into a shawl of new information to comfort herself.

"I can't play a thing," she told them at last. "Not a single note on a traveling harp or whatever. No, it's the store I'd love."

"I never knew that, Ma."

"Your father thought it a foolish dream, and I never mentioned it after we were married, he being a farmer, a practical soul. Handled the books. Didn't need me, and then I got addled and all. But I might again, now. Mention it to myself."

"Well you should," Elizabeth said. "Now ain't this fun? Who's next?"

"I'll go," Sister Esther said.

"You gonna tell us what's in the letter now?" Jason asked. He and his brother stood outside the circle until the women finished, listening intently.

"No. I am not," she said. She had thought long and hard about this task, thought it silly at first, but liked the effort it took to clarify, keep her mind from always judging. "First. I am frightened of bees, of being stung as I have been since I was a small child. That's the first statement. And second, I studied the same classes as my brother Harold, who was a divinity student in the East." She looked straight ahead, did not want to catch the eye of anyone.

"Why, that's easy," Adora said. "You're not afraid of bees. You've ridden with them all this way without a peep. That's silly. They're supposed to be hard to guess, like Lura's was."

"Is she cheating, Mama?" Sarah asked.

"Shush. Pay attention," Betha said.

"If it is the bees, if that's the truth, then you are a remarkable woman," Suzanne said. "To live each day with a fear as that, surrounded by the thing that terrorizes you. How could you do that and still be a useful person?"

"Perhaps as you do, Suzanne," Sister Esther said. "By faith and grace."

"By faith," Mazy said. "But then that would make the second statement seem the truer. I could imagine Harold training for the ministry. He was a very kind man."

"Yes, he was," Esther said. "They both were good men, my brothers." She sighed heavily, the mark of hanging on to something that drained the soul.

"Are women allowed to read divinity?" Tipton asked.

"She didn't say she read it, just studied the same stuff her brother did," Mariah corrected. "That could be."

"I'd rather she told us about the letter," Ned said.

"In due time," Esther said. She smiled. The banter was a comfort she had not known she needed.

"We give," Elizabeth said. The others agreed.

"I wish it was that I had read theology along with my brother, but neither brother did, and yes, Tipton, as a woman, I could not. Not that

I didn't try to get one or the other to do it. How I badgered. My father was a minister, and he, too, pressed his sons before he died. In the end, they consented only to come with me, to help me carry out my mission." She looked away. "And so you see what happened."

Deborah broke the silence with her tiny voice. "So is lie you…read same like brother?" The girl's left eye was almost swollen shut from her bee stings. "And truth you fear bees?"

"The truth is that."

Deborah put her fingers to her lips, blinked quickly.

"And still you stay with the bees and help," Mazy said. "You ride beside your fears."

"Ride beside them, yes. As do we all who chose to make our way along this trail."

filling up

Mazy sat beneath the shade of a hardwood tree. The green canopy offered rest; a book lay open on her lap. She had written a word, some quality of faith. Then she heard the agitation of wings.

They'd flown like hawks diving for rabbits, tearing toward the soft spots of her face. Her heart pounded, eyes enlarged by the sight of the black swarm in the sky.

Sit very still, sit very still, don't let them know you're here.

They'd swarmed onto the trunk and over her eyes, her mouth, her nose. She couldn't move. She couldn't breathe! She felt her throat constrict, shut off the air that committed her to life. She'd die if she didn't move, didn't change, whether they stung her to death or not! She melded into the solid but unmoving trunk, and the bees blackened over her, made her one with the tree. She fought, knowing to move was to die of their stinging; but to stay, just a lump on the trunk, that was a death over time.

"Wake up, darling. You're dreaming bad," her mother said, moving the muslin cover from her daughter's face, shaking her.

Mazy fought through the ooze of nightmare, blinked to see herself on a dusty trail far from home.

"What was that all about?"

"Bees."

"Stinging you, were they?" Elizabeth stroked Mazy's cheek, moved wet strands of hair back behind her ears.

"They didn't sting," Mazy said. "I felt more…choked, more suffocated and sad than anything."

"Just a bad dream," her mother said. "They pass, in time."

The dream stayed with her through the day. She struggled to understand the meaning of the sadness, the lack of stinging. And she wondered what the word was that she had written in the book but could not read through the suffocating bees.

⟿

The ferryman stared, moved a plug of tobacco from one cheek to the other, waiting while the group of them congregated at the Green River. He spit. Betha cringed. Such filth, they were surrounded by filth.

They'd come a good distance, crossing the streams that meandered, over and back again as though they had not gotten it right the first time and were forced into repetition. Here at the Green River, Betha just wished Adora would make up her mind.

"I won't pay that," Adora said, arms crossed over her chest. "Six dollars a wagon is too much! Only paid fifty cents to cross the Desmoines."

"It's either pay or find our own way, " Elizabeth told her. "He's already come down a dollar." There were shouts from other wagons yelling about "holdups."

The ferryman smiled a tobacco-stained smile. "I got lots of time, ladies," he said, "but you ain't. Winter's coming."

Adora dropped her arms. "I haven't any money," she said in a whisper. "We never found the purse."

"Tipton! Your mother needs you," Betha called to the girl, gazing at the swirling water.

"Could you have left it in Laramie?" Lura asked. "I'm just terrible myself about misplacing things."

"No, I had to borrow money for laudanum and whiskey, and—"

"I didn't know you bought lauda—"

"I couldn't find my purse, remember?" Adora snapped at her approaching daughter.

"When did you have it last?" Betha asked. "Let's go back to that."

Tipton rolled her eyes. Adora turned to Lura. "I guess when your Matt and Joe left."

"We were both giving out money that day," Lura said. "Charles was there, too."

"I doubt it has anything to do with Charles," Adora said. She turned to Lura and glared.

"You surely can't think my Matt had anything to do with it. Not Joe either. They're good boys. Don't point your finger at them."

Such a dirty finger it was, too, Betha thought, dirt all caked beneath the nails. She looked at her own. She could plant a garden in the dirt residing there.

"That leaves just one explanation for your lost wealth, Mother," Tipton said.

Adora frowned, replaced her arms across her chest. "I do believe you're right, if truth be known." She took one step forward and pressed her long finger against the chest of a very startled Zilah.

"Aiee, no!" Zilah said. Her eyes were huge, and she backed up, her bare feet catching on the shredded hem of her dress. She pushed Clayton to her side, safe behind her.

They had to find a way past this, Betha thought. She knew that small bites of distrust not spit out would starve them of all they needed to complete this journey. Where was Mazy?

"What's happening?" Suzanne asked. Pig pressed against the woman's leg.

"My mother thinks Zilah took her money," Tipton said. "It's easier to believe than that her son betrayed her."

"And we're crossing the Green," Mazy said, arriving from the back of the line.

"On the ferry?" Betha asked hopefully, looking at Adora.

"On the ferry only if Adora—or someone—pays the ferriage," Mazy announced. "Adora, I don't believe Jeremy ever repaid you the Tipton-watching money, so I'm doing that now, beginning with the six-dollar ferriage. Agreed?"

"Charles wouldn't. I know him," Adora whined. "Zilah had time. Tipton wasn't watching—"

"Adora? Will you take the money or not?" Mazy said.

"What? Oh yes, I suppose."

"We can attend to your charge against Zilah later," Mazy added, pulling coins from her own purse to get their party moving.

"My money would certainly set her up nicely in California," Adora mumbled as the wagons rolled onto the ferry.

⊱

Mazy realized she shouldn't have offered the money to Adora, now that she suspected that the "extra" Jeremy left did not belong to her or to her mother, either.

Too much time to think. That's what the monotony of dusty travel offered up. War had its monotony, that's what Mazy's father once told her, after the glorying turned morbid and real. They were in a war to survive, to endure. But they lacked a rallying force to spur them. Mazy's mouth tasted of grit. Should she endure it or rinse with the putrid water? She questioned everything, even something so basic. After the letter, she questioned most of all what she knew of her husband.

The official-looking missive from the lawyer said he represented Jeremy's brother and his wife. She didn't know Jeremy even had a brother. How could she not have known? It spoke of money, money sent Jeremy to purchase cattle for "their operation." So Marvel the cow brute might not even belong to her, nor the cows. How had she lived in such a fog beside this man who claimed to love her? Was she blind in what mattered between people? Was she just safer with dogs? Perhaps this was why she didn't form friendships; she misread people. Mazy shook her head. Perhaps Tipton was the wisest of them all, just slipping away. Perhaps that was why in her dreams Mazy felt choked and blinded by bees.

And then the second half of the letter—she hadn't even told her mother about that. There was a child, it said. Jeremy's child. Now residing in Oregon.

"If you can't stand something, you'll pass out," her mother'd once said. Mazy was getting ready to pass out.

Suzanne made her way beside the wagon, the first in the short line. Still the dust billowed up, and their neckerchiefs muffled their words. Wild roses and the last of tiny pink carnations grew as though fed by reddish rocks. Pig walked in service with Suzanne's fingers gripping his harness. Mazy stepped back to check the chickens' cage. No eggs. When she turned back, the oxen had stalled. She walked to the front to confront a fat rattler. It was bigger than those in Wisconsin, and by now Mazy knew the thing to do was to let it pass, not try to kill it but let it make its way.

"What's the holdup?" Suzanne asked, Pig keeping her back by the chickens.

"Just a snake," Mazy said. "Take a breath. He's moving on and so will we."

❧

"I'd feel useful doing it," Suzanne said when they'd resumed. "Are you listening?"

"We're all so tired," Mazy said, turning her face toward Suzanne.

"Zilah, Deborah, they all liked it before."

"You got to speak up so I can hear you over these ox tails swatting at flies," Elizabeth shouted coming up from behind. "Liked what?"

"The English classes," Suzanne told her. "I want to resume them, as we walk along. It would destroy the monotony of this trail, if nothing else, and give their fiancés English-speaking wives."

"Like the classes Sister Esther and her brothers taught with that white-collared man," Elizabeth said. "Seth something. I remember. What ever happened to him?"

"Went on to Oregon, didn't he?" Mazy said. "Or was it California?"

"South, I suspect. Greater gambles to be had down there," Elizabeth said.

"We could do it while we walked," Suzanne said. "Just take a few nails and a little time."

"Maybe after we cross over this next mountain," Mazy answered. "Until then, I think we need to conserve everything we have for that big push."

"A good challenge has a way of removing tiredness," Suzanne said. Her mouth turned upward into a smile, revealing dimples Mazy hadn't seen before.

"Only if it's met," Mazy added.

⁓

In the evening Jessie begged for cookies, and the boys aided and abetted, as Betha called it, as they made camp in a wide grassy area. Several others heading west had chosen the spot to camp at as well. "You dig the hole and gather up the firewood by the river bank there, I'll see what we can rustle up," Betha told them. In a day or two, they'd begin the heavy crossing up two miles of steep hill. They needed something homey to nurture them.

"Put your stitching down and help," Ned told Sarah.

"You don't have to be mean," Sarah said.

Betha took out her brass matchbox with a boxer dog on the lid. "Go ahead, Sarah," she said.

Sarah laid her stitchery down, and Betha wondered how she

grieved, whether the aching legs the girl complained of in the evenings were somehow related. She'd never complained before her father's death.

Betha set the fire, and while it burned she gathered up her last eggs from her flour barrel, handling them like fine porcelain. She cracked the eggs into a bowl and forked them, then fluffed them with Mazy's butter. She added sugar and stuck her finger in. "The milk gave it a strong taste," Betha said quietly so as not to sound complaining.

"Probably all the alkaline water," Ruth told her. "They may not give much more milk until we reach good grass and water country. Best we enjoy this while we can."

Flour, dried apples, and raisins went into the batch. The pan set over the trench the boys had dug to be just the right width. Ruth shoved a rifle ramrod into the dirt at an angle. When she pulled it out, the empty shaft formed a natural draft. Just the scent of baked goods drifting over them brought smiles to the bonnet-shaded faces.

Should do more of this, bring a little flavor of the usual to the journey, Betha thought.

The cookie aroma drifted in the breeze.

"I'll prosecute and put an end to any too burned to serve, Ma," Jason said, his missing front tooth showing, "and consume any evidence of my efforts."

Betha laughed. "Just like your father," she said, the first time she had thought of Jed without tears choking in her chest.

⟜⟝

"I hope the carpet tacks'll do," Mazy said. Tipton pounded with one of Tyrell's hammers. "Here," Mazy said. "Adora had a few and so did Lura and Betha to add to yours. No nails anywhere to spare."

"They should work fine," Suzanne said, her fingers moving across the brass heads. "I can feel the *A*," she said. "There's *B*."

"What're you doing?" Mariah asked, coming up beside the cluster of women.

"Putting letters on the side of the wagon, so I can feel them and you children can see them. Deborah and Naomi and Zilah, too," Suzanne said.

"Want me to write the words in the sand, too, as we go?" Mariah asked. "If I'm such a child."

"No offense meant," Suzanne said. "Just anything to teach the alphabet and the sounds. You can take the word back down the line and the Celestials can spell it out, take little short hikes to the alphabet wagon."

"We can do some visitin' that way, too," Elizabeth said. "About something other than our feet and how food's moving through us."

"Bryce always wanted me to try Braille dots. I told him I was too old, my fingers too insensitive to pick up something so subtle as little pokes in paper." She rubbed her fingertips together, and Mazy noticed calluses. "He said if Barbier could teach the French military to use dots for night communicating, I was certainly not too old to acquire similar skills."

"Always said life's a lesson," Elizabeth noted. "We're always in a classroom."

"Pig's keeping me in mine."

The dog looked up at Suzanne as she spoke, an act that ambushed Mazy's heart.

❧

Sister Esther smoothed her skirts over her knees, set her writing desk on them, and opened her Bible. She needed some kind of assurance that she was not alone in this paradox of trust and faith and now betrayal. What would she tell the girls, their families? When?

She sat at the low fire, the others not yet up. She missed the time she used to have with Mazy before the girl stopped writing at the fire after her husband died. Esther opened her Bible to Jeremiah, the prophet, at 29:11: *"For I know the thoughts that I think toward you, saith the LORD, thoughts of peace, and not of evil, to give you an expected end."*

She had expected the joy of accomplishment, the satisfaction of service in taking four young girls to California. But one was now dead and two of the contracts had been dissolved. What was peace in that? They were all adrift on this overland sea. She could only trust in the Scripture; all else felt confusing and frail.

⁓

Worthiness, that was the word. Tipton remembered now. It arrived on the twitter of a bird, so loud beside the trail she heard it above the wagon clangs and crunch. Worthiness. That's what they'd been discussing there in that desolate place not long before he had left and then died.

"Living to the utmost of one's powers or ability. That's what being worthy is," Tyrell had told her. "You've been given much, Tip. We all have. All we need." A bird had chirped so loudly they both turned to it. He laughed. "Like that fellow. No worries. Careful, now."

He worked on a wheel, Tipton remembered. Whose was it? That Dr. Masters, a wheel that helped him desert.

"Sometimes I think folks are afraid of what they're worth," Tyrell had told her. "So they hide behind themselves." He'd looked up at her and smiled. "You're like that, Tip. Such a light you'd shine."

"You think so?" She'd been both filled and frightened by his words.

"Shine as far as you'd let it." He'd continued to work, sweat glistening off his arms from the effort and the heat of the fire he'd built. The force of his hammer vibrated against her feet. Tipton fanned herself with her handkerchief, not having bothered with a parasol. He slid the flat iron rim onto the wooden wheel, tapped it into place.

"We're all like the spokes of a wheel, seems to me," he said then, straightening, looking her in the eye. "Rolling along on a journey around a strong and sturdy hub. With a good iron rim acting like a bond to keep it all in place."

"Sometimes the spokes break," she said. "Wheel runs over things, gets hung up on rocks. There are accidents."

"Just keep rolling, Tip. Stay attached to the center." He bent to kiss her nose, right there, for anyone looking to see. "God's the center," he'd said. "We're all just the spokes in his wheel."

Oh, how she missed him! She took the silver combs from her hair, pulled off the clumps of brittle blond she found there. She walked up beside the alphabet wagon next to Suzanne and Pig and wiped her eyes with the back of her palm.

"Tipton? You always smell so good. Pick a word," Suzanne said. "One to ask Mariah to take back to the others."

"*Light,*" Tipton said. "I'm trying to think on worthy things."

❧

It surprised Mazy, all the traffic. People passing them from behind; trappers heading to Fort Laramie; Californians heading back east. It wouldn't have been so strange if they'd stayed on the trail back to Wisconsin. She would never have gotten the letter then, there was always that. And she wouldn't be experiencing this odd fleeting feeling of wondering what lay ahead not with dread, but with a prickle of anticipation.

More than once they met traders with pack animals heading east who declared they'd be returning to California or Salt Lake. Most tried to buy up their mules and extra oxen.

"Aren't worth much mor'n a nickel in California," a bearded man with a grease-stained shirt added. "Take your carpet tacks for ya, too," he said, pointing with his bearded chin toward the green and yellow wagon that wore the alphabet on its side.

He moved on to other camps, and Mazy noticed in the morning that he rode southwest with a string of thin mules just purchased.

"Maybe we should do that," Elizabeth said. "It'd help Adora out with her cash if she got rid of the mules. They aren't likely to make it anyway."

"If they survive they may be more valuable than anything else," Mazy told her. "Might be her starting fund. No, something about his offer sounded less like hospitality and more like hunger."

"His interest in the carpet tacks, that's strange, I ponder that," Elizabeth said.

"I'm too tired to ponder anything," Mazy said.

"A lie if I ever heard it," her mother said and smiled.

Perhaps the most important message from the traders, trappers, and eastbound travelers was that if they headed south instead of north toward Oregon, they'd find trading posts and people faster and friendlier, have less risk of being caught in the early severe weather.

"Still got mountains and all, but it's like the Lord himself has placed help for you, to get just what you need when you need it," one man told them. "To get to California, you just got to commit to the trail."

Just commit, Mazy thought while she milked Mavis, avoiding the cow's tail as it swished. She did seem to have trouble with that notion. Each time the opportunity appeared, she reconsidered, chastised herself: *We could have gone back; We should have gone back. I should have.* And soon there'd be another big decision. And they had yet to cross the big mountain.

◦≈≫

The road leading toward the rocky crag crossed the river several times. In between, they drove through stretches of road littered with pounds of bacon now gutted by flies and yellow jackets, tins of jam, carpets, trunks, and sometimes whole wagons, discarded. Often they'd seen a carcass first, fallen amid blue lupines, followed by the signs of hard choices, later made.

"The good thing about crossing so many rivers," Ruth told Betha, "is that the wheels tighten good with the swollen wood." Betha rode in the wagon, clutching the sides. All she could see was the drop toward the swirling water, the swiftness of branches that bobbed and dipped in the stream, the shimmer of rocks and hidden holes beneath the surface.

"Look toward where you're going, not down," Ruth told her.

Betha remembered Suzanne's accident back at Kanesville. The crossings since terrified her, even on that little ferry at the fort, with just the women, the horse, Koda, and her one faithful ox aboard. She almost envied Suzanne who never had to see uncertainty.

"I think it's the same with this whole journey," she told the group in their necessary circle that evening, their backs to each other while one woman squatted, protected, inside. Betha's truth had been of her fear of water; her lie that she didn't like to eat chicken. "Every day starts out with sweaty hands and my heart pounds. Then we get on the road. I hear people talking and chattering, and my legs work and my feet keep going even when I wake up so tired I don't think they can."

"Is that a truth or lie?" Lura asked.

"Just fact."

"You too?" Elizabeth said.

"I didn't know that starting out was troublesome for you, Mother," Mazy said. She stood next to her mother in the circle. They shared the same view of an imposing mountain, one they'd soon be overcoming.

"Not that, just that I wonder if my hip'll work. Always a moment of gratitude when I can bear my own weight."

"Is nights for me," Deborah said. "I lay wake, legs twitch, then sleep chase."

"Because you kneel all day," Adora told her. "You girls need to start doing things the American way, not hang on to old habits so much."

"We're not in the States here, though, are we?" It was Mariah speaking.

"Not until we reach Oregon Territory. Or California," Sister Esther answered, "though the latter is the only actual state out west."

"Where's the ladder Sister Esther always talks about?" Sarah whispered to her mother. Several heard and chuckled. The child blushed.

"Mornings trouble me the most," Lura said. She stood and stretched stiffly, tapped Suzanne on the shoulder, took Clayton's hand as he stood beside Zilah. "Just step straight back, dear," she said over her shoulder. "I kept hoping that once we knew for sure we were heading west, that it wouldn't be so—"

"I can't picture it real clear, where we're headed, even yet," Betha said.

"Do we ever know that?" Esther asked. "Even when we think we know our destination, change arrives. We are shaken up again."

Mazy heard something she hadn't noticed before in Sister Esther's words. Or was she reading in her own discomfort, living in that place where indecision reigned?

"What are we to count on, then?" Tipton asked.

At first, no one responded, then Sister Esther said, "We're told in Scripture 'not to worry,' not to be afraid, and still we are. We do things out of fear we ought not do. But we also endure fearful things, if we can believe God walks through them with us."

"I worry my faith isn't strong enough," Lura said.

"Worrying's what a mother's supposed to do," Adora said. "What would we do if we weren't doing that?"

"Laughing and having fun," Elizabeth told her.

Adora scoffed and swatted at mosquitoes buzzing about her ears. Mazy could hear the slaps of women's hands against their necks, the futility of trying to kill the insects off.

"I think faith polishes us," Betha continued. "Just shines us up. We have to be rubbed a bit, a little spit and vinegar put to the cleaning cloth so all the heavy dirt we pick up in living every day can be taken off. Suppose that's what happens when I make it across those rivers without throwing up my supper. A little polish's been applied. It leaves behind a shiny treasure with all the nicks and dents that make us...special," she said.

"Stretched maybe," Suzanne said. "Into risky things."

Elizabeth laughed. "I'm stretched all right. Everyone else seems to be dropping weight while I'm picking it up." She patted her stomach.

"We've all been drawn out," Mazy said, more to herself than anyone in particular. "Moved further than we thought we'd ever have to go."

"Perhaps so we can find the boundaries of more pleasant places," Esther said.

Mazy stared at her and wondered if Esther had somehow eavesdropped on the journal she used to write in.

≈

"You've got to throw things out," Mazy told Adora. "Leave that chest of drawers. We've got a very long and steep mountain to go, and you'll likely lose another mule unless you lighten up. This mule didn't have to die."

"I could leave out that big table," Lura said. Her voice quivered as she stared at the mule.

"So those traders or that ferryman can come by here after we've gone and get it for themselves? I've got the mules, we'll use them."

"This delays us, Mother," Tipton told her.

"Leave that big anvil of Tyrell's if you want to lighten the load."

Tipton rubbed at her arm. "I suppose I—"

"For now," Ruth said, leading a mule forward, "we've got to unharness a dead animal, get it out of the road, and then get these others around it. That's going to take us a good bit of time, even working together."

Naomi put her strong back to the effort of unharnessing the mate to the dead mule and then the dead creature itself. The trail narrowed here. Their faces dripped in sweat, those who had pushed and pulled; the rest wore anxious looks as they lumbered past the dead animal.

"Maybe we should butcher it, dry the meat before we go," Mazy said. She wiped at her face with her apron. She'd taken to wearing her wrapper again as it was easier in the necessary circle.

"Pretty thin," Ruth said. "The wolves'll eat it. We need to move on." Her felt hat shaded her face from the hot sun, but she still rubbed at her eyes with her hand. "Eyes hurt," she said to Mazy's look of concern. "All the sun."

Mazy said, "We might wait for help."

"Or just decide," Ruth said. "Let's move. They look to you for answers, Mazy."

"I don't believe that's true," she said.

"You don't do any of us any favors pretending to be less than what you are," Ruth said as she dismounted and pulled on the mule.

～～

"You're not eating?" Lura asked. "Oh, looks like half your food's been eaten. But no beans?"

Tipton shook her head. "They make me…well, you know." Tipton felt her face get hot. "And I'm gaining weight." She patted her swollen stomach. "We need to lighten the loads, according to Mazy."

Lura lowered her voice. "Not my beans, girl. I cook 'em in vinegar. You can join the circle and not worry a bit when you eat from my pot."

Tipton blushed, her cheeks the color of snapdragons.

"Looks like you're getting skimpier, to me," Lura said. "Hair even looks…brittle. You got to keep your strength up if you're going to survive. My Antone said we got to eat."

"But my stomach," Tipton told her.

Lura squinted at the girl's abdomen. "Reminds me of a child I saw once back in New York. Abandoned by his family, living in a rat-infested barn, surviving on grain 'til they found him. Almost starved to death, all limbs and bones and a fat belly. The only thing that kept him

337

alive was the will to live and finding someone else who wanted him to. Sure you don't want my beans? I sure want you around to try them."

∽

At the evening gathering on that early August day, Mazy said, "Tomorrow we make the mountain. We'll be taking one wagon at a time with double the teams. Each has to be pulled up with eight animals then unharnessed and the wagons lowered over the other side with ropes. You'll see trees up there." She pointed. "They have marks around the trunk that're from the ropes that hold the wagon as it's lowered down, at least that's what the book says. The oxen pull us up then they're put to work easing the wagons down over the side. They serve as both momentum and brakes."

The women sat like schoolchildren, intent and staring at their teacher.

"Then we'll have to drive the loose stock around the side. The first question is, Are we ready?"

"Sister," Sarah whispered. "Ain't you gonna pray first?"

Esther looked at Mazy, who nodded.

At the joint "amen," Adora spoke. "We're ready."

"Are we really? Some of us still have too much weight."

"Don't point your finger at me, Mazy Bacon," Adora said. "I don't have any more'n the rest of you, if truth be known."

"Truth is, you do," Mazy said. "I think we all have to go back and see what else we can discard from our wagons."

"That'll trouble me," Ned said, kicking at a hard clump of dirt.

"Wish I had someone to take Bryce's clothes," Suzanne said. "The scent…" She swallowed.

Tipton said, "I'm not sure I can throw out any more. What's left is all I have of Tyrell."

"I agree," Adora said. "Good thinking, daughter."

"No, it isn't," Mazy said. "I'm sorry, but that's what all those beds and barrels we've seen dumped out along the way have been saying to us. We've got to give 'things' up if we want to have our hopes met, if we truly want to get there, all of us together. We've got to decide what it is that matters and make room for that and only that. The more we hang on to, the less room we have for what will see us through."

"We've fared well," Sister Esther said. "Since we agreed to head west again and pared down to four wagons, we've had no illness, lost only a few animals. Do you really feel we should eliminate more?"

"We haven't crossed the first big mountain yet," Mazy reminded her. "That's the test. Maybe someone else should look at our things. Strip us. It might be easier having someone else point at my…bucket of dirt from Wisconsin, for example, and ask me if it's really needed." Mazy sighed. "If we carry only what we must, I believe the mountain will be ours."

"We've never done this before," Lura said. "It's the first mountain. I used to celebrate my 'first times,' first parties."

"Virginal, are we?" Elizabeth said, and the group laughed, even Esther.

Ruth said, "I read an unusual definition once, of a virgin."

"Please, Ruth, the girls," Betha cautioned.

"They can hear it. The word meant 'a woman who was complete unto herself, who was neither the property of nor dependent on a man.' Not a brother, husband, father, or son. Just herself."

"That's a strange thought, Ruth," Esther said as she leaned over the boiling water to see if the dragonflies and other critters swimming there were dead, then strained the liquid into a tin cup.

"It was a definition in Greek and Roman times," Ruth said. "When virgins sacrificed themselves to heal wounded nations. Their sacrifice made no difference; but that they *could* make every decision about their lives, life or death, made them fully complete."

"Wasn't Mary a…one of those?" Mariah asked.

Mazy said, "Of course God would select a woman complete, one able to make the choice to accept what was offered her or not. To be willing."

"Interesting to ponder," Elizabeth said.

"And she took it," Sister Esther said. "Made the decision to bear the Messiah."

"I never thought of her having a choice about it," Mariah said.

"It's a precious gift, the ability to choose," Suzanne said.

"But we always can," Mazy said. "No matter what, we can always choose what's important and how to act to make that happen."

"As we must now. What we take and what we leave behind," Esther said.

"I'd adjust that definition a smidgen," Elizabeth said. "Mary was dependent, just not on anyone earthly."

⁂

Mazy found Suzanne crying, the dog asleep at her feet. His ears perked up and he stood, his tongue hanging out, ears partly up, his face happy when he saw his master. She scratched his ears.

"Must be Mazy," Suzanne said, wiping her eyes. "Pig has a certain sound for you."

"I'm glad I'm unique to him," Mazy said. She buried her face in his fur. It smelled of smoke and leather. She sat down beside Suzanne. "I can sort your things, unless Zilah has," Mazy said.

"Just feeling sorry for myself," Suzanne said. "The sewing machine has to stay, I know. I don't even mind except that it was Bryce's last insistence to me. And the camera and the musical instruments. They're such heavy things. I wondered if maybe they could be lowered over separately and put back in afterwards, but Elizabeth said no, this was really the first of many crossings and how we prepared ourselves for this one would be a portent to the rest."

"Mother said *portent?*"

Suzanne laughed. "My word." She removed her dark glasses,

dabbed at her eyes. The corneas of both eyes were scar-crossed pits. "It's as though I keep reliving the loss, not just Bryce's death, but my accident. Every time change drops by and wants to be fed, I wonder if I'll have enough or if it'll eat me out of house and home."

"Grief's ravenous, isn't it? I suppose that's where the emptiness comes from, and we keep trying to fill it with…food and blame, irritations and what all. Keeping busy." Mazy chipped at a spot of dried beans clinging to her apron, picked at her torn nails. She patted the dog who had lain down between the women. "We have to throw out things that get in the way of our going forward."

"I know," Suzanne said. "It's just so painful."

"I wanted to plant something at Jeremy's grave," Mazy said. "But it wouldn't have grown." Suzanne fumbled across the dog for Mazy's hand, squeezed it. Mazy felt the tears well up, spill over onto the dog. "Letting go of things in order to fill up. It's an essential I hadn't really thought of."

❧

Mazy woke to the soft strain of a troubadour harp's strings. The artist was accomplished. She chose a mournful Irish tune, and the singer's voice skipped up, low note to high. "He's like the swallow that flies so high. He's like the river that never runs dry. He's like the sunshine on the lee shore. I love my love and love is no more."

Mazy woke her mother, and the two of them raised their heads to peer outside the tent. Moonlight filtered across a heap of chairs and chests, and barrels, Lura's table, Tyrell's anvil and small bellows, even a spare wagon tongue. A parasol lay there too, and pottery pots. A camera and sewing machine and the blanket chest that had belonged to Mazy's grandmother. Mazy hung on to a photo album, a few clothes, a small chest of blankets, and Mrs. Malarky's seeds in her decorated gourd. She'd dumped the Cassville dirt.

The crescendo of the harp's plucked strings brought an orchestra to mind. The conductor was key. He—or perhaps she—helped all those independent musicians play together, bring their gifts to the same song. How could she do that herself? Respect what each could give and yet make of them a moving composition?

Mazy scanned their gathering. Ruth lay on her stomach in her tent, arms crossed but head raised to the song; Betha and Lura stuck their faces out of their wagon, one over the other. Even Tipton stepped down, shivering in the cooler mountain air, but drawn to the plunk and blend of harp strings. Adora slipped out behind her, wrapped a shawl around the girl's thin shoulders. The Asian women, every one, knelt, eyes closed in concentration. Sister Esther towered above them in her nightdress, her nightcap pulled over a long braid cascading down a shoulder. The singer moved on to a tune they all knew, "Down in the Valley," and they sang as one, all together. Only the children slept, and that was as it should be. These were women sharing and preparing for a crossing, God willing. Women, together, complete unto themselves.

sason's song

Mazy watched Suzanne as she stepped back into her wagon. She stopped halfway. Her back arched, and she dropped down beside the discards.

"Something's wrong," Mazy said to her mother's turned back. Mazy scrambled out, her bare feet cool on the damp ground, doing the calculations, her hands clammy with knowing.

"Is it early?"

Suzanne shook her head, reached out, then gripped Mazy's hand. "No. Just not now, I didn't want it now, before we crossed the mountain." She gulped in a breath, held it, then exhaled in a moan. "I'm scared," she said. "So scared."

"We're all here together, Suzanne. That's how we'll get through it."

"Out of the way, Pig," Elizabeth said behind her. "This is one you'll have to let us handle. Birthing's as natural as wind." The dog whimpered.

"Find his sock," Suzanne said. "He likes Bryce's old sock."

Elizabeth laughed. "Not put in the discard pile, I'll wager."

His whining roused Zilah, who was dispatched to find Pig's sock, and then the others rose, their breaths puffs in the air as the starlit night dissolved into sunrise.

Surrounding camps began to stir. Wagons beginning the ascent passed the women by, word reaching them of a baby making its way to the world. That a baby was being born gave an unexpected lift, joy wrapped inside dusty uncertainty. New meanings scrubbed away the past. Life continued. Here arrived a baby as proud proof.

"Who'd a thought we'd use our skirts for more than the necessary circle?" Betha said, standing in front of the tent opening to protect Suzanne's privacy. Pig lay in front of her with his wide paws crossed over a dirty, knotted sock.

"I hope nothing goes wrong," Lura said, looking behind her.

"*It is of the* LORD's *mercies that we are not consumed, because his compassions fail not.* Lamentations 3:22," Esther said.

"I hope he's got lots of those compassions," Lura said. "We seem to be needing them."

"The next verse says 'great is thy faithfulness.' So I believe we have nothing to fear. I will boil water now. For hyssop tea," Sister Esther said. She walked the short distance to stir the fire and gather up her tea caddy.

"She doesn't know there's no real use for hot water till after the baby comes," Betha said, "and then just to clean up."

"Heating kills those squiggly tails at least," Adora said, approaching. "I'll be most grateful for well water once we reach the West."

"Straining bugs with every swallow. I'll remember this trip for that, if nothing else," Betha added.

"Now we can remember it for a birthing," Mazy said, crawling out of the tent. "A new beginning, everything going as planned."

"Still so many fearful things," Betha said. She swatted at flies.

Mazy surveyed the landscape, inhaled a deep breath. "I don't ever want to fear the face of tomorrow," she said, "or put features there that ache away the hope."

❧

"Who you talking to?" Ruth asked Mazy later in the morning.

"Jennifer." Mazy scratched at the wide bone between the cow's horns. The cow lifted her head, pushing against it as though to make Mazy repeat the scratching.

"Good-natured, at least," Ruth said. "We could start yoking animals around the base of that mountain. Maybe figure out how to get the bees there." She lifted the bucket of milk Mazy'd set aside from Mavis. Not much there.

"Everything in its own time. I think that was one of the things I was meant to learn here, to stop trying to push it all into my time, and trust I'm not alone in it. We'll get the wagons over, the bees moved. I feel it. Besides, we need the celebration of this birth."

"Bringing a baby into this world may not be wise," Ruth said. She swatted at the dust on her pants with her felt hat and looked away.

"What eats at you, anyway?" Mazy asked her.

" 'Who?' is the truer question," Ruth said. "But I'm not sure you'd like to know, not really."

Mazy heard something in Ruth's voice, saw the clenched jaws, the protected eyes shadowed by the felt hat. She wanted to think of the joy of the birthing, but something in Ruth's posture, the challenge in her offer, told Mazy that this was Ruth's moment to stretch.

"Let's see if Esther has her tea caddy handy, and you can tell me what you will."

The women dropped leaves in their tin cups, and Esther poured hot water over them. Then the two, one dressed this morning in bloomers and the other in her husband's buttoned pants, sat off to the side.

"I'd tell it as a truth or lie, but no one would believe it. And it would be more…painful spoken there." Ruth sipped. "He's been released. May be right behind us. My husband," she said to Mazy's questioning eyes. "He's served five years for the death of our son. I was the witness against him. He's coming after me." Her hands shook around the cup. "Oh, he's charming, always 'in awe' of me until I gave birth and the baby…died. Zane said I was as guilty—I didn't get up when I should have, to save my baby. So he's right. I should have gone away as soon as he was sentenced, but I couldn't. I kept putting it off, the leaving. Maybe as penance."

"I assumed your interest in horses drove you west."

She nodded. "I wanted to escape...to follow...I'm as bad as Suzanne," Ruth said, shaking her head. "Starting out and not finishing thoughts."

"I think Suzanne's coming out of that, getting clear inside her mind."

Ruth took a deep breath.

"Jessie's my daughter. That's what drove me west."

Mazy's heart skipped a beat. Her mind raced back to the love she'd seen in Ruth's eyes when she gazed at the child, the love and the longing. "How hard for you," Mazy whispered, the ache of her own loss piercing. She swallowed. "I didn't know."

"Good. I don't want anyone to know. I came in part to win her back, to tell her that I was her mother, who gave her up to save her. But I don't believe I can. Not now, not after I see all that Betha is to her. And then she'd have to know about her father, and why...I let her go. And that I didn't save...I'm not sure she could forgive me."

A pink dawn had blushed its way across the camp, washed up onto the western mountain, revealing a straggle of wagons. They caught the shouts of men and women and animals straining their way up. Mazy heard anticipation in their banter, doing it all together, strangers helping strangers, turning them to kin.

"My mother's always told me that forgiveness begins at home, not that I listened," Mazy said. "We seek it, receive it, and savor it, and it turns into love. Then, we can give it away."

"It's too much to forgive," Ruth said. "My son died by my inaction. I hoped Jessie might forgive, someday. Now I'm not sure if I want her to ever know. I'm constantly arguing with myself about something, about whether the truth is helpful or harmful, whether to stay with her or leave them be."

"Whether to forgive yourself." Mazy paused. "If you'd like," she said, surprised at her own offer, "I could pray that you'd know."

Ruth's breath vaporized in the morning air. "I don't think anyone has ever prayed for me," she said. Her jaw unclenched.

"Maybe not that you've known about," Mazy said. "Not something folks talk of much. Do you ever pray?"

Ruth coughed, fidgeted, brushed at her pant leg. "A few weeks back, when we rounded up the stock, after the storm, something strange happened. I prayed, that Mariah and I...that we'd go unseen by one of the Sioux warriors. And it was so odd, but he didn't see us. I...it couldn't have been an answered prayer, though. I would have felt something, some power, wouldn't I? All I felt was relief."

"An answer," Mazy said. "Relief from worry and fear and hurt feelings and frustration and misery and guilt, all there." She wondered if she was speaking to herself. "I suspect you could be forgiven, too, Ruth, for still loving your children's father."

Ruth swallowed and tears pooled in her hazel eyes. "It's that obvious?"

"I think we're destined," Mazy said. Ruth looked at her, such large, disquieting eyes. "We're drawn by...difficult men, you and me. Now there's a truth I'd rather not confess to. I wish it were a lie. Jeremy wasn't always...forthcoming. I don't even know how much I don't know about him. It's strange to love someone who could be two people almost." She sighed and wondered if sighing meant she was hanging on or letting go. "Don't suppose that'll change until we figure we're worth someone different, worthy by ourselves."

They heard the baby cry then, born worthy all at once.

❧

"I want a word that means joyful," Suzanne said, holding her son in her arms. Her fingers explored the child, his ears and nose. Zilah hovered over her, and from a pottery dish marked with dark shapes drawn on the butternut bowl Naomi handed her, she took a damp rag and wiped Suzanne's forehead with sweet-smelling herbs.

"*Sason*," Sister Esther told her. "It is a Hebrew word that means rejoicing, gladness, joy that comes from the Lord."

"*Sason.* Lovely. Musical and strong. With his father's middle name. Sason Bryce Cullver." She repeated the name to her son, her fingers memorizing. "Let me see your face, Sason," she said. "Let me see your face." She looked up, and Mazy realized she did not have her glasses on. "Describe him, Tipton, would you?"

"Dark hair, like yours," Tipton said. "And a mouth that's perfect and lifts upward at the ends. Bright blue eyes, the color of a spring morning. Your nose. Looks like he's got everything, all his fingers and toes. He's so alert," she said then in wonder. "Just watching you and your face, your eyes. I didn't think a baby could be so watchful, so early on," Tipton said.

Elizabeth had wrapped the boy in a portion of quilt, but Tipton handed over now a fringed shawl the color of snow. She'd taken it from the single trunk still remaining in her mother's wagon.

"That's your best shawl," Adora said, pushing against her daughter's hand. "You'll need it when we reach—"

"It's a gift, Mother," Tipton interrupted, extending the cloth. She tucked the silky alabaster wrap around his tiny face, and the baby cuddled into the cloth. "See? He likes it. Look at how he stares at you, Suzanne."

Suzanne clutched at her eyes then, patted around for her glasses.

"No. Let him see you," Mazy said. "You're beautiful. He knows." She thought of something. "Let's plant a columbine seed in Sason's honor. I'll get my seed gourd, grab up a handful of that Wisconsin soil, and plant it in a cup. You can plant a new one every year, no matter where you are, and when they bloom, you can think of us." Suzanne nodded her approval.

Jessie made her way over then, shy behind Betha, holding the cup while Mazy retrieved dirt and pressed a seed deep inside.

"First time I ever saw you holding back," Betha said, pulling the girl into her skirts.

"He won't break," Suzanne told her. "Bryce always said they don't break unless left untended."

The girl stepped forward. "I got the seed," she said and ran a small finger over the baby's forehead. Clayton squeezed between the women and came to lean into his mother, pushing Pig to the side.

"Meet your brother," Suzanne said, and she lifted the toddler's hand and placed it like a summer's leaf drifting, caressing the baby's head. "Feel your brother's fuzzy hair?"

"Fuzzy hair?" he repeated.

A thin scar marked the spot where Jumper had struck Clayton's head. Mazy thought it a miracle he walked and talked and laughed. Sason was a miracle. She looked around. They were all miracles together, in one place.

~

Lura made up a batch of hot cakes and bacon, and Clayton ate his fill. Then he led Naomi and Deborah, and they clustered around Suzanne suckling her baby. Behind them rose the final discards from their lives back home including a tidy stack of men's clothing bearing the sign: "Please take."

We needed this time of rest, Mazy thought. *This pushing, pushing doesn't make the gains that stillness does.* Perhaps it was having something to celebrate first that gifted them with vigor. She would try to remember that, to look for moments of gratitude and joy and convert them into fuel to propel her through difficult days.

Deborah turned to the group. "I tell bees of baby," she said. "They rest."

"Praise the Lord," Sister Esther said, lifting her eyes and hands to the heavens.

"Bees go way if not like you," Deborah told her. "They—"

"Choosy about their traveling companions," Mazy said.

"Aren't we all?" Betha laughed.

"Or should be," Adora said, stretching as she walked toward the newborn baby. Zilah walked with her wide, flat-footed gait to hand Adora a cup of hot coffee, her eyes lowered as she made the offer. "If truth be known," Adora said, taking the cup, "we couldn't have selected a better crew than what got chosen for us." She sniffed at the coffee. "I do believe I can almost smell this brew," she said. "Now, wouldn't that be a miracle?"

～

They began now the hard labor of the day. Mazy thought of Adora's words as she and her mother lifted the heavy yoke around the oxen's necks. They had been given a gift with these women, chosen as though for a reason. Despite their uncertainties and irritations, they each had gifts offered just as they were needed. Even she offered something that had nothing to do with gardening, with planting seeds of columbine or peas. She could sort things out, excavate the gifts of others, encourage people to reach beyond their usual hesitations, work together as one.

And she'd discovered another: There was nothing wrong with wanting to please, to care for others as she did, to be ready to listen to Ruth or Tipton. But it was meant to be a gift freely given, not one offered out of obligation. She wished Jeremy were alive for her to tell him that, to show him that she was still learning, that seeds had been planted in her soul that had not yet begun to germinate. The world needed people who could both till fresh soil and break new ground to expand the boundaries of a field, but who could also nourish the turned clods of worn-out dirt. Both promised places for seeds to grow with proper tending. She had found something essential.

～

Emigrants moving on by offered to assist them.

"Do we take their help?" Mazy asked. "We've had delays."

"Could do it ourselves," Ruth said. "But I guess being independent doesn't mean being alone, just being responsible."

"Even you're willing to accept the help of men?" Adora asked. "Well, that is a sign of things changing."

They accepted. With a word from Mazy, Ruth began hitching Lura's wagon to go up and over first because it was the sturdiest, her oxen the steadiest wheelers. Eight animals were engaged to pull and they entered the loose line of wagons moving toward the mountain. The women cracked whips over the oxen's heads and pushed at the wagon at the same time, though the latter merely gave them something to do while the dust swirled around their feet, hung on sweat-stained wool.

Tall pines with barklike thick scales rose on either side of them. Rocks spit from underfoot; animals strained against the wagon weight. The air hovered hot and heavy. Dampness seeped at Mazy's seams, and she longed for a breath of wind to cool the bloomers that hung from her hips. She pressed the woolen jacket against her breast to pat some of the moisture.

At the top of the grade, even Ruth cringed.

"What'd you think?" Mazy asked.

"It's going to be a killer." Ruth leaned toward her. "But I'd only say that to you."

"We'll make it, ladies." One of the men helping at the top pointed over the side, at wagons already settled safely. Mazy guessed his face hadn't seen a razor since he'd left Missouri. "Be surprised what can be accomplished with tobacco and spit." He signaled and other men removed their hats, wiped their brows with their forearms, then began the task that would consume the remainder of their day.

❧

"Zilah, you best go help Mazy and Ruth," Adora said. "I lack your strength, truth be known. I'll look after Clayton and Sason when he wakes."

"Miss Suzanne, too?"

"Of course." She motioned with her fingers until Zilah handed her the baby, who slept in Tipton's alabaster shawl. Adora tucked the fringe beneath his tiny chin, and the child yawned in his sleep. "Go on," she told Zilah, and the Celestial left, looking back over her shoulder.

Adora tied the shawl so a big knot formed over Sason's body, making a handle for carrying. She walked toward the last wagon, set the baby down in the shade, then leaned back against the wheel. Drool formed at the corner of her mouth as she sank into sleep.

Ruth chocked the wheels, then helped unhitch the oxen, careful not to step too close to the outer edge of the rockface. Mazy walked the oxen off to the side, patting and talking to the faithful beasts while Naomi and Sister Esther moved to the back of the wagon, swapping ropes with Ruth and Mazy. Even Tipton began throwing parallel lines, then tying them underneath. The callused hands of two men reached and tightened beside them.

The wagons would swing out and away from the rockface like a child's toy sliding across two ropes stretched between the trees high on the cliff and others down below. But these would be real wagons, not toys, holding all that they had. The men tied huge knots buttressed out to the side, and then they brought the ropes to the trees, already showing yellowed, jagged scars around their girths.

"Others have done it before," Ruth said, reminded by the marks on the trees.

"Wish that were more comforting," Tipton said.

More activity as four oxen were hitched to secure the rope around the cliff tree. Mazy looked down the slope at Sister Esther, who seemed to be praying. Then with a massive thrust and jerk and a shout from the men, the wagon eased over the sheer face.

Elizabeth and Betha waited at the bottom, staring up. They'd walked the mile or so around the mountain's base on a shady trace too narrow for wagons. Their shoulders rubbed against the inside rock wall. Following behind, Mariah rode Jumper and pushed the cows, mules, and oxen single file along the path.

Betha pressed pudgy fingers against her mouth, still staring upward. The wagon swung out and then, like a spider suspended on a double strand of web, it was lifted by the wind, then pushed back against the rockface.

"Let out some slack!" Mazy shouted.

The bearded man grinned and nodded, repeating the call.

"Let out some slack!" Ned and Jason repeated, their job being to carry the message down the line like buckets passed along a water brigade.

Inch by difficult inch the wagon made its way down the twenty-five feet until it jerked on the hard rock bottom below them. The ropes held. The wagon survived.

A cheer went up from the women and the men at that end. One wagon down: three to go. It had taken two hours.

❧

"Today you move," Deborah said, speaking in soft English to the bees. "Much activity in household. Not frightening. Queens sleep and sleep. The word *sleep,* it is spelled with eyes, yes?" Deborah asked.

"I guess a double *e* looks like eyes," Ruth said, wiping her forehead of perspiration. "Alphabet wagon goes up next. Then yours. Do you want to leave the bees to go over in the wagon or…?"

The girl smiled. "They all I have, the bees," she said. "I carry. One hive. You help please?" She lowered her eyes as though embarrassed to seek it.

Sister Esther inhaled. "I almost sleep with them, so perhaps I could carry a colony."

Deborah crawled inside and handed out a box to the Sister. "Maybe Adora could carry one. Where is she?" Sarah had an active Clayton in tow, his bells jangling. They looked around. No one could see her.

Deborah began carrying the bees, taking time with her painful quick, quick steps, talking as she moved. She didn't anticipate trouble.

❧

"The horse took the baby!" Adora shouted, running toward the base of the hill. "Your horse," she yelled and pointed at Ruth.

Beyond, Ruth could see Koda walking with his white treasure, the shawl clamped between his teeth, Sason apparently still asleep inside. The horse set the baby down and ripped at grass beside it. Adora turned and ran toward the horse, which promptly picked the bundle up, moved four or five feet with it until Adora stopped. Then Koda set it down.

"He's playing a game," Ruth said. "Back off. He'll tire soon enough."

"But if he steps on that baby…" Adora wailed. "How irresponsible of you to teach him to steal babies!"

"Tell me what I can't see," Suzanne said, holding her side as she approached without Pig.

"It's all right," Ruth told her. "It's the white shawl Koda likes."

"Where's Zilah?" Suzanne asked.

"I sent her off to help Ruth and Mazy," Adora admitted. "And I fell asleep."

"Speaking of irresponsible," Ruth snapped.

Koda did tire of his game, and Ruth retrieved the child. As she did she made a decision: she didn't belong; she brought trouble wherever she went. She'd help them over this mountain, ride to the deciding place, and then go on north—hopefully alone. If she was lucky, Zane would follow her, a last good thing she could do for Jessie.

❧

They pulled Adora's wagon up next. The oxen instead of the mules were hitched to it. That might have been the cause. Or perhaps it was the oxen resisting the strange men on an unfamiliar wagon, or perhaps it was as it was meant to be, no one's fault at all; an opportunity, Mazy thought later, to walk by wisdom instead of certainty.

They had just unhitched the animals at the top when a chock slipped or a chain came loose at the tongue or who knew what. But before anyone could stop it, before the ropes had been secured to the trees, Adora's wagon lurched then slid then lumbered backwards, gaining speed.

Shouts of "Hold on!" and "Out of the way!" tangled with frantic jerks against the ropes, then people slipping, rope burning against gloved hands and then "Let 'er rip, boys, she's a lost one!" Men standing back, their hats perched back on dirty brows as Adora's green and gold careened back down the mountain, heading straight for Esther's wagon. And the four remaining colonies of bees.

Deborah heard the shouts and turned in time to see the wagon rattling backwards, watched with huge eyes as it struck Esther's team, two oxen bellowing from wounds inflicted by the now shattered wagon.

"The bees!" Deborah gasped. "The queens!" She set her own colony down, trying to run in her blue silk slippers. "Wait, please, wait," she said. Sister Esther stood alone with the bees now, swallowing, her hands trembling.

"What's happening?" Suzanne asked, turning back. She held Sason, Clayton roped to her side. Esther told her, her mouth dry and scratchy as she described the wagon, her oxen. They could hear the high-pitched humming of bees spilling from a box knocked out of the wagon's back. "I'm setting these down," Esther said. "Don't stumble on them."

Esther called the names of her oxen as Deborah found one box slammed against another and the lid loosened, allowing the bees to spill then swarm away. Deborah spoke in her calmest voice, in her native language, straightening a box, a dozen stings at her wrist, near her eyes. She watched the open lid of the other turn black with a swarm of escaping bees.

"Leave wagon here," Deborah told Mazy, who arrived breathless from atop the hill. The bees hovered around her face. "They fly away! Home no move or bees lose way. Not come back." Her reedlike voice shook.

Deborah told Mazy to be calm, to send no signals of fear. It looked as though only one colony'd been freed. The others, though humming loudly, appeared to be intact. Mazy stood still, not batting at the bees that fluttered over her nose, buzzed near the pasteboard of her bonnet.

"They come back," Deborah said, crying softly. She pulled an already swollen hand from within the hive, setting the small box upright. "The queen still lives inside. They die we move box. Need come home same place."

"They sure don't accept much change in where their home's at, do they?" Mazy said. "Must be related to me." A black cloud of bees lifted away. "All right," Mazy said. "We'll find a way."

With effort, they unyoked the two wounded oxen as extra hands helped move aside the wreckage of Adora's wagon. She and Tipton picked at the spillage of photo albums and hats, flour and shoes. A blizzard of destruction, of wounded oxen and what was left of Adora's precious things, littered the side of the trail. Adora sobbed, moving splintered wood, sucking at fingers full of slivers.

The white bee box remained in the dirt where it had spilled out, set as Deborah told them. They worked around it.

Ruth, Naomi, and even Tipton tended the oxen's wounds with vinegar splashed on the gouges and flaps of loose skin. Lura's sewing kit was requisitioned for the task, and Tipton drew the needle and thread as the oxen permitted.

Then they took Betha's alphabet wagon up the hill, leaving Sister Esther's for last.

Deborah, eyes pinched nearly shut from the stings, still managed to return along the trail that skirted the mountain's rocky base. She'd carried one box and delivered it to safety. Mariah and Naomi each moved a box while Esther led her precious oxen. Then Deborah came back and remained in the exact spot where the wagon had been hit, sat in the dirt near the white box while other wagons moved on around them.

And she'd been right. At dusk the bees returned, retracing their flight, landing backwards as they did, Deborah talking, talking until she closed them inside the small, square hive. She'd waited until almost dark and then Suzanne and Pig had joined her to walk back. "But it is dark," Deborah protested when she saw them.

"We all need to rest in a place we're familiar with," Suzanne told her as she listened to the girl pick up the precious box of bees and carry them along the trail to meet the wagons successfully lowered over the mountain's shear face.

The crossing had destroyed the Wilsons' wagon but left Esther's usable, though the contents inside suffered. One of Sister Esther's oxen, mangled beyond doctoring, had been put out of its misery by Ruth's pistol and then butchered, the meat shared with those who'd helped their crossing. Ol' Snoz survived.

"At least we feast tonight on fresh beef," Adora said as they sat at the evening campfire.

Elizabeth said, "I am as tired as I have ever been in my life and not even hungry." She set her plate down.

"You could have bartered or sold the beef," Lura told Esther. "What you won't need and can't dry ourselves you could sell, even at reasonable prices."

"Some of those wagons serve very lean people," Esther said. "A little beef before heading into these last weeks might make the difference to some of those grizzled-looking children I've seen. No, I'll give away what we don't use. I believe it is the Christian way," Esther said.

"Antone said the Californians and the Oregonians had to send relief parties out almost this far the last two years," Lura said. She chewed on a biscuit, brushed the crumbs from her cheeks.

"Those traders we met awhile back said there are relief stops set at the Humboldt Sink and Carson and on the Oregon route, too," Ruth said.

"Doesn't speak well of what's ahead, does it?" Mazy asked. Rethinking she added, "On the other hand, it's nice to think that someone's out there, preparing if we need to be rescued."

"Antone wanted us to be sure to have enough supplies so we wouldn't need charity," Lura said.

"Got enough bacon, but he didn't pack enough tobacco, right, Ma?" Mariah asked, giggling.

"Oh, pooh," Lura said. "I've decided to give that up anyway. Bad habit. Makes me cough."

Adora looked at her. "Another piece of discard? Well, maybe we should all forgo our attachments." She looked at Tipton.

"Like your sugar tooth, Mother?" Tipton asked.

"Hard to believe I can't taste much when I crave that maple candy. Deborah's promised to introduce me to honey dishes, haven't you, Deborah?"

"How'll you get the goo out without wrecking the hives?" Elizabeth asked, addressing Deborah.

"She has a special way of designing the hives," Esther told them.

"That'll be a fancy thing, all right," Lura said. "Make raising bees a sweet and profitable proposition."

Adora would never have made it alone, Mazy thought. She needed help more than most, always hanging tighter to what was. Still, on this big mountain crossing, she'd seen most of these women shift to accommodate each other, put memory and useless baggage aside in order to make room for the new. Even Sister Esther seemed to soften her certainty.

Perhaps that wasn't fair. They needed the Sister's assurance of God's presence when it wasn't obvious he was there.

By the campfire light, Adora and Tipton moved what things they thought essential into Betha and Naomi's wagon while Lura joined Mazy and her mother, Suzanne and Zilah, too.

"I thought you might like these," Tipton ventured, handing a small package to Lura.

"What?" The woman loosened the string. Her face became a question as she held up two silver combs. "These aren't mine," she said.

Tipton shrugged. "They don't stay in my hair much. And I thought you could…in return for your cooking, you know…" Her eyes dropped. "I know they're not what you lost. Couldn't find what you lost, nor what Mama lost, either."

"My, oh my," Lura said and wrapped Tipton in her arms, still clutching the girl's hair combs. And Tipton let her.

❧

"I kind of like lying close to Mavis," Mariah said. "She chews her cud and those sounds and the coyote's howling just drop me to sleep. Ruth likes my company back there with her too. I'll see you in the morning, Ma."

"At least you have plenty of room to sprawl out," Adora told her. She had that indignant tone in her voice, and Mazy wasn't looking forward to the evening's sleeping arrangements.

How odd, Mazy thought as she walked to milk the cows, that Adora should be in the company of her and Suzanne and thus with Zilah, the woman she once charged with theft.

"Distance breeds distrust," Ruth told her when Mazy expressed the thought out loud as the two finished the milking by lantern light.

"But isn't it amazing how it worked out, with the very people needing—whatever it is they need—forced together. Just funny how that

happened. Like it was meant to be. Love and loss and betrayal, all a part
of life, but we're given gifts to get us through."

"Through to what, I wonder."

"Maybe understanding," Mazy offered.

"I'd like a safer place," Ruth said.

"Kinship. Kindness. Security. Strength. Guess they go together,"
Mazy said, the words coming to her like the scents of favorite flowers.

❧

"Adora," Lura said, "If one of those Californians comes by, you can sell
what mules you have now and make good money." It was the evening
after the mountaintop experience, and Tipton's combs sat on Lura's
head like jewels in a rat's nest, packed inside the snarls of her unwashed
hair.

"Mules are all I've got," Adora protested. "Grieving everything but
what I can stuff in a corner of someone's else's wagon. That's what it's
come to."

"And me," Tipton said. "You still have me. If you're interested."

Adora looked startled. "Why wouldn't I be interested?" she said.

Tipton shrugged her shoulders.

Adora poked at the fire for a time. The women swatted at mosquitoes. Deborah brought out some muslin to drape over Suzanne and
Sason, and the women made the sounds of getting ready for rest. Mazy
had almost forgotten what Tipton had said by the time Adora spoke
again.

"I have a truth and a lie," Adora said.

"Oh, good," Betha said. She threw the dirty sock for Pig, who
chased it and trotted back to the fire with it. "I like this game." The others assumed the position to listen.

"I came all this way from Wisconsin, went through all this trouble
to get here because I was interested in my Tipton. That's one." She

threw pebbles toward the fire, their plink causing a flicker in the flames. Pig's ears alerted. "Now two. I followed my daughter here because I didn't want to go unnoticed." No one spoke. "Now you're to guess, isn't that right?"

"And one of those is a lie?" Elizabeth asked.

Adora thought. "No. I have to change one. Wait. I *didn't* come here to follow Tipton, that should have been the first one. Oh, I can't do this right."

"Then the lie is that one," Mazy said. "You came here because of your daughter and because you didn't want to go unnoticed."

"Yes," Adora whispered. "If truth be known. I would have been, back there in Cassville. You were always the honey that brought the bees by, Tipton, gave me things to talk about." She reached across the log they sat on and patted her daughter's hand. "Truth be known, I came here for me as much as anyone. But I'm glad to have found someone more important to be with than myself. If that makes sense to you." Tipton held her mother's hand. "And I'm worried over you, how thin you are. Scared, I am, to lose you."

"I'm next," Tipton said. She swallowed, but her voice held firm. "I have laudanum hidden, I'm afraid to eat more, and I make my arm go numb."

"Huh?" Jason said, looking at his hand. "That's three."

"I've seen those fingers of yours," Lura said. "I don't think you could cause that. But there's no laudanum around. I'm sure of that. And I've seen beans terrorize you."

"It's the hand," Ruth said. "You can make it go all contorted like that." Tipton nodded, her face turning pink. "Amazing what our minds make us do, isn't it, Tip?"

"Any more guesses?" Suzanne asked, not being able to see Tipton's nod.

"Elizabeth told me that someday I'd know why my hand numbs," Tipton told them. "Why my arm ached and hurt. She made me mad when she said that. But it's true. When I breathe real fast it happens. I could make it happen right now."

"No, don't," came a chorus of protests.

"I breathe that way so I don't have to think about how scared I am of something else. Of being alone, I guess. Of Tyrell going away, of eating too much, of everything being in a swirl."

"I believe if you hold your breath, it'll stop that," Elizabeth said. "The tingling part in your hand and your nose."

"Tyrell said to let out long breaths. And I want to, now. To stay…here, to find some other way, so my hand doesn't do that. As for the eating—"

"We'll do it," Adora said, holding her daughter's thin hand. "A little bit at a time. We'll sit together and just be. Without our full span of mules, no wagon of our own, we still got something to hang on to we didn't know we had."

"I believe this is cause for celebration," Elizabeth said. She walked to the back of Betha's wagon and reached inside. She carried the troubadour's harp to Suzanne. "Play us a joyful song," she said, "if you feel up to it."

Suzanne's hands knew the instrument. She strummed an Irish melody, quick and light.

Mazy looked at the strings, all separate but playing together, held in tension by the curve of the wood, the lines of a pleasant place.

"I put this on the discarded pile," Suzanne said quietly when she finished. "A harp is not essential."

"I brought 'er back," Elizabeth said, "because joy is."

where we love

They awoke with renewed vigor, Mazy in the pattern of her past. She found her journal and began writing. She read a Psalm, then thought of a quality of God's character. "Anticipation," she wrote. Expectation, foreknowledge. *As though something has been planned ahead, prepared.*

What they'd needed on this journey west had been prepared for.

They needed to laugh, and Elizabeth had provided the occasions, even if sometimes Mazy felt older than her mother. *She looked forward to how joy would appear. She anticipated something pleasant.*

She wrote it down, surprised at what words and quiet brought to question.

Betha swept the ground around the campfire. She nodded at Mazy. "Good to see you writing in the morning again."

Had everyone noticed?

Mazy finished, then headed toward the cows. Ruth's independence, her handling the stock so skillfully with never a complaint—they needed that commitment, to see it every day, this woman doing what she knew best while she struggled inside.

Mazy bent her head to Jennifer's udder. It felt different. One last milking, then no more 'til she delivered a calf. More changes. Mazy thought of her traveling companions, how they had changed, as her hands stripped milk into the bucket.

Lura had offered to alter the silk dress that Zilah wore, after Mazy expressed concern that the loose cloth would catch on one of the oxen's horns when she leaned over them to adjust the yoke. Suzanne described a way to take the tucks in that gave the girl a look of curves when everyone knew she leaned slender as a bean. Their joint efforts cheered her, and the other Celestials came forward asking for ways to salvage their hems shredded by walking through stickers and sage.

Even Tipton—having given up her parasol to the discard, her combs to Lura, and absent the laudanum—displayed new spirit, biting back at the now gentle jibes her mother gave her about her still needing "Tipton-watching," only now because she'd stumbled over Fip and nearly squashed the pronghorn.

And they needed her, Mazy decided as she swung the bucket at her side. Yes, they did. They needed her own good mind, her ability to bring independent spirits together into one place. She could make decisions. She smiled at that. She did that "deciding thing" well for other people. She just had trouble making compassionate choices for herself.

But she'd changed, too, unveiled herself—as had they all—like petals of flowers unfolding to light. Maybe in her life with Jeremy that unveiling had not existed. He had never unfolded himself to her. The letter just confirmed it, telling her of things she neither knew nor imagined. Had she wanted him to be elusive? She realized that she, too, had been elusive—in her way. Had it been too painful to know herself and so she'd let him define her boundaries, kept herself so privately engaged at pleasing him—and other people, too—that she had failed to recognize who either of them was?

❧

The guidebook said they would encounter another difficult mountain within the next two days, but instead by midmorning, they were given the choice of paying a toll for using a road "just completed the end of July," said a young man who introduced himself as Buck.

"McAuley's cleared it round so you don't have to go over. Get some service berries along the way," he said and grinned. They paid the toll happily, shortening the journey through the efforts of others.

Rain fell on them that night while the mules munched on good grass. "We're supposed to have no water now for seventeen miles," Mazy said. But they were blessed with fast-flowing rivulets throughout the next day and arrived at Soda Springs where they camped near what Jessie called "fuzzy water."

A Mormon up from Salt Lake stopped at their campsite, loaded with two baskets of fruits and vegetables, and everyone splurged and sank their teeth into onions and even corn.

"Corn," Mazy said. "Mine would be ready back in Wisconsin." They boiled it and spread the last of the butter over the plump kernels, marveling at this feast.

"My mama told me once that all the little silk of corn is connected to each little kernel," Elizabeth said. "God made 'em so the silk catches the light and brings it inside the husk. And where they're missing kernels—that's where a silk got pulled out to the wind and that little thing didn't grow up, didn't get to play its part."

Lura pulled her cob back to stare at it. "Could that be true? God attending to detail like that?"

"Think of his planning for us, if he's put so much thought into each kernel of corn," Esther said, licking her fingers.

"He anticipated," Mazy said. "Gave each of us a place."

"Hunger makes a good sauce," Betha said, butter oozing over her palm. She looked around, then wiped her hand in the grass. "My mother used to say that."

"Mine always said this little poem," Lura remembered. A kernel dropped off her chin. *Ich bin klein. Mein Herz ist ganz rein. Wiemand wohnet darin Jesus allein.*

"What's that?" Jessie asked, wrinkling her nose.

"Well, if I remember, it means, 'I am little. My heart is all pure.' She patted her heart with her buttered fingers. "'Nobody lives there, except Jesus alone.'"

"Nobody's home except Jesus?" Jessie asked.

"Hadn't thought of it that way, but yes. When we love, pure in our hearts, then nobody's home there but him."

∾

They made good distance the next day. Rain, heavy at times, slowed them but also settled the dust. The trail moved steadily uphill on these traveling days, but the oxen had good grass and water when expected.

This was good, Mazy thought. She knew that, once they reached the deciding place and beyond, they'd face expected miles of barren, burnt earth without water. Night travel, too. Then they would reach the place on the Council Bluffs trail where each would decide whether to go north to Oregon or south to California, the parting of the ways. They should have discussed it earlier, but Mazy put it off and the others let her. Maybe they thought they'd never really get this far.

But Mazy knew: Like the desert and the Sierras ahead, it would take all their strength and effort, all their faith together, to get them up and over and then onward to the place where they belonged.

∾

Ruth walked Koda more than rode him, still protecting his foot. She could pull the bar shoe, but it had been nailed well back at Laramie. Laramie. She shivered. Had it been Zane? Had he recognized Koda there? She wished she could shake this feeling of dread, that someone rode with evil intent along the trail beside them.

366

She walked up on Lura, doubled over in laughter.

"She's got an easy gait," Tipton told her. "All mules do. Better than horses. It'll help your legs."

"I've never been a-horseback before," Lura said. "Just walking and in a wagon or a buggy since I was a little tyke."

"We're all doing new things now, Ma," Mariah reminded her. "Come on. You can ride back with Ruth and me."

They'd made a stirrup of their hands and helped Lura step in, then attempted to flop her onto a Wilson mule. The jack stomped. Lura soared. She crumbled into a heap on the other side of the mule, the animal gazing in seeming disgust at her backside.

"Don't get scared now," Mariah told her, covering her smile.

"You talking to me or the mule?" Lura asked, straightening her bonnet.

"You have one steady mule, Adora," Ruth told her.

"I told you they were good ones," Adora said. "The ones you gave away were…" She stopped herself. "If truth be known, they're the"— she looked at Tipton—"the second best thing I got."

Lura rode to Sinking Creek on the mule and talked Betha, too, into riding a mule off and on, if Adora allowed. "Save your shoes," she told them.

"We look like pumpkins on a rail," Betha said.

"Speak for yourself," Lura told her. "My Antone would be proud I learned something new. Well, at least Mattie will be."

They covered good miles, and then Mazy halted the lead wagon.

"Why you stop?" Zilah asked. She walked beside the oxen, talking to them, and did not often look ahead, her eyes accustomed to watching her feet.

"It's almost noon," Mazy said. "We've got good grass here. And up ahead is the junction to Fort Hall or California. We either head south toward the Humboldt Sink, maybe the Applegate Trail or Sacramento, or we make our way north to Oregon. We can't go farther without a decision, and I, for one, don't plan to make it by myself." She heard Sason cry and smiled. "Besides, we've a baby that needs tending."

～

Ruth wanted Oregon. That's where her horses were, that's where the Schmidtkes' cattle were. North, to Fort Hall, then along the Snake River into Oregon and free land. Three hundred and twenty acres. That's what she needed. That, and to be in as a remote a place as possible from Zane. Yet she had to lure him after her, not the rest.

She watched Jessie hold the drinking dipper to Suzanne's lips. The girl was kind. Kind but small and young. She suspected that the California trail, though it crossed a great desert and the Sierras, would be the better route for Jessie and Betha, Sarah and the boys. The relief stations were well established if they had trouble, and opportunities greater in the gold country, in a state already added to the Union. There were posts along the southern route, trails made by the gold seekers, traders willing to supply them. They'd have a better chance to make it south with three wagons. Certainly the occasional people arriving out from the camps with their vegetables and newspapers told her civilization stirred a good stew in the south.

They would make it without Ruth.

～

"So what's your pleasure?" Elizabeth asked as her eyes scanned the wagons. They'd pulled off to the side to allow room for others to pass. The parting of the ways, as it was known, would cut into a dusty, treeless area, and both roads led forlornly from each other, like dance partners separating to opposite sides of the hall. Through sage and dust, the roads disappeared toward different horizons. Here, near water and grass, they would talk.

"Seems like we could use a prayer, maybe," Tipton said.

"Who'd like to offer one?" Lura said.

"I would," Ned said. He spit on his hand, slicked his hair back, then offered up, "Now I lay me down to sleep. I pray the Lord my soul to keep. If I should die before I wake, I pray the Lord my soul to take. Amen."

"Well said," Sister Esther said, and she smiled.

Mazy hadn't often seen the woman smile. "Suzanne, would you like to summarize for us?" Mazy asked. "Keep us on track if we get off?"

"If Sason doesn't keep me too distracted."

Clayton poked a finger toward his little brother, but Zilah's hand gently touched the toddler's finger to her own. The boy looked up, and Zilah kissed his pudgy hand.

Wispy clouds like angel's hair wafted across the sky. Few natural sounds could be heard, though Mazy thought she recognized the high-pitched cry of a hawk lifting in the distance, smelled something dry yet fragrant from the grass. She adjusted her bonnet and looked at the women settled like colored squash in the shade of the wagons. Her mother fanned herself with her hand.

"Let's see if we have any agreement," she said. "If you're Oregon bound, raise your hand."

Ruth and Adora raised their hands. Lura did too.

"Does that mean the rest are for California?" Ned asked. "This voting thing is chirk."

"Not if it goes against you," Betha said. "Just wait."

"Who voted?" Suzanne asked.

"Three. Ruth, Lura, and Adora. Oh, four. Tipton just raised hers. Oh. And Betha, too. No? Yes. So, California then?" Mazy asked.

Sister Esther raised her hand as did Deborah, though so timidly Mazy almost missed it. Naomi and Zilah raised theirs. Elizabeth's hand went up for California as well.

"Really, Mother?" Mazy asked. "I thought you wanted the land claim?"

"Not strong either way," Elizabeth said. "Just thought when you didn't vote for Oregon, I…"

"No. Let's each vote our hearts." She gave the totals to Suzanne.

"Lots of people didn't raise their hands, Mommy," Jessie said. "They're not paying 'tention, are they?"

"No, they aren't," Betha said.

"It doesn't matter to me," Mariah said. "Pa said we could get into Oregon by way of California and wouldn't be nearly so rough a trail. Avoid the Columbia that way. Mattie might've gone that way to Oregon City." Both Ned and Jason nodded in agreement. "Suzanne?" Mazy asked.

"I…no." Suzanne swallowed. "I would like to go to California, but I anticipate needing help."

"There is way I help?" Zilah's voice carried desire across the landscape in a way none had heard before.

Sister Esther clasped her hands before her apron smudged with bacon grease and dirt. "You are committed," she said. Zilah dropped her almond-shaped eyes. "The contracts." She cleared her throat. "There is a problem. Of course, Cynthia's must be redeemed, and now there is another unwilling to accept his bride. I have not shared this earlier. He will want his payment back. I do not know who or why. I have no way to know until we reach Sacramento to make the matches, or somewhere I can contact the Agency. But I know I must go into California. There is no choice for me in that."

❧

For the first time, Esther realized she needed the Celestials. If they changed their minds and went another way, she would be spending her life finding a way to redeem their contracts. Worse, living with failure and loss, all alone.

"But you may not need to," Suzanne said, her voice high with infrequent joy. "If Zilah wishes to go with me, I'll pay her contract, send the money back to her family and she'll have worthy employment."

"She was contracted to a worthy man," Sister Esther said. "That is what our agency does, and she may still be expected."

"But only two are needed now," Mazy said. "From what you say."

"Yes. Only two."

"The bees?" Deborah asked, her voice faint.

"I do not know," Sister Esther told her, her palms to the air. "I am so sorry, but I do not know."

"I leave," Zilah said. "Or I go with Missy Suzie. I not go to husband."

"But why not?" Esther turned her body stiffly toward the young woman.

"I know this not time," Zilah said, "but I have truth. I not send photograph to new husband. I send cousin's, a woman of beauty."

"Good grief," Lura said. "You're lovely. Don't know any man who wouldn't find your face attractive, even if it isn't of the daguerreotype you sent."

Zilah brought her fingers to her cheeks. "The bumps…" she said.

"Oh, pooh. Any man who takes issue with those doesn't know he's got a survivor on his hands. That's all those mean, that you were tough enough to live through illness. So are we all. We should all have marks on us after this journey. We lived through the worst of times." Lura's voice cracked. "I would have just stayed there and died next to my Antone, without each of you."

Betha patted her shoulder. "We all helped each other."

"I go with Missy Suzie. If she have me," Naomi said. "If not Zilah."

"I thought you'd stay with us," Adora said, her voice a whine.

"You didn't want any of the Celestials around, Mother," Tipton said.

"Well, if truth be known, I think I can smell better with Naomi's cooking. Might not be those herbs and all, but, well, I don't think I want to take the chance."

"Tasted success, have you?" Elizabeth said.

"And the accusation?" Mazy said. "Of Zilah taking your money. Should we settle that now, too?"

Adora squirmed. "Truth is," she said, picking some unseen lint from the hem of her dress, "I think Tipton's right. The purse and money that disappeared had Charles written all over it."

"Money had name on it?" Zilah asked, turning to Naomi.

"Just a way of speaking," Elizabeth told her. "So you want your sense of smell worse'n chasing the scent of bad money? Bad enough to go to California to get it?"

"What do you think, Tipton?"

"Let's head for California for now," Tipton said. "We have time to settle up with Charles. Truth is, I'd like to be...stronger when I do. So I don't shake when I tell him that he was wrong about Tyrell. He knew about being worthy. He was worthy, and he wanted the same for me." She rubbed at her arm and squeezed her fingers open and closed.

"But what'll we do for money?" Adora asked.

"The mules," Lura said. "They'll stay alive if we're not hauling with them. And if we stop riding them into swaybacks, they'll be worth plenty."

"And I'll replace the ones I gave away," Ruth said. "When I get my horses and sell them. I promise you that, Adora. I had no right...I'm sorry."

"Well...I never expected that. I accept," Adora said, making it three words.

"Not sure what we'll do about our own resources," Lura said. "But I still got my knife sharpener. All the way from London. I can go to work doing that, if we can board with one of you folks for a time."

"Where'd you stick it, Ma, so no one knew to toss it out?"

"Under the wagon where the extra wheels used to be." Lura grinned. "Hope you all don't mind. I'll do your knives for free."

"I want someone clever living near me," Elizabeth said to Lura's blush.

"Either way, you have a place, Zilah," Suzanne said.

"Deborah and me. We keep duty contract, Sister," Naomi said. "Find way help."

"Well, I'll vote for California, then," Adora said. "We can always go on to Oregon when we've worn out California, now that we know how to travel light."

"Ruth? What would you say if we went to California too?" Betha said. Her words were tentative. "I could hire on as a cook and house-keeper until I'd saved enough to buy my own place for the children. A boardinghouse of sorts. I could do that. It'd be a little easier south, to do that, I think."

"Not so many rivers to cross either," Ruth said. "No Columbia."

"I wasn't thinking of that, but yes, maybe that too. I've met my share of rivers. I just think I'm getting on in years, old to be carving out land to farm and horses to trail. I know that's what you want and I don't blame you, but I think maybe I'd head south if I listened to my heart, as Mazy says we should. I think Jed would approve. It'd be hard alone, without both of you, but—"

"I kind of thought you'd head south," Ruth said. "It'd be better for your…girls. The boys, too. I can join on with folks going to Oregon, pack Jumper and ride Koda 'til I hear of Matt and Joe Pepin and find my string. I'll get by."

"Seems so dangerous, you going alone," Mariah told her.

"Oh, being alone's no problem," Ruth said. "I'm used to it."

"But you don't have to be, it sounds like to me," Mazy said.

"Are you going to Oregon?" Ruth asked. "I'd be happy for the company."

"I meant that there's invitation in Betha's voice. For you to stay with them. That it would be all right to need them, just as they need you."

A hot breeze flapped at the canvas of Esther's wagon. Sarah swatted at a horsefly, sighed, and leaned against her mother.

Ruth imagined the horses, the vigor of traveling on alone. She could always choose aloneness. But the eyes of those circled in the wagon shade said that kinship and connection waited here.

"It is…appealing to be invited," Ruth said. "But for good reasons, I think it best if I just head north. It'll be safer. For everyone."

"Safer?" Adora asked.

"Trust me."

"Can't we change your mind?" Mazy said. "Go where all of us go? We've done so well helping each other."

"Don't make it harder," Ruth said, "now that I've finally made up my mind."

"We haven't heard from you, Mazy," Suzanne said. "Or are you still undecided?"

＊

It felt like failure, Ruth's insistence on going north. Mazy could see what would be best for each of them. It was always easier to see other people's paths, point out potential boulders and nourishing resting places for them. It was knowing what she, Mazy Bacon, wanted at this moment that brought the most discomfort. Deciding what was best for her took courage, made her insides shimmer and shake like the last leaf of fall clinging to the branch. She might want to go north, but they needed her, this group. They needed Ruth, too. She just couldn't convince her that they weren't alone now. They were stronger with each other. They were a community, all together.

Deciding as though she was alone was as awkward as when she'd worn the bloomers the first time, maybe worse. She'd felt a little child-ish, naughty almost, and surely frightened, but she had done it. Never mind that wearing them that day ended in tragedy. The act of donning them had splashed invigoration on her skin, brushed stimulation across her senses, and brought a burst of independent joy. The difficulties that happened after didn't take away what once had been.

"Cracked earth keeps opening and opening until rains come to heal it," Mazy said. "This journey's been like that for me. We've had our share of misery—cracked-open soil. But the tragedies have led us to each other."

"Challenges covered by faith convert people into kin," Sister Esther nodded. "It's been my experience."

"That sounds exactly right," Mazy said.

"So will you go with us to California?" Lura asked. She glanced at Ruth, looked back. "I'm starting to get antsy sitting here."

Mazy said, "I want to find a piece of land that I can nurture and invite others to, or ask them to leave if I wish, just for a bit. I want to have my own little plot. My own home. I wonder if that wasn't what Jeremy looked for, after all, what any of our men went hunting for, a place to belong to, surrounded by ones they loved. I don't know." She shook her head. Others dropped their eyes, looked thoughtful.

The mention of the losses appeared to set each woman looking backward. Mazy wanted to move ahead.

"I want to grow things that taste wonderful or that fill the air with fragrance. I want bees and butterflies and birds all around my home, not just tall timber in shadow, but open spaces with a creek or river or the promise of a spring. I want a place that feels like I belong there and that maybe, someday, if I'm ready and wanting, I'll invite another man into, but only because I chose it." She swallowed. "But it scares me that I'll go back to my old ways, that I didn't really turn around, that I'll get bogged back down in muck."

"Sure sign you got good soil, you get into muck," Betha said.

"Everything that happens has another side if we just trust it's there," Elizabeth told her, "and not spend too much time blaming the muck before we trudge through it."

"I will ask new husband loan you bees," Deborah said.

"Thank you."

"Thinking back on those vegetables we ate, coming from the south," Lura said. "Corn on the cob. It'll grow good in California, won't it, Mariah? Think we should let Mazy and Elizabeth take us toward Sacramento?"

"They got to go with us, Ma. They don't even have a wagon."

"Never thought of that," Elizabeth said. "Nothing to sell. Have to bribe Lura to let us stay on."

Lura brushed her palm as though to say "not to worry."

"'Course we got that money Jeremy left. And the cows," Elizabeth mused out loud.

Mazy grimaced. "There is this matter, Mother. Some unfinished business. With Jeremy's brother and sister-in-law."

"Jeremy had family? Ponder that. Where?"

"In California, according to the letter. Possibly that brother even owns my cows and who knows what else. We might even owe him for the wagon we left behind."

"Well," Elizabeth said, her voice a low whistle, "I guess we have good reason to head south, if nothing else, to settle up."

"That lawyer's letter mentioned another…issue, too. I've been reluctant to share it until, well, I knew what I might do. But here's a truth. Or maybe it's a lie. Jeremy has a daughter, living somewhere in Oregon Territory."

The group sat silent, staring.

"Imagine," Tipton said, finally, "a daughter, and Mr. Bacon leaving out something that essential."

Suzanne moved uneasily, handed Sason to Zilah, reached for Pig's brace and pulled herself up. "So it looks like a California route we're taking, into Placerville or Sacramento, somewhere south. Except for Ruth—and Mazy hasn't yet said."

Mazy took a deep breath. "I'm scared to death, but I'm determined," she said. "I choose California."

Elizabeth stood and pulled her daughter to her chest. "And you didn't say you was sorry and you didn't ask my opinion of what you should do or nothing before you said it. I'm proud of you, my turn-around girl. I'm proud of you as picked peas!"

"You'll find adventure in California, Mother?"

"I find that wherever I am," Elizabeth said. "Long as I'm with those I love."

Ned took out a tin whistle and began to play. The women clapped their hands to the music. Even Sister Esther cupped her hands, stiffly, with precision.

This journey, Mazy thought, had given her a gift that staying in one place, at home, would have deprived her of. She could survive; she could go on; she could make decisions for herself and others as she needed, and she could learn from past mistakes. She could even anticipate the future and not be frightened by it. She didn't journey alone; none did. The Lord provided and maintained her lot. With his help, she could plant new seeds in soil as yet untilled.

⋙

Ruth moved away from the group, placing grain into pack bags, pulling out dried beef and other supplies. Jessie wandered over. "Can I help?" she asked, and Ruth let her toss the rope as Ruth tied the diamond hitch over the packs on Jumper's back. She wouldn't think about the empti-ness of her leaving; she was protecting them, that was what mattered.

"I'll miss you, Ruthie," Betha said. "You're good kin. You'll let us know when you get your horses, maybe come south then?" She brushed at her now-stained apron, held Jessie at her side. "I wouldn't think of going on without you if I didn't have the others."

They held each other, and soon the other children joined them, then the other women, all saying good-bye, respecting Ruth's right to decide.

"Sure you don't want to ride with us to the deciding point at least?" Elizabeth asked when she hugged her.

Ruth shook her head, straightened her hat. "Best I head out while I can."

~

They waved at Ruth until they could no longer see her, Mazy staring the longest. Ruth said she'd parallel the trail, not go where all the rest would, just for safety, her being a woman alone. *A woman alone,* Mazy thought. But only by choice.

They decided to camp there, worn out by deciding and Ruth's having left. Nearby, a puddle of standing water flirted with dirt, and a splash of tall grass promised comfort to the stock. That night as she heard Pig turning before dropping to sleep, Mazy wondered where Ruth laid her head.

In the morning, they yoked up to the music of meadowlarks. Mazy would remember that later, the contrast of pause without premonition.

Zilah helped Suzanne, made the offer to assist Betha. Cicero, Betha's ox, wandered farther from the other stock, stood beyond the dirty water in the tall grass.

"I'll get him," Betha said, "then gladly take your help."

Sister Esther stood, shading her eyes with her hand, watching as Betha waddled off toward her ox, her hands waving at mosquitoes.

Suddenly, Betha was consumed by a black rush and a hum of buzzing insects. Not mosquitoes, something larger, rising up from the grass, circling her skirt, covering her apron, her bodice, her face.

"Yellow jackets!" Betha screamed. "Stay away!"

Mazy and Elizabeth rushed toward her. Esther ran toward the wagons.

She shouted at Suzanne still in the wagon. "The lantern!" Esther said. "Hand me the kerosene lantern."

Suzanne swung her arms around, grabbed at the straight chimney of glass.

"That's it!" Esther shouted. "Quickly! Quickly!"

They could hear Betha crying and slapping, screaming as the insects feasted and stung.

Esther ripped the lantern from Suzanne's fingers with such force that Suzanne fell. "Go," she said. "I'm all right."

Esther looked in, hesitated, thought she saw something wet near her writing desk, then turned and ran toward Betha, pulled the chimney and threw the liquid on the woman's hair while the others slapped at the wasps still clinging.

But it was too late. Betha's face swelled, her breathing collapsed, and within minutes she died, held closely in Esther's wide arms.

dance of the turnaround women

Ruth had made a dry camp in a dip behind bunch grass and sage. She'd slept uneasily, dreaming of footsteps and small children's cries. She awoke, saw the stars and wondered if she should have left, turned away from the light in her life. *Will I ever be sure of anything?* She said a prayer for guidance, then fell back asleep. She awoke with a start just at daylight.

A sound. Her eyes sought out Koda, hobbled nearby and still. Jumper slept, standing. She whispered Koda's name, and the horse moved to her, nuzzled her bedroll, nickered low. A wagon train? No, someone riding, that's what she heard, the thump of hooves against earth. On her belly, she eased her way toward the sound, her heart pounding. She was alone, no one else to turn to, no one else to help. Her hand shook as she pushed aside the sage. A rider trailing a pack animal rode beyond her, wearing white. She pressed her hand against Koda's nose to keep him from whinnying. Without looking, she patted the ground for her whip.

❧

As Mazy rode out on Ink, she focused her grief on the task at hand—finding Ruth and bringing her back. Mazy had to bring her back.

"Not good, your going out alone," her mother said.

"You tend to the children, bury Betha, then head out. It'll give purpose. If I don't find Ruth by tomorrow, I'll turn back. You may be at the turning place by the time we head back."

"Seems like we should wait," Adora said. "Grieve here."

Mazy shook her head. "Need to keep moving. I'll catch up with Ruth, I know it. She needs us and the children. She just doesn't know it."

Mazy's eyes watched the earth. The sandy soil promised tracks if she could just find some sign that she hadn't ridden past Ruth, that she paralleled north and not south. She had to bring her back, should have worked harder at keeping her with them. *It wouldn't have prevented what happened, but we weather life's storms better together.*

Her eyes hurt from straining to watch the trail. She rode back and forth as though on a switchback, a prayer on her breath. Then she found what she needed: the track of the bar shoe still on Koda's foot!

❧

All white. Zane had always worn black, but she was sure Tipton described him, sure he trailed behind them—or perhaps he'd already passed her by. She watched. This rider sat his horse more forward. It wasn't Zane. Maybe he was still behind them and would head to California anyway, her sacrifice at going on alone now worth nothing. As the rider faded away, Ruth's heart stopped pounding in her head, her breaths slowed, she stopped gripping the whip. She crawled back into her bedroll and lay staring up at the cloudless sky. So frightened she'd been, over nothing, no one. All because of Zane. The man controlled her life, her very breath—and she hadn't seen him in years. It was crazy. It hadn't been this hard in the presence of the others.

Morning light washed over the landscape, and she rose, fixed a fire, drank some hot coffee, ate one of Betha's biscuits, chewed a chunk of Esther's dried beef. She thought of them, the women and children, and felt tears press behind her nose. But for Zane she could be with them instead of about to turn north, alone.

Koda nuzzled her. "It isn't Zane that pushes at me, is it? It's my own doing, being afraid and thinking that if I lean on Betha and the others I'm weak." She thumbed her eyes. "This is weak," she decided. "Being myself *with* the others, that's what takes strength."

She'd get her family to California, settle them in and then head north for her horses. Yes, she'd choose differently, not let Zane decide her course. Then maybe what she got from her life would change too. She blew her nose on a white handkerchief. "Let's go back," she told Koda. "I'm tired of being alone."

❧

Mazy watched the rider approaching and knew at once that it was Ruth.

"Whither thou goest," Mazy said when she was within earshot. Ruth looked confused, and Mazy smiled a wistful smile. "I've got sad news for you," she said. "But you've made it easier to tell with your turning back." She spoke then of Betha's passing and that the women followed hoping she'd be found by Mazy, sure they would fare better all together as one.

They met the wagons by the evening circling, their reunion tempered by the shadow of their loss. Ruth held the children, exchanged glances with the others. "It'll be all right," she said. "We've got each other."

❧

They headed south. "Some of those little stones I piled at Mama's grave I brought with me all the way from home," Ned said.

"She'll like that," Ruth told him.

Elizabeth had planted a columbine seed, she said, and Mazy told again the story of its meaning, "I will never give thee up."

Ruth left a different marker at the turning place when they reached it the next day. On it she wrote: "To Zane Randolph. Your family headed to Oregon." It was her lie, but she knew he could read and hoped he'd stay out of California.

They walked as they had the weeks before, and in the travel, they grieved Betha's passing, remembered the others, how their lives and loss had stretched each woman's heart. But the dreariness lessened, at least for Mazy. A new goal led them: to get to California, settle legal issues, contract matters, find new beginnings. A smile even crept across her face as she kicked at dust. The pain in her side eased. She still ached inside when she thought of Jeremy, gone; felt a rush of blood at the memory of his betrayal. But leaves of forgiveness grew too. Forgiving him would let her forgive herself; or perhaps as her mother implied, if she was kind to herself, she'd have more to give away.

Time healed, and so could looking forward. Who would have guessed that she, Mazy Bacon, would someday not only accept the unknown but find excitement, a hope, wrapped within?

The women now knew they would settle close to each other, be together. They already resided in that place of friendship fired by difficulty, in the shelter of faith and each other. But to be physically near each other, to share the work of washing or the chatter of their days, where they could continue to nourish the broken clods of each other's spirits into ready soil, that would be a miracle. Another one of many, if truth be known, as Adora might say, as Sister Esther would surely agree was certain.

⁂

Sister Esther held the writing desk, a black splotch of ink staining the oak.

"What happened?" Mazy asked her. It was morning, a time for writing.

"I don't know for certain. Deborah?"

Deborah came on her quick, quick steps.

"Do you know anything of this?" Esther held the desk to her, shaking it like a shaming finger.

"No," the girl told her. "I not see before."

Her protests drew Ruth, then Lura, Pig, and Suzanne. And when Suzanne asked, Esther described the stain. "It's recent," she said, her fingers touching the grain raised from the wet. Then remembering, she caught her breath. "Oh, I am so sorry to accuse you, any of you," Esther said. "The day that Betha died. I reached too sharply for the lantern in Suzanne's hand. The ink bottle…I did it myself."

"Paper?" Deborah asked. "Paper inside?"

"Oh, my," Esther said as she lifted the lid, her fingers shaking as she opened the hinge. Inside lay the white linen, blotched black as sin. Esther moaned as she lifted the cloth. Beneath lay Deborah's future, the parchment now nothing but a blotter for ink.

"Maybe it can be redrawn," Mazy said. She stared at the parchment's edges revealing portions of letters and lines.

"By whom? How? Oh, I'm always judging someone else, and it's me, my errors, my penance to pay," Esther said.

"You were overcoming a fear," Suzanne told her, "hoping to save a friend. Accidents happen."

"Well spoken," Mazy told her, touching her hand. Then, "Tipton draws. Maybe you and Deborah can remember some of the design and tell Tipton."

"I saw it, too," Ruth said. "When Sarah made it her kite."

"You could describe it to Tipton, you and Deborah? I would be so grateful."

"Better," Ruth said. "I'm a lithographer. We can draw it together."

Several days after the parting of the ways place, they crossed a deep, white, windy valley with no water. They walked well into the night, the bugs and mosquitoes constant companions, their throats parched. The moon rose high above them, casting shadows of sparse sage on sand; no grass, nothing to stop for; water promised only when they made it through this.

Mazy moved past Sister Esther and heard her praying beneath her breath. Mazy patted her shoulder, dragged her own feet through the dust beside Suzanne and Pig, Sason still in Tipton's shawl sling. No one whipped the oxen. They did all that they could on their own.

"Do you need to ride, Suzanne?" Mazy asked her.

"I'm thinking of calling myself Suzie," she said, adjusting her dark glasses. "Suzie's not so formal. Something new. And no, I'm fine walking."

Tipton reached for Sason, to relieve Suzanne.

"You've stayed with us, Tip. We've needed you. I'm grateful," Mazy said.

Ol' Snoz, Sister Esther's favorite ox who had survived the crash and journey this far, did not stay with them; he expired from thirst in the night.

"Leave him," Esther said, wiping her nose, sniffing in the moonlight. "Nothing can be done for him." They clustered around the fallen ox, offering comfort to the straight-backed woman. "I'm too tired to butcher it, too weary without water to care."

"And we've no time," Mazy said. "Need to keep pushing or we'll lose another ox, or worse."

Esther grieved for the beast long after they left him.

At last, while it was still dark, as the moon set without the rise of the sun, they reached a campsite, recognizable by its single water hole that looked dark and still, but wet. They unhitched the remaining oxen, which sucked at the water, their noses deep in. Lura lay on her stomach and splashed her face. "Stinks and it's warm," she said, "but it's wet."

"Close your eyes and pinch your nose," Adora told Tipton. "Won't even taste it."

Tipton sighed and dipped a cup in. "The critters…" she said.

"Oh, nothing can live in that," Elizabeth told her, "even without boiling."

The women hobbled the mules and horses, offered them and the milk cows buckets of the putrid stuff, which they took grudgingly. Suzanne gave her share of hoarded water in the lidded bucket on Lura's wagon to Clayton, made sure the other children had enough, then gave the rest to Pig.

Tipton watched Adora swallow before she let the warm water trickle down her own throat. She grimaced. "What a body won't do to survive," she said, then tried not to think of what she'd just put inside her.

Each woman fell into a deep and hungered sleep.

They awoke to the sounds of an ox bellowing in the distance.

"Must be another group gaining on us," Elizabeth said, blurry eyed.

But when she stood up, she saw no other wagons, no other emigrants close behind. Instead she hurried to Sister Esther's tent. "You ain't going to believe this, Sister, but we've got us a resurrection."

Sister Esther peered into the moonlit night, her eyes pinched from the long day in the sun. "Can it be?" she said. "Snoz?"

"He must have found some old alkaline hole, and here he is," Mazy said.

The animal bellowed and shook his big head, but he did not stop to greet his surprised and grateful owner. He lumbered past her to the water hole just beyond.

"Praise God?" Deborah said, softly making her way beside Esther.

"Oh my, yes, do that," Sister Esther answered.

They found a good watering spot farther on in the morning though with little grass. Nothing grew here, it seemed. The cracks in the white baked earth were wide enough in places to catch the children's ankles, scratch them deep as they pulled their bare feet back out.

"Hope we didn't make a mistake coming this way," Ruth told Mazy.

"What's done is done," Mazy said. "I don't have any fuel to give to the wondering of what I might have done different, at least not at this moment, while we're in it. Have to evaluate when we get where we're going. Decide what I've learned then."

"I'm working on that too," Ruth said.

Within days, they looked down into a wide valley marked by the slender ribbon of what Mazy said had to be the twisting Humboldt River.

"There'll be some rough places yet," Mazy said. "They say the water gets worse instead of better and the river gets thinner. But beyond is a meadow and then, California and the high Sierras. Good water there, not to mention the cool of the mountains."

"I like the way you think on pleasant things, child," her mother said. "Keeps us moving."

Mazy's lips were blistered and cracked and the bloomers she wore shredded, but she didn't care. She wasn't frightened anymore, at least not of indecision. She'd chosen on her own, and she'd been faithful, not apologized or blamed the others or herself when things got rough or wrong. They were here, on the verge of achieving what they'd set out to do, find a new home, a new place to be.

She looked at each of the women. They all wore caked blisters, dirt ground into their skin. Lura's apron hung like a limp brown rag against her faded dress, and Mazy sent a prayer of remembrance for Betha and her tidy ways.

"We look so wretched," Tipton said. "Just look at us."

"What was that little poem you said, about it being a gift to be simple and to come down to where we ought to be? Sarah, what was that?"

"And when we find ourselves in the place that's right, 'Twill be in the valley of love and delight."

Mazy started to laugh at the faces of caked dirt, the sun-streaked clothes, blistered feet, and yet how beautiful each woman was, from the inside, where things were essential. "We're in the valley, all right. And each of you looks as full of love and delight as any I ever knew back in the States. Though to some, we might just look like buzzard bait."

Elizabeth looked up at the hot sky. "See any?" she asked. The other women looked up. "No? Well, we've got something more to offer then. Let's keep going, simple and free as we be."

They looked wretched, but it was a temporary state. It was all temporary. All the misery and worry, all the hardship and strain. Just temporary. All the good things too, Mazy supposed, the moments of joy and lightness, of love and delight. Those didn't last either, but time was better spent musing on them.

The best we have is the present, what happens right now, with all these women given to each other to help us survive, keep going. It was almost worshipful, watching their thin calicos move across the desert. Like the Israelites, wandering and dusty as they sought the Promised Land. Only when they came to trust, only when they stopped demanding on their own, did they discover the water of the Jordan. But even there Moses had made them stop to remember the past, what they'd learned, so they could take the stories and truths with them and not wander uncertain again.

What had she learned so far? To make the best of the moment with people she'd come to care for, was willing to change for; and to thank God for the choice, and trust him for the rest.

Mazy smiled.

"What is it, darling?" Elizabeth asked her.

"I'm just counting my joys. Finding such good people out here in the middle of nowhere. Friends. Ten times more than I had back in Cassville. And thinking of what Jeremy told me once when I got tangled up in the reeds in that cold spot in the Mississippi. He was right. Things aren't always as they seem. Sometimes they're even better."

∽

They began meeting more people: traders on horseback, Californians asking about relatives from Missouri or Wisconsin, from New York or the Ohio Valley. Their animals sometimes carried supplies, dried beef and fresh spring-fed water. Several said they were hired by relief groups, out from Sacramento and other places, to bring the emigrants in, to welcome them with "open arms," those who had spit in the elephant's eye.

"They must want something," Lura said, chewing on her empty pipe.

"It's only for the destitute," one man said as he tipped his hat at Tipton.

"Which you aren't," Tipton said, eyeing him dressed all clean and covered.

"You don't fit that description either, ma'am," the man said, his ears turning red.

"Why, that's the nicest thing anyone's ever said to me, I'm sure," Tipton told him and curtsied. She batted her eyes at the man, her face a mass of scabs from insect bites, her skirt shredded, dirty and limp, her bodice stained with sweat. Her bare feet had the look of sausages, all swollen and red. But she was upright and walking and sassy, and she could still make a man blush.

"Where you coming from?" one of the men asked.

"Oh, from all kinds of places. Along the North Platte," Mariah told him. "How about you?"

"Sent out to let you know about Beckworth's largess and to avoid the Lassen Cutoff," he said. "Just stay on this route, head into Sacramento," he told them. "South around Ragtown, along the Carson River. You'll be in good shape."

He'd tipped his hat again and ridden on, but his presence was the subject of the evening circle around their necessary time.

"Wouldn't it be nice if we just could make a choice and then go with that and never waver? Never have to change course?" Ruth said.

"Like on a ship?" Mariah said.

"Even ships make adjustments, go around storms if they can and have to steer through what they can't control," Sister Esther said. She was in the center of the circle. Outside, Mazy watched the boys looking after Clayton while Sarah and Jessie sat like little statues, being allowed to hold Sason for the first time on their own. The children were cleaner than they'd been for a while, a stream having provided a needed place for bathing and for a good scrubbing of their threadbare clothes. They cried less as each woman made time to hold them and wipe their tears. The women had pitchered water over each other's heads, the feel of cool water on their dirty scalps like a balm to a wound.

"We are on a course," Mazy said. She inhaled deeply the clear, cooler evening air. "A good direction. It's a little exciting to see what's around the next bend, don't you think? We'll just have to weigh what these men have to say to us before we veer off in one direction or another. What matters is that we've made the commitment. We have to trust Providence for the rest."

In the morning, they met three riders touting various routes, offering to buy up Adora's mules. They eyed a thin Ink as well.

"If you're willing to give me that kind of cash out here," Adora said, "think what I can get in California."

"Your mules've got to make it. They're looking pretty slim."

"They're tough as tacks," she said.

"Speaking of them," the man said, scratching at his hairy chin, "we'd buy them up too if you had 'em, which I see you do there, on your lettering wagon."

The offer came more than once.

"What would they do with those?" Suzanne asked when Mazy told her what they wanted. "My carpet tacks? And Lura's? Everybody's?"

"He's wearing white," Tipton said. "I can see that. And he's about the same size as that Laramie man." The women stared, wary of the distant rider with a high top hat.

"Time I faced him," Ruth said. "Mazy, keep Jessie and the others in the wagon, will you? I don't want them seeing him or him seeing them."

"Seeing who, Auntie?" Jessie said.

"He must have taken the Salt Lake trail to be coming at us from the west like that, doubled back."

Suzanne asked, not certain of what she heard, "He's riding in from the west, heading east?"

"Well, ponder that," Elizabeth said, squinting her eyes into the distance. "We all know who that is."

"Charles?" Adora said.

"Not…Charles," Tipton said.

"No," Elizabeth told them, beginning to wave her arm in a wide and welcoming arc. "It's that gambling man turned teacher, Seth Forrester."

"Why, Seth," Mazy said as the rider pulled up his horse before them. "You white-collared man. What happened to your quality beaver-skin hat?"

Seth grinned at her. "The quality comes from what's under the hat, not what material's in it." He removed the white hat, said, "It is my pleasure to encounter you again. Where's that giant dog of yours?" His eyes cast across her, searched them all. They stopped at Pig standing beside Suzanne, and then his eyes moved back. Mazy could tell that he counted no men.

"What happened?" he said, his voice low, his eyes holding hers.

"Sit a spell with us at our nooning and we'll tell you," Elizabeth said.

And so he nooned with them, and they told him of the sorrow and the losses, the burials and the moving east and then west again like a dance. There was a tenderness in the telling, for he was someone who

391

could hold their loved ones in his mind. It made the giving richer, the remembering deeper. And as they spoke, the men and women they'd lost filled their lives again, Jeremy and Antone, Jed, Hathaway and Tyrell, Bryce, Harold and Ferrel. Betha. Cynthia, too. All entered their conversations.

"We'll bring our memories with us, to new places," Elizabeth said.

"You've been through much," Seth said. "Worthy of admiration." He fingered his hat as he sat on the milking stool Mazy offered him, set in the shade of a wagon. "I'm sorry to learn of your losses."

"Thank you," Mazy told him, "but we've been well provided for, beyond measure really, if truth be known."

"And now you," Sister Esther said. "Tell us your truths. Weren't you headed to the California gold fields?"

"I was. I did." Seth extended his long legs before him as he leaned back against the wheel, scratched his back at the hub. "What I'm doing now is under contract to William H. Nobles of the Shasta City diggings. I was traveling with a train he met up with. Told us all of his new venture. From Minnesota he is, of German stock. He's made a shortcut to the northern mining regions. But it meets up with the trail heading on south, to Sacramento, or you can take an easier route north, along Applegate's Trail on up into Oregon. Uses portions of Lassen's Cutoff."

"You took the Lassen?" Lura asked.

"It was a gamble, but I am a gambling man." Seth grinned. "We took it, and as luck would have it, we learned later we were the first on Nobles's venture. Shasta residents had raised two thousand dollars to improve the trail and bring a train on in, and there we were, the first to be feted at the principal hotel."

"What's *feted*, Auntie?" Jessie asked.

"Celebrated," Ruth said. "Like a big party."

"And he's hired you to bring other wagons in?" Mazy asked.

"So he has. It's a good little town. Timber, pines, oak, meadows along the river. Trinity River country is unparalleled in beauty. Good water. Producing mines. They're needing everything a mining town needs: progress and people. It even has three, no four, bookstores. Just getting ready to open up a school."

"We know our letters already," Jason said.

"I see you've been working on them." Seth nodded toward the wagon.

"You're one we can ask. Why do people want the tacks?" Mazy said. "Several have offered to buy them from us."

"Are the letters made up of carpet tacks?" Seth said. "Brass ones?" He stood, walked to take a closer look. "Well, I'll be."

"What's the interest?"

"Of all the things you could have discarded, it's amazing you kept these." He shook his head in disbelief.

"Why? What's so unusual?" Mazy said.

"Hanging muslin on the walls is the big craze in mining towns," Seth said. "All over Northern California. Their nod to civilization. But they've got no tacks to hang it with, no little nails or anything to spare, so they pay their weight for tacks. In gold."

"Gold?"

"You've got a fortune spelled out there," Seth said.

"And we didn't even know it," Adora gasped.

"I'd like to be feted," Jessie said and swung her legs as she sat on the wheel. She smiled at Ruth, who winked back.

"I think you'll have good reason," Seth said.

"Soon as we get to California we'll really have something to celebrate," Adora chirped.

"Why wait? You're awful close," Seth told her.

"We are?" Several spoke at once.

"You are. Allow me," he said, "to be the first to officially welcome you. On behalf of William Nobles, I extend this invitation to consider making Shasta City your California home. I'll take you there myself, if you'll allow. And you can celebrate being back in the States, now."

"What's the vote?" Jason shouted.

"We have prayer first," Deborah announced.

"Thank you, Lord, for carpet tacks," Adora intoned, her hands in the air. "Amen."

"And for good mules and good people and for providing just what we needed when we needed it," Lura said.

"I still need to fill my contracts," Sister Esther told him. "In Sacramento."

"Direct trail south from Shasta City. I can help you find what you need to know," Seth offered.

"There are others of us needing contact with lawyers," Mazy said.

"I can get you that, too," Seth said, his eyebrow raised at the tone of her voice. "Almost anything you want we've got at Shasta City, or it's a gateway to it."

"Except carpet tacks," Mazy said. "Who would have thought them essential?"

"They weren't," Sister Esther said. "They're just the whipped cream on the cake of good eating God always provides."

"I was just wonderin'," Elizabeth asked him, "if there're any big trees in this Shasta City." She spread out her arms as though they were an oak or maple swaying in the wind. Fip lurched toward her on his leash and bunted at her skirts.

Mazy laughed. "Why do you want that?"

"Why, to build a tree house in," Elizabeth said. "Ponder that."

She gathered up the troubadour's harp then and handed it to Suzanne. Jason fished his tin whistle from his pocket, and the two began to play.

Seth bowed low, offering his hand to Mazy. She hesitated, then took it. He stood taller than she, and it surprised her as it always did to be looking up to someone.

"Hey!" Ned said. "Everybody didn't vote. So are we going to Shasta City or not?"

Suzanne stopped playing. "Mazy? It's up to you," she said.

"We're going all together; all together," Mazy said. "Some questions though, Mr. Forrester: Will cattle thrive there? Will my garden give a bountiful harvest?"

"Yes to the first; no doubt to the second. It's a good little town, with orchards already planted. I plan to stay awhile myself. Not a better gamble in all of California."

"Well, get the bucket," Mazy told Ned as she dropped Seth's hand to make his dancing offer available to someone else.

"You going to milk the cow now?" Ruth asked. "I don't think she's got any milk to give."

"Nope. I'm ready to plant Mrs. Malarky's seeds. One of them's a maple tree. Might as well start it so we can transplant it for your tree house, Mother, soon as we find a home."

~⊱~

They decided to rest for the day and let Seth lead them on in the morning. The big man cooed over Sason, holding the child cradled in the cup of his elbow. The baby stared up at him, sucked on the man's little finger.

"Careful now," Lura told him. "My mother said men holding babies was catching as a cold."

Seth laughed. "A man could catch worse things."

He handed the baby back, and the Celestials circled him and spelled out English words to his deep-voiced praise. He stood, his hands smoothing the silk neck scarf that hung down his chest while he chattered with the boys. Ned slapped his cap on his knees to brush away dust the way Mazy'd seen Seth just do it. Jason stood smoothing a red neckerchief that had been his dad's. Mazy'd never seen him wear it before. She blinked back tears. *How those boys must miss their dad. Now their mother, too.*

Seth brought a blush to Lura as he offered to dance with her. Adora and Elizabeth acted as each other's partner. Ruth stood off to the side, her arm draped over Sarah's shoulder. Mazy caught her eye and the woman smiled. A burst of laughter and both women turned to see Mariah helping Jessie onto a defenseless Fip, whom Ned tried to hold with a halter. Clayton, who perched on Tipton's hip, reached out, saying, "Me, now. I ride now. Me!"

Jessie lasted only a second, sliding west as the antelope jerked east. She landed laughing in the dirt. The children acted, at long last, just like children.

Mazy clapped and tapped her toes and watched the women, these turnaround souls, her friends worthy of celebration.

Deborah stepped out of the wagon, carrying a box of bees. Five colonies made it. That was a miracle in itself, though one more box was quiet, and Deborah told her, eyes cast down, that the queen inside had died.

"You took such good care of them, Deborah. Such good care," Mazy said. "It's all any can ask for."

In the other boxes, the tiny insects hovered around the opening Deborah made for them to go about their work in the dusk. They moved in a pattern back and forth, this way and that as though memorizing where they'd been before leaving, seeking and searching the area for the nourishment they needed to bring back to the queen. They danced as they darted.

When they were sure they knew their way back home, the bees dotted into the distance.

"Another dance?" Seth asked, offering his hand.

Mazy shook her head. "But you're welcome to rest your feet," she said. "And sit beside me while I work."

"Work?" he said, his chin lifted in question. "What is it that you're doing?" He squatted down beside her, watching her face.

"Helping Deborah."

"I ask one more thing," the girl said. "You call me Mei-Ling?"

"Of course," Mazy said. "I didn't know."

"Does it have a meaning, in English?" Seth asked.

She blushed. "Beautiful. My mother say so."

"As do all mothers, I suspect, Mei-Ling, as do they all."

Mei-Ling step-stepped away, and Seth turned back to Mazy. "Are you still helping? Looks like you're resting to me."

"I'm talking her bees back home."

Home! Her face lit up. That was the word Mazy had been unable to read in her dream, the word the bees had kept her from seeing! They'd almost suffocated her in the dream because she didn't stand out, wasn't unique, wasn't at home in her own heart.

Mazy laughed, but didn't explain it to Seth—how could she? This journey had been like the bees, a dance to remember, readying her soul to live at home, not in the past or the future but here, where she was.

"We played a game, to distract ourselves from the miseries getting here," she told him then. "Of guessing a truth and a lie. It entertained us in our necessary circles. Revealing at times too. I'll share one with you, see if you can guess."

"Sounds intriguing," Seth said.

"I wish I'd never left Wisconsin. That's one. And I'll always be at home when I'm truthful with myself."

Seth sat thoughtful. "I hope the lie is that you wished you'd never left Wisconsin because the other, to be truthful to yourself, that's a truth worth leaving home for."

Mazy nodded. "To be true to yourself—and to love your neighbor as yourself. I never realized what that meant before." She ran her hands through her hair, rubbed at the back of her neck. "The lie is that I wished I'd never left Cassville. I never would have believed that, I so hated to leave. But if I hadn't or we hadn't turned back around, I never would have known…this." She nodded toward the people dancing before her.

"They say in Europe that vintage wines give up the taste of their origins," Seth said, "that a discriminating palate tastes the place the vines were first nurtured. Just a sip prompts memories of the terraces of grapes under a hot sun, then moves from their tongue to their taste buds to their memory and mind. I think people are like that, some of us. The vintage ones who bring that first sense of place with them no matter where they go."

Mazy stared at him. "Bringing it with us, from the earth itself."

Sarah approached her with a sampler in hand. "I finished it, Mazy. See?" The girl held it up, and Mazy read the verse from Acts, the second chapter that she'd stitched across the plains. *They were all together in one place.* Blue columbines and birds surrounded the words.

"It's beautiful," Mazy said. "Your mother would have been proud."

Sarah left to share her treasure with another, and Mazy said, "That verse—it's from the day of Pentecost, when people from different places came together, waiting to obey. Wind and fire followed, but it was those together that made the difference, became a community of faith. Just as we're doing, risking being known and yet remaining together. The best kind of friendship, wouldn't you say?" Seth nodded. "I might never have known that, nor the joy of the Psalm, either, that the Lord maintains my lot, how he makes the boundaries fall on pleasant places. If I hadn't left home I'd have read them but never believed them as I do now. I'd never let it live in my heart if I hadn't left my familiar place."

"Quite a truth," Seth said. "Some folks live a lifetime and never find it. They die fearing the future more than anything else, never feel the joy of what's now."

They watched the women swinging, their faces reflecting life's challenge and change. Pig bounded over and nuzzled beneath Mazy's hand. "Oh, you remember me now, with Sason to compete with." She buried her face in his fur. He made his growling, slobbery sounds, pushing his big head into her, tugging at her wrist, his tail wagging. "You're a good friend, Pig," Mazy said, "and always will be, even if you do go off and look after another." She smiled up at Seth, who reached out to scratch the dog's neck.

Who knew what tomorrow would bring? But, more, did it matter? They had mountains to cross, new places and people to meet, the loss of the past to put down, replace with hopes woven inside. What mattered was that they were all together in one place at this moment. The Lord knew their lot.

Mazy trusted that. And herself. And she knew in her heart, that as long as her soul was filled, she'd always be safely at home.

Author's Notes and Acknowledgments

"I am a part of all I have read," wrote John Kieran, and so am I.

All Together in One Place began when I was a child reading Laura Ingalls Wilder and Caddie Woodlawn. Then Willa Cather, diarists, compilers, historical society documents and psychological speculations, and the stories of women I came to know and write about, all nurtured this story through the years. The responsibility, however, for what's been woven—with its errors and speculations—remains all mine.

All Together in One Place as a novel began in 1994 while researching *A Sweetness to the Soul.* A friend loaned me a copy of Ezra Meeker's *Ox Team Days on the Oregon Trail,* originally published in 1912. In it, Meeker related his encounter in 1852 with eleven wagons heading east, all driven by women, their men having died and been buried on the trail. "What happened?" became the question that formed this story of triumph and tragedy, of community and connection, of kinship and faith.

Aside from Meeker's account, no record exists of eleven women turning back, though there are numerous accounts of turnarounds, people heading east instead of west, congestion on the trail because of directional change. These women may have dispersed back in the States; they may have turned west again and gone into California, as none are recorded as having entered into Oregon as part of a group of eleven women. Eleven women together are not recorded at Fort Laramie or Kearney or in Oregon as having arrived that year either, though registrations are said to have dropped off in certain years. Ezra Meeker may not have remembered well; 1852 was his first journey. He was a young married man accompanied by his wife and six-week-old child. The weight of the choices that faced him may well have affected his counting of wagons and women.

I am especially grateful to the westward diarists themselves, the women who recorded their days on the Oregon Trail, and most of all to Eliza Ann McAuley's recordings from 1852. To historians (and fellow Wrangler Award Winners) Merrill Mattes, author of *The Great Platte River Road,* and John Unruh, Jr., author of *The Plains Across,* I owe much. I am indebted as well to Jim Tompkins, historian, Portland State University, and consultant to the End of the Oregon Trail Interpretive Center, Clackamas County Historical Society, for his e-mail messages to me, his commentary on this incident, and his exceptional research on diarists writing at the same time and as part of the same company as Ezra Meeker.

Caroline Fry did indeed begin a Marriage Association in 1852. Langsforth did patent the design in bee hives in 1852. The French military did introduce night communication through Braille-like dots. *The Cholera Years* by Charles Rosenberg proved useful for medical information on the nature of disease in 1852 and the commonly held disparaging view of some physicians. The 1937 edition of *Old California,* a book by Stewart Edward White, both provided lithographic information and told the true story of mining camps and carpet tacks. William Emerson's work *The Applegate Trail of 1846* offered sound maps as well as data about what people carried and the inner workings of wagons. Christina May's book *Pioneer Clothing on the Oregon Trail* and Keith May's conversations with me from their vast knowledge and passion about the trail provided valuable details about everyday life. *Discovering the Oregon Trail,* a publication of the Nebraska Historical Society, and the PBS series *The West* were invaluable resources, as was the Oregon-California Trails Association, composed of people who are passionate about the stories of the West and willing to share them.

Susan Butruille's collections of women's voices gave depth, I hope, to mine. Sociologist Lillian Schlissel's book, *Women's Diaries of the Westward Journey*, provided my first image of what I came to call the "necessary circle" among other insights. My own circle of women spent hours in speculation about what might have happened and how these women might have responded, who they might have met, what help was offered and accepted, and at what point would they have known that life as they knew it had ended. The value of these women in my life as nurture and protection from self-doubt cannot be counted; from them I accept the wages of care.

The series *Covered Wagon Women, Diaries and Letters from the Western Trails, 1852, The California Trail,* Volume 4, edited by Kenneth L. Holmes, proved especially helpful. Unique features of the 1852 crossings are noted there by Ball State University history professor and author Glenda Riley. These factors helped set the stage for this community of care. Among them are these: encounters with native peoples in 1852 lacked the hostilities of earlier—and later—years; the bloomer costume made its debut; cholera continued to leave graves in its wake; and more women and families crossed that year than any year previous.

The effect of more women on the trail, according to Dr. Glenda Riley, was significant. Their relationship with other women, the social and cultural mores that rode with them, gave meaning and purpose to their journey. Many women heading west did not wish to go at all and chose to make the trek only to preserve their families; more rare were those making the trip by themselves, a sign of independence.

The year 1852 is notable also for the entrepreneurs wanting to lead emigrants onto newly developed trails and for those providing relief parties when needed. The Shasta City story of raising money and celebrating new arrivals is based on fact, as is the Nobles Trail information, both from John Unruh's book.

Special thanks go to my Web site manager Michelle Hurtley for all she does to spread the stories in ways I will never understand; Web site managers for Cassville, Wisconsin, and to the State of Wisconsin for maintaining the replica of Stonefield, a village near Cassville that recreates the past; to Kathy White, site manager at the Western Historic Trails Center in Council Bluffs, Iowa, for helping get my characters across Iowa in April. My Norfolk, United Kingdom, beekeeper resource, Mark Turner, advised me via Internet on a cross-country transport of queen bees, their care and connection to home. I am grateful also to Cal Thayer, beekeeper in Eugene, Oregon, for providing me with U.S. Department of Agriculture data on the history of beekeeping which offered dates and paths of likely transport and for letting me don the hat and netting of beetender so I could mingle with the bees.

Special thanks go to Kay Krall, Blair Fredstrom, Sandy Maynard, and Jack and Carol Tedder and our friends in Sherman County, Oregon, for faithful support; to Jean Holly for her candid and gracious answers to my questions about the loss of sight and the challenges and joys of parenting sighted children; and to Dave Larson for details of the farrier's life. My deep appreciation goes to writer friends (and manuscript readers) Bob Welch and Wade Keller for their encouragement, time, and thoughtful suggestions; and to writer Harriet Rochlin for unwavering nurturing and inspiration. Such thanks go as well to my literary agent Joyce Hart of Pittsburgh and my signatory agent, Terry Porter of Flat Rock, Indiana.

The little German poem is a memory of my father's and I thank him for it. The Ayrshire information came from Barb Rutschow, herd manager and sister-in-law extraordinaire who, along with my brother Craig, loves columbines and the bluff country of Wisconsin.

It is my hope that the women encountered in these pages pay tribute to those who faced what those eleven faced and honor the strength of their spirits, their lessons of learning to let go, living in the present, and trusting in the words of Scripture. *All Together in One Place* is a phrase from the book of Acts, describing the bringing together of divergent voices and people into a family of service. It seemed a fitting title for this triumphant story of kinship and courage and the hope woven into all loss.

This *Kinship and Courage* series is inspired by Psalm 16:5-6 and is based on the belief that to find the pleasant places of our lives we must be willing to expand our boundaries, spiritual, emotional, physical, and relational and to trust as Mazy did that "the Lord maintaineth my lot."

I hope that the wonder of how these women live their lives in Shasta City, how they find themselves on the Applegate Trail into Oregon and south to Sacramento, perhaps even back to Cassville, keeping community and sustaining their faith, will return the reader to additional books in the series.

Finally, a word of thanks and gratitude goes to my editors Lisa Tawn Bergren in Colorado and Traci DePree in Minnesota and to the fine team at WaterBrook Press, a division of Random House, for their belief in the power of stories and in my capacity to tell this one. And to my husband, Jerry, I give my deepest thanks, for teaching me about hope and faith, and of boundaries and their necessary expansion; and for the love and shelter he provides to make that happen.

Last, but not least, appreciation goes to each of you, the readers, for spending time with these women, for sharing their stories. May you find your own strength and courage reflected in the hope woven inside.

Jane Kirkpatrick
www.jkbooks.com

The following is an excerpt from Jane Kirkpatrick's
No Eyes Can See
Book 2 in the Kinship and Courage series

~

Along the trail to California, 1852

His arms outstretched, he called to her, his voice deep and far away. "Look up here then, at me. I'll catch you if you fall." Suzanne found his gaze behind round lenses, the sun glinting off the wire frames.

Suzanne heard, wanted to believe, but she hesitated, watching her husband brace himself against the current as he stood in the middle of the stream. He'd rolled the legs of his butternut-colored pants up to his knees. Water splashed and stained his suspenders, two lines of cedar-red tracks across his bare chest. He looked…boyish, hair falling over one eye, a wide grin of encouragement given just for her. "Put your foot on that rock, there." He pointed with his chin to a gun-gray stone smeared with moss of green.

"It looks…slick," Suzanne said above the water's rushing. "I'll fall." Something made no sense. Her husband wasn't here; she couldn't see him.

"It's not so bad out here in the middle," he said. "Just look up. Keep your focus, just like the good photographer you are. You'll be fine."

Focus. Her mind drifted with the word that seized meaning from the Latin, *hearth,* the hub of home, the pivot point for family. "Keep your focus," he'd said. That's what she must remember. Maybe then, she would truly learn to see.

~

Join the women of *All Together in One Place* as they discover the meaning of family and what truly makes the center of a home. Come with Suzanne and Mazy, Ruth and Elizabeth, Seth and Tipton, too. Even Zane Randolf and Charles, Tipton's petulant brother, are thrown into the turbulent times where gold rules and ruins those who lose their focus. Mazy winds her way through betrayal while Ruth journeys deeper into the wilderness of spirit and what brings true gratitude to her life. Meet David Taylor, driver for the Hall and Crandall stage company, and cheer him on as his life intertwines with the All Together women and one lone Wintu woman named Spring. As they all converge on Shasta City, can they remain together? Or is life made up of joining and separating, of taking new risks in the wilderness of relationship and landscape, savoring the experience and then moving on? Find out and journey with these remarkable women as each seeks to quench their thirst for meaning—and discovers it in the promise of a spring.